BATTLE STATION PRIME

THE DRAGONMASTER'S REVENGE

AN UNOFFICIAL GRAPHIC NOVEL FOR MINECRAFTERS

CARA J. STEVENS

ILLUSTRATED BY SAM NEEDHAM

SKY PONY PRESS
NEW YORK

This book is not authorized or sponsored by Microsoft Corp., Mojang AB, Notch Development AB or Scholastic Inc., or any other person or entity owning or controlling rights in the Minecraft name, trademark, or copyrights.

Sky Pony Press books may be purchased in bulk at special discounts for sales promotion, corporate gifts, fund-raising, or educational purposes. Special editions can also be created to specifications. For details, contact the Special Sales Department, Sky Pony Press, 307 West 36th Street, 11th Floor, New York, NY 10018 or info@skyhorsepublishing.com.

Sky Pony® is a registered trademark of Skyhorse Publishing, Inc.®, a Delaware corporation.

Visit our website at www.skyhorsepublishing.com.

10 9 8 7 6 5 4 3 2 1

Library of Congress Cataloging-in-Publication Data is available on file.

Cover design by Kai Texel
Cover and interior art by Sam Needham

Print ISBN: 978-1-5107-5987-9
Ebook ISBN: 978-1-5107-6587-0

Printed in China

#6

BATTLE STATION PRIME

THE DRAGONMASTER'S REVENGE

MEET THE

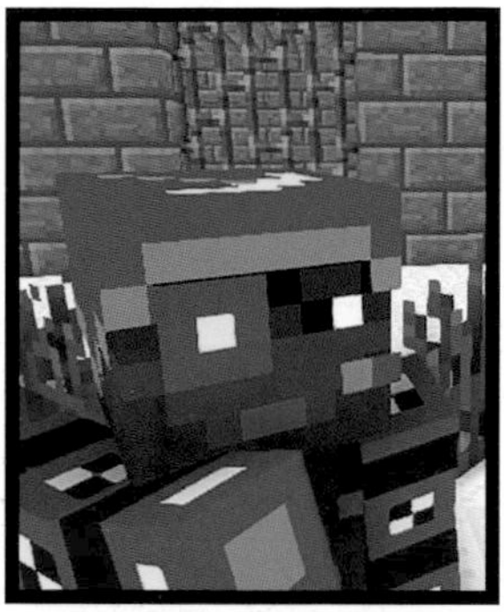

PELL: A boy with a talent for getting lost and for making the best of every situation.

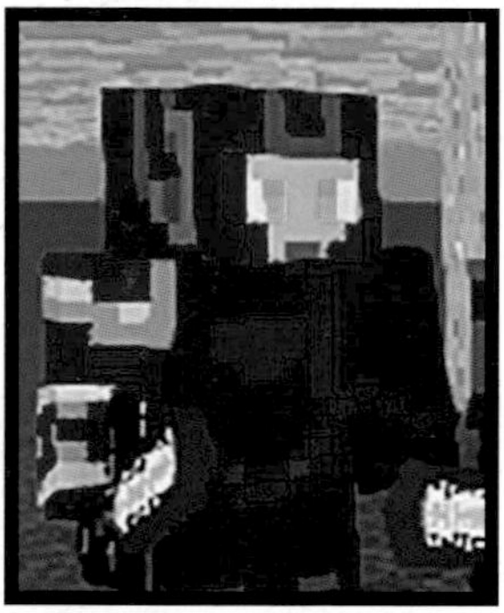

LOGAN: Pell's best friend, who is an expert hacker and redstone programmer.

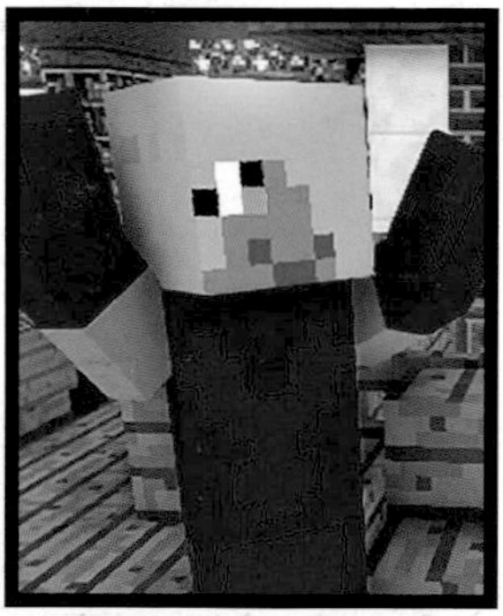

MADDY: Logan's very smart little sister, who has a talent for enchanting objects.

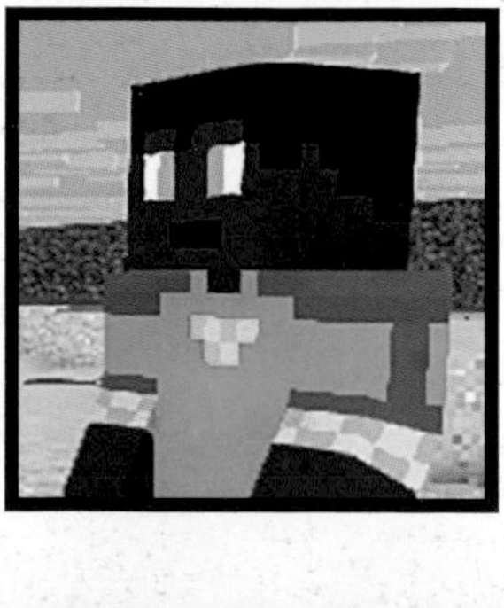

UNCLE COLIN: Pell's uncle, who is an excellent politician and leader.

CHARACTERS

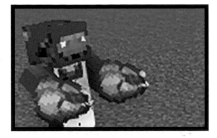

MR. JAMES: The leader of Battle Station Prime.

NED: A great chef who has a mysterious past.

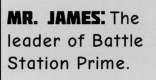

BEN FROST: A programmer who has a talent for inventing clever solutions.

CLOUD, ZOE, AND BROOKLYN: Residents of Battle Station Prime.

INTRODUCTION

With the skeleton armies gone, trading is a breeze and life returns to somewhat normal for the kids of Battle Station Prime. But there's one thing that keeps them up at night: the threat of the dragonmaster's revenge.

The Ender Dragon egg had been a carefully guarded secret until it hatched and the young, powerful, dragon inside imprinted to an evil sorcerer named Borin. The kids know it is only a matter of time before this dangerous partnership threatens their existence.

We resume our story as the kids introduce their new friend Percy to life at the Battle Station.

CHAPTER 1

NEW
BEGINNINGS

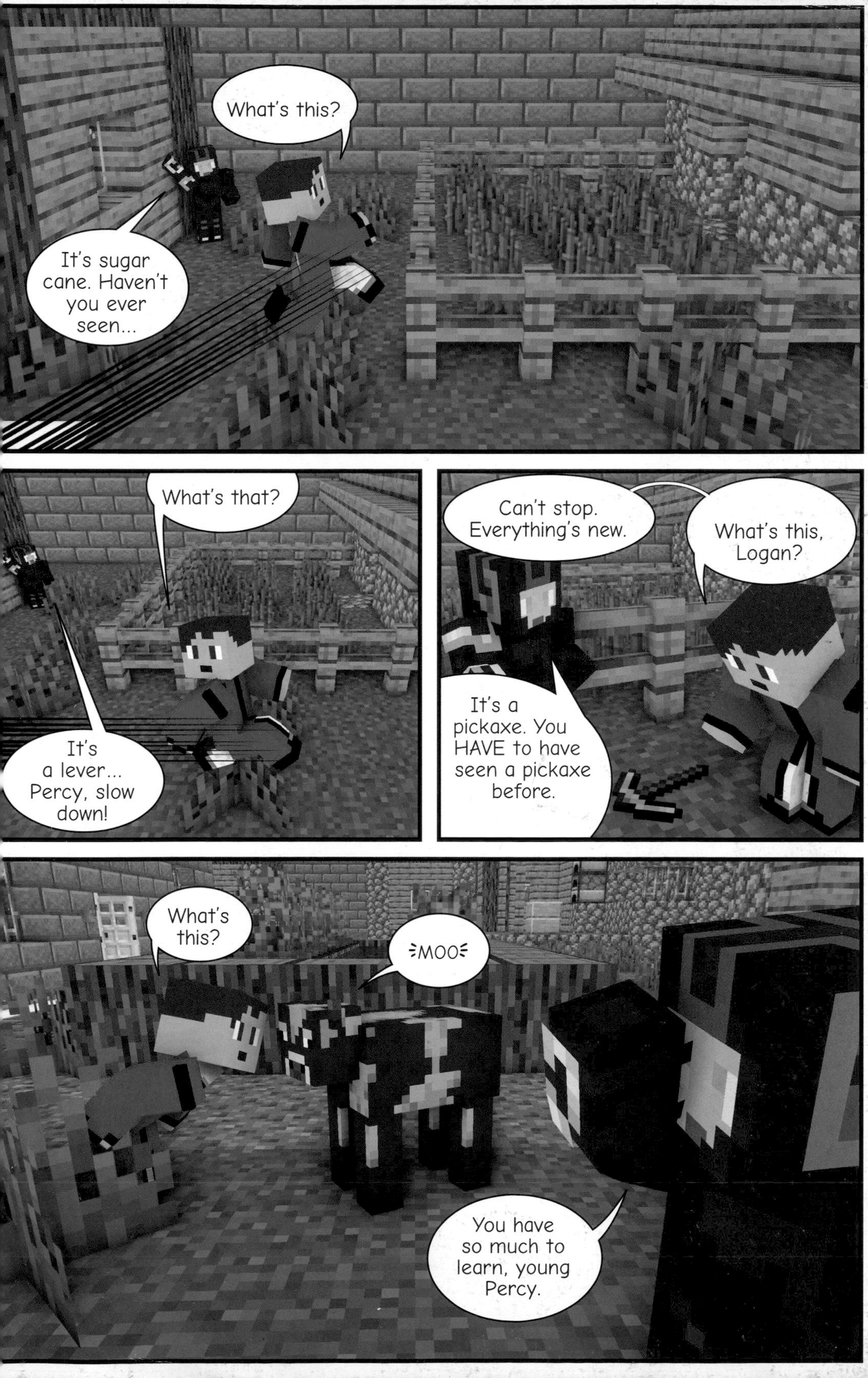
What's this?
It's sugar cane. Haven't you ever seen...
What's that?
It's a lever... Percy, slow down!
Can't stop. Everything's new.
What's this, Logan?
It's a pickaxe. You HAVE to have seen a pickaxe before.
What's this?
MOO
You have so much to learn, young Percy.

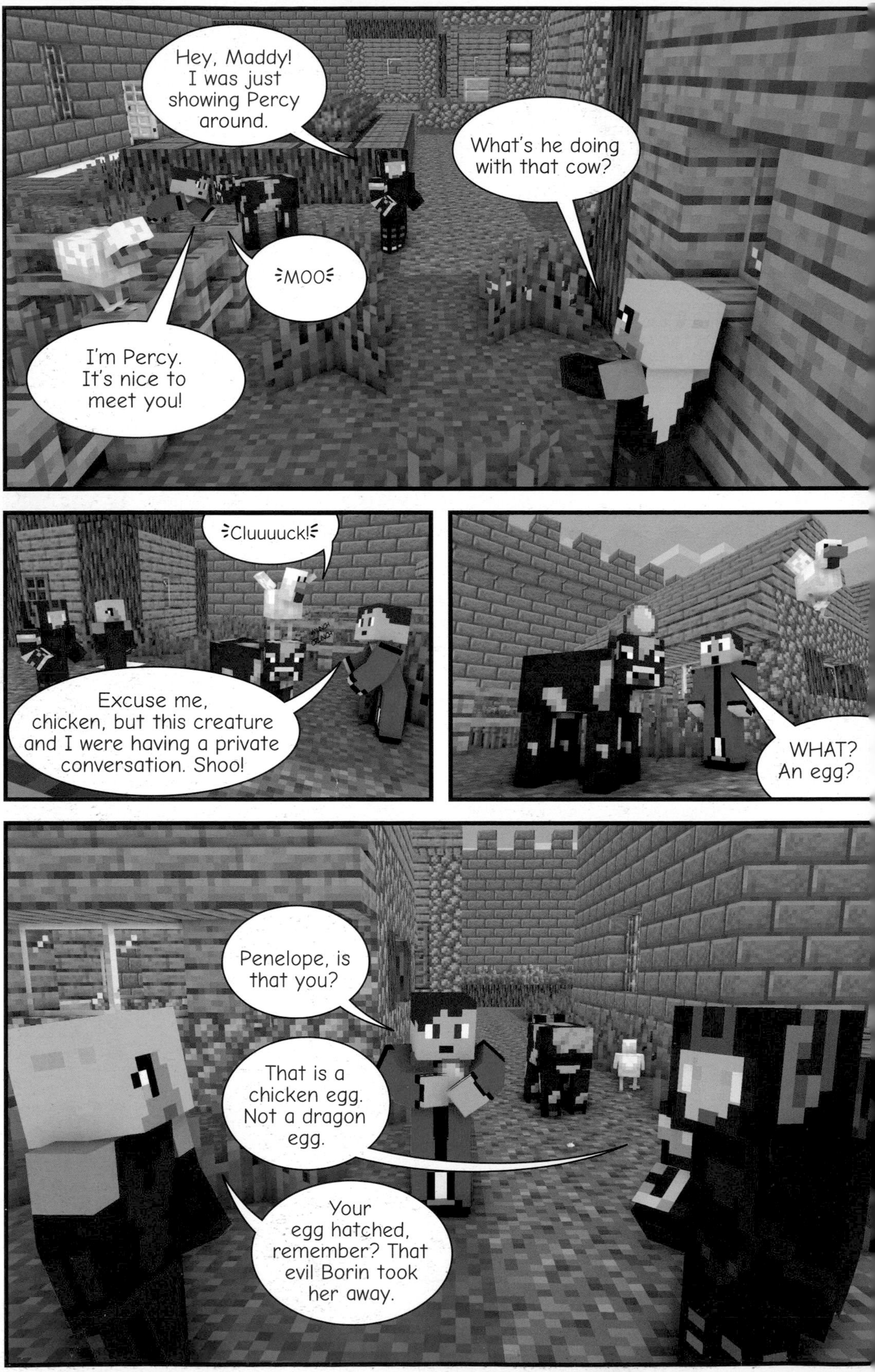
Hey, Maddy! I was just showing Percy around.
What's he doing with that cow?
MOO
I'm Percy. It's nice to meet you!
Cluuuuck!
Excuse me, chicken, but this creature and I were having a private conversation. Shoo!
WHAT? An egg?
Penelope, is that you?
That is a chicken egg. Not a dragon egg.
Your egg hatched, remember? That evil Borin took her away.

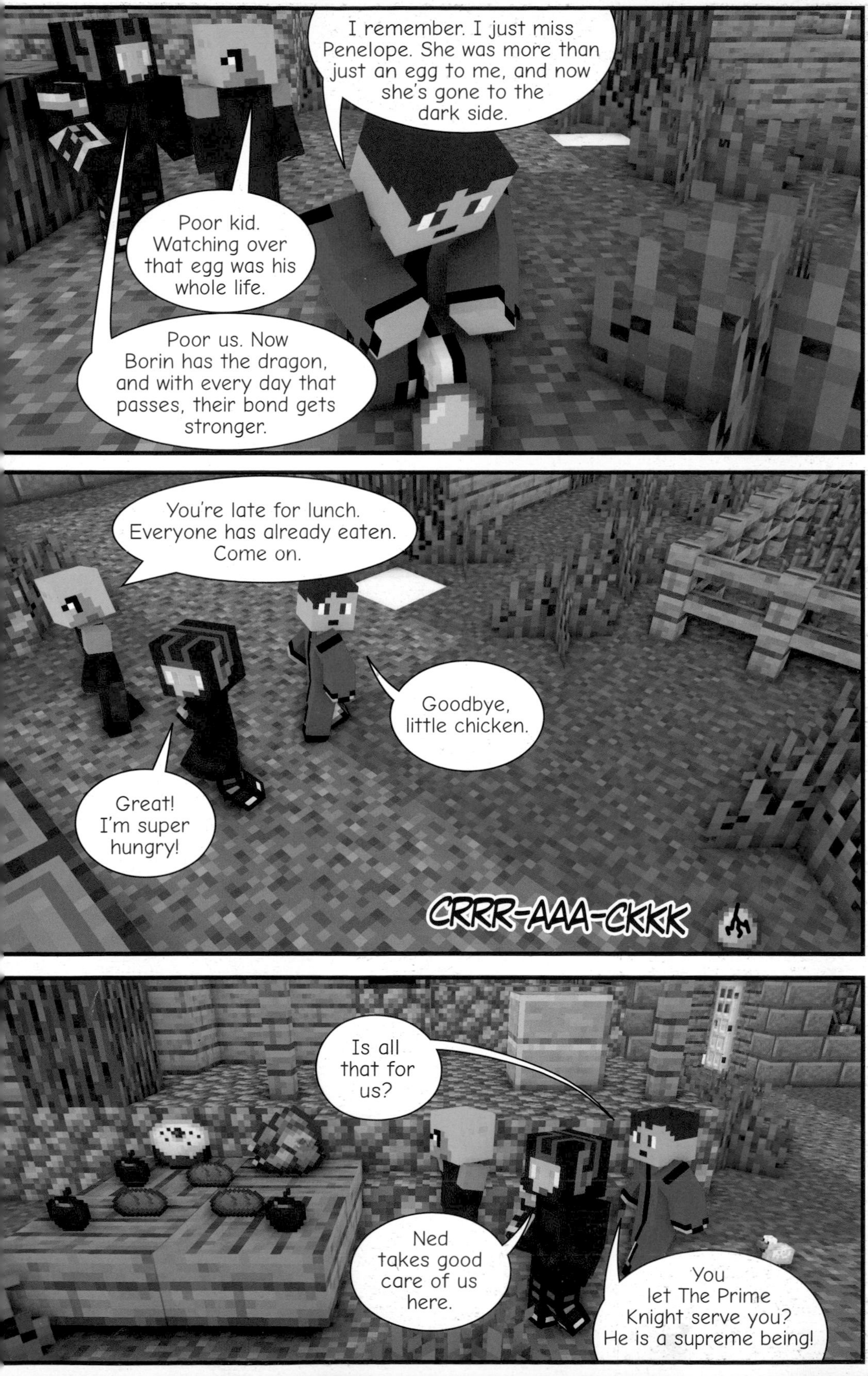
I remember. I just miss Penelope. She was more than just an egg to me, and now she's gone to the dark side.
Poor kid. Watching over that egg was his whole life.
Poor us. Now Borin has the dragon, and with every day that passes, their bond gets stronger.
You're late for lunch. Everyone has already eaten. Come on.
Goodbye, little chicken.
Great! I'm super hungry!
CRRR-AAA-CKKK
Is all that for us?
Ned takes good care of us here.
You let The Prime Knight serve you? He is a supreme being!

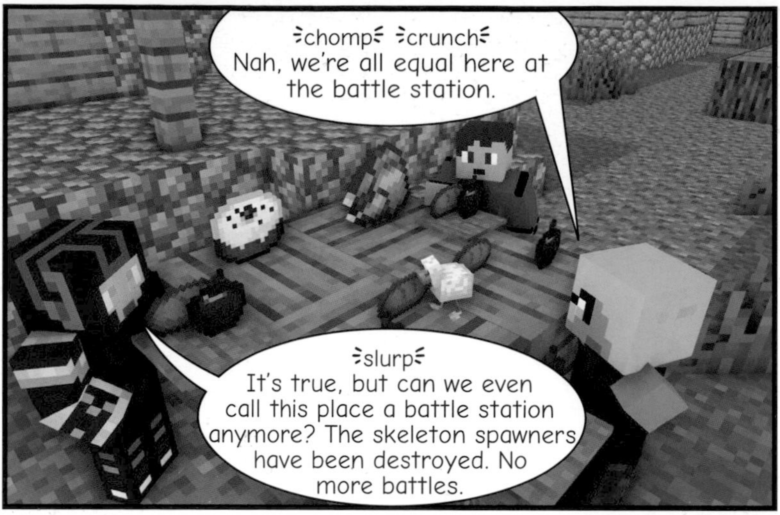

=chomp= =crunch= Nah, we're all equal here at the battle station.
=slurp= It's true, but can we even call this place a battle station anymore? The skeleton spawners have been destroyed. No more battles.

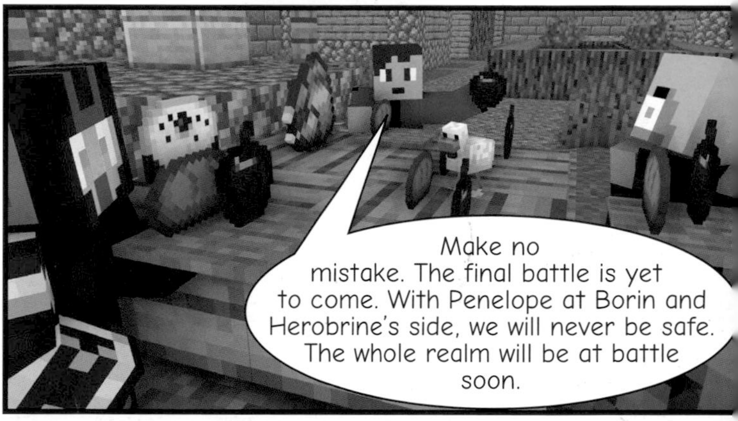

Make no mistake. The final battle is yet to come. With Penelope at Borin and Herobrine's side, we will never be safe. The whole realm will be at battle soon.

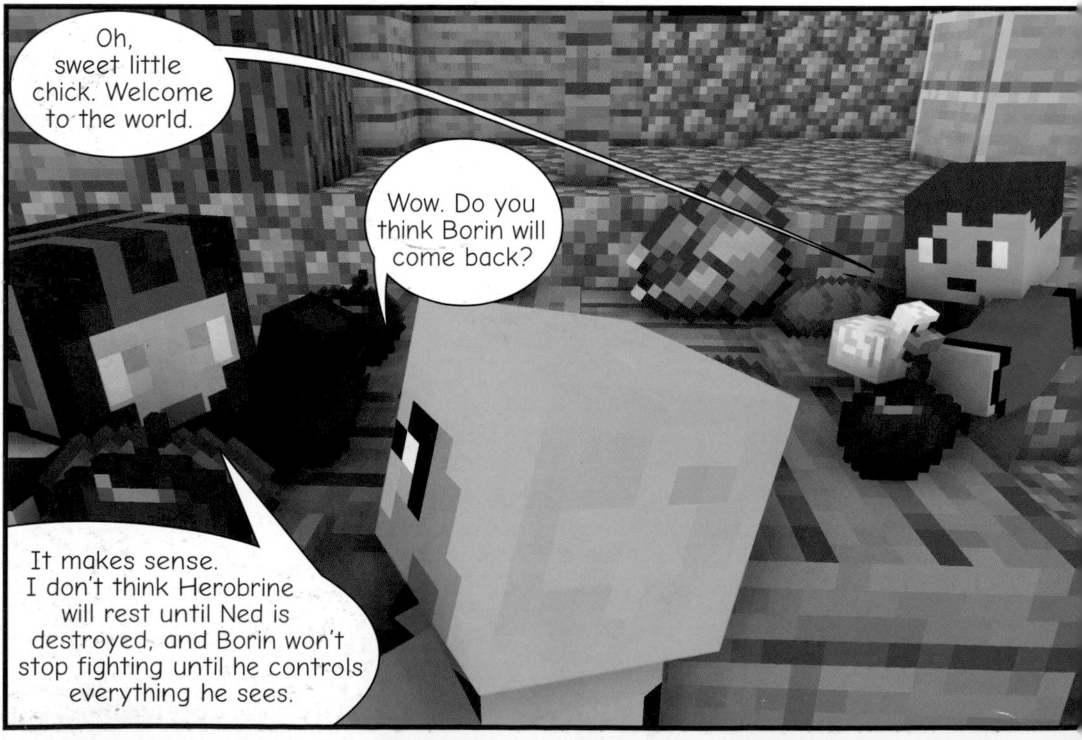

Oh, sweet little chick. Welcome to the world.
Wow. Do you think Borin will come back?
It makes sense. I don't think Herobrine will rest until Ned is destroyed, and Borin won't stop fighting until he controls everything he sees.

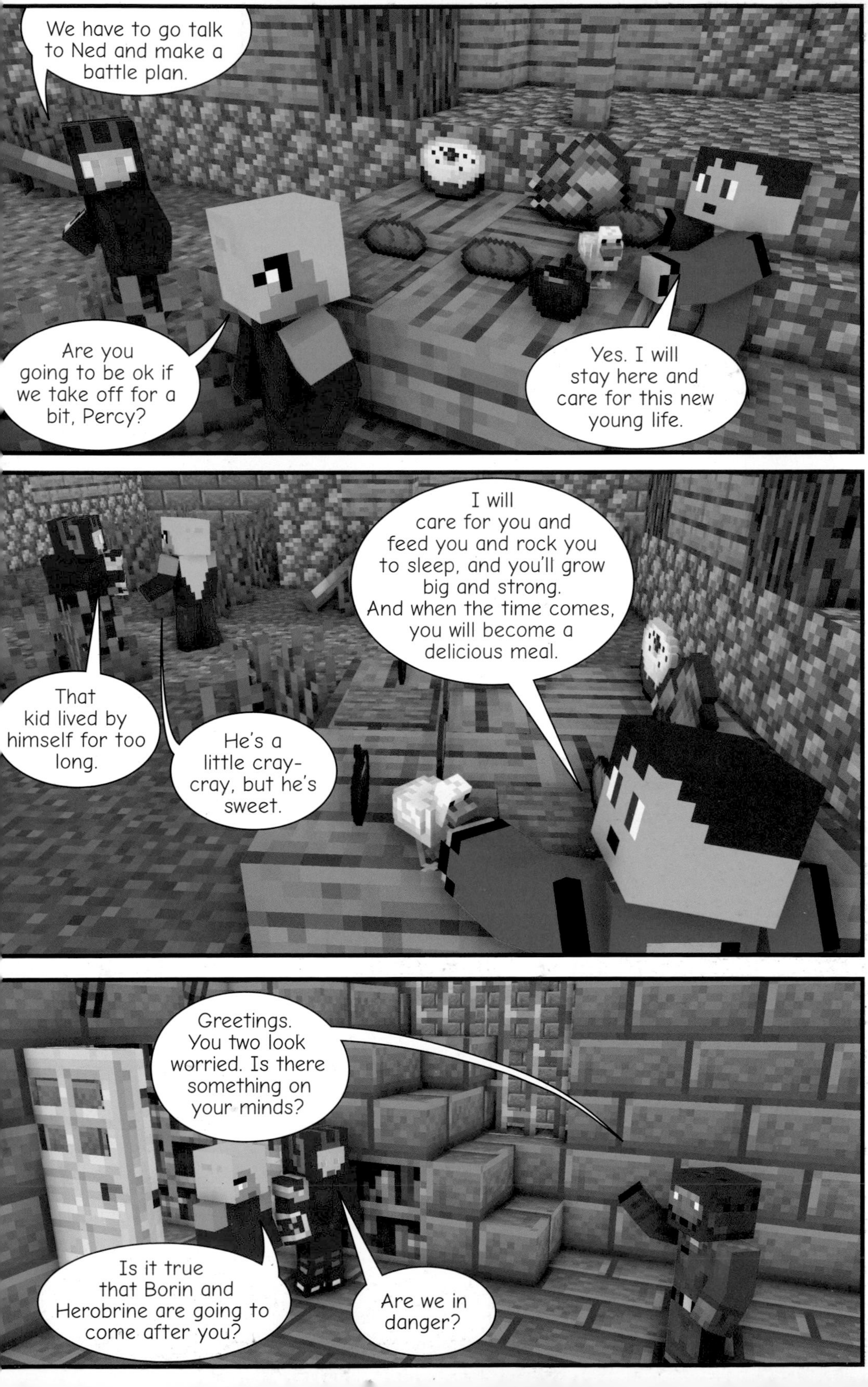
We have to go talk to Ned and make a battle plan.
Are you going to be ok if we take off for a bit, Percy?
Yes. I will stay here and care for this new young life.
I will care for you and feed you and rock you to sleep, and you'll grow big and strong. And when the time comes, you will become a delicious meal.
That kid lived by himself for too long.
He's a little cray-cray, but he's sweet.
Greetings. You two look worried. Is there something on your minds?
Is it true that Borin and Herobrine are going to come after you?
Are we in danger?

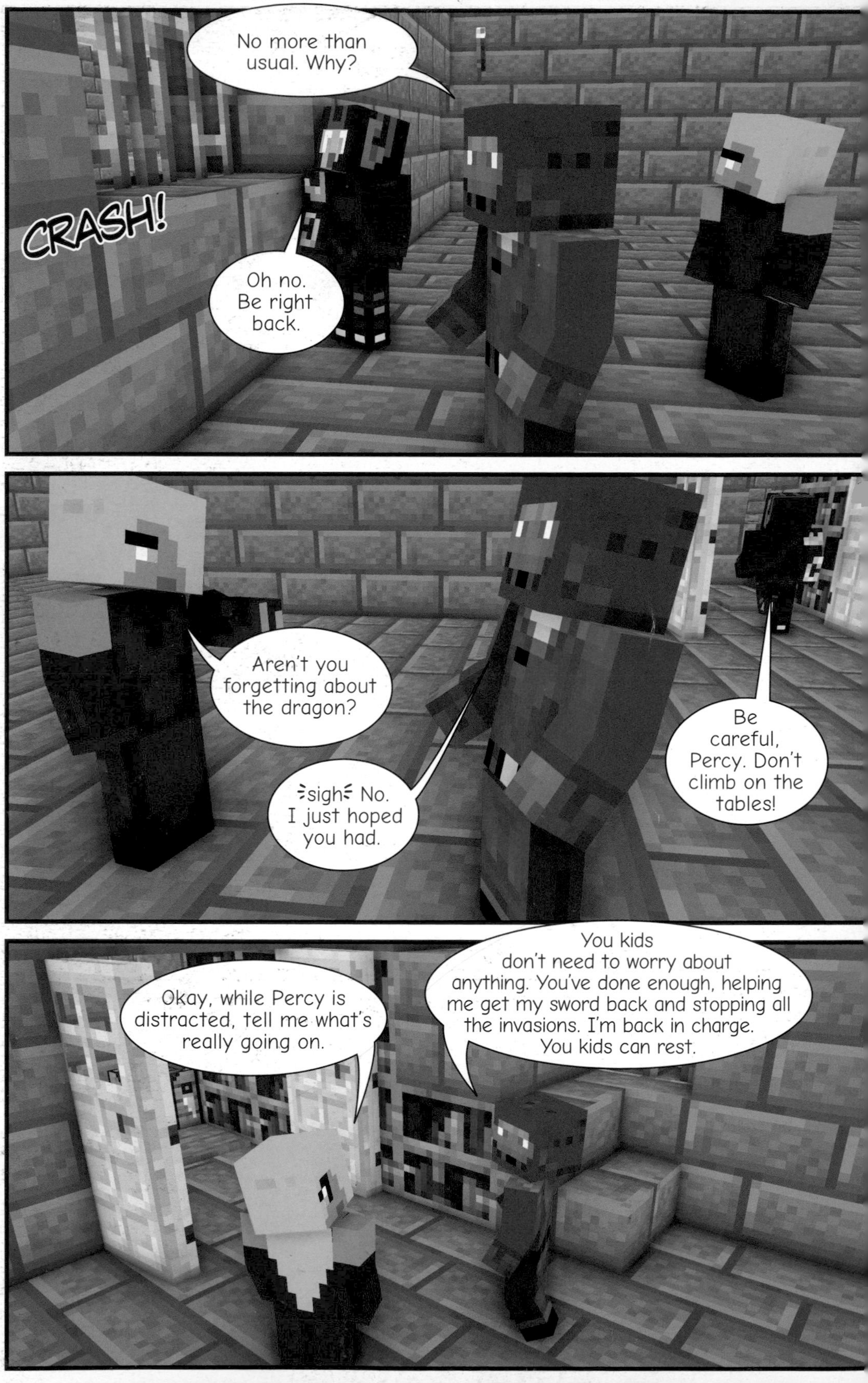
No more than usual. Why?
CRASH!
Oh no. Be right back.
Aren't you forgetting about the dragon?
≷sigh≶ No. I just hoped you had.
Be careful, Percy. Don't climb on the tables!
Okay, while Percy is distracted, tell me what's really going on.
You kids don't need to worry about anything. You've done enough, helping me get my sword back and stopping all the invasions. I'm back in charge. You kids can rest.

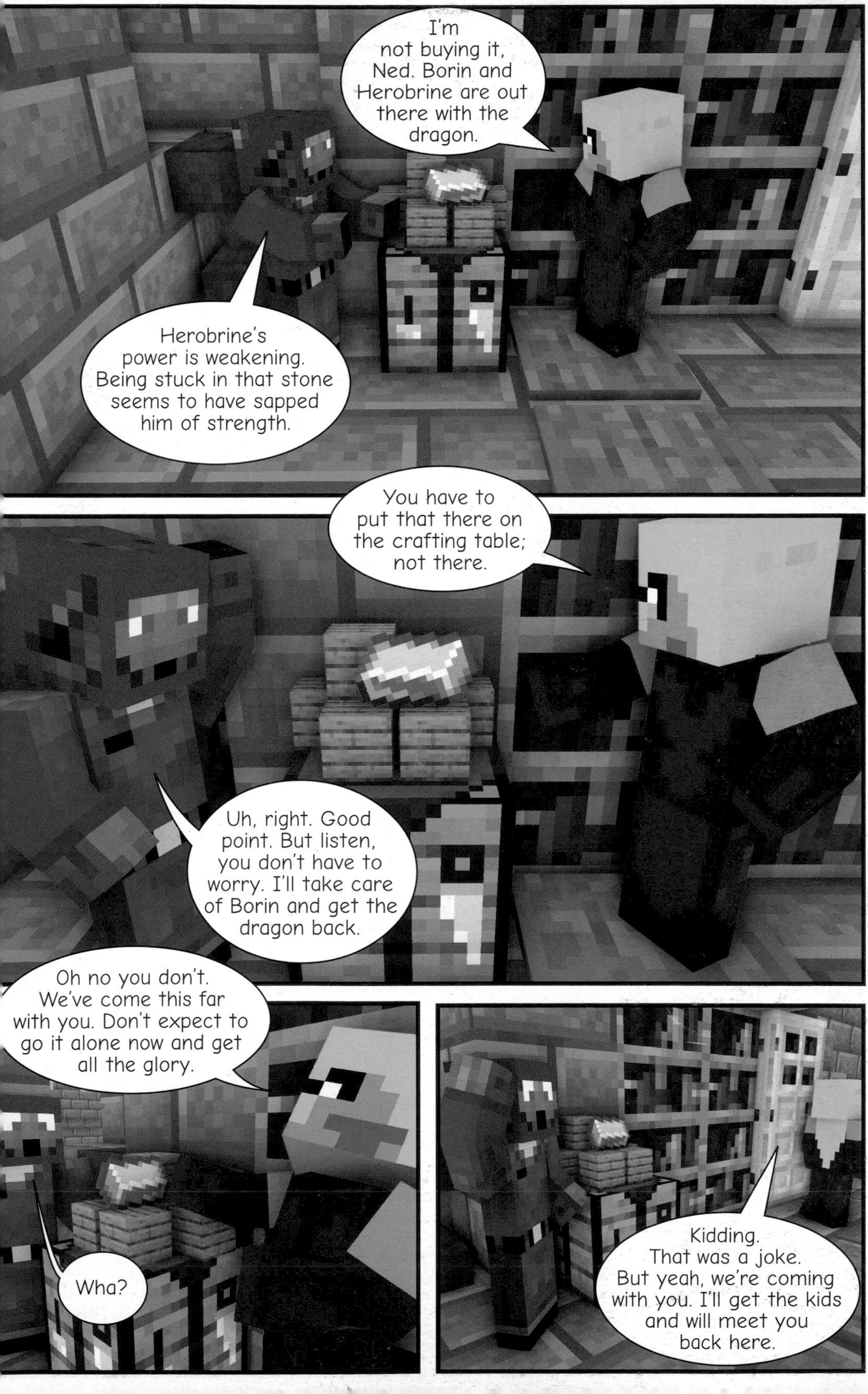
I'm not buying it, Ned. Borin and Herobrine are out there with the dragon.
Herobrine's power is weakening. Being stuck in that stone seems to have sapped him of strength.
You have to put that there on the crafting table; not there.
Uh, right. Good point. But listen, you don't have to worry. I'll take care of Borin and get the dragon back.
Oh no you don't. We've come this far with you. Don't expect to go it alone now and get all the glory.
Wha?
Kidding. That was a joke. But yeah, we're coming with you. I'll get the kids and will meet you back here.

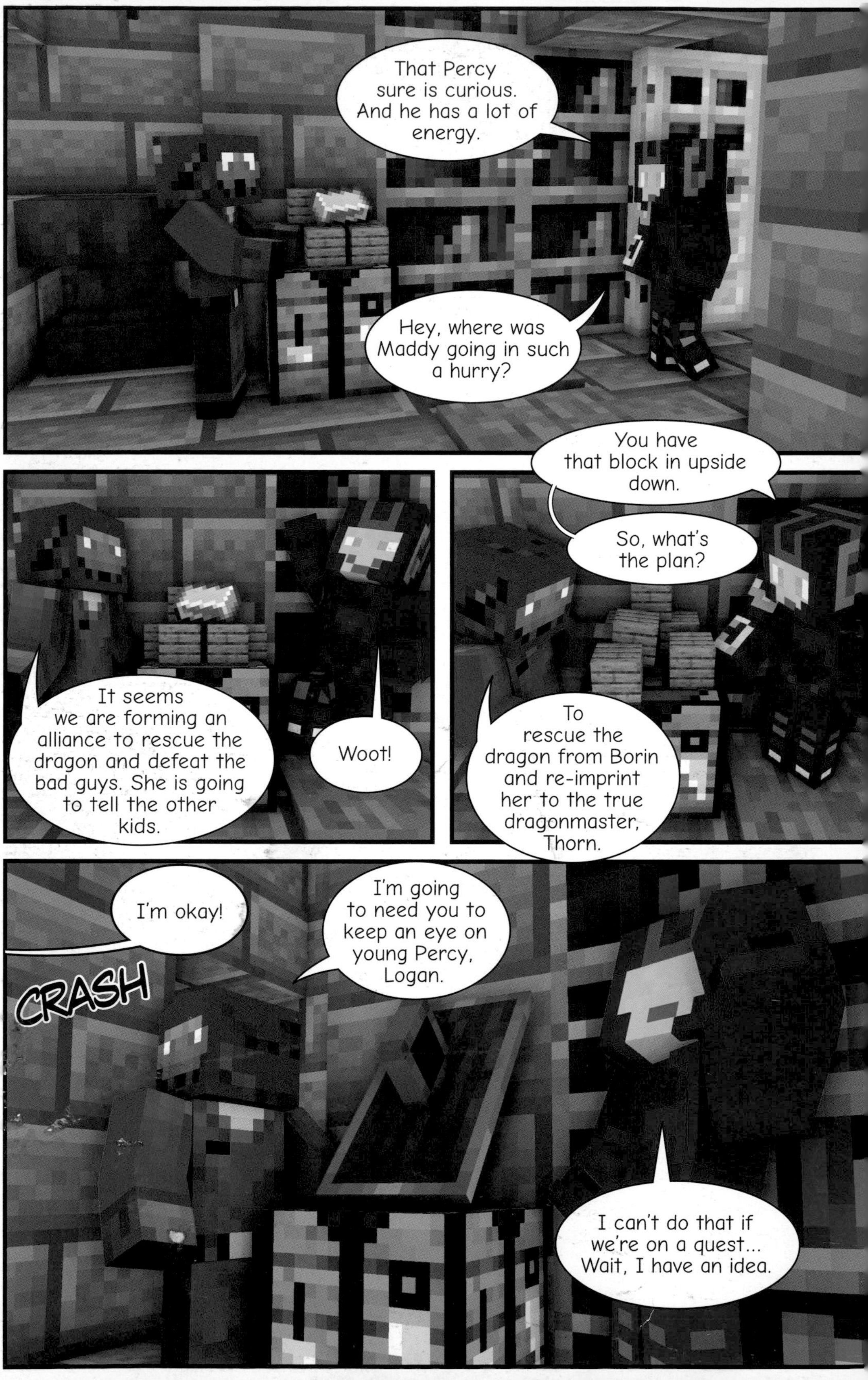
That Percy sure is curious. And he has a lot of energy.
Hey, where was Maddy going in such a hurry?
It seems we are forming an alliance to rescue the dragon and defeat the bad guys. She is going to tell the other kids.
Woot!
You have that block in upside down.
So, what's the plan?
To rescue the dragon from Borin and re-imprint her to the true dragonmaster, Thorn.
I'm okay!
CRASH
I'm going to need you to keep an eye on young Percy, Logan.
I can't do that if we're on a quest... Wait, I have an idea.

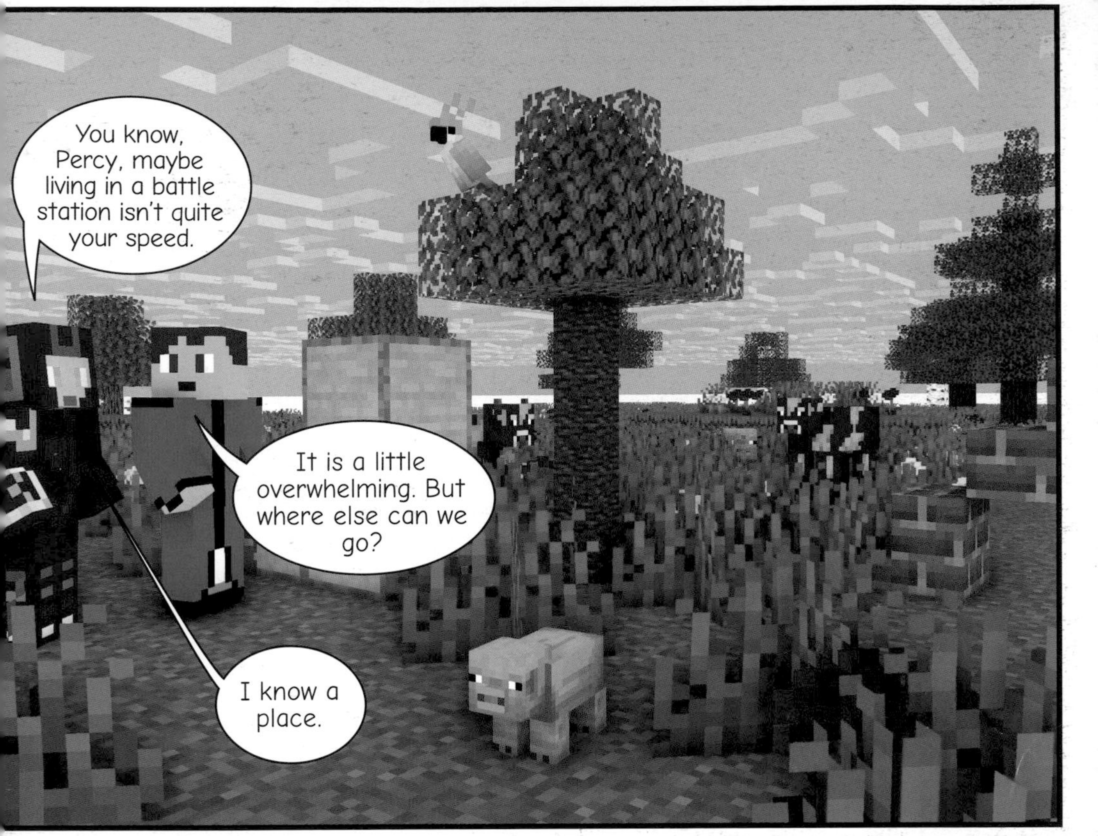
You know, Percy, maybe living in a battle station isn't quite your speed.
It is a little overwhelming. But where else can we go?
I know a place.

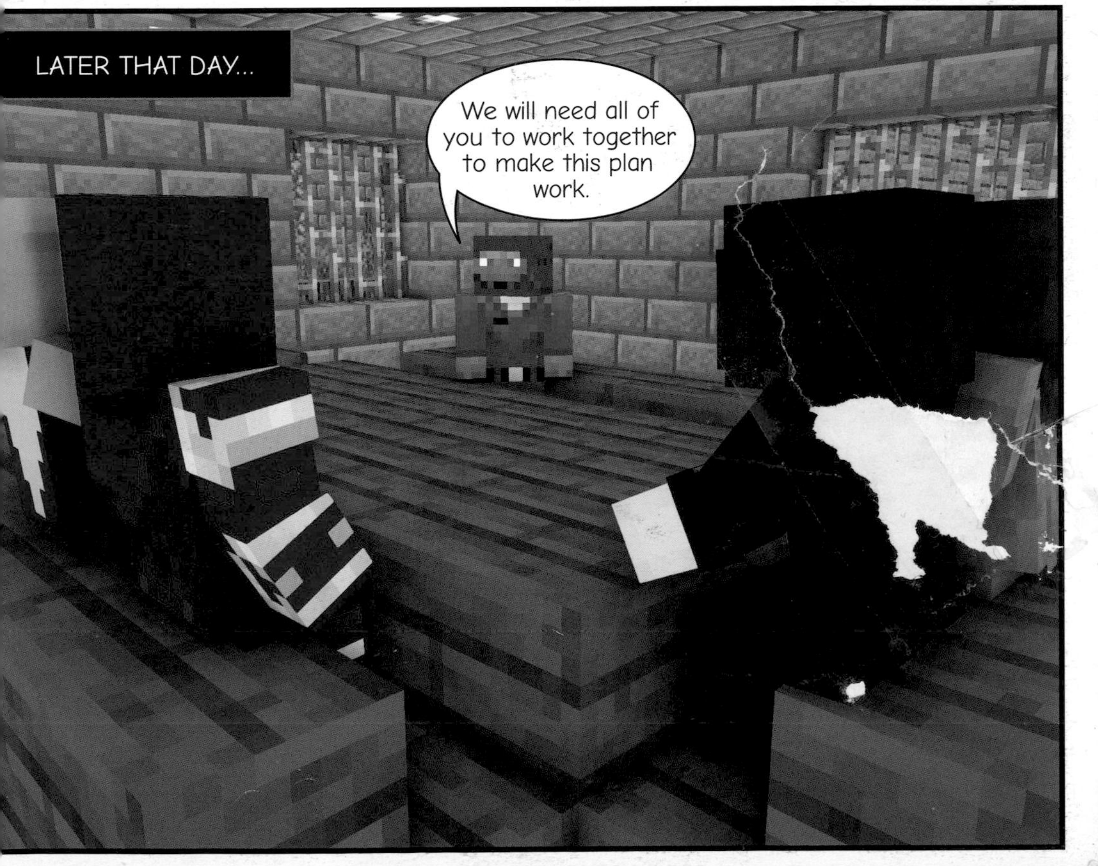
LATER THAT DAY...
We will need all of you to work together to make this plan work.

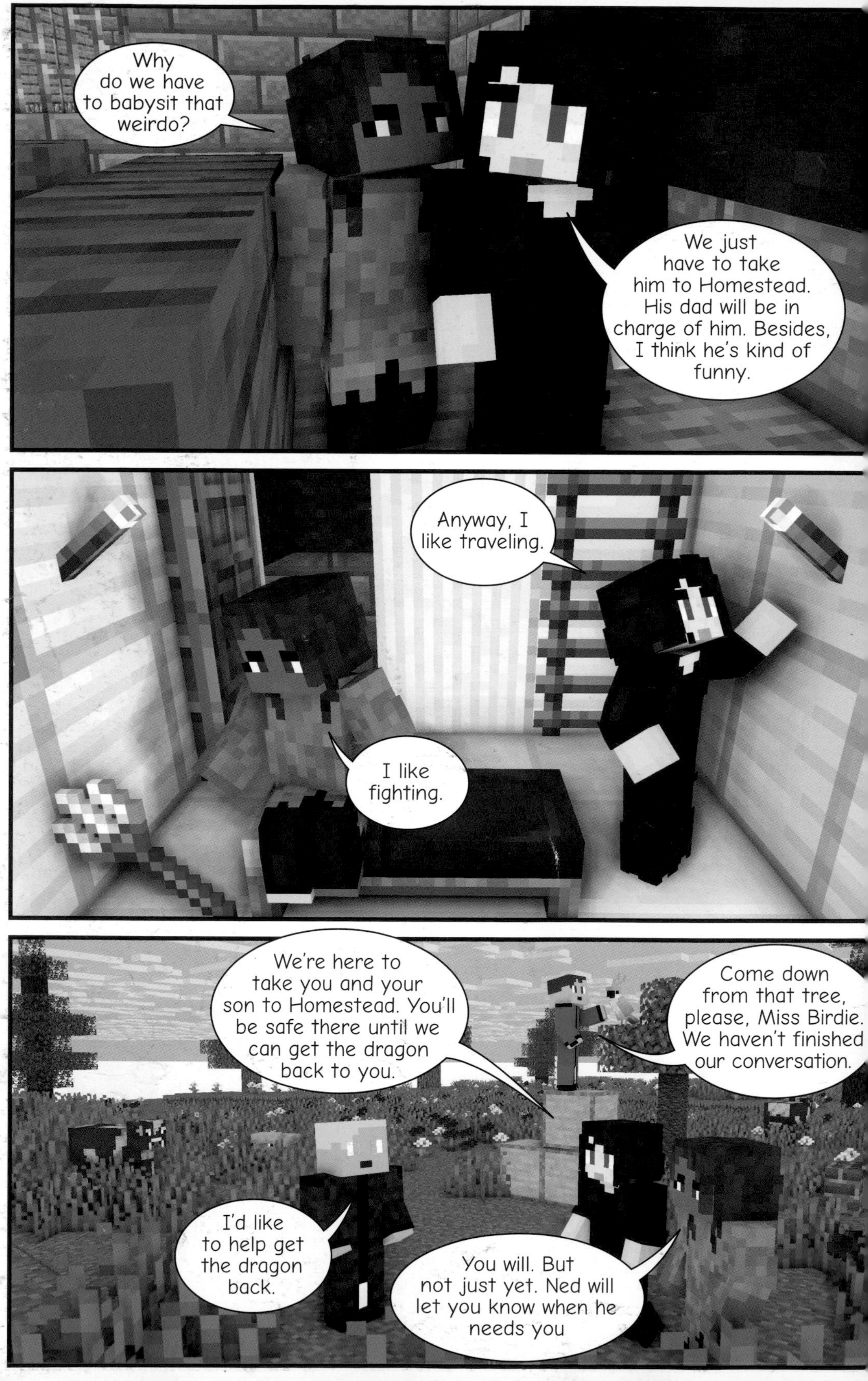
Why do we have to babysit that weirdo?
We just have to take him to Homestead. His dad will be in charge of him. Besides, I think he's kind of funny.
Anyway, I like traveling.
I like fighting.
We're here to take you and your son to Homestead. You'll be safe there until we can get the dragon back to you.
Come down from that tree, please, Miss Birdie. We haven't finished our conversation.
I'd like to help get the dragon back.
You will. But not just yet. Ned will let you know when he needs you

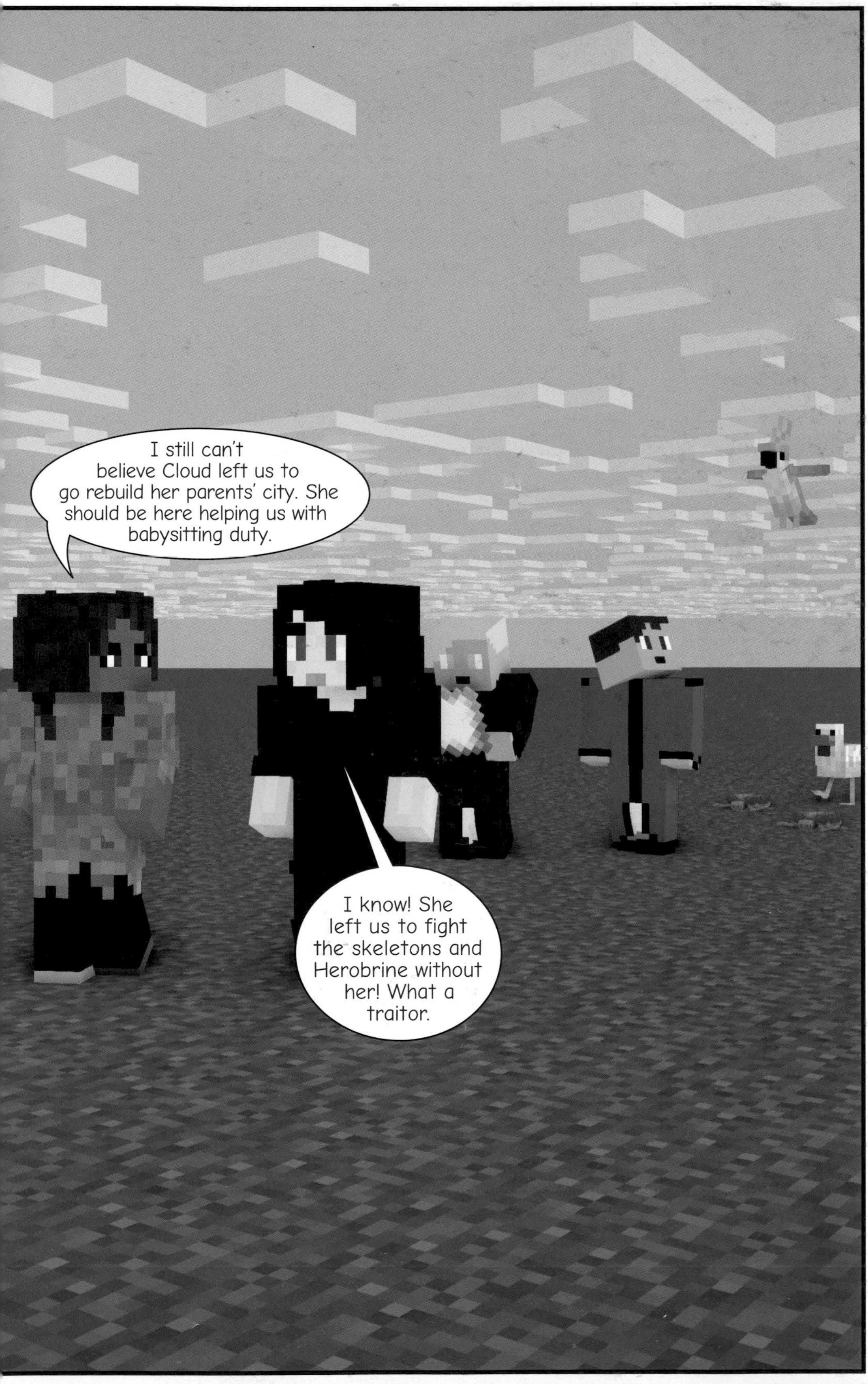
I still can't believe Cloud left us to go rebuild her parents' city. She should be here helping us with babysitting duty.
I know! She left us to fight the skeletons and Herobrine without her! What a traitor.

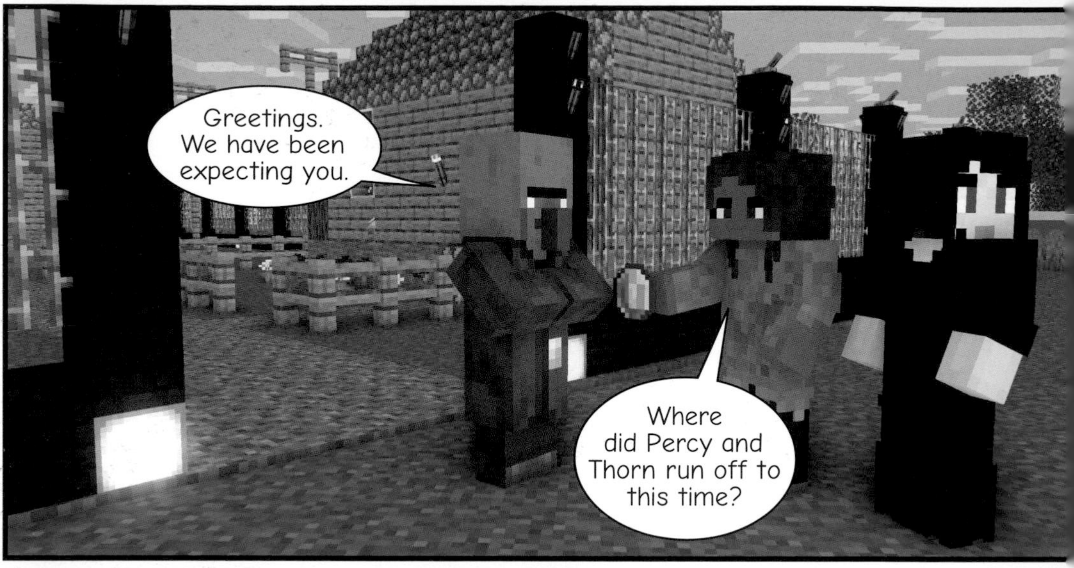
Greetings. We have been expecting you.
Where did Percy and Thorn run off to this time?

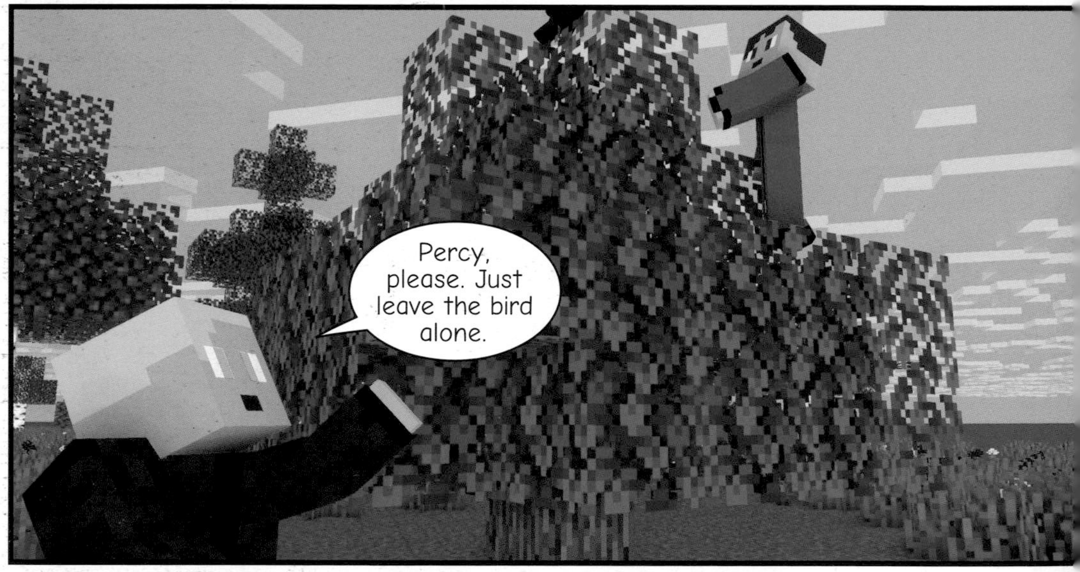
Percy, please. Just leave the bird alone.

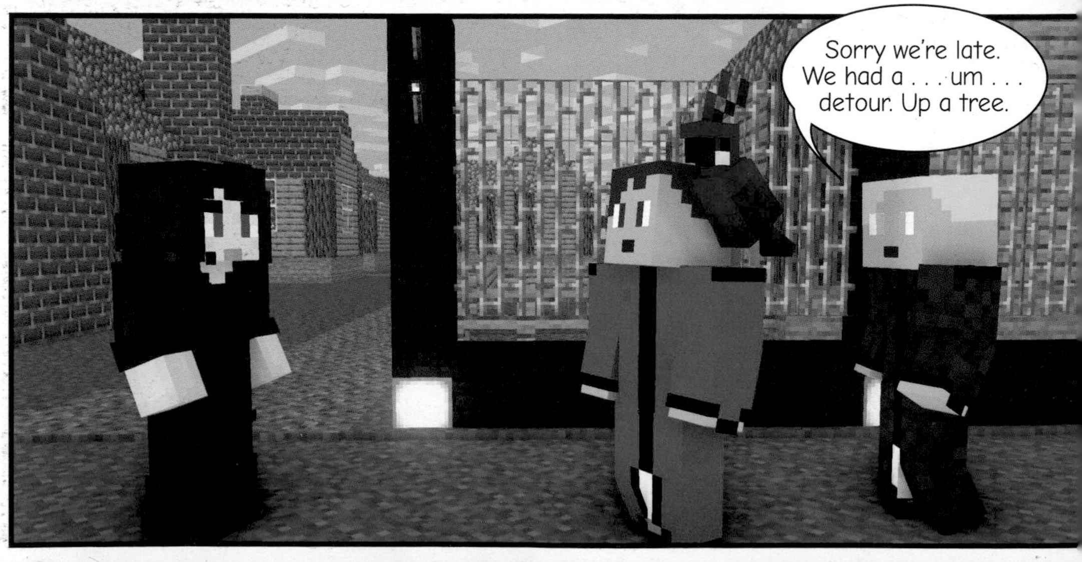
Sorry we're late. We had a . . . um . . . detour. Up a tree.

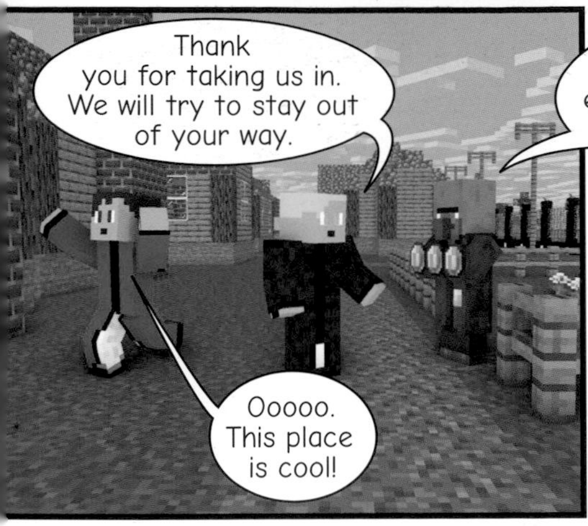
Thank you for taking us in. We will try to stay out of your way.
Your friends have paid us well in exchange for keeping you here. Stay as long as you'd like.
Ooooo. This place is cool!

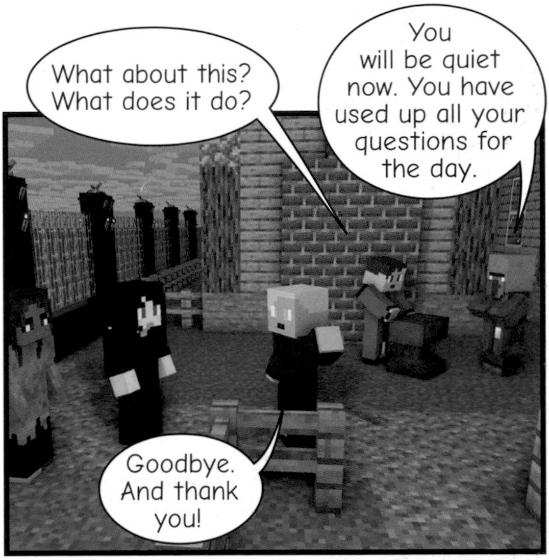
What about this? What does it do?
You will be quiet now. You have used up all your questions for the day.
Goodbye. And thank you!

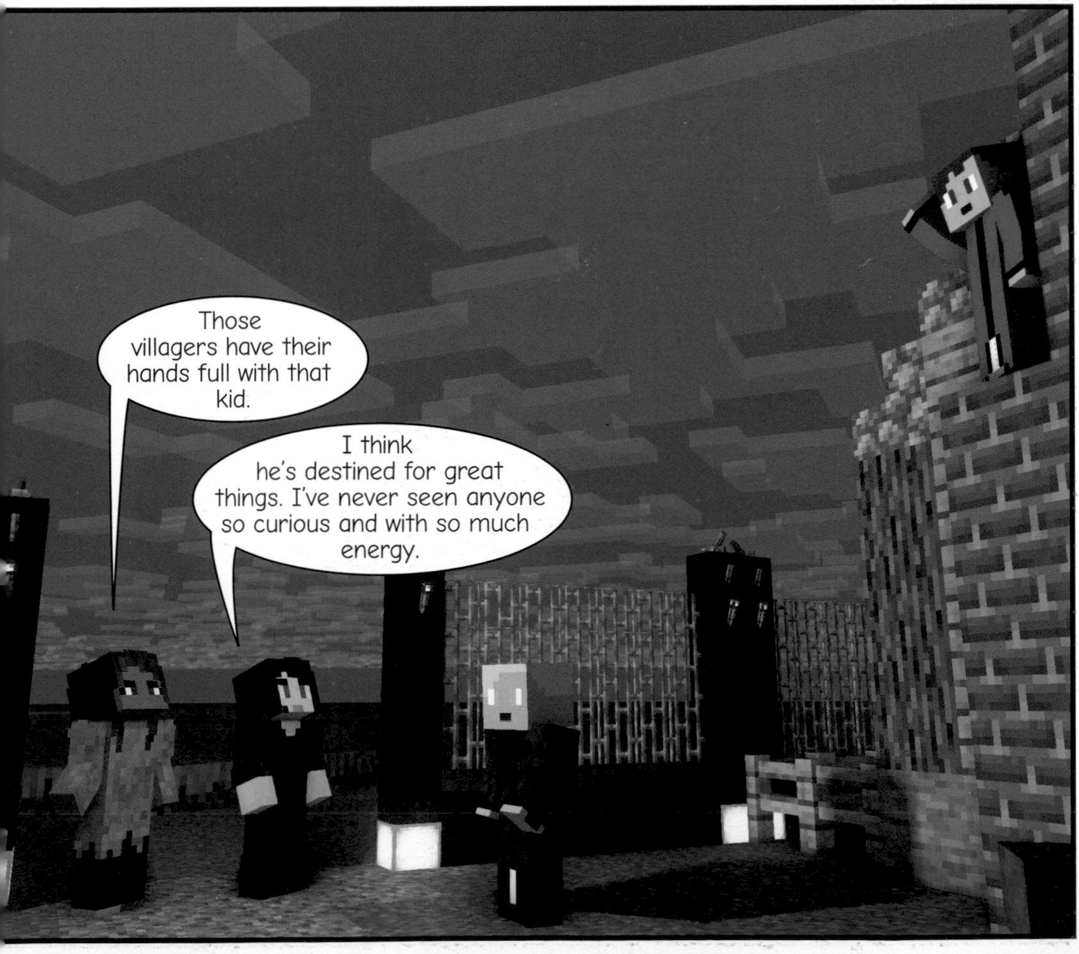
Those villagers have their hands full with that kid.
I think he's destined for great things. I've never seen anyone so curious and with so much energy.

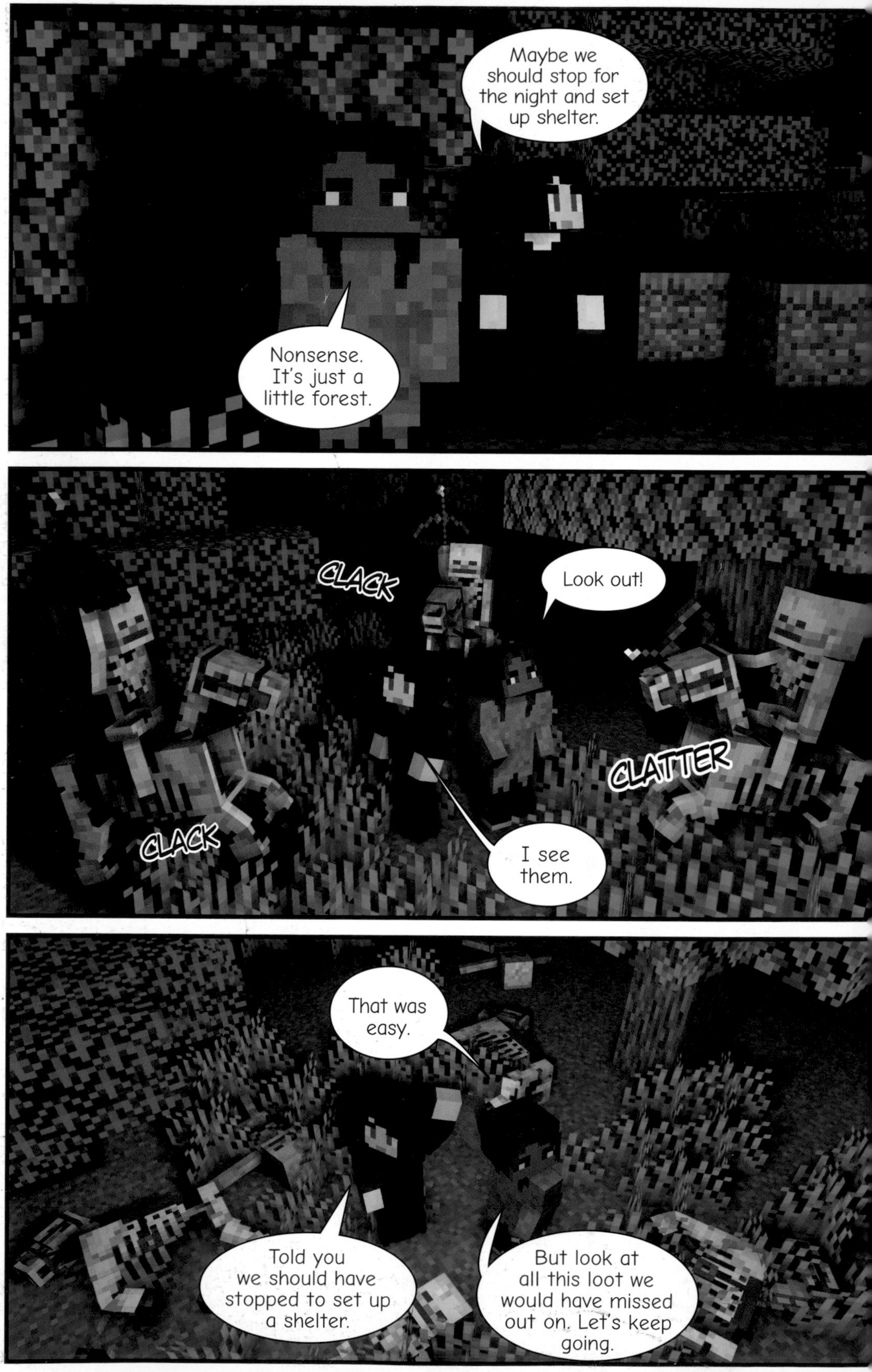
Maybe we should stop for the night and set up shelter.
Nonsense. It's just a little forest.
CLACK
Look out!
CLATTER
CLACK
I see them.
That was easy.
Told you we should have stopped to set up a shelter.
But look at all this loot we would have missed out on. Let's keep going.

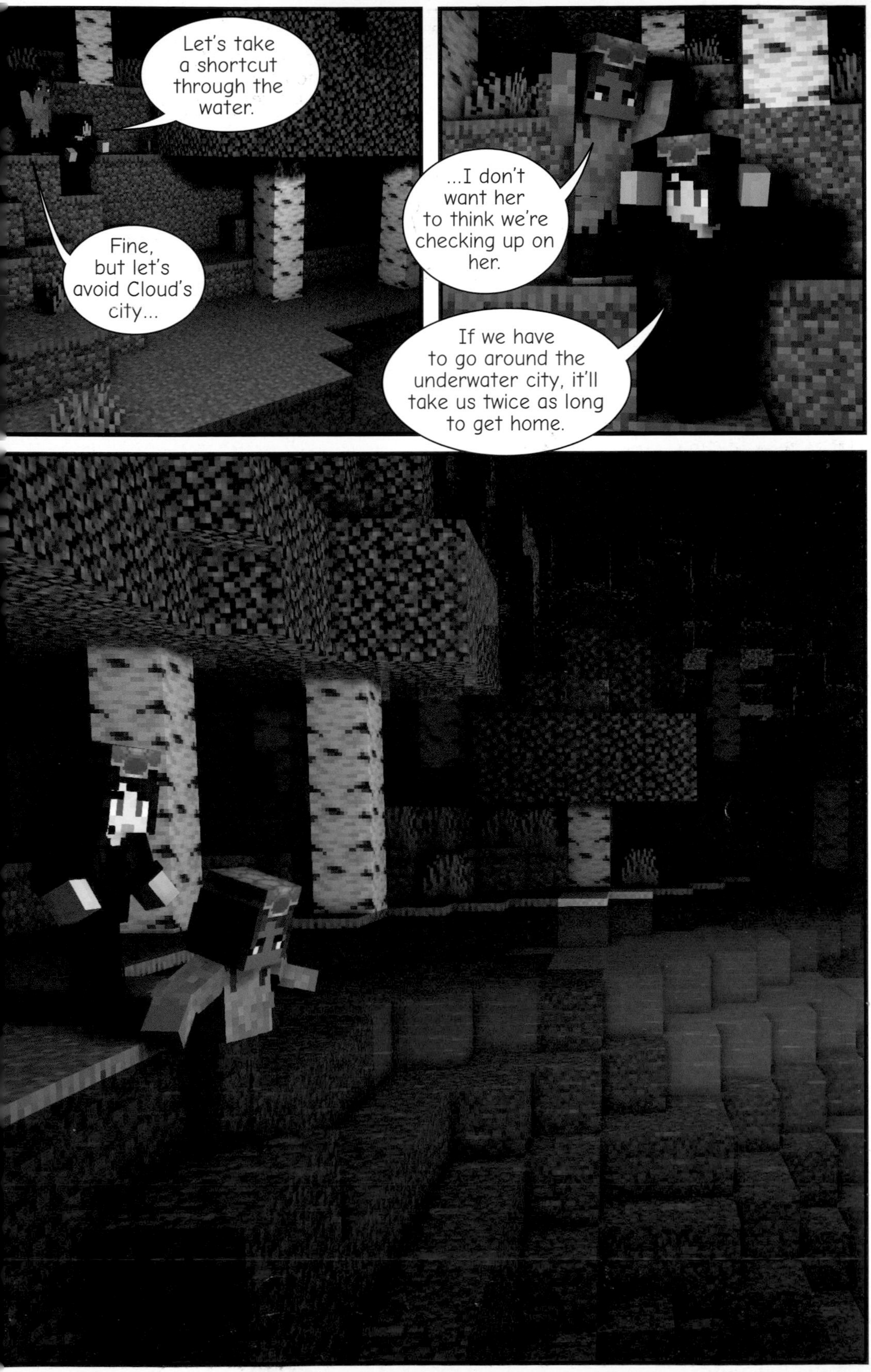
Let's take a shortcut through the water.
Fine, but let's avoid Cloud's city...
...I don't want her to think we're checking up on her.
If we have to go around the underwater city, it'll take us twice as long to get home.

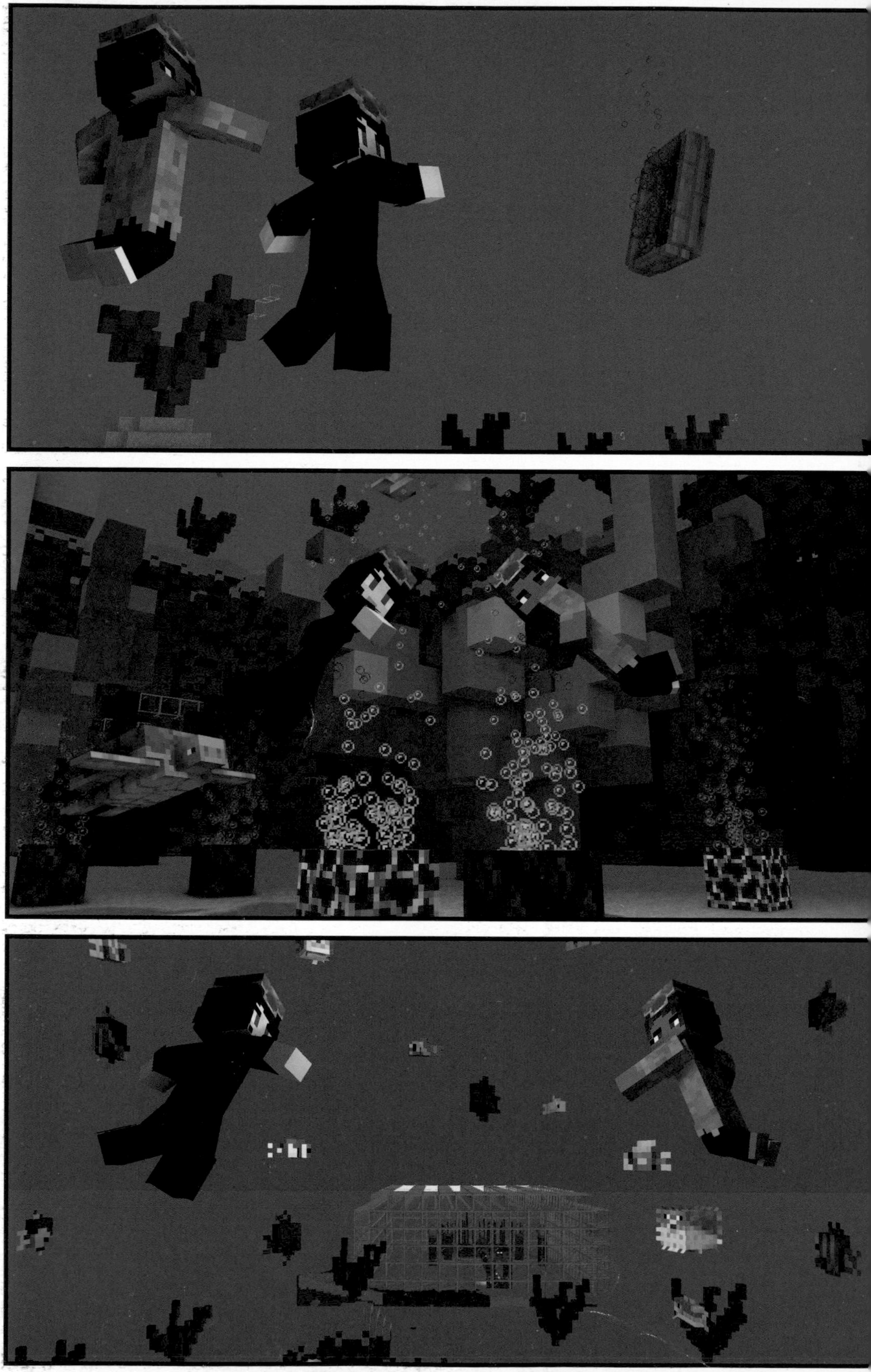

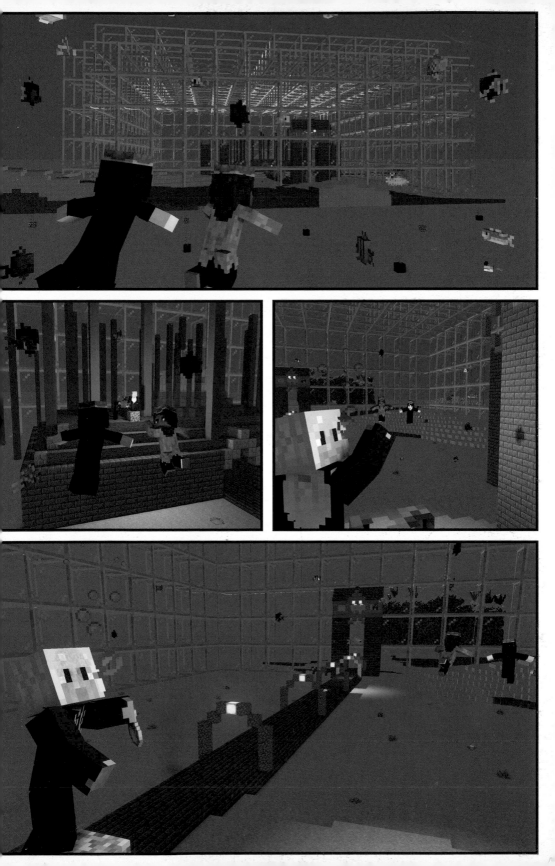

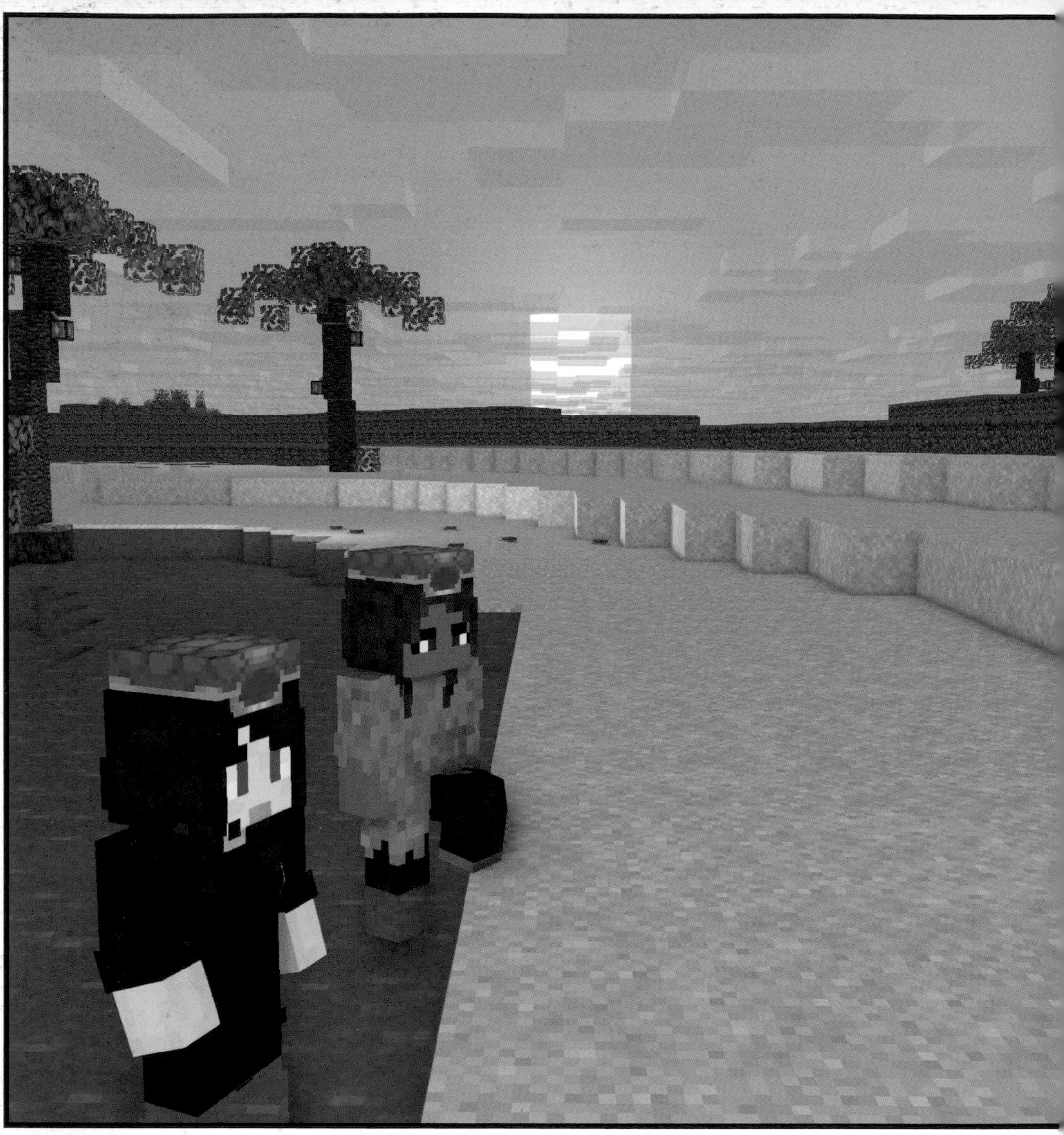

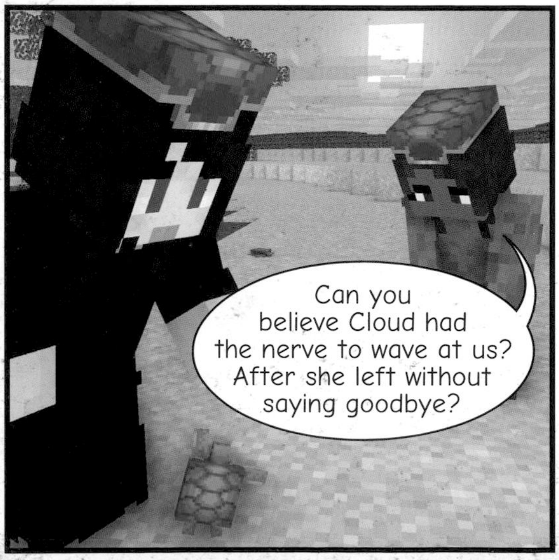
Can you believe Cloud had the nerve to wave at us? After she left without saying goodbye?

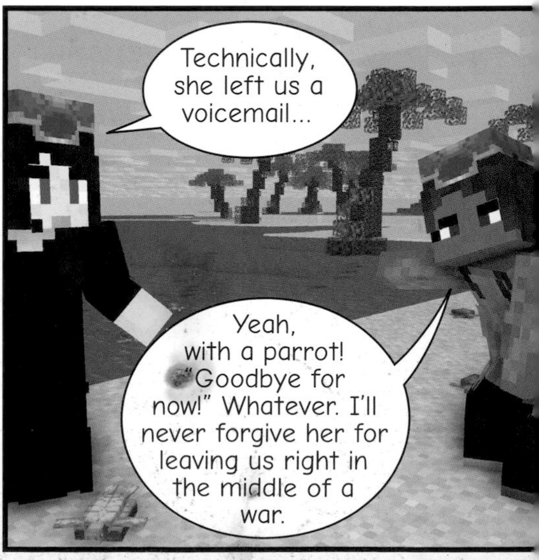
Technically, she left us a voicemail...
Yeah, with a parrot! "Goodbye for now!" Whatever. I'll never forgive her for leaving us right in the middle of a war.

CHAPTER 2

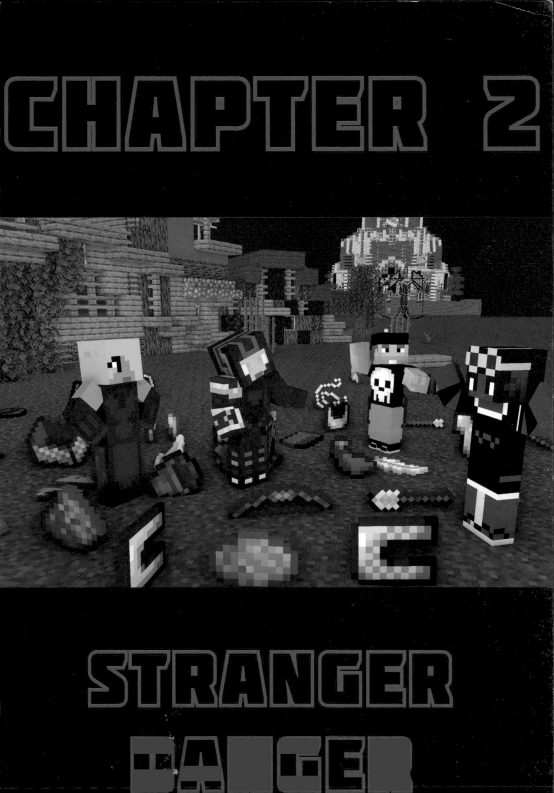

STRANGER
DANGER

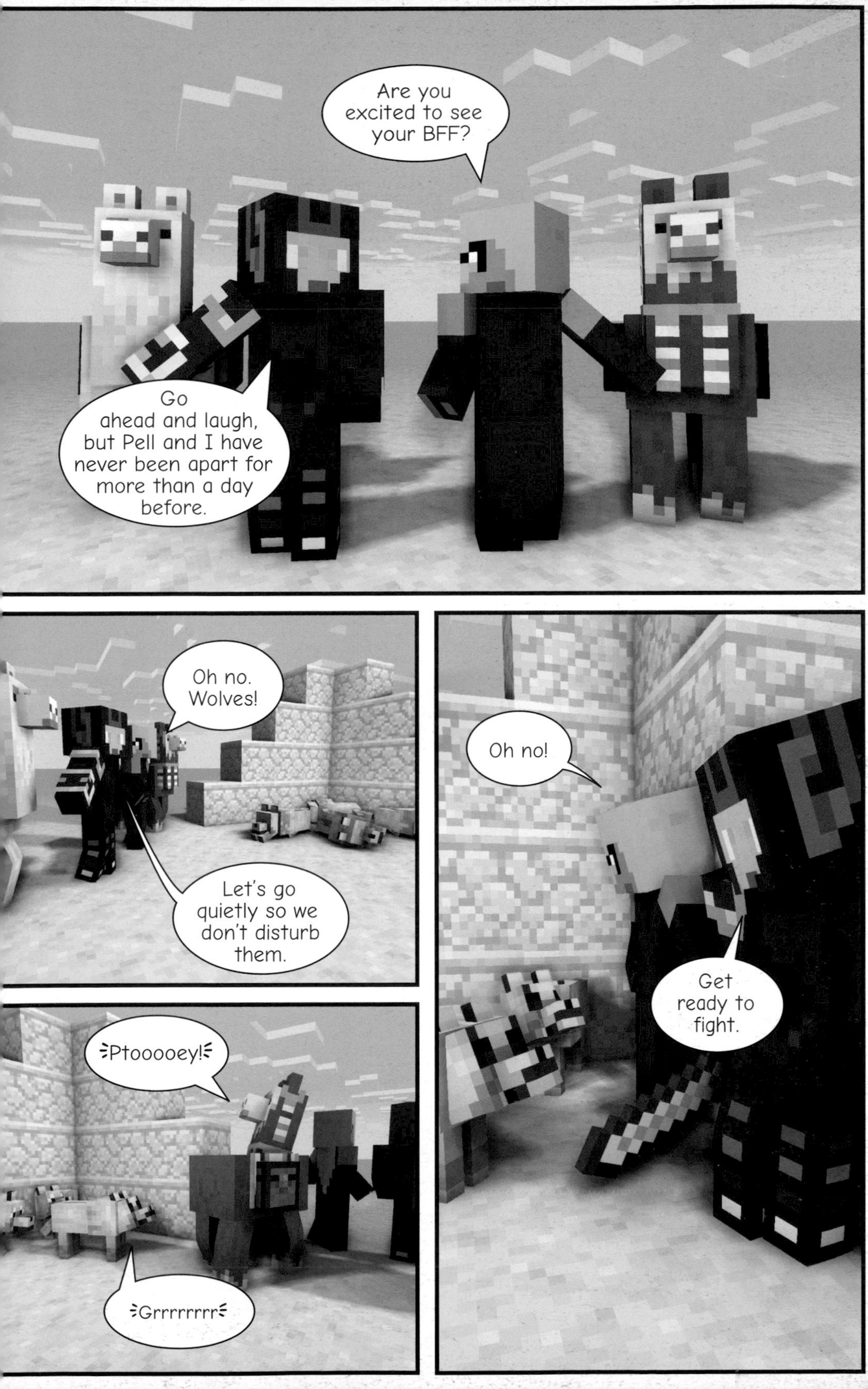

Are you excited to see your BFF?
Go ahead and laugh, but Pell and I have never been apart for more than a day before.
Oh no. Wolves!
Let's go quietly so we don't disturb them.
Ptooooey!
Grrrrrrr
Oh no!
Get ready to fight.

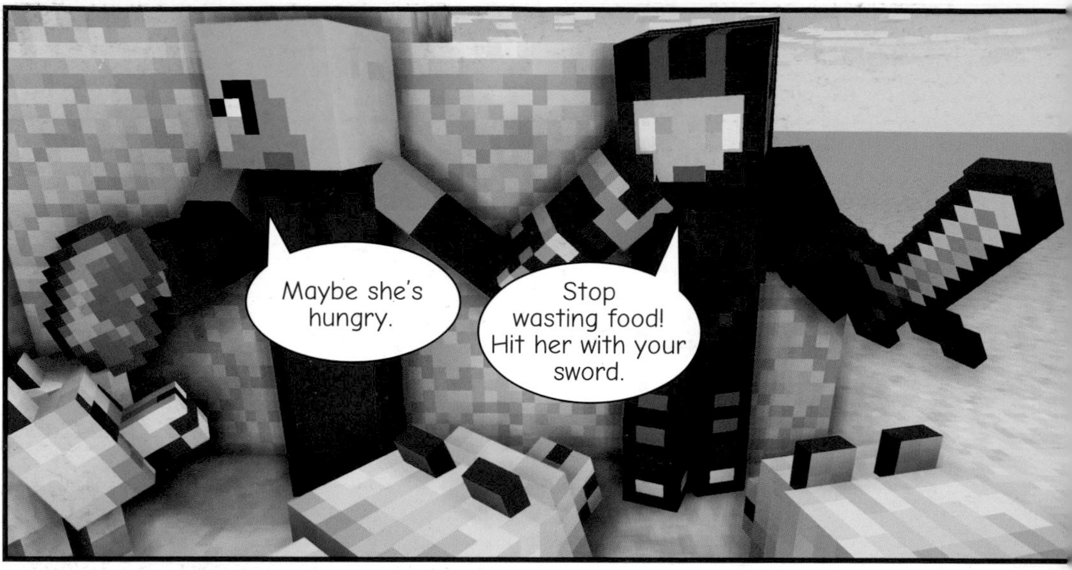
Maybe she's hungry.
Stop wasting food! Hit her with your sword.

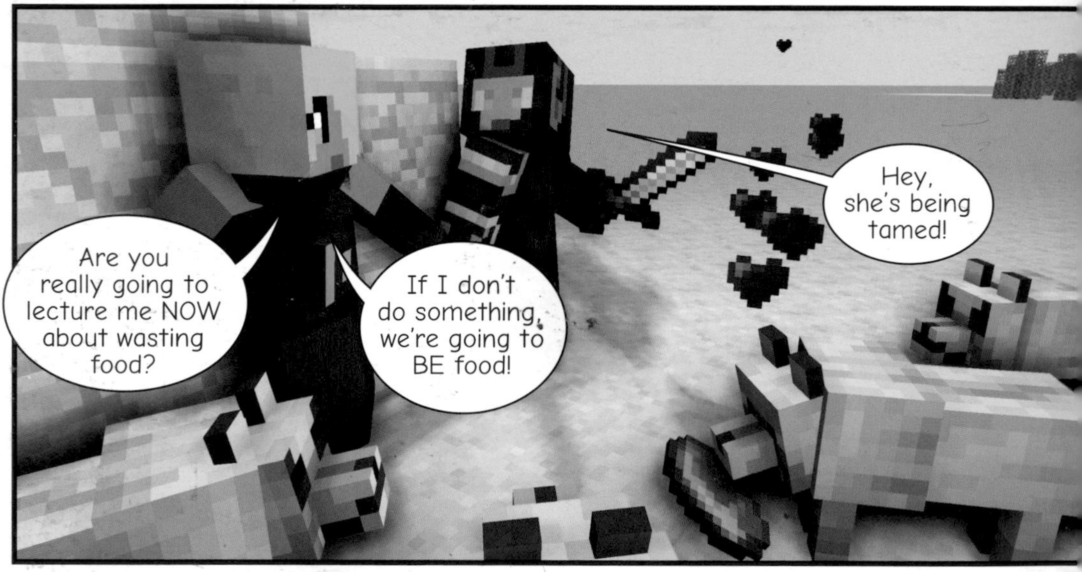
Hey, she's being tamed!
Are you really going to lecture me NOW about wasting food?
If I don't do something, we're going to BE food!

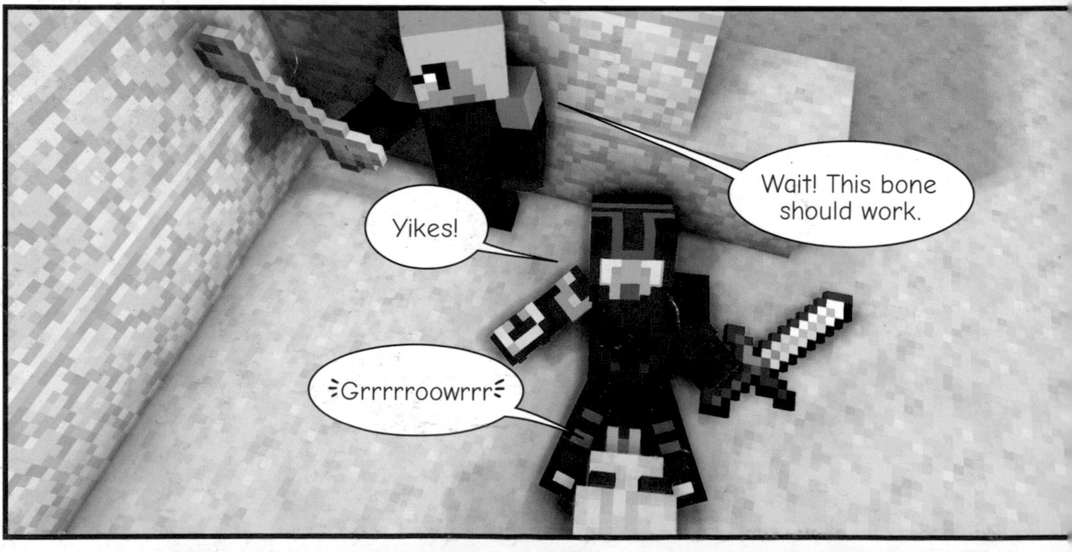
Wait! This bone should work.
Yikes!
Grrrrroowrrr

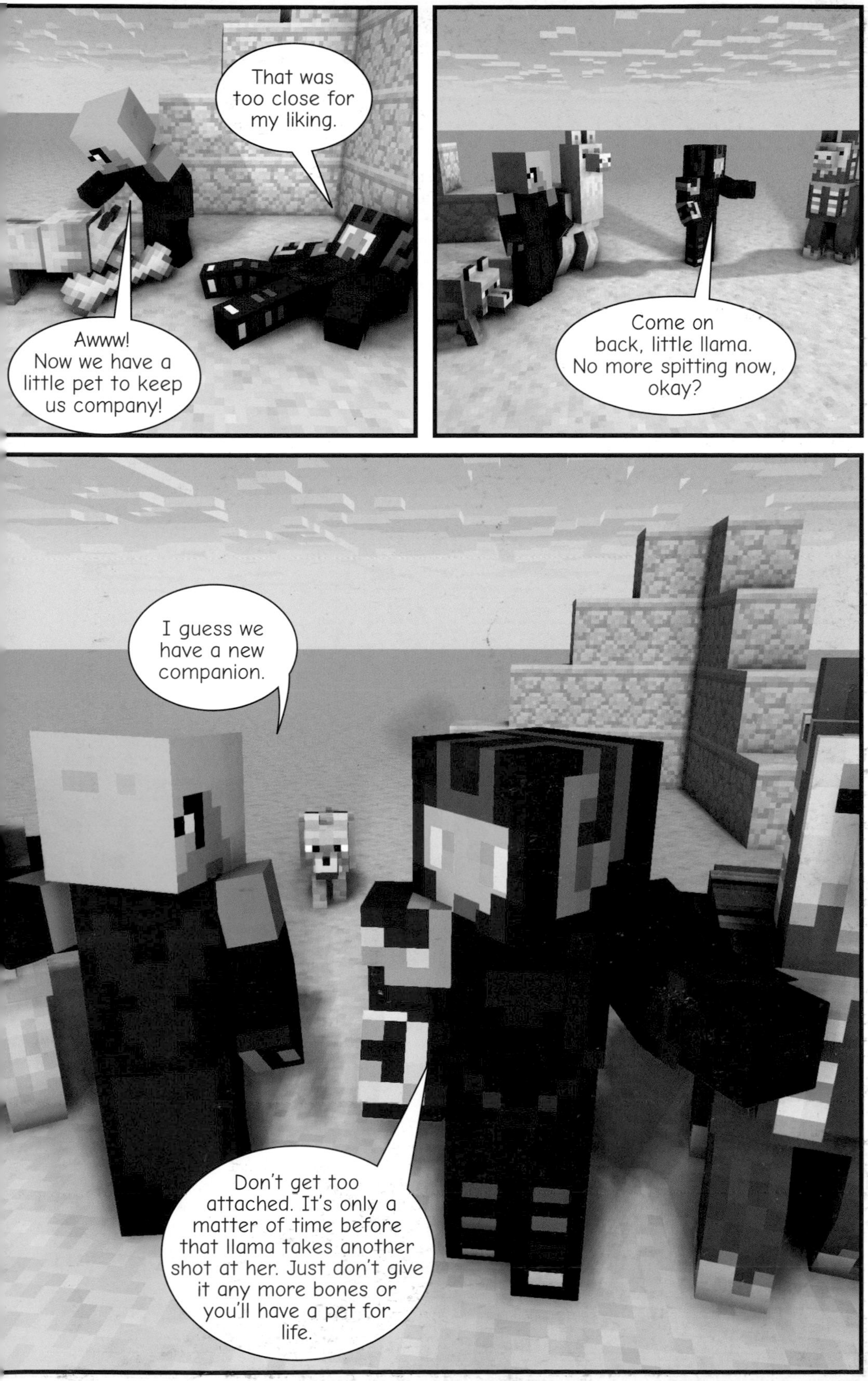
That was too close for my liking.
Awww! Now we have a little pet to keep us company!
Come on back, little llama. No more spitting now, okay?
I guess we have a new companion.
Don't get too attached. It's only a matter of time before that llama takes another shot at her. Just don't give it any more bones or you'll have a pet for life.

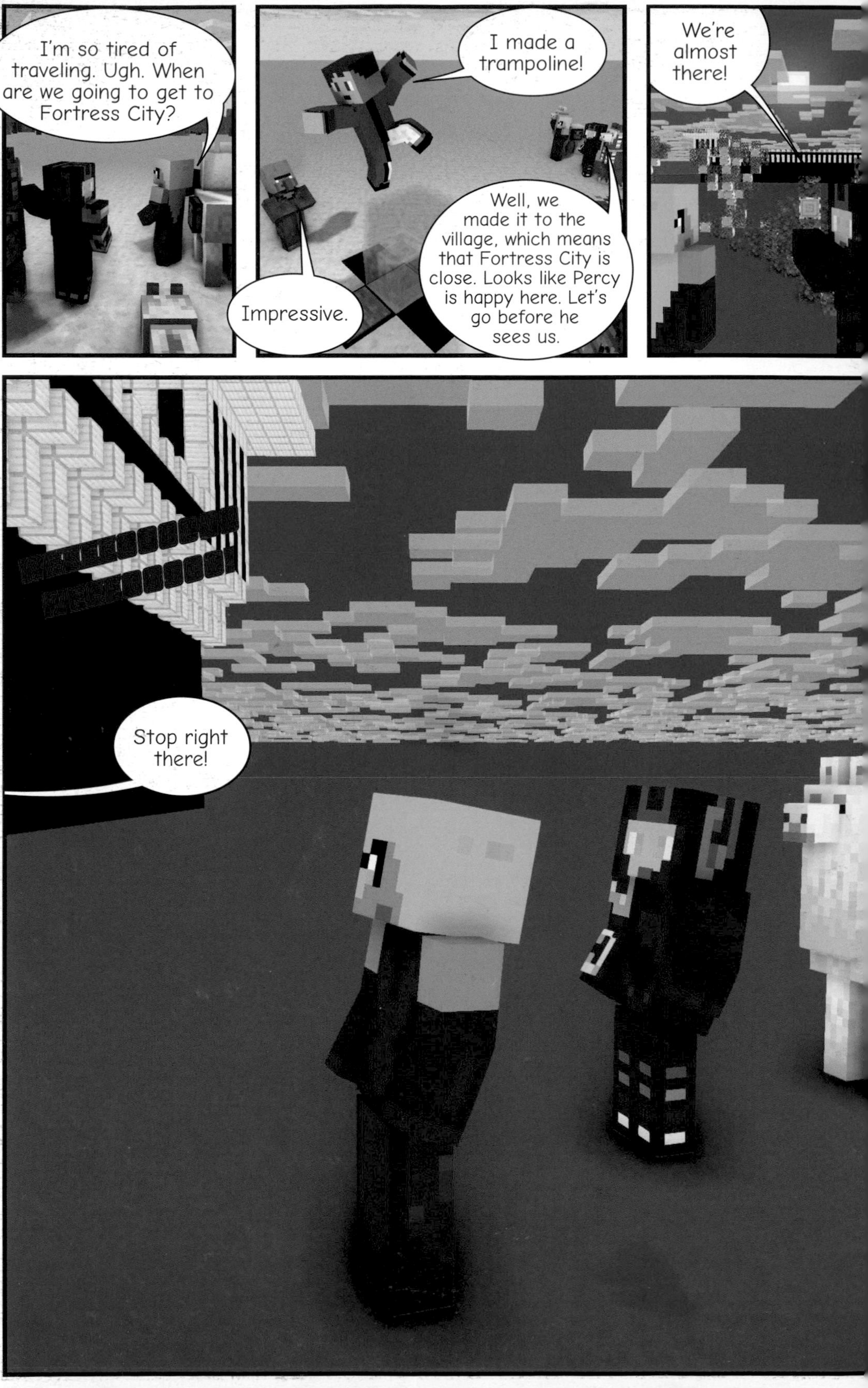
I'm so tired of traveling. Ugh. When are we going to get to Fortress City?
I made a trampoline!
Impressive.
Well, we made it to the village, which means that Fortress City is close. Looks like Percy is happy here. Let's go before he sees us.
We're almost there!
Stop right there!

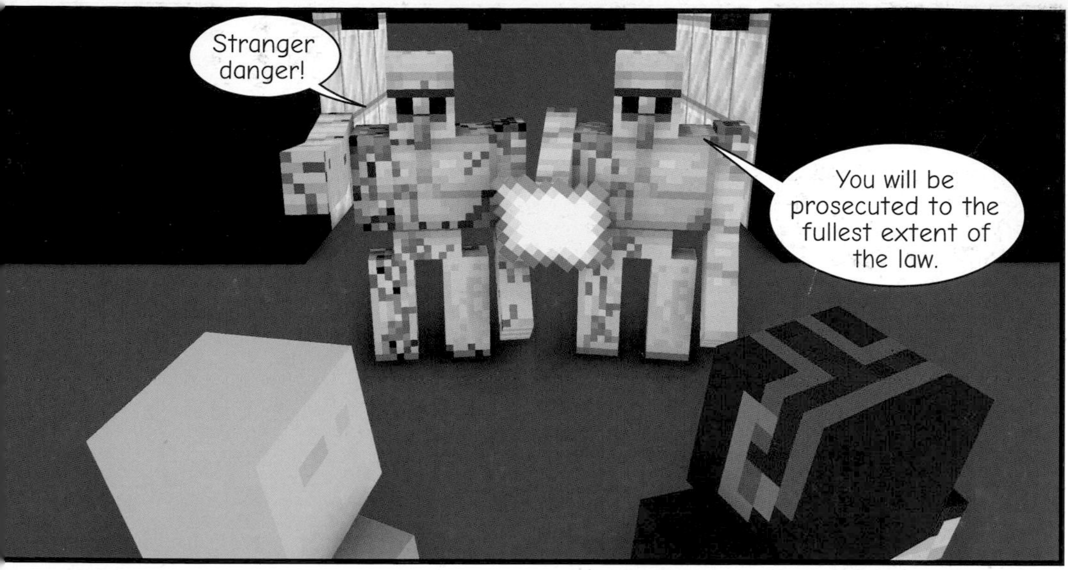
Stranger danger!
You will be prosecuted to the fullest extent of the law.

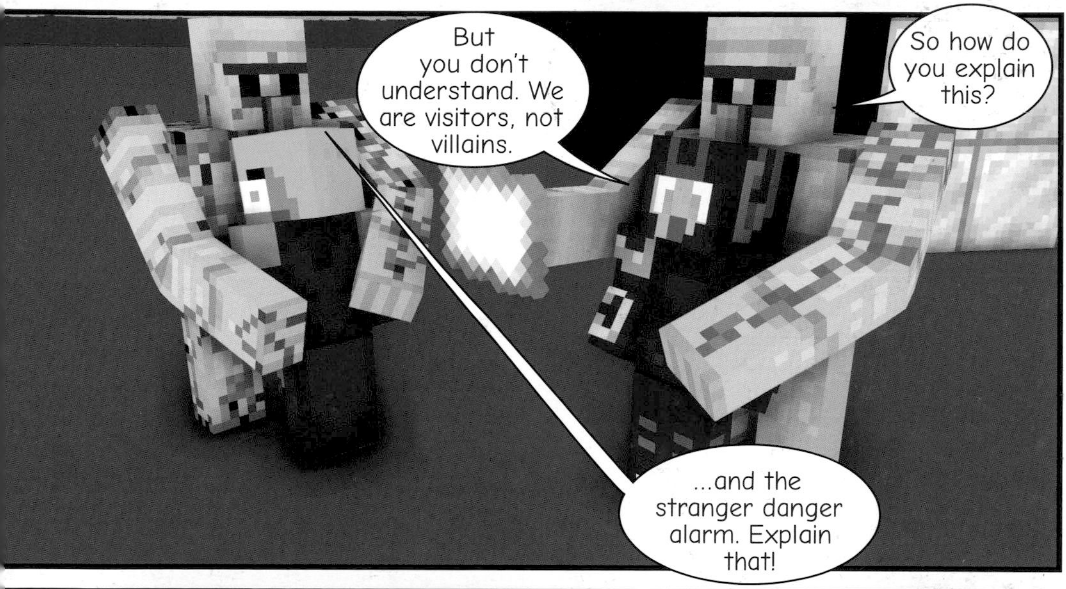
But you don't understand. We are visitors, not villains.
So how do you explain this?
...and the stranger danger alarm. Explain that!

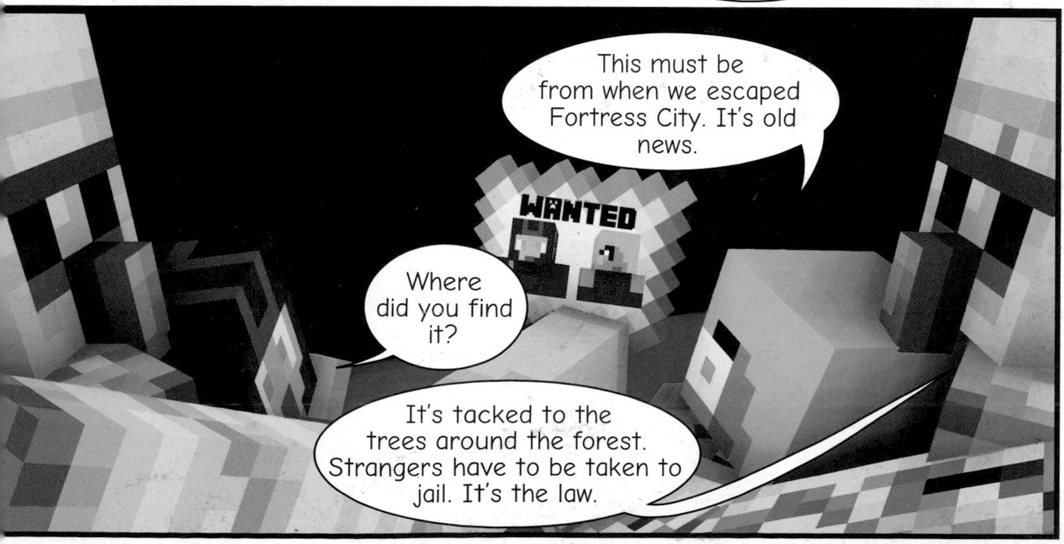
This must be from when we escaped Fortress City. It's old news.
WANTED
Where did you find it?
It's tacked to the trees around the forest. Strangers have to be taken to jail. It's the law.

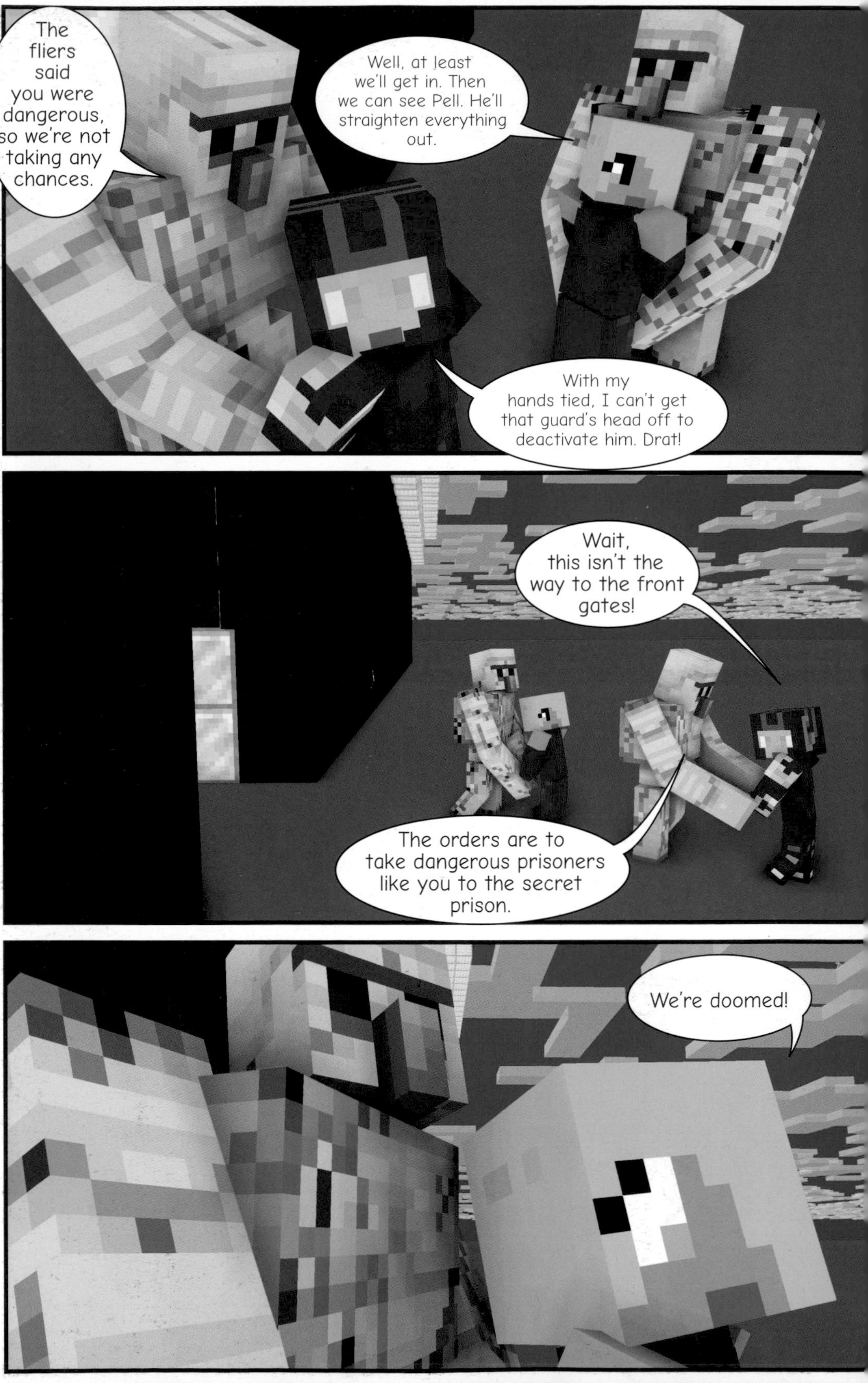
The fliers said you were dangerous, so we're not taking any chances.
Well, at least we'll get in. Then we can see Pell. He'll straighten everything out.
With my hands tied, I can't get that guard's head off to deactivate him. Drat!
Wait, this isn't the way to the front gates!
The orders are to take dangerous prisoners like you to the secret prison.
We're doomed!

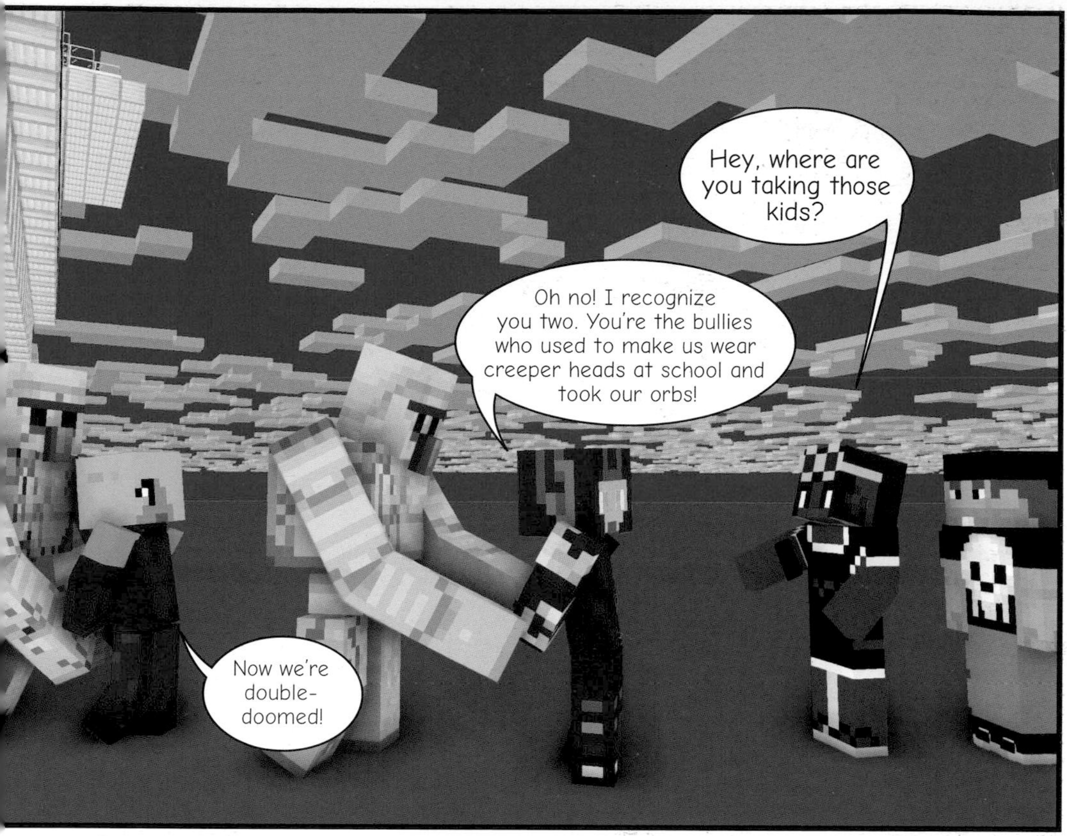
Hey, where are you taking those kids?
Oh no! I recognize you two. You're the bullies who used to make us wear creeper heads at school and took our orbs!
Now we're double-doomed!

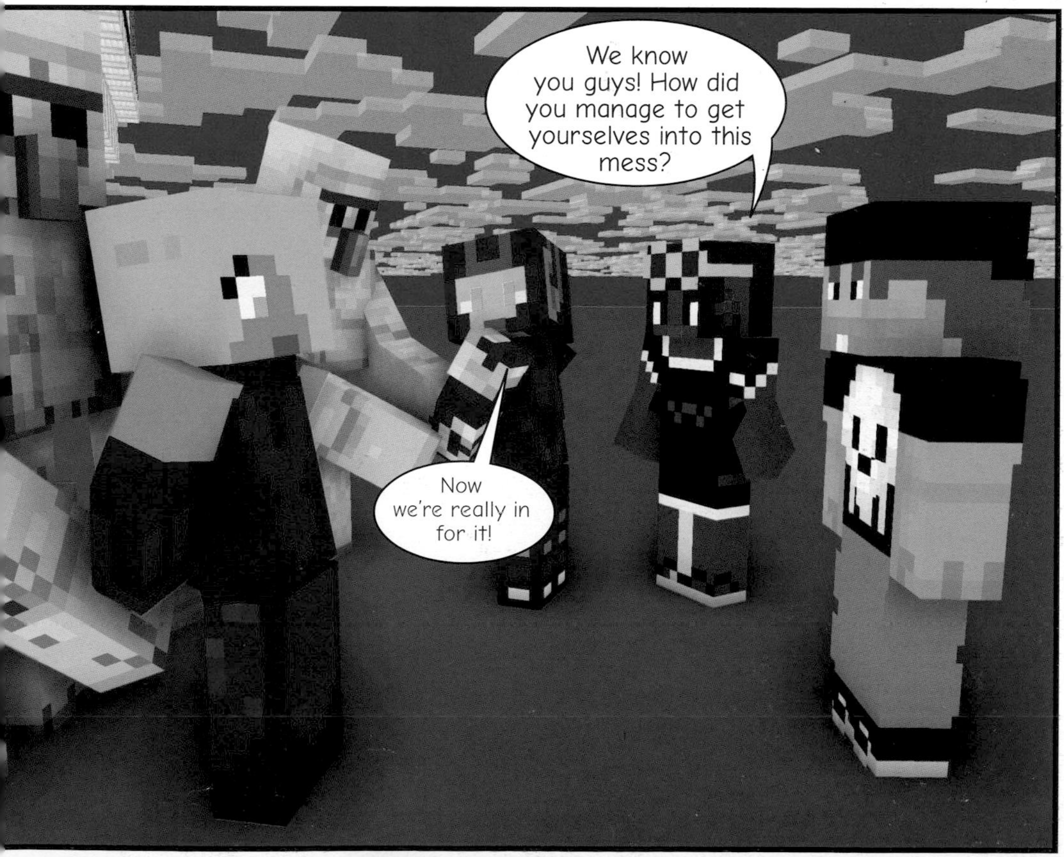
We know you guys! How did you manage to get yourselves into this mess?
Now we're really in for it!

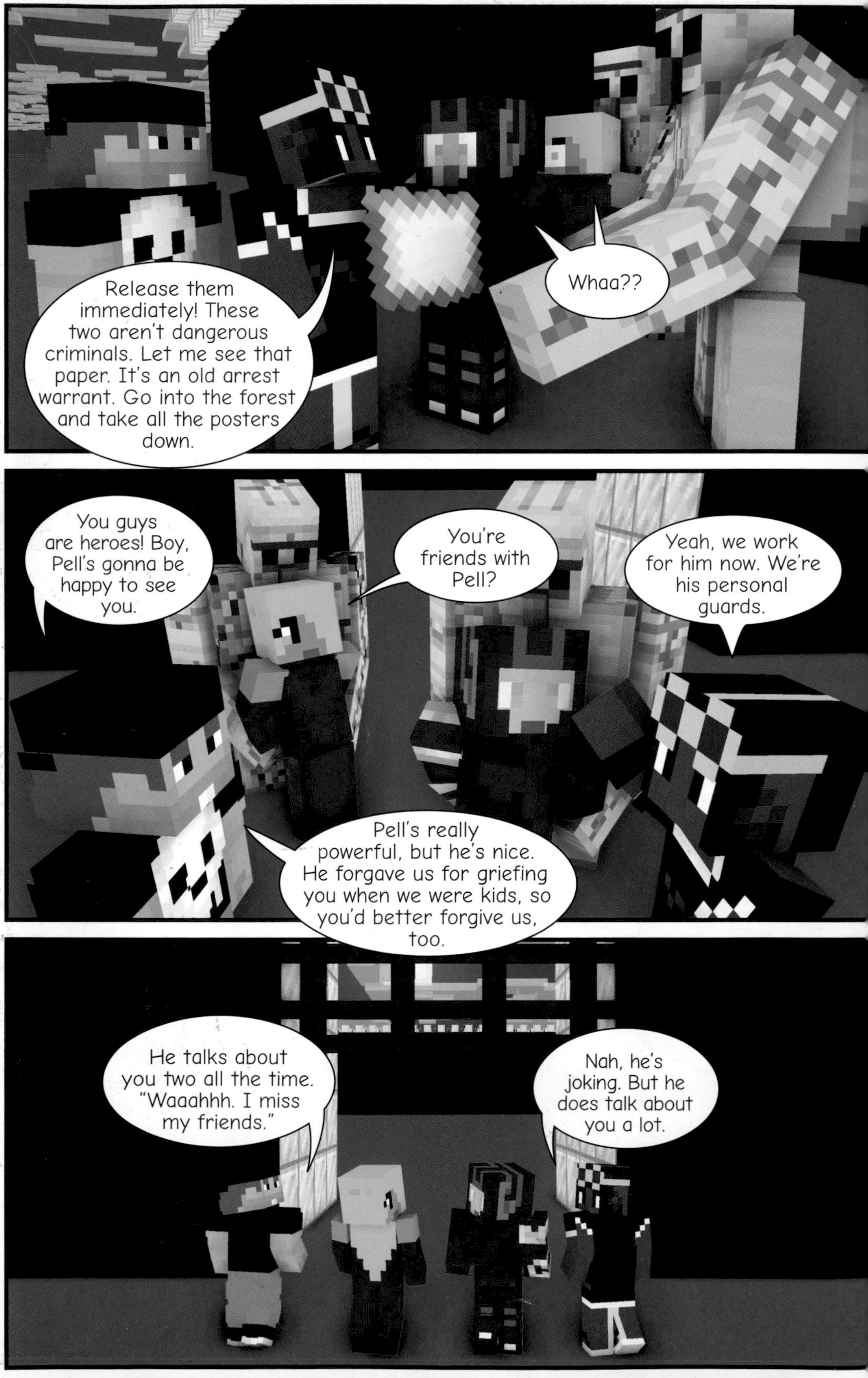
Release them immediately! These two aren't dangerous criminals. Let me see that paper. It's an old arrest warrant. Go into the forest and take all the posters down.
Whaa??
You guys are heroes! Boy, Pell's gonna be happy to see you.
You're friends with Pell?
Yeah, we work for him now. We're his personal guards.
Pell's really powerful, but he's nice. He forgave us for griefing you when we were kids, so you'd better forgive us, too.
He talks about you two all the time. "Waaahhh. I miss my friends."
Nah, he's joking. But he does talk about you a lot.

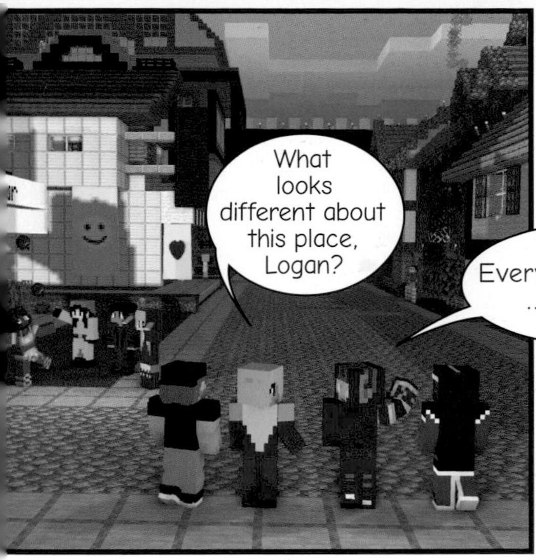
What looks different about this place, Logan?
Everyone seems ...happy!

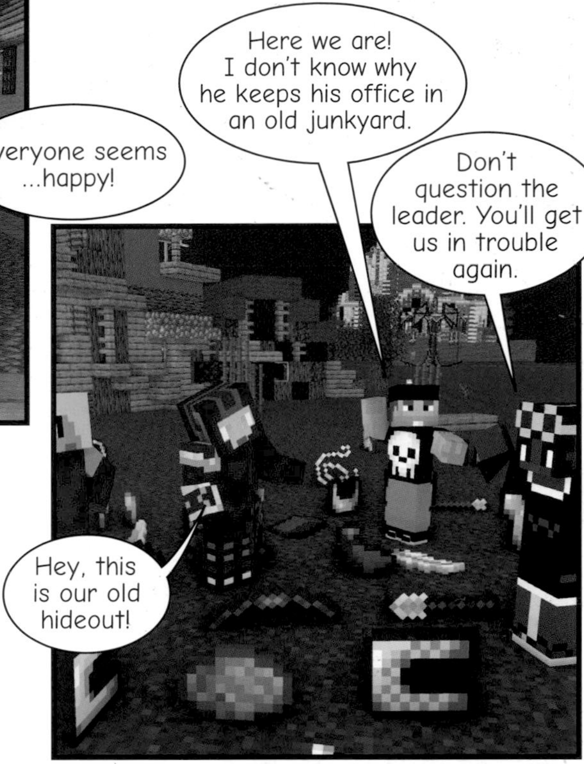
Here we are! I don't know why he keeps his office in an old junkyard.
Don't question the leader. You'll get us in trouble again.
Hey, this is our old hideout!

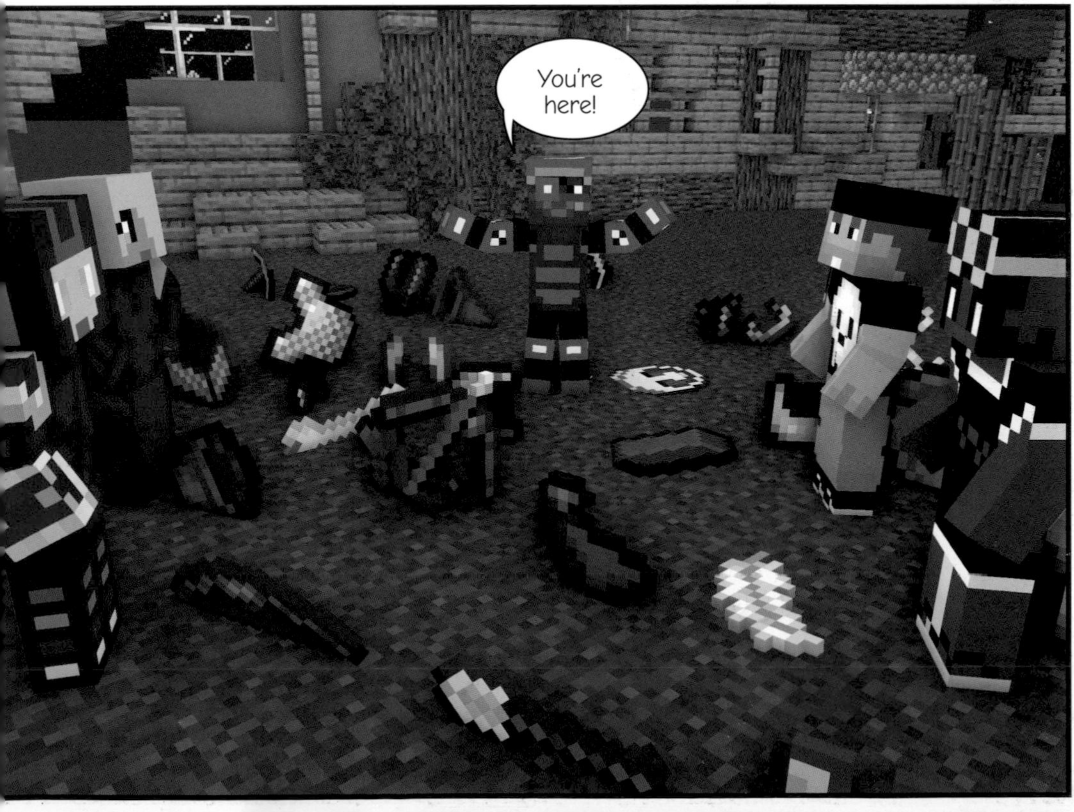
You're here!

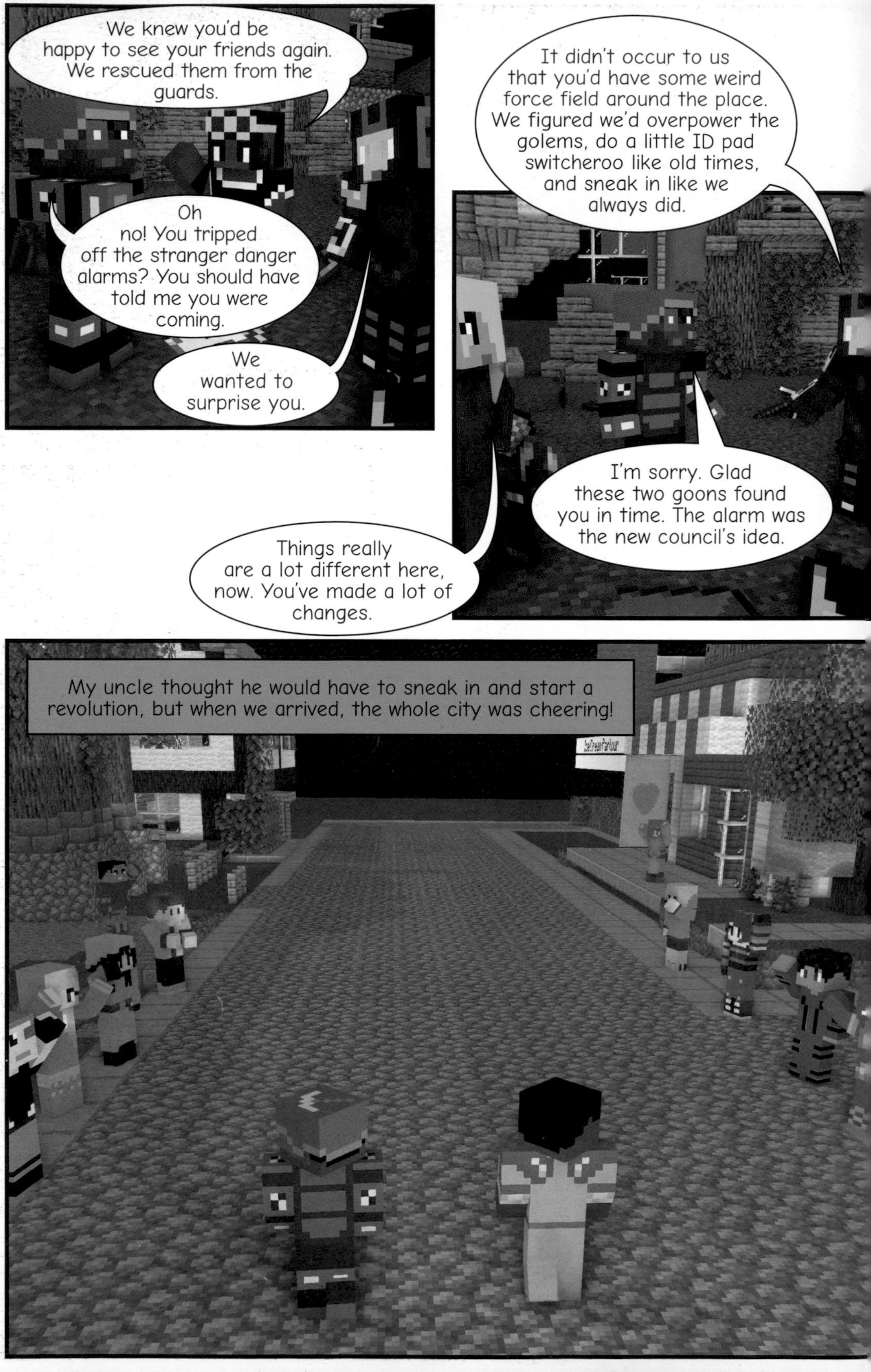
We knew you'd be happy to see your friends again. We rescued them from the guards.
Oh no! You tripped off the stranger danger alarms? You should have told me you were coming.
We wanted to surprise you.
It didn't occur to us that you'd have some weird force field around the place. We figured we'd overpower the golems, do a little ID pad switcheroo like old times, and sneak in like we always did.
I'm sorry. Glad these two goons found you in time. The alarm was the new council's idea.
Things really are a lot different here, now. You've made a lot of changes.
My uncle thought he would have to sneak in and start a revolution, but when we arrived, the whole city was cheering!

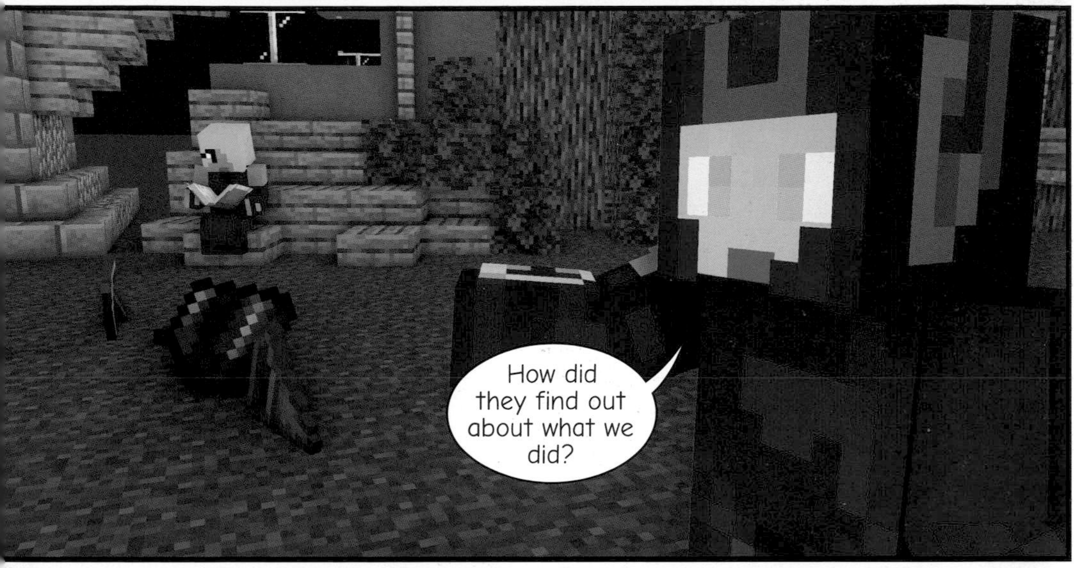
How did they find out about what we did?

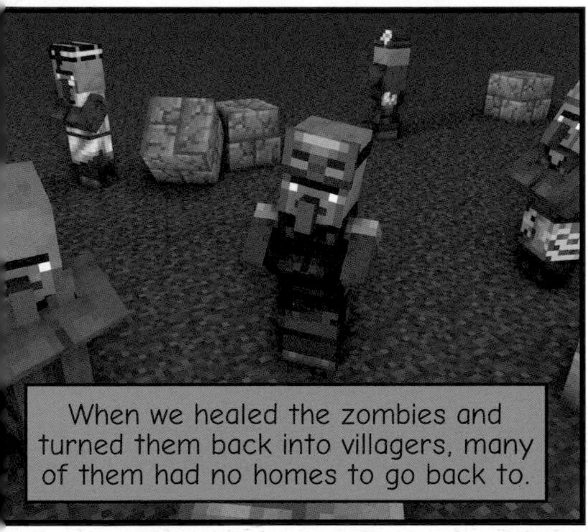
When we healed the zombies and turned them back into villagers, many of them had no homes to go back to.

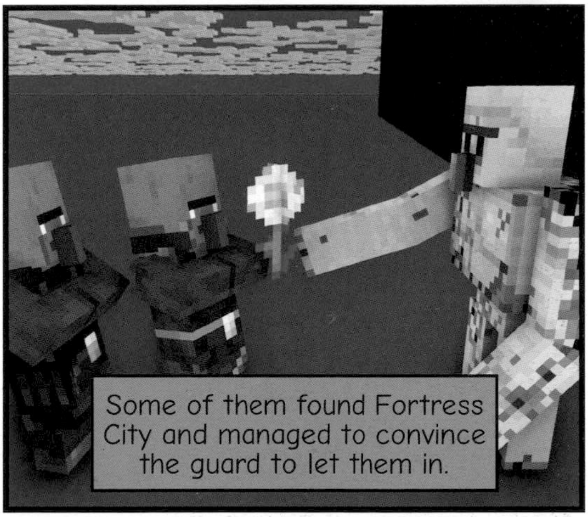
Some of them found Fortress City and managed to convince the guard to let them in.

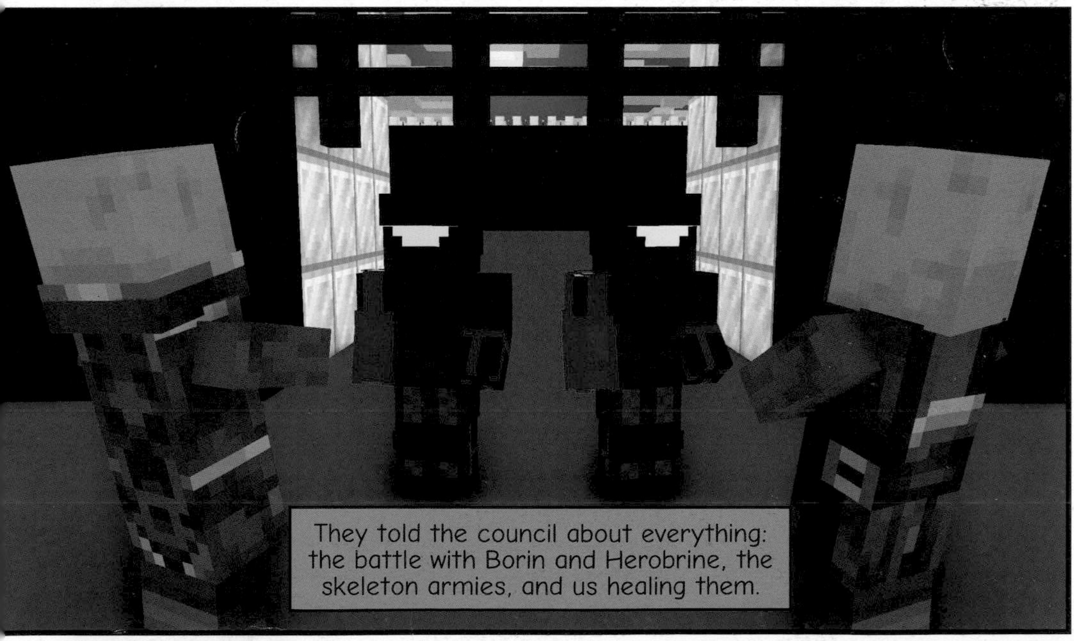
They told the council about everything: the battle with Borin and Herobrine, the skeleton armies, and us healing them.

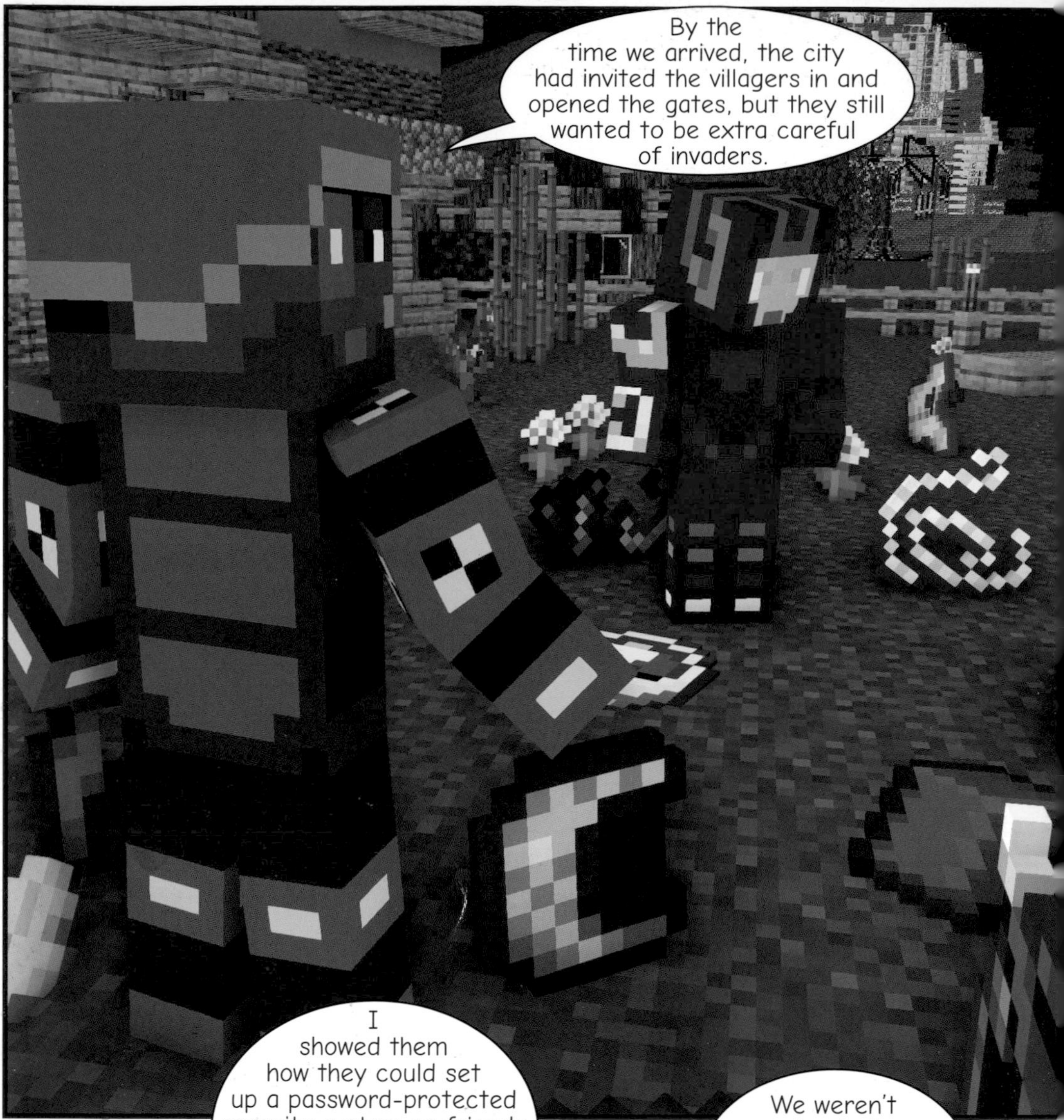
By the time we arrived, the city had invited the villagers in and opened the gates, but they still wanted to be extra careful of invaders.

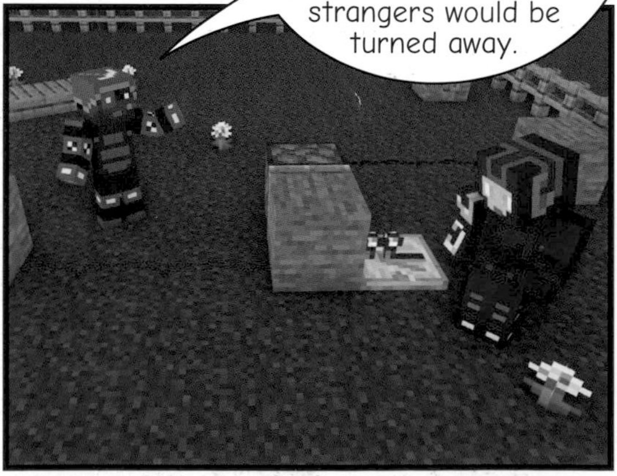
I showed them how they could set up a password-protected security system so friends of the city could come and go as they pleased, but strangers would be turned away.

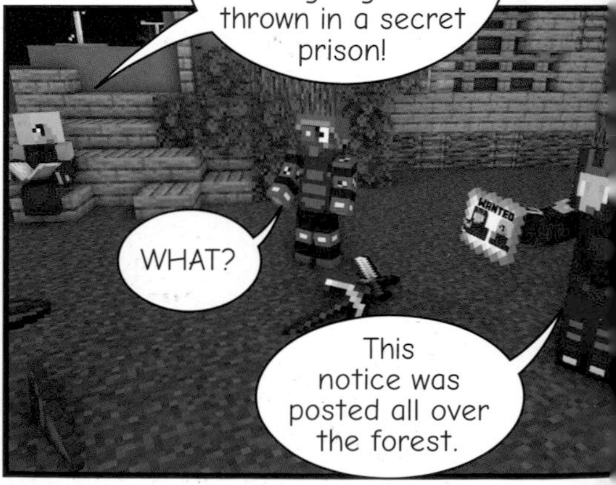
We weren't going to be turned away. We were going to be thrown in a secret prison!
WHAT?
This notice was posted all over the forest.

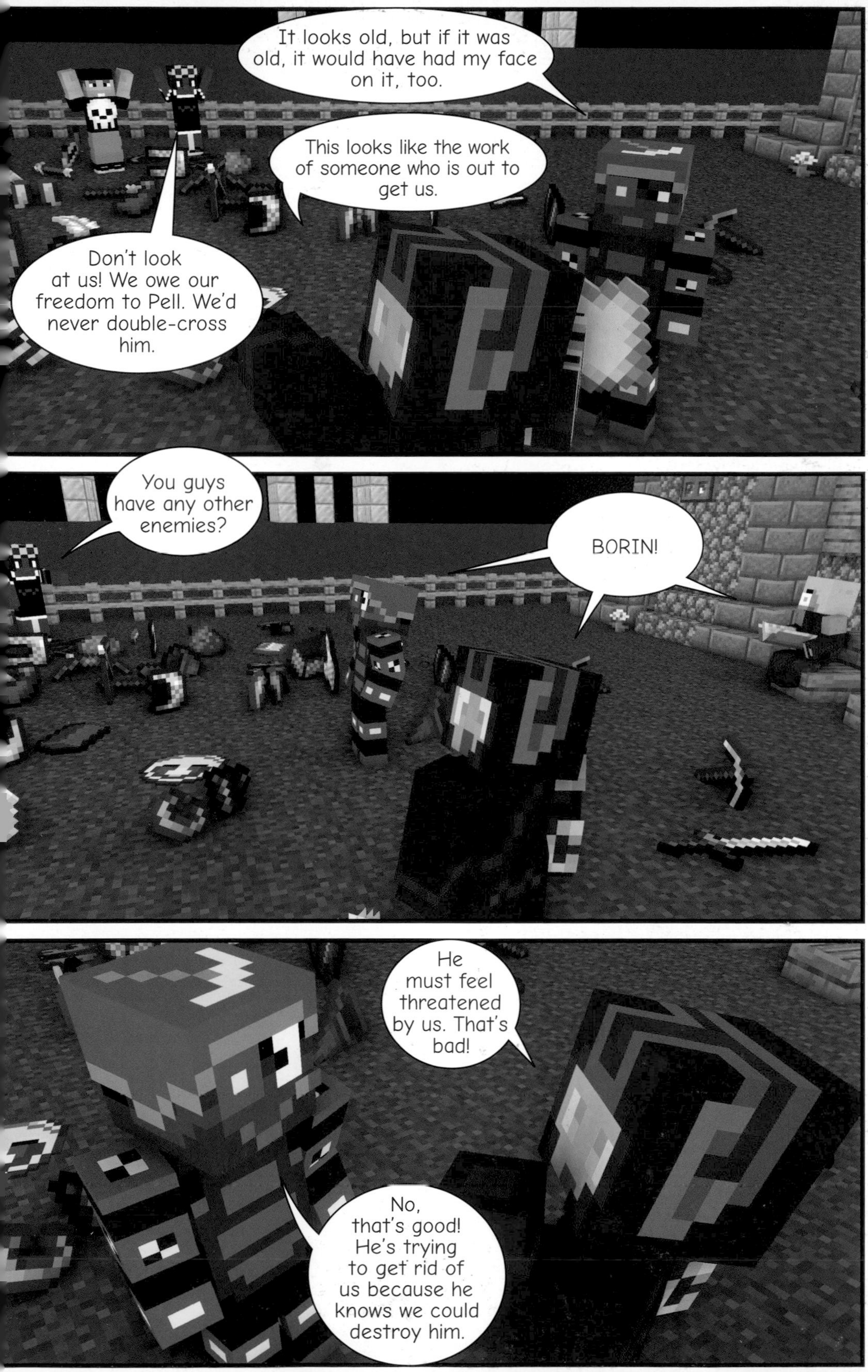
It looks old, but if it was old, it would have had my face on it, too.
This looks like the work of someone who is out to get us.
Don't look at us! We owe our freedom to Pell. We'd never double-cross him.
You guys have any other enemies?
BORIN!
He must feel threatened by us. That's bad!
No, that's good! He's trying to get rid of us because he knows we could destroy him.

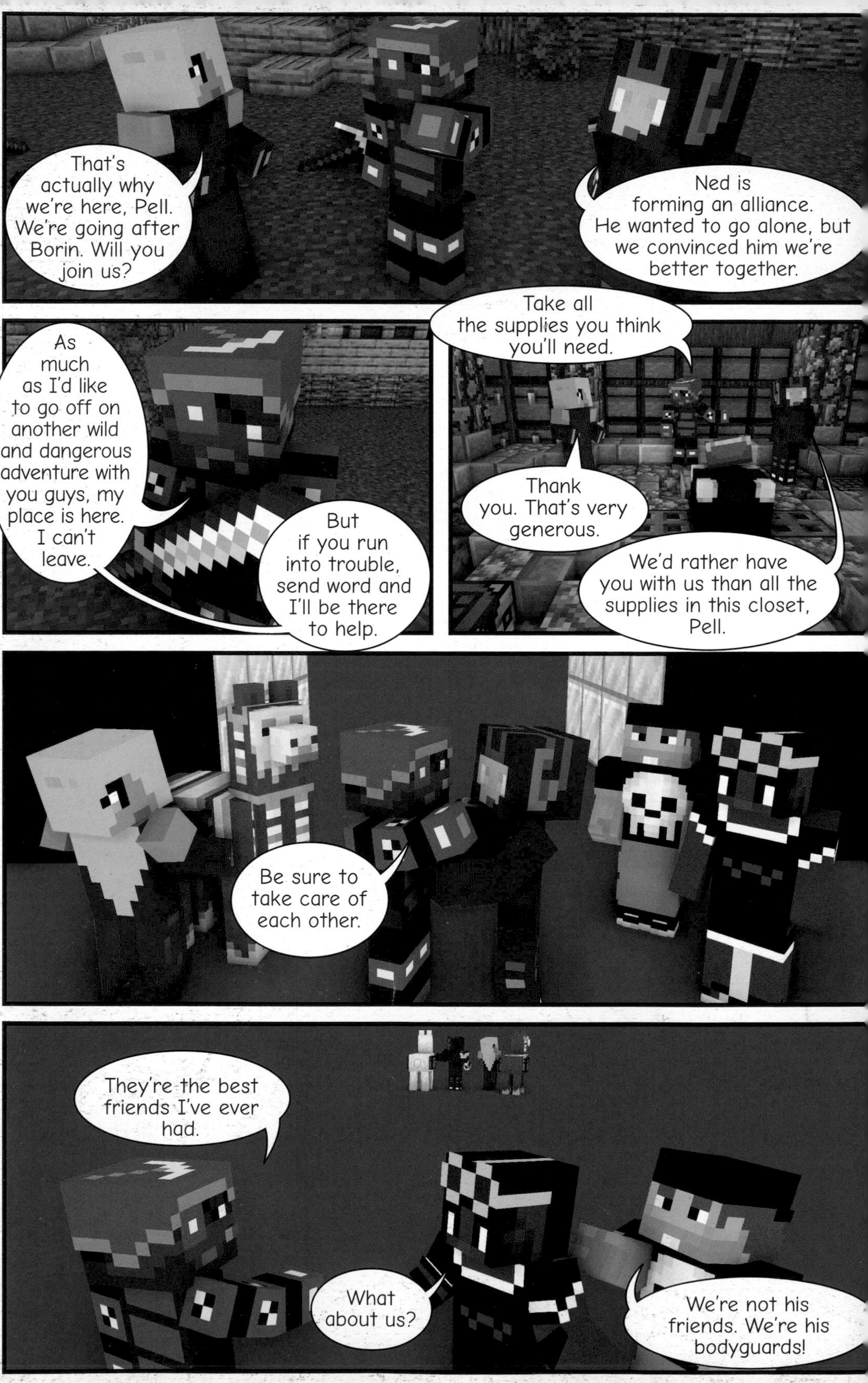
That's actually why we're here, Pell. We're going after Borin. Will you join us?
Ned is forming an alliance. He wanted to go alone, but we convinced him we're better together.
As much as I'd like to go off on another wild and dangerous adventure with you guys, my place is here. I can't leave.
But if you run into trouble, send word and I'll be there to help.
Take all the supplies you think you'll need.
Thank you. That's very generous.
We'd rather have you with us than all the supplies in this closet, Pell.
Be sure to take care of each other.
They're the best friends I've ever had.
What about us?
We're not his friends. We're his bodyguards!

CHAPTER 3

A HERO'S WELCOME

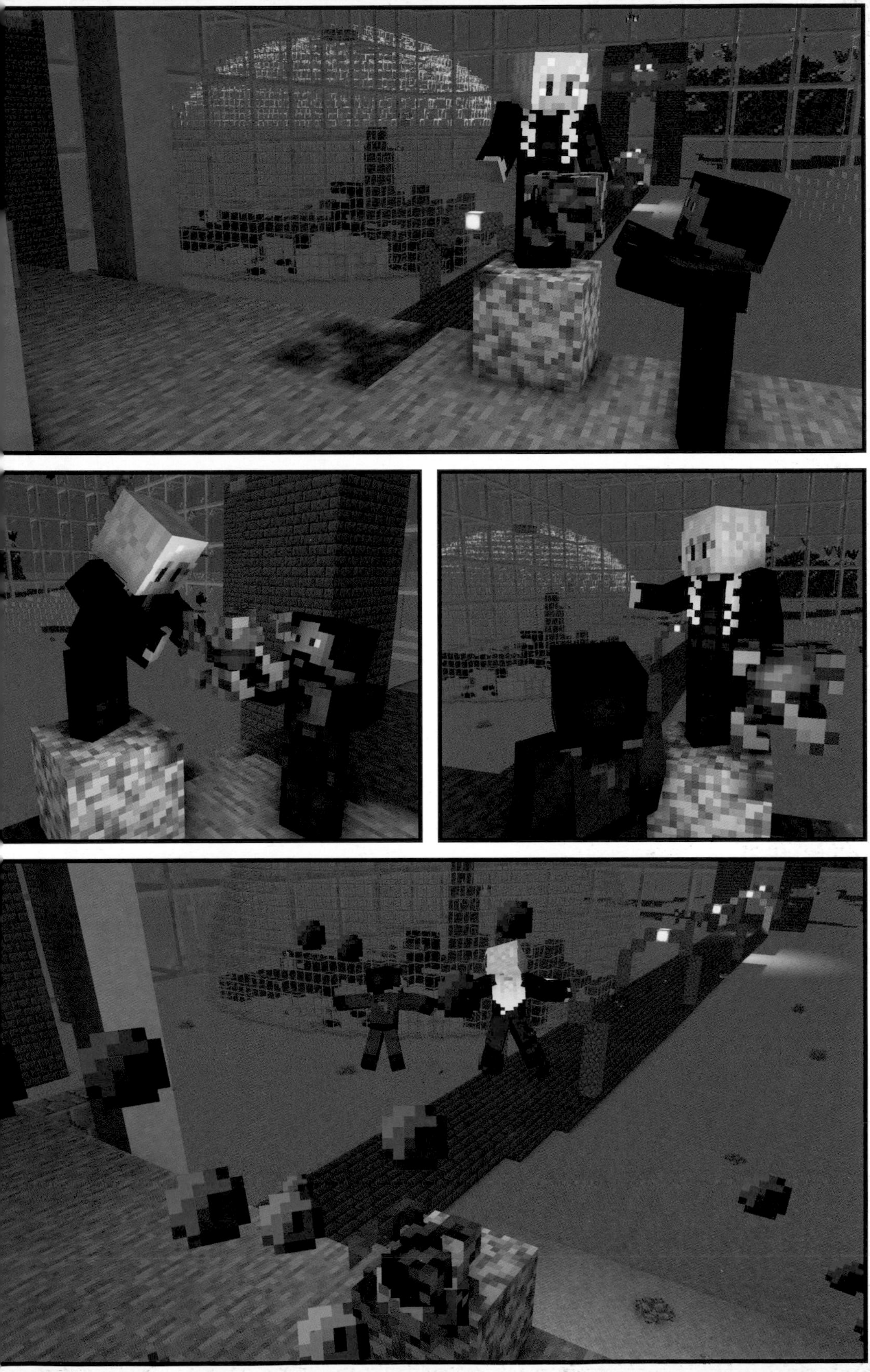

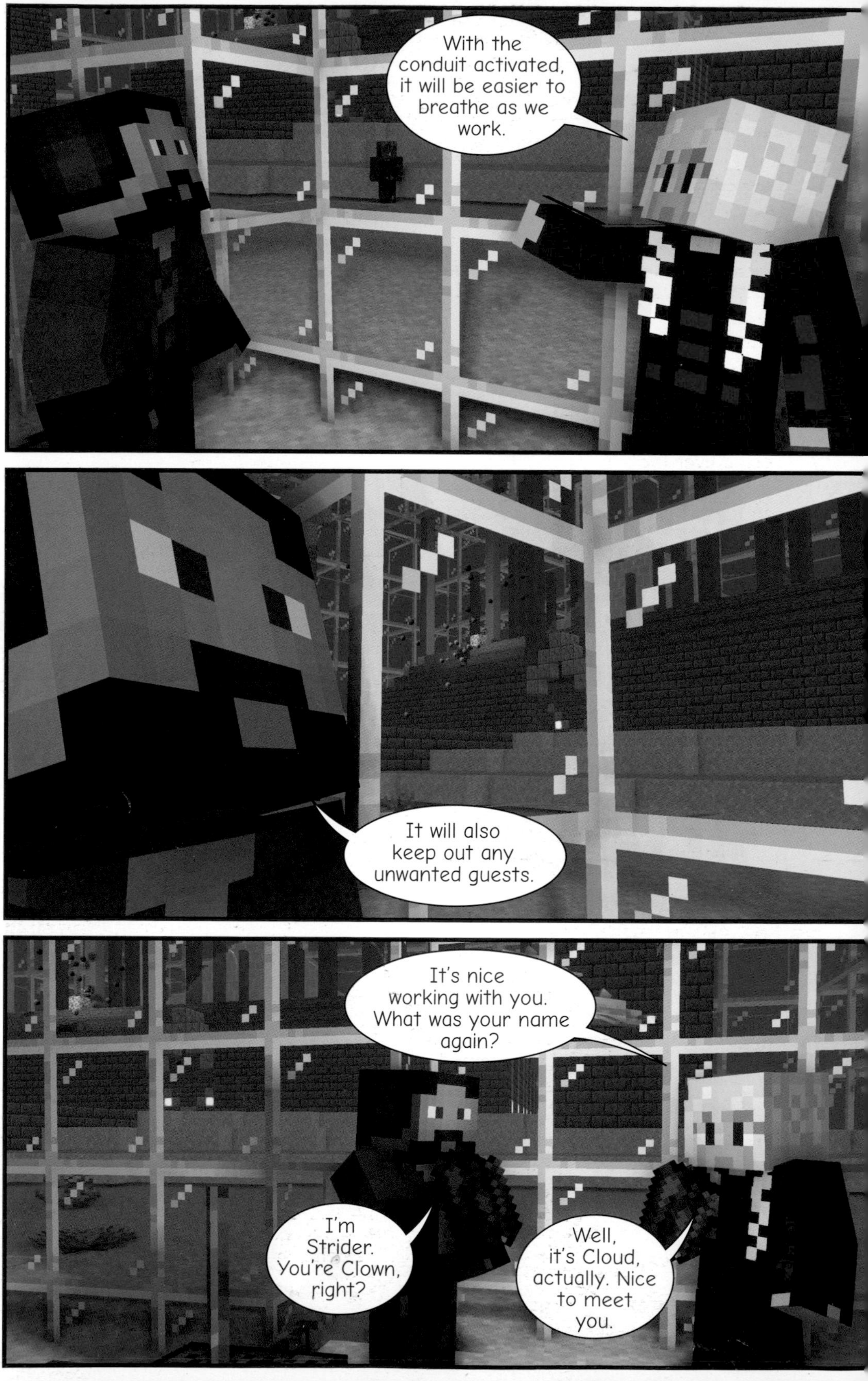
With the conduit activated, it will be easier to breathe as we work.
It will also keep out any unwanted guests.
It's nice working with you. What was your name again?
I'm Strider. You're Clown, right?
Well, it's Cloud, actually. Nice to meet you.

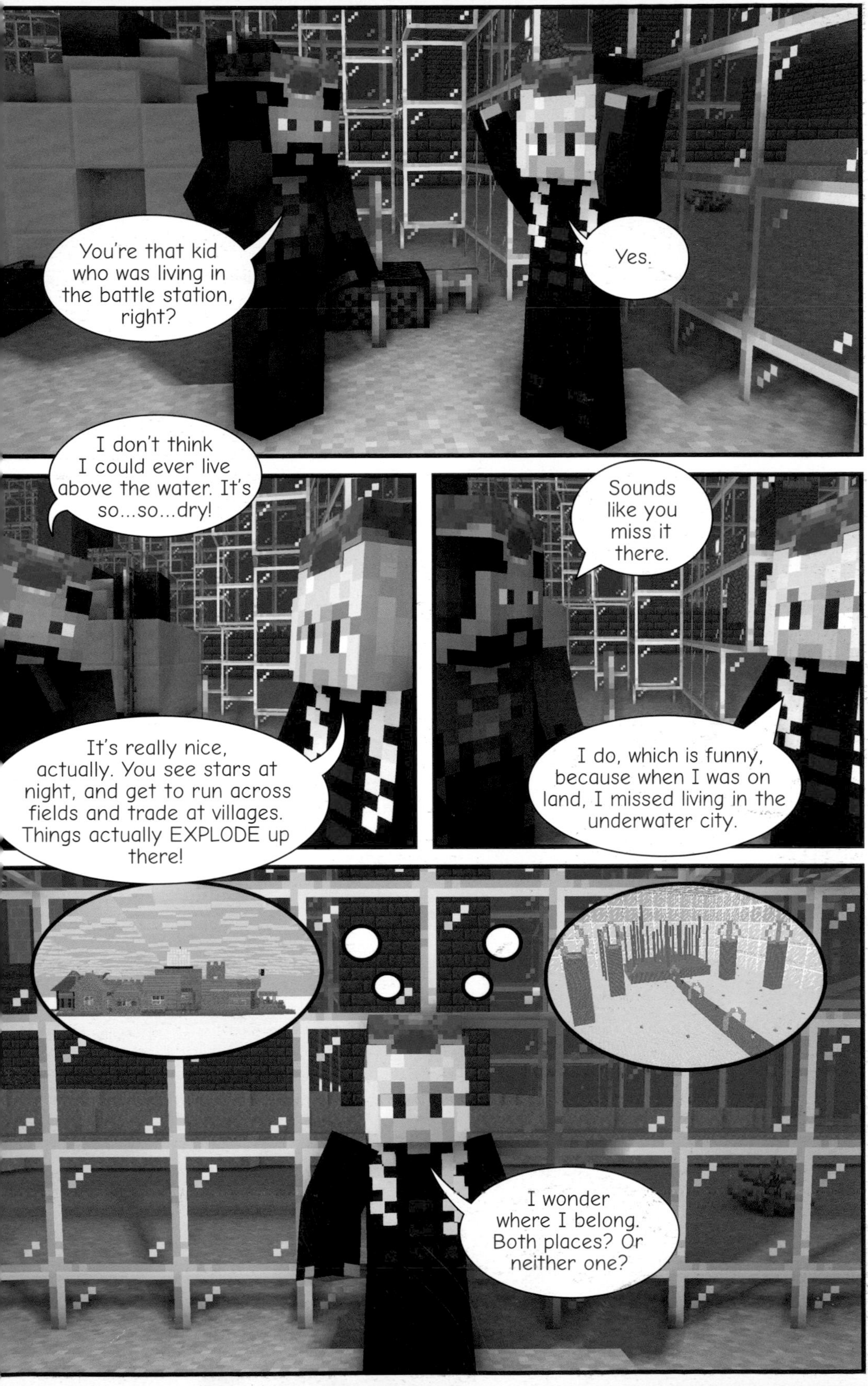

You're that kid who was living in the battle station, right?
Yes.
I don't think I could ever live above the water. It's so...so...dry!
It's really nice, actually. You see stars at night, and get to run across fields and trade at villages. Things actually EXPLODE up there!
Sounds like you miss it there.
I do, which is funny, because when I was on land, I missed living in the underwater city.
I wonder where I belong. Both places? Or neither one?

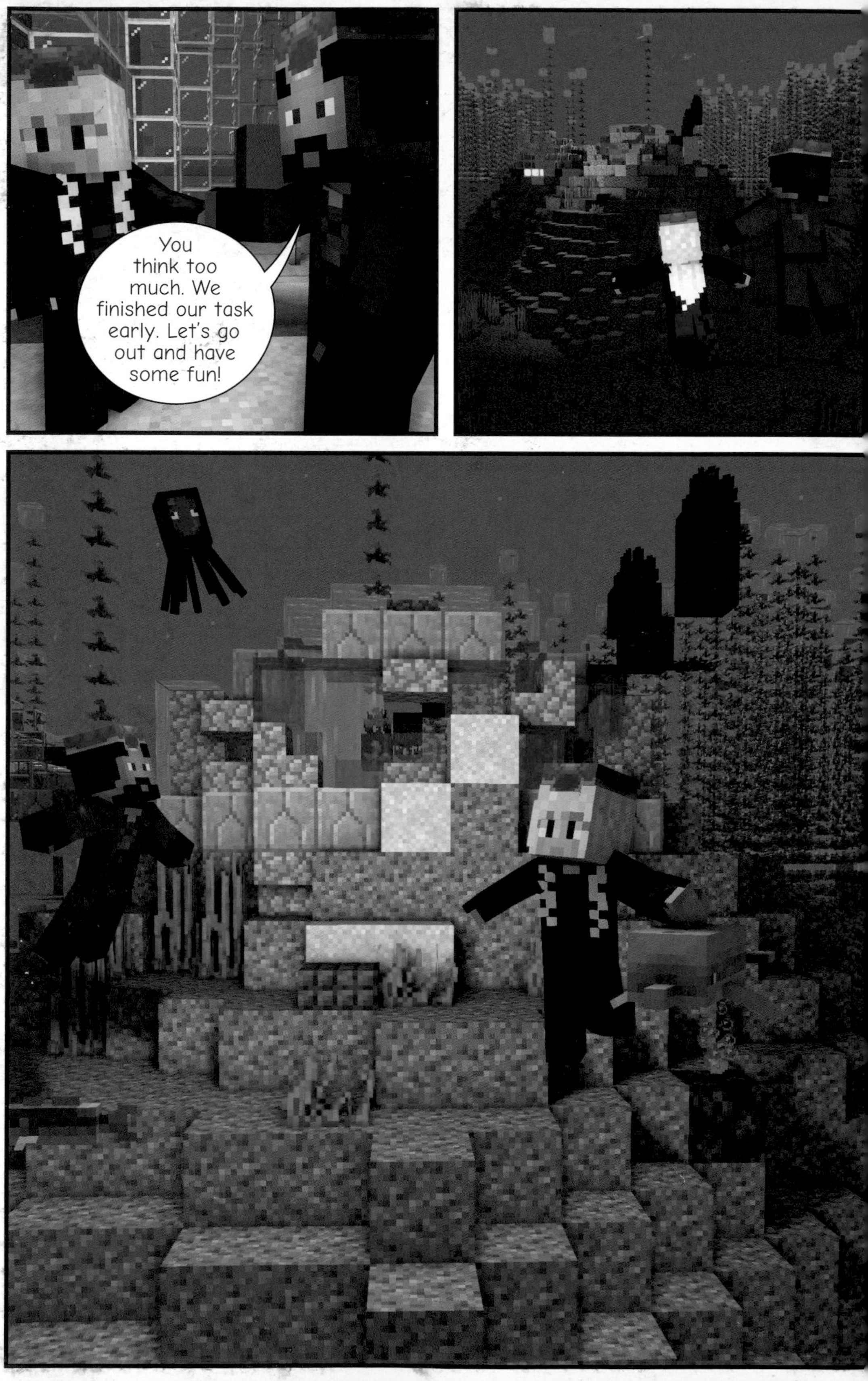
You think too much. We finished our task early. Let's go out and have some fun!

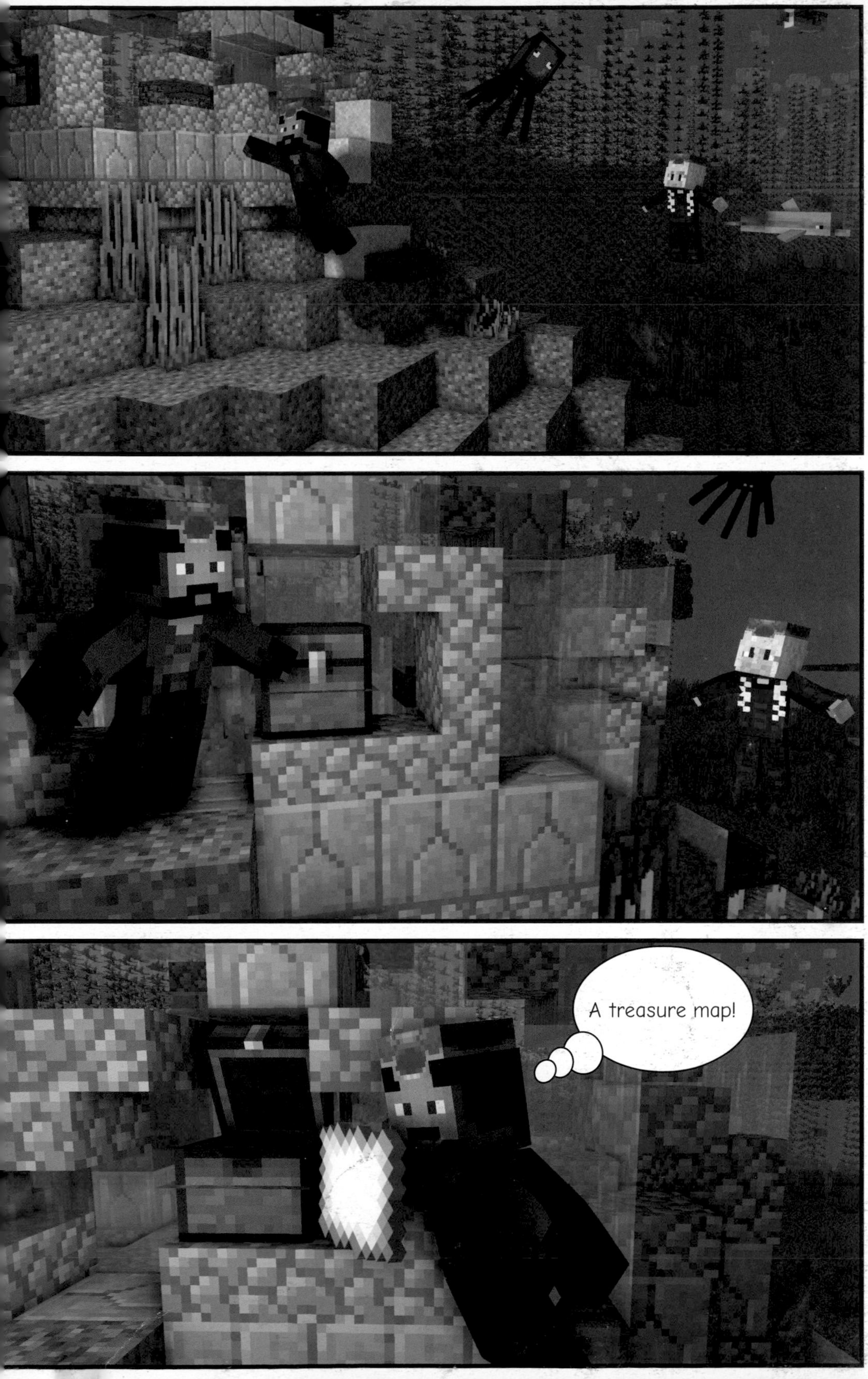
A treasure map!

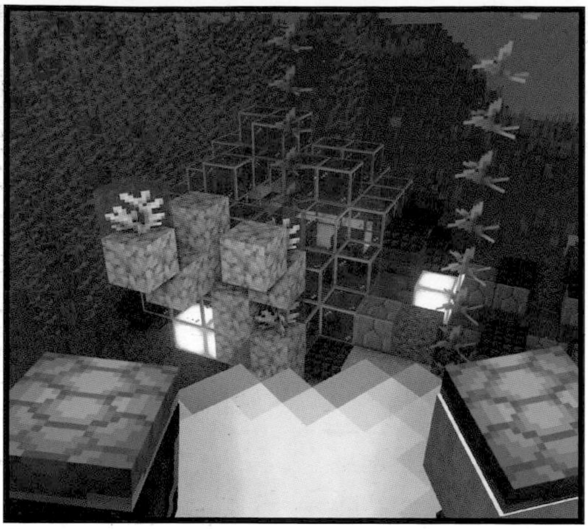

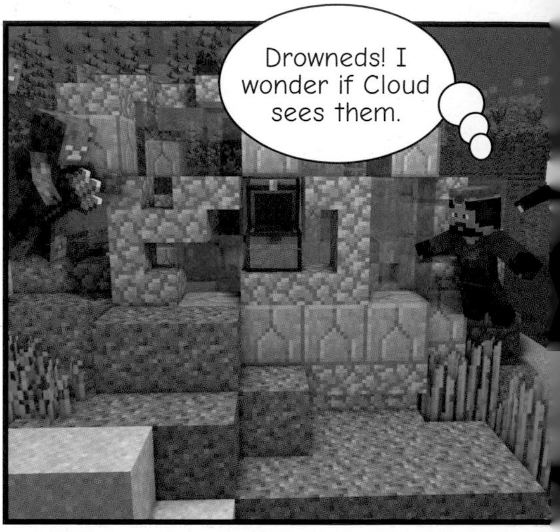
Drowneds! I wonder if Cloud sees them.

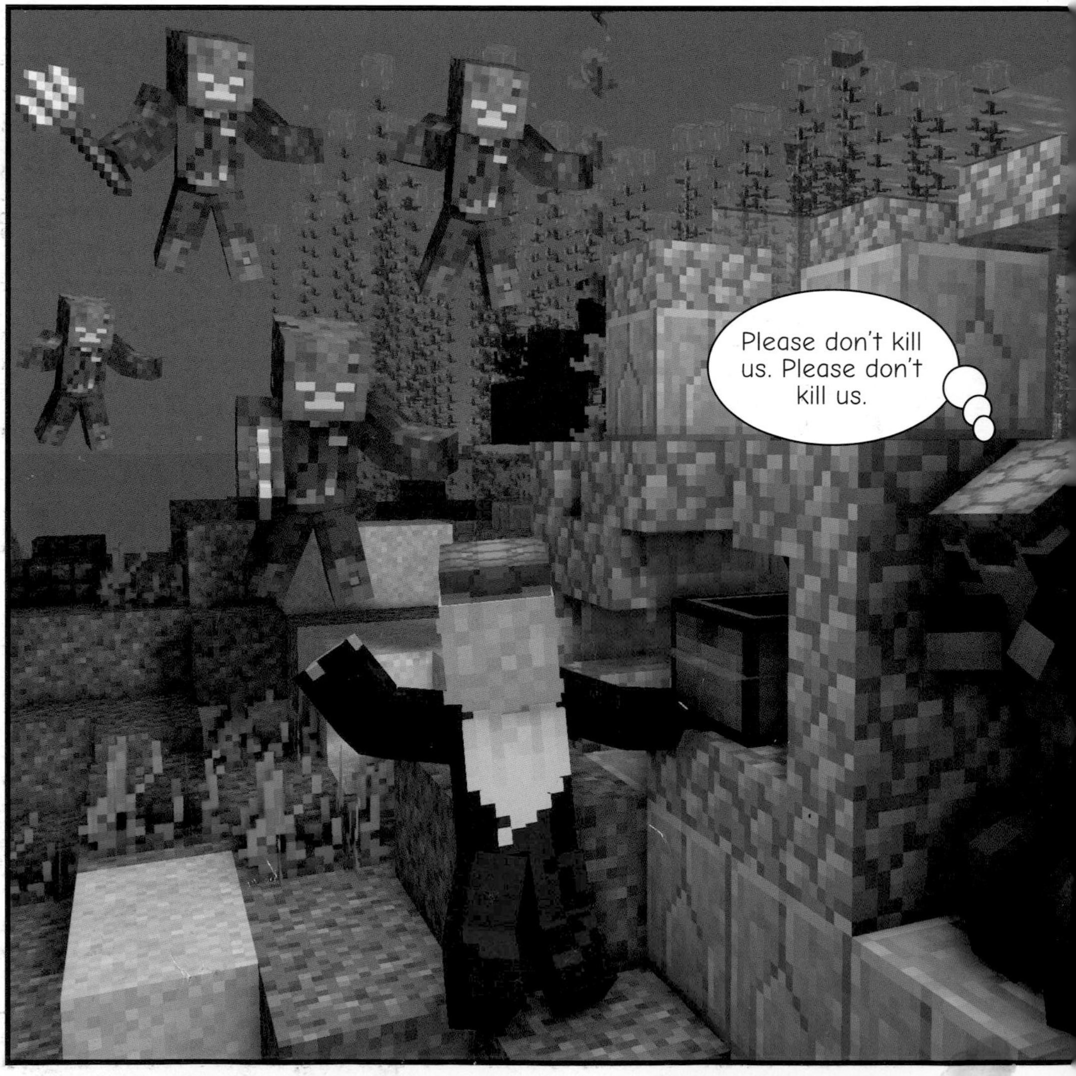
Please don't kill us. Please don't kill us.

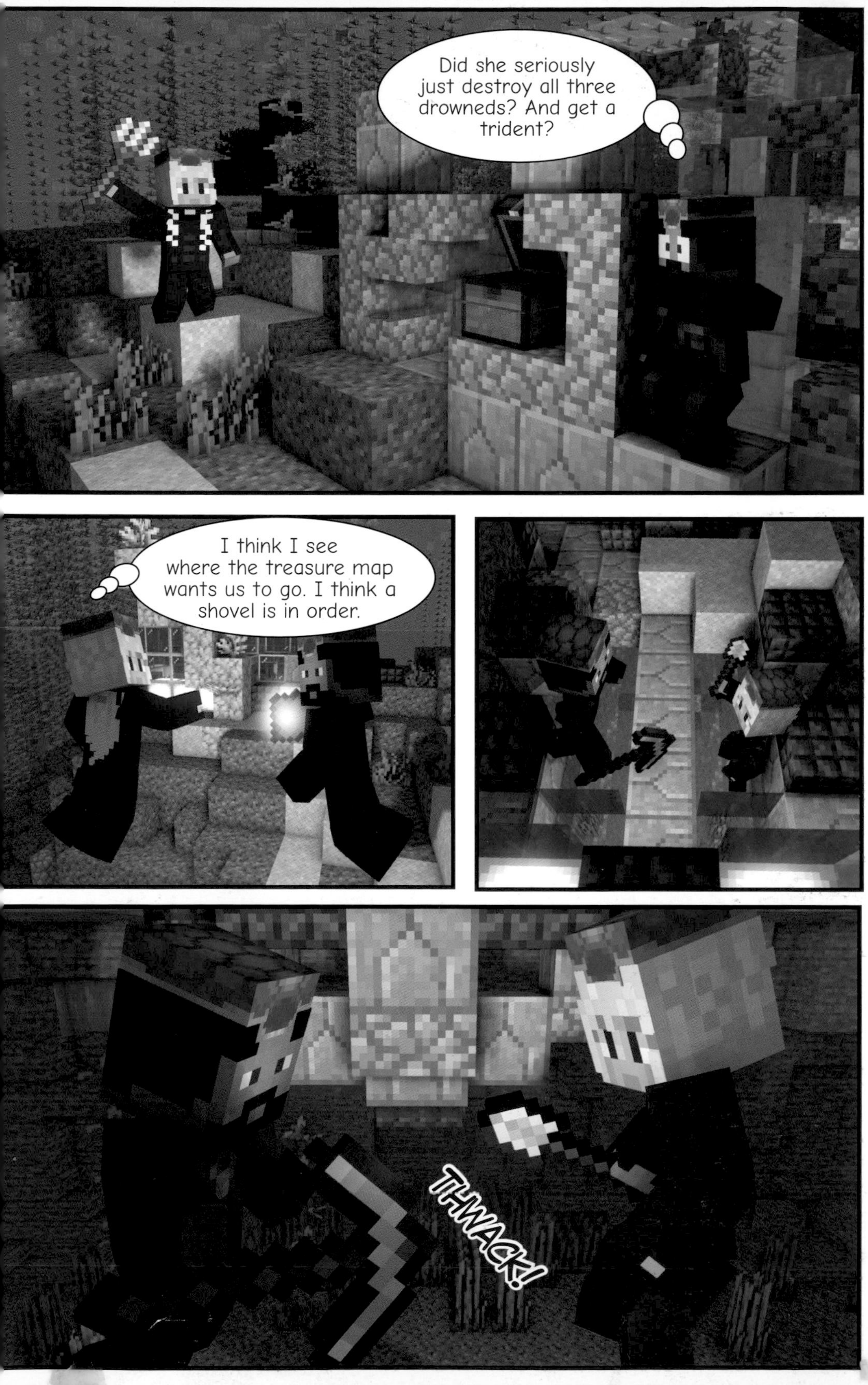
Did she seriously just destroy all three drowneds? And get a trident?
I think I see where the treasure map wants us to go. I think a shovel is in order.
THWACK!

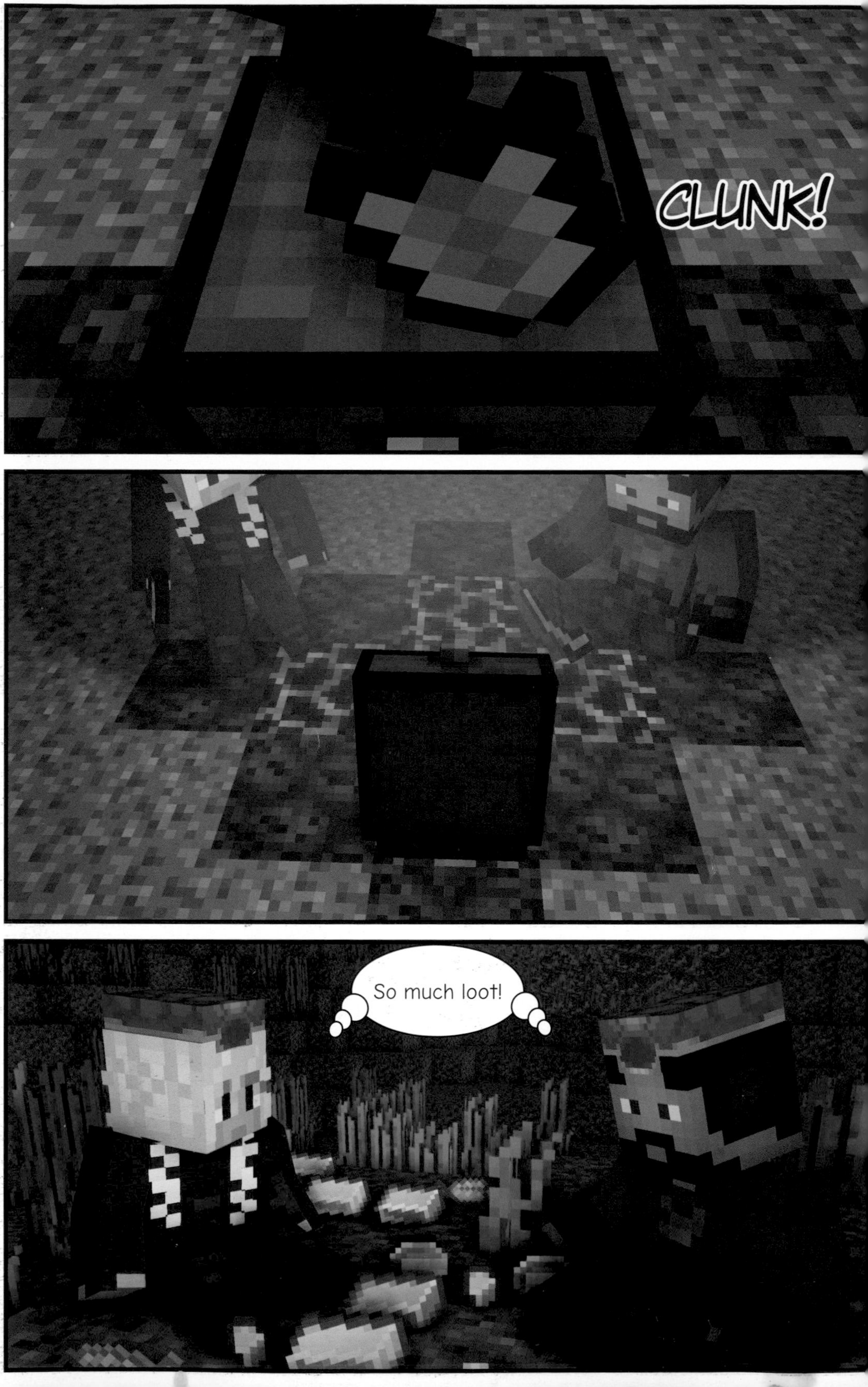
CLUNK!
So much loot!

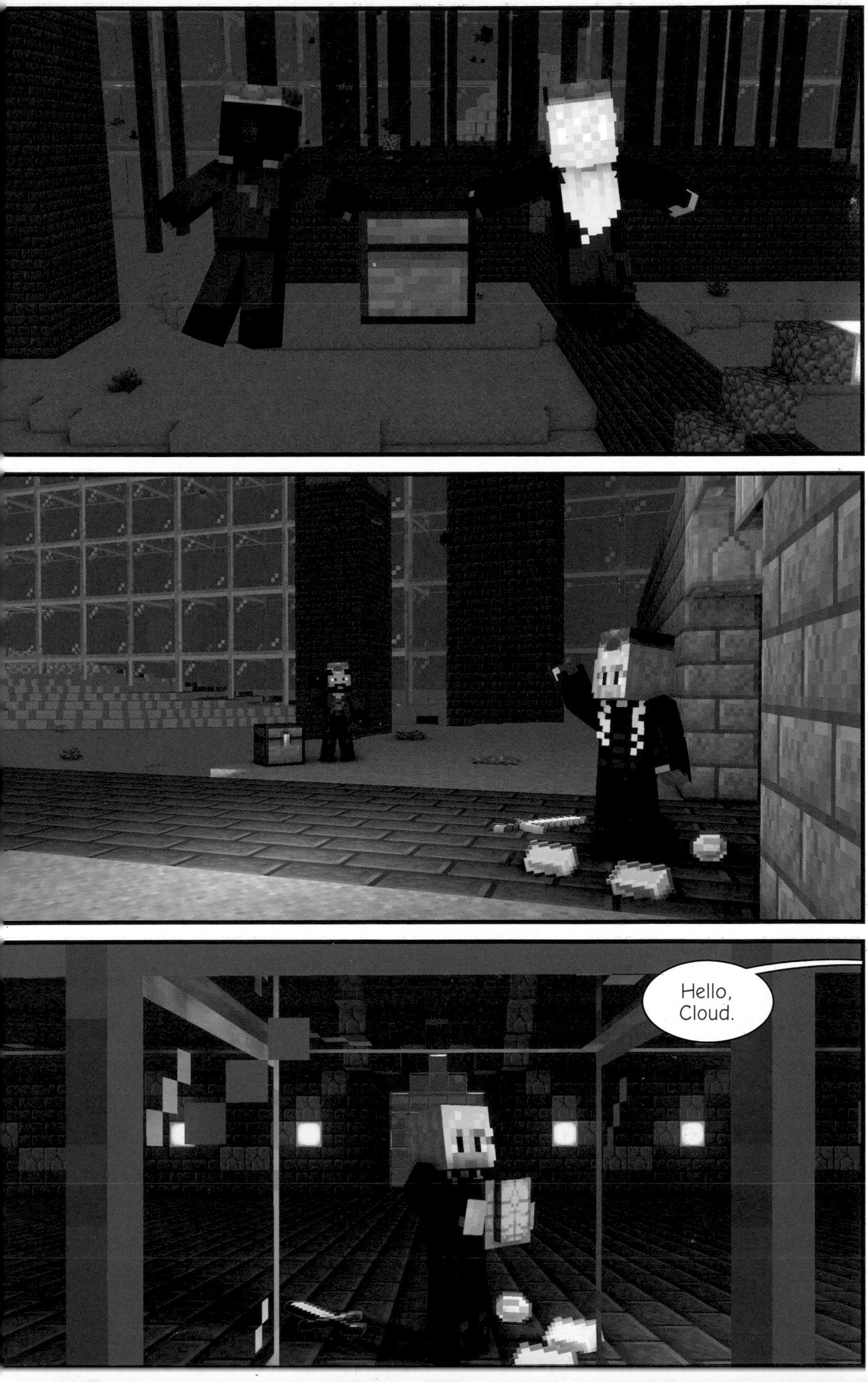
Hello,
Cloud.

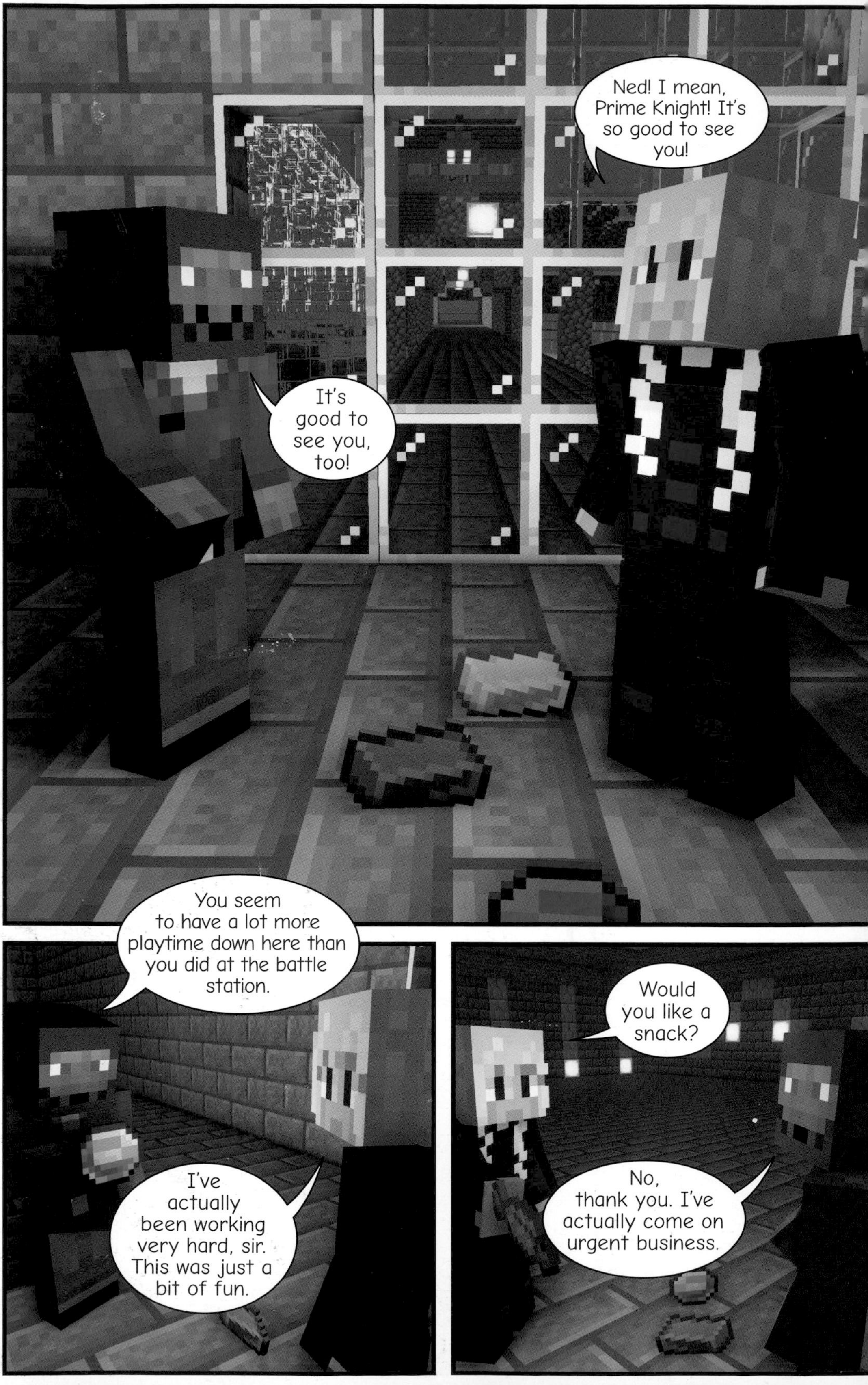
Ned! I mean, Prime Knight! It's so good to see you!
It's good to see you, too!
You seem to have a lot more playtime down here than you did at the battle station.
I've actually been working very hard, sir. This was just a bit of fun.
Would you like a snack?
No, thank you. I've actually come on urgent business.

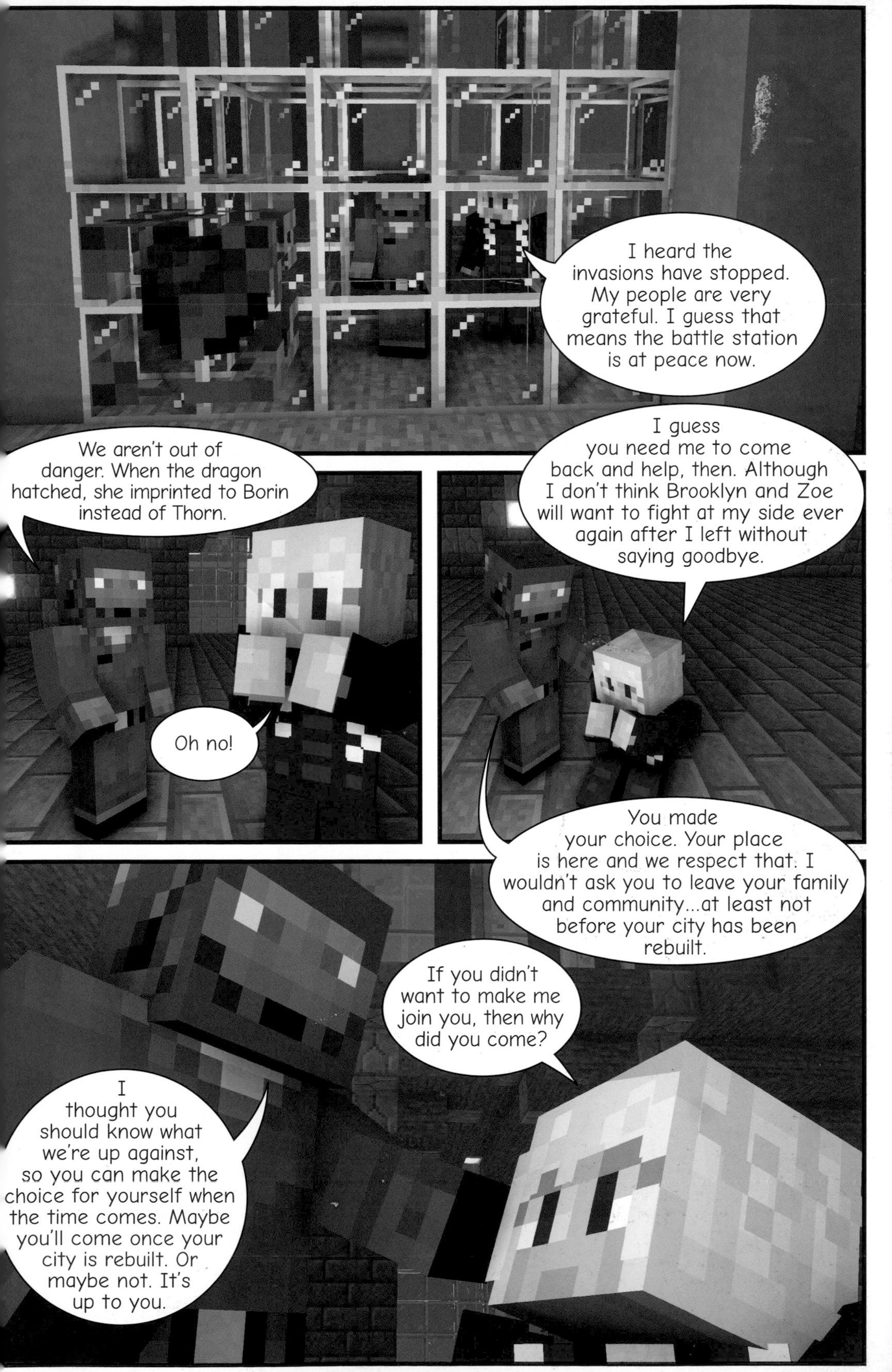
I heard the invasions have stopped. My people are very grateful. I guess that means the battle station is at peace now.
We aren't out of danger. When the dragon hatched, she imprinted to Borin instead of Thorn.
Oh no!
I guess you need me to come back and help, then. Although I don't think Brooklyn and Zoe will want to fight at my side ever again after I left without saying goodbye.
You made your choice. Your place is here and we respect that. I wouldn't ask you to leave your family and community...at least not before your city has been rebuilt.
If you didn't want to make me join you, then why did you come?
I thought you should know what we're up against, so you can make the choice for yourself when the time comes. Maybe you'll come once your city is rebuilt. Or maybe not. It's up to you.

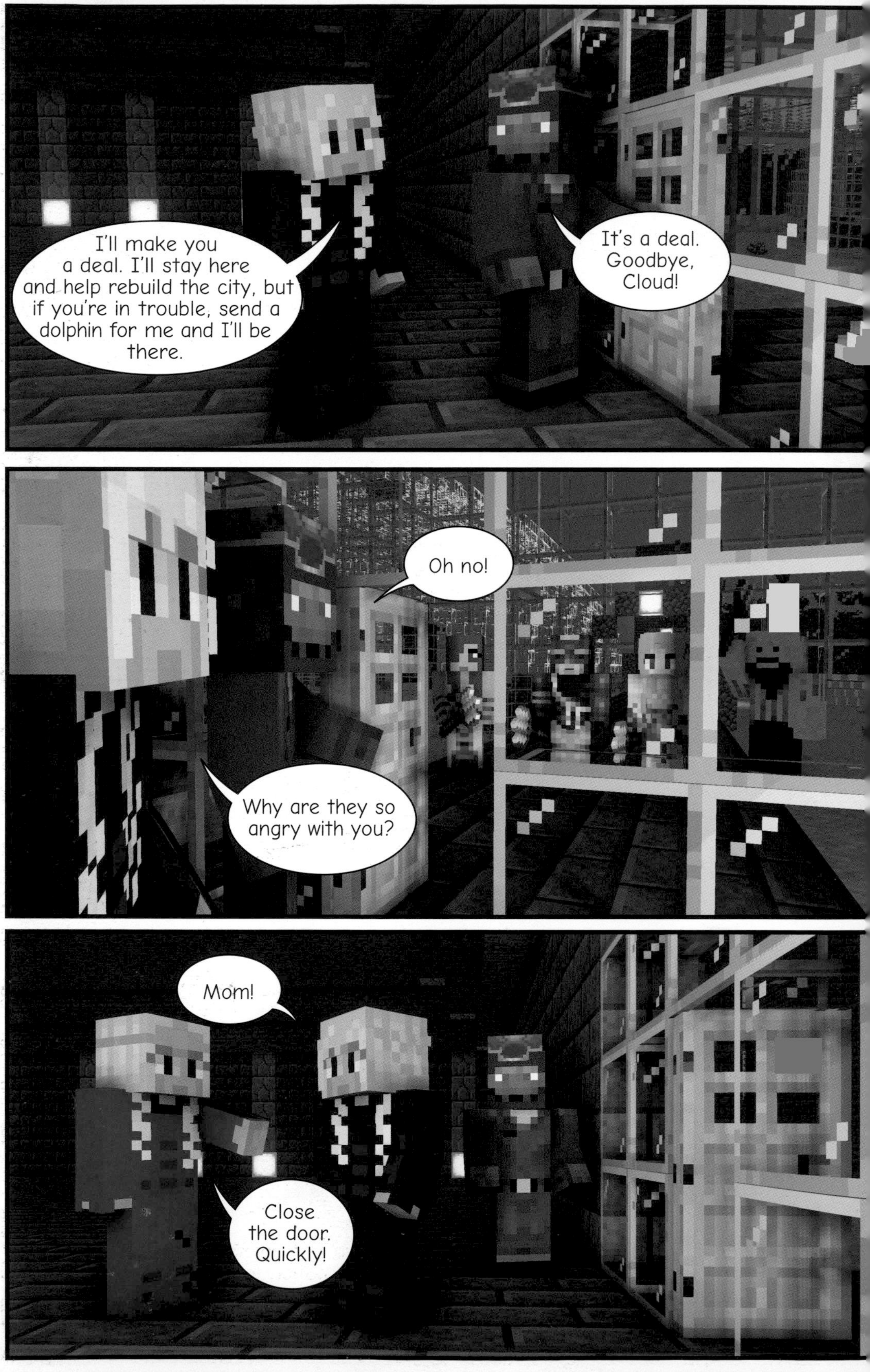

I'll make you a deal. I'll stay here and help rebuild the city, but if you're in trouble, send a dolphin for me and I'll be there.
It's a deal. Goodbye, Cloud!
Oh no!
Why are they so angry with you?
Mom!
Close the door. Quickly!

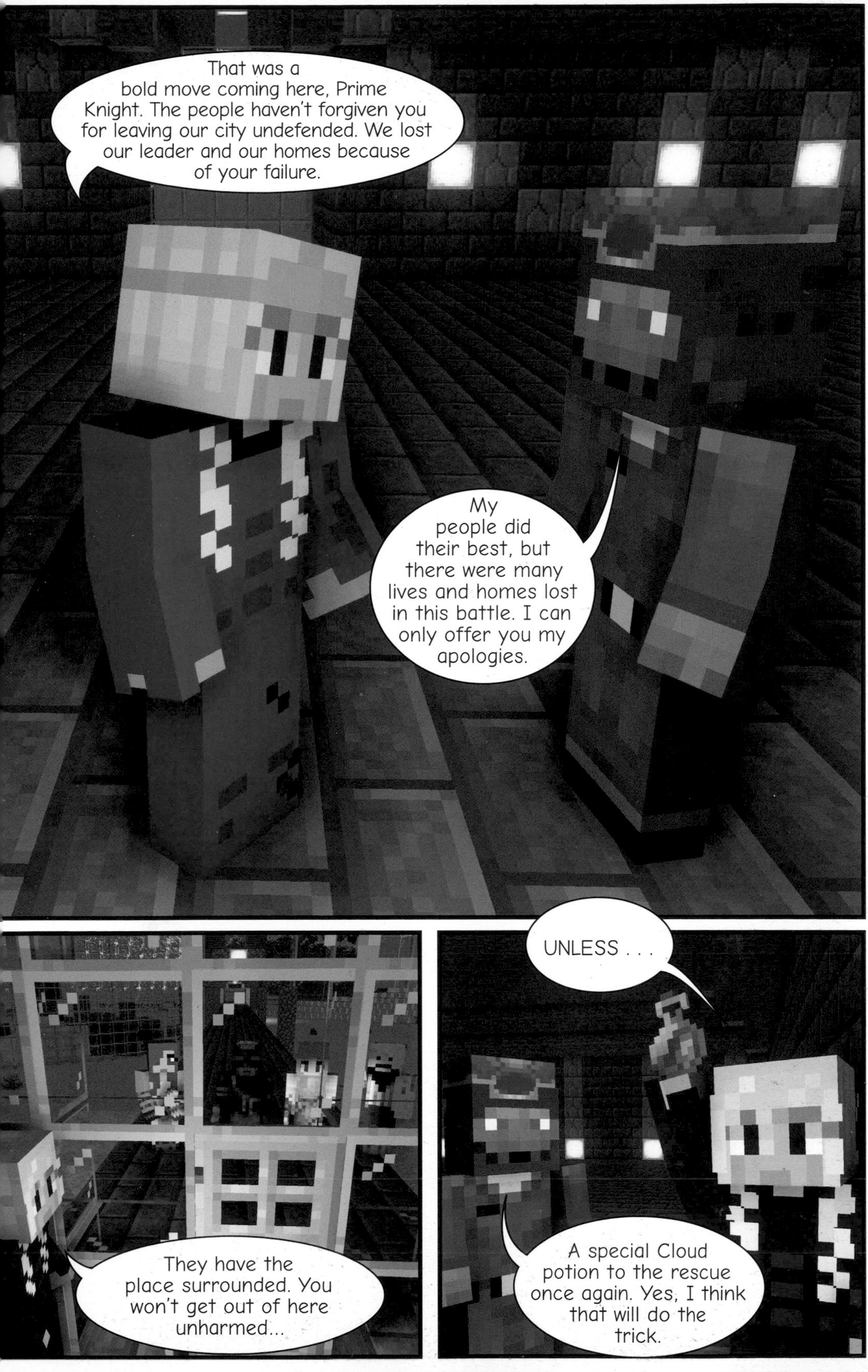
That was a bold move coming here, Prime Knight. The people haven't forgiven you for leaving our city undefended. We lost our leader and our homes because of your failure.
My people did their best, but there were many lives and homes lost in this battle. I can only offer you my apologies.
They have the place surrounded. You won't get out of here unharmed...
UNLESS . . .
A special Cloud potion to the rescue once again. Yes, I think that will do the trick.

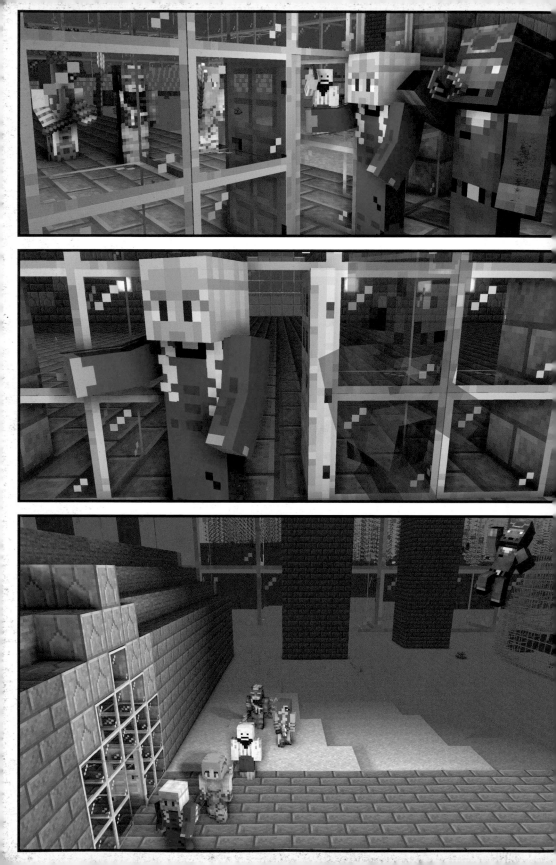

CHAPTER 4

BREATH
OF FIRE

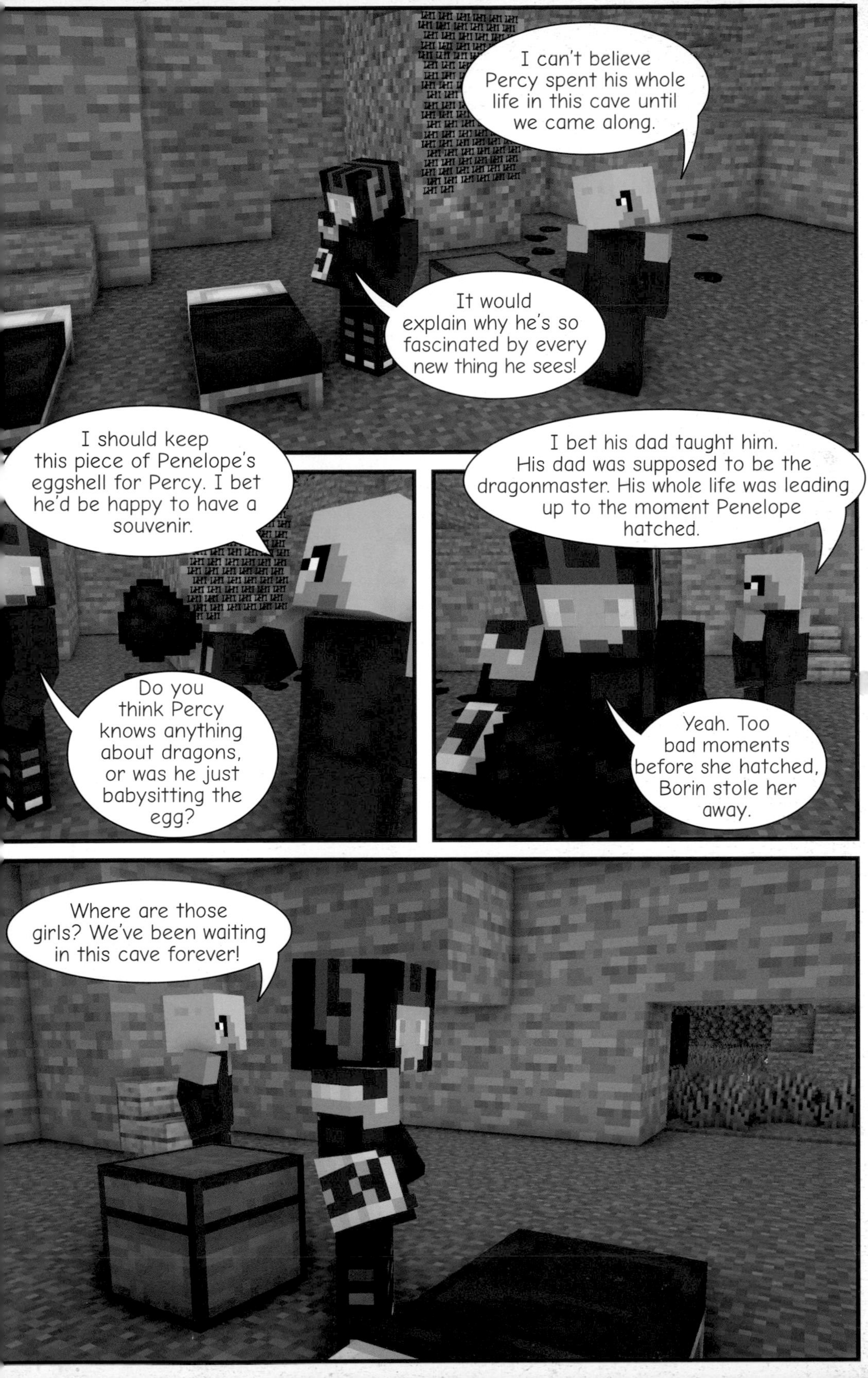
I can't believe Percy spent his whole life in this cave until we came along.
It would explain why he's so fascinated by every new thing he sees!
I should keep this piece of Penelope's eggshell for Percy. I bet he'd be happy to have a souvenir.
Do you think Percy knows anything about dragons, or was he just babysitting the egg?
I bet his dad taught him. His dad was supposed to be the dragonmaster. His whole life was leading up to the moment Penelope hatched.
Yeah. Too bad moments before she hatched, Borin stole her away.
Where are those girls? We've been waiting in this cave forever!

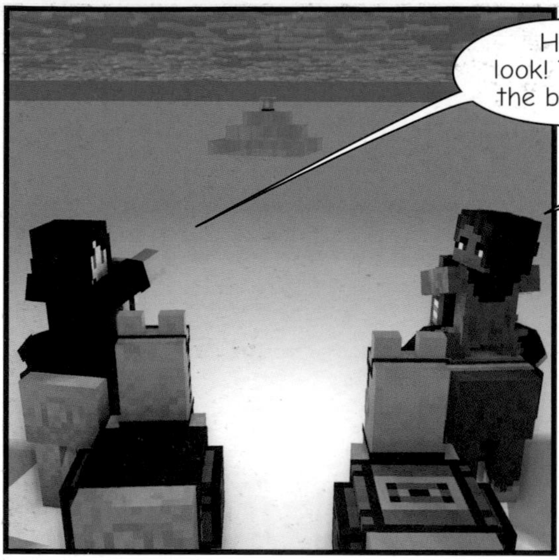
Hey, look! There's the beacon!
We're almost there. We just have to avoid...

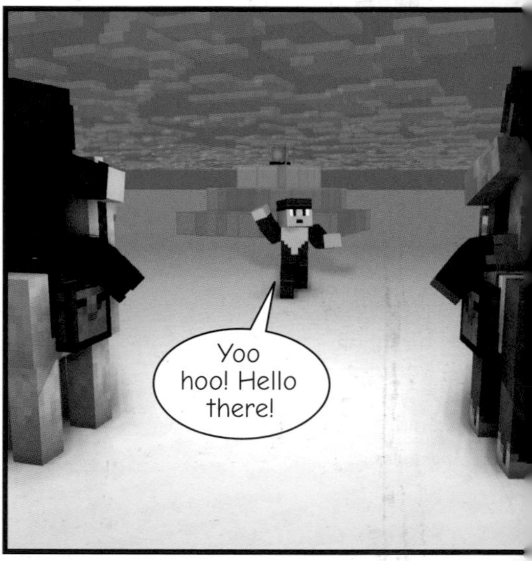
Yoo hoo! Hello there!

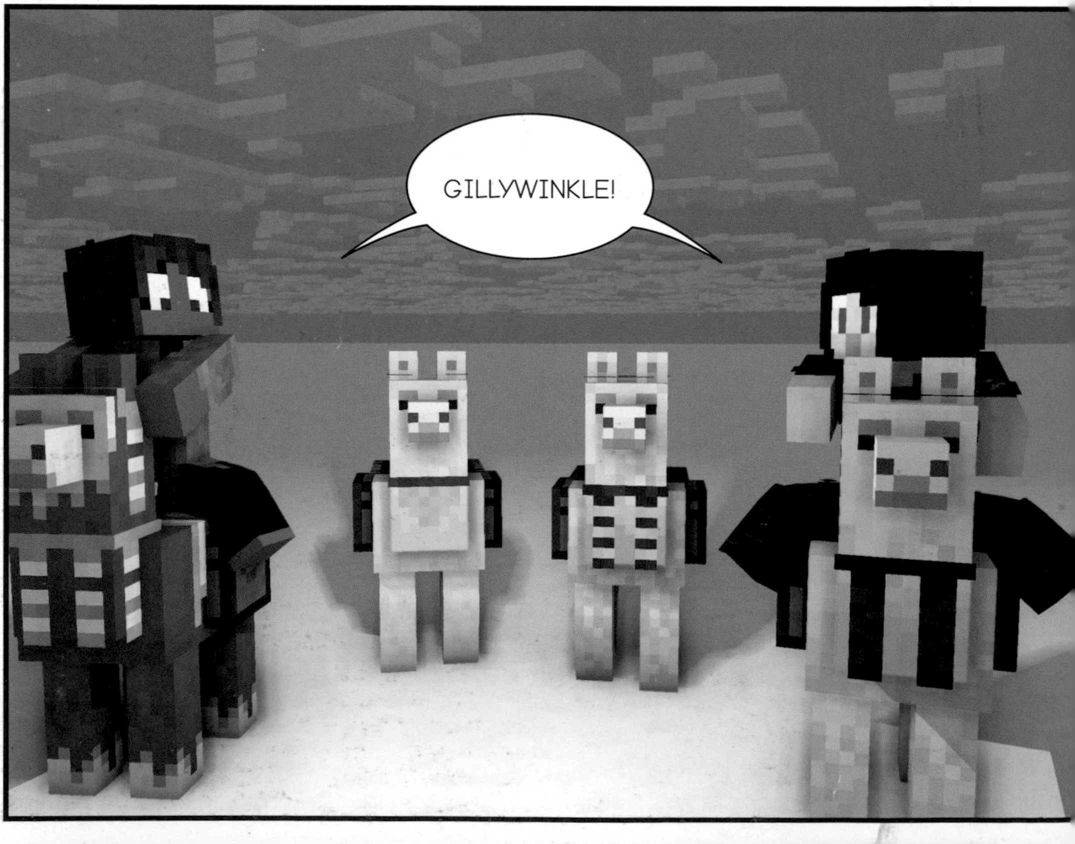
GILLYWINKLE!

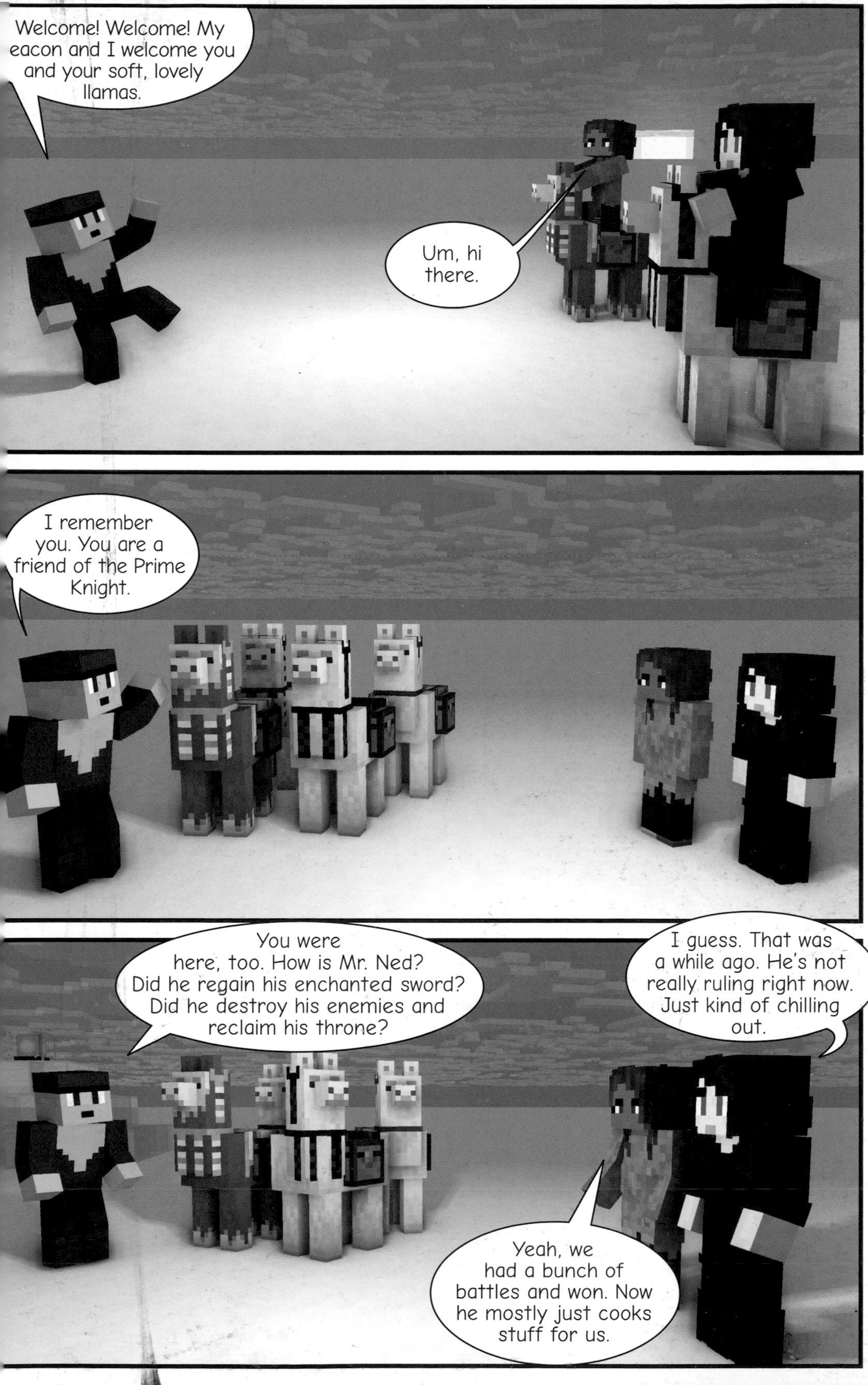
Welcome! Welcome! My eacon and I welcome you and your soft, lovely llamas.
Um, hi there.
I remember you. You are a friend of the Prime Knight.
You were here, too. How is Mr. Ned? Did he regain his enchanted sword? Did he destroy his enemies and reclaim his throne?
I guess. That was a while ago. He's not really ruling right now. Just kind of chilling out.
Yeah, we had a bunch of battles and won. Now he mostly just cooks stuff for us.

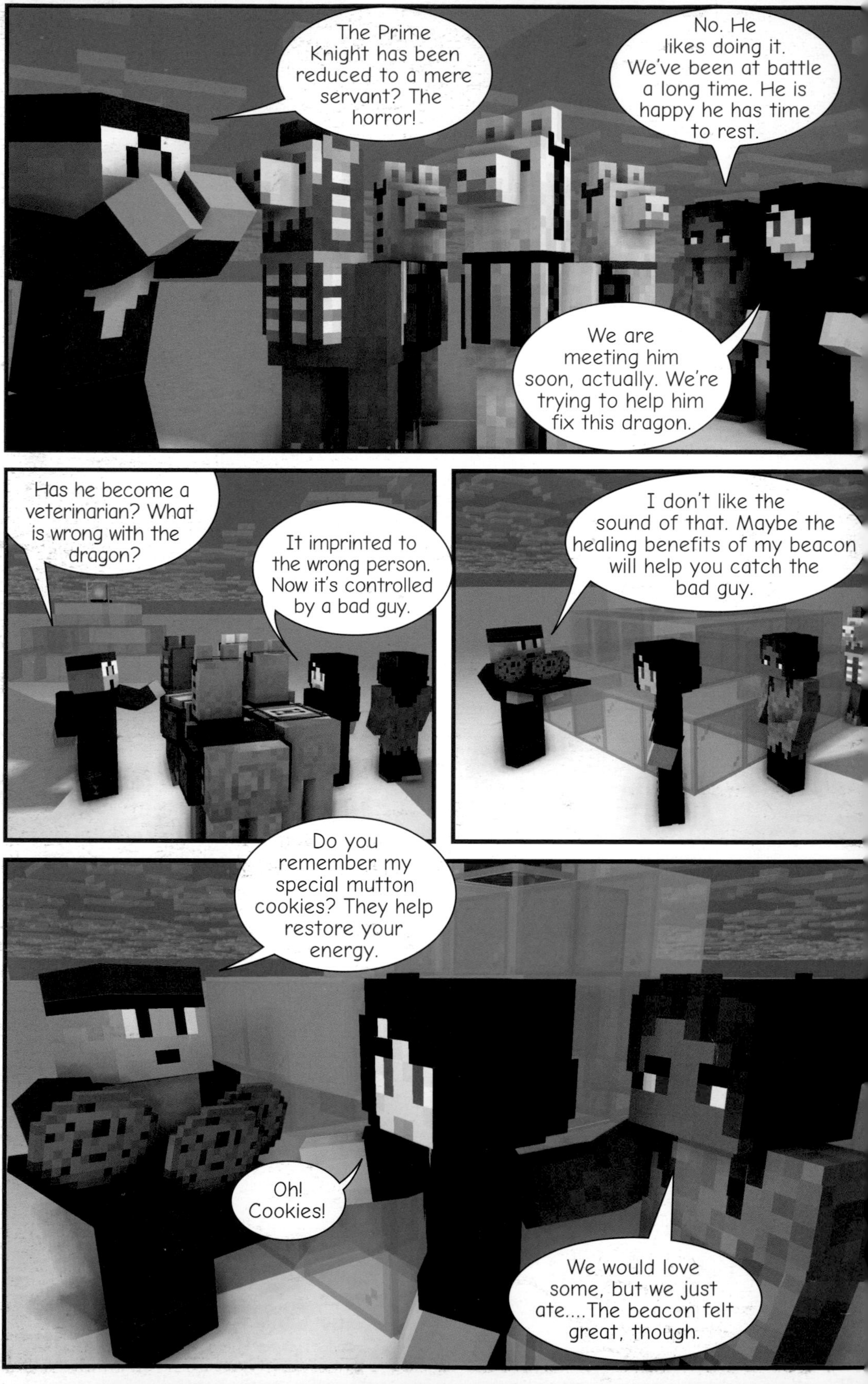

The Prime Knight has been reduced to a mere servant? The horror!
No. He likes doing it. We've been at battle a long time. He is happy he has time to rest.
We are meeting him soon, actually. We're trying to help him fix this dragon.
Has he become a veterinarian? What is wrong with the dragon?
It imprinted to the wrong person. Now it's controlled by a bad guy.
I don't like the sound of that. Maybe the healing benefits of my beacon will help you catch the bad guy.
Do you remember my special mutton cookies? They help restore your energy.
Oh! Cookies!
We would love some, but we just ate....The beacon felt great, though.

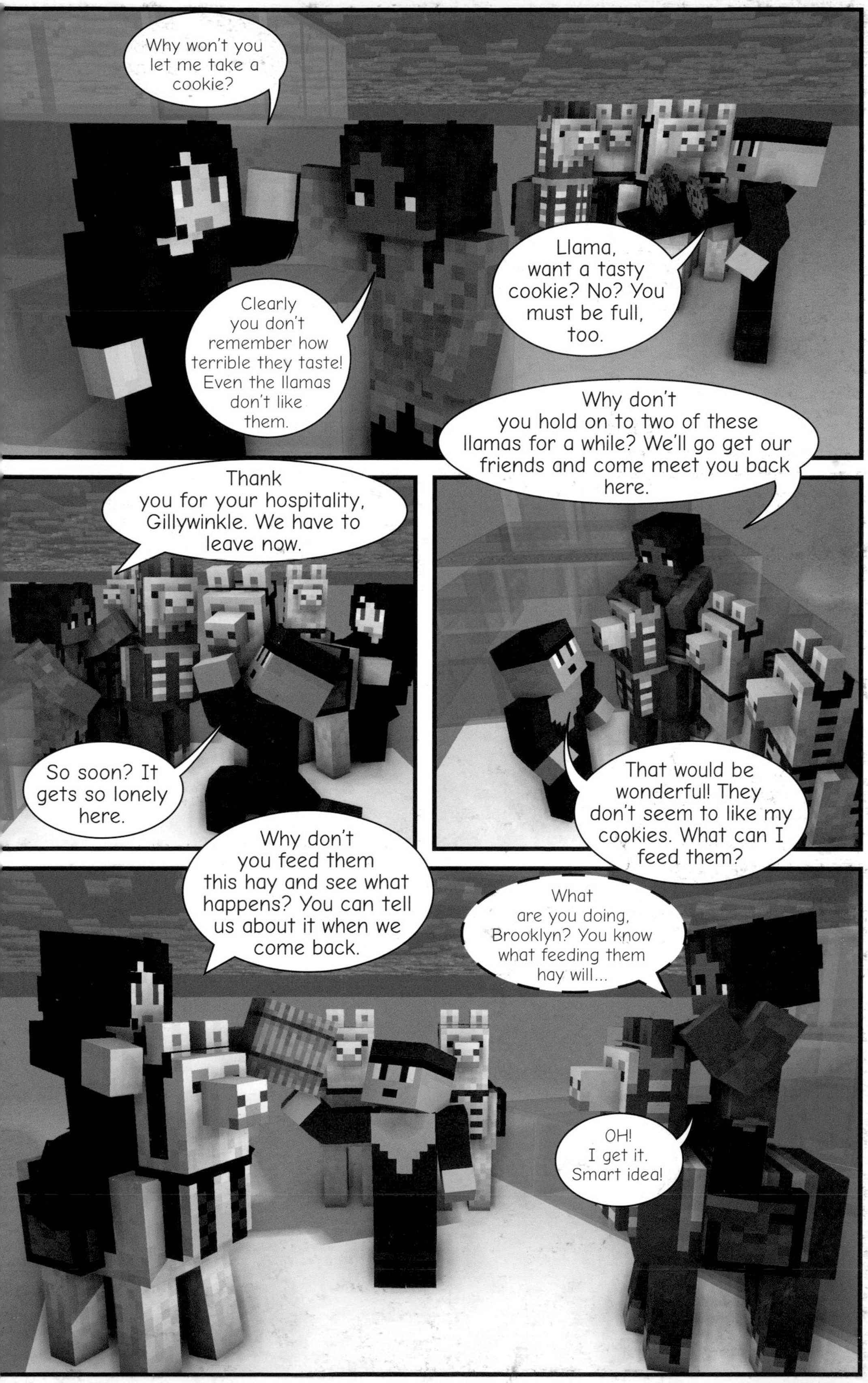
Why won't you let me take a cookie?
Clearly you don't remember how terrible they taste! Even the llamas don't like them.
Llama, want a tasty cookie? No? You must be full, too.
Thank you for your hospitality, Gillywinkle. We have to leave now.
So soon? It gets so lonely here.
Why don't you hold on to two of these llamas for a while? We'll go get our friends and come meet you back here.
That would be wonderful! They don't seem to like my cookies. What can I feed them?
Why don't you feed them this hay and see what happens? You can tell us about it when we come back.
What are you doing, Brooklyn? You know what feeding them hay will...
OH! I get it. Smart idea!

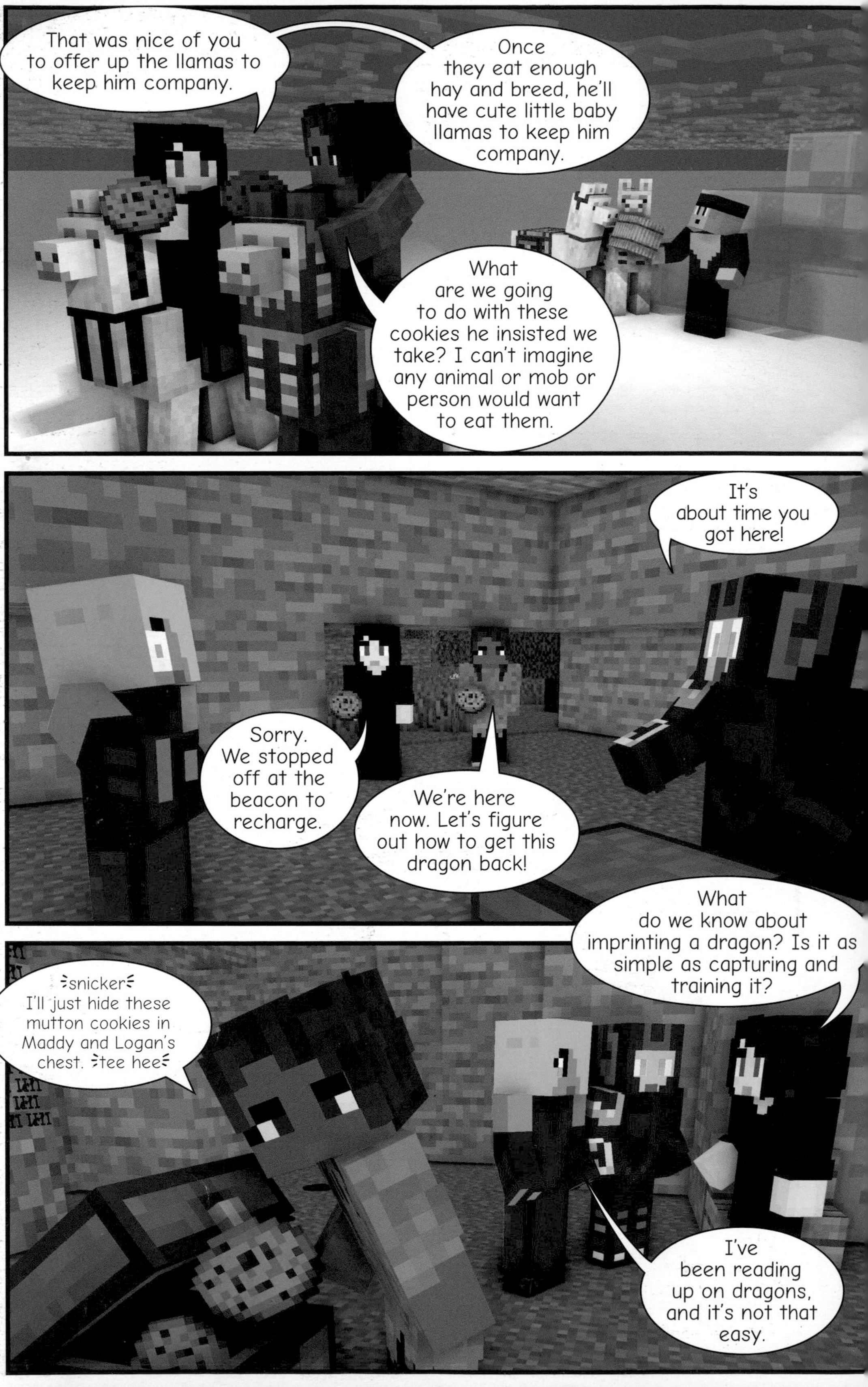
That was nice of you to offer up the llamas to keep him company.
Once they eat enough hay and breed, he'll have cute little baby llamas to keep him company.
What are we going to do with these cookies he insisted we take? I can't imagine any animal or mob or person would want to eat them.
It's about time you got here!
Sorry. We stopped off at the beacon to recharge.
We're here now. Let's figure out how to get this dragon back!
snicker I'll just hide these mutton cookies in Maddy and Logan's chest. *tee hee*
What do we know about imprinting a dragon? Is it as simple as capturing and training it?
I've been reading up on dragons, and it's not that easy.

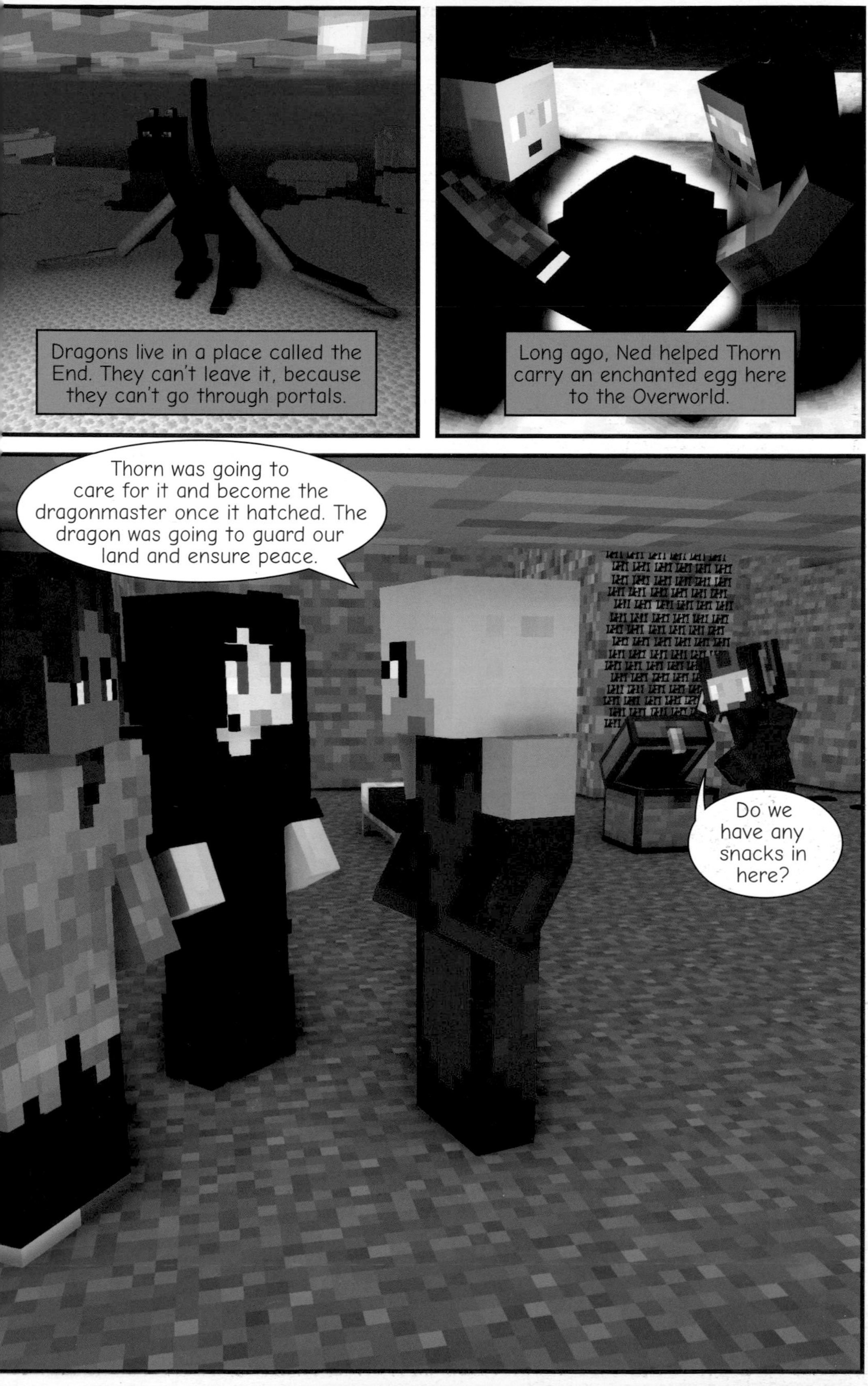

Dragons live in a place called the End. They can't leave it, because they can't go through portals.
Long ago, Ned helped Thorn carry an enchanted egg here to the Overworld.
Thorn was going to care for it and become the dragonmaster once it hatched. The dragon was going to guard our land and ensure peace.
Do we have any snacks in here?

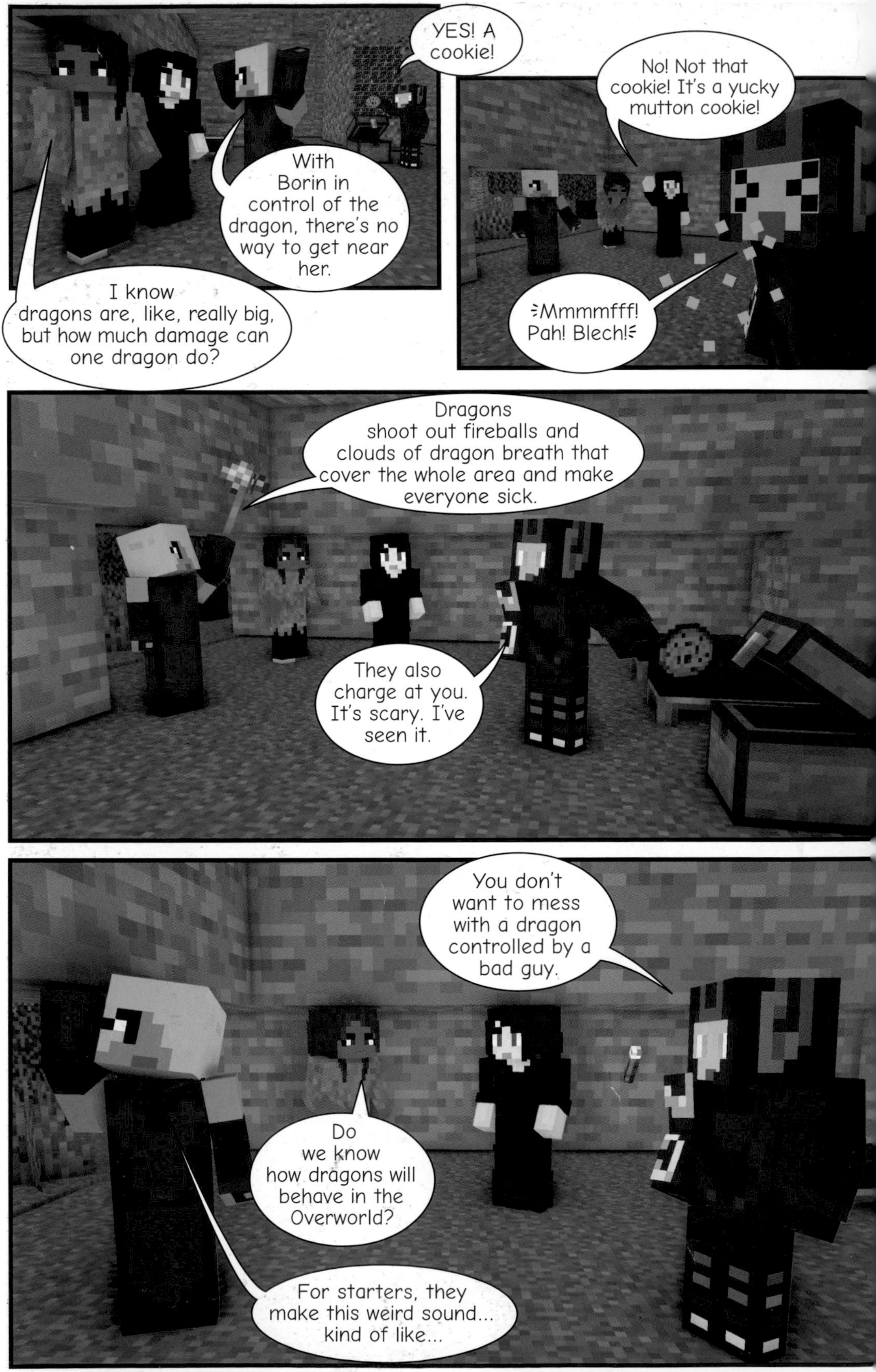
YES! A cookie!
With Borin in control of the dragon, there's no way to get near her.
I know dragons are, like, really big, but how much damage can one dragon do?
No! Not that cookie! It's a yucky mutton cookie!
Mmmmfff! Pah! Blech!
Dragons shoot out fireballs and clouds of dragon breath that cover the whole area and make everyone sick.
They also charge at you. It's scary. I've seen it.
You don't want to mess with a dragon controlled by a bad guy.
Do we know how dragons will behave in the Overworld?
For starters, they make this weird sound... kind of like...

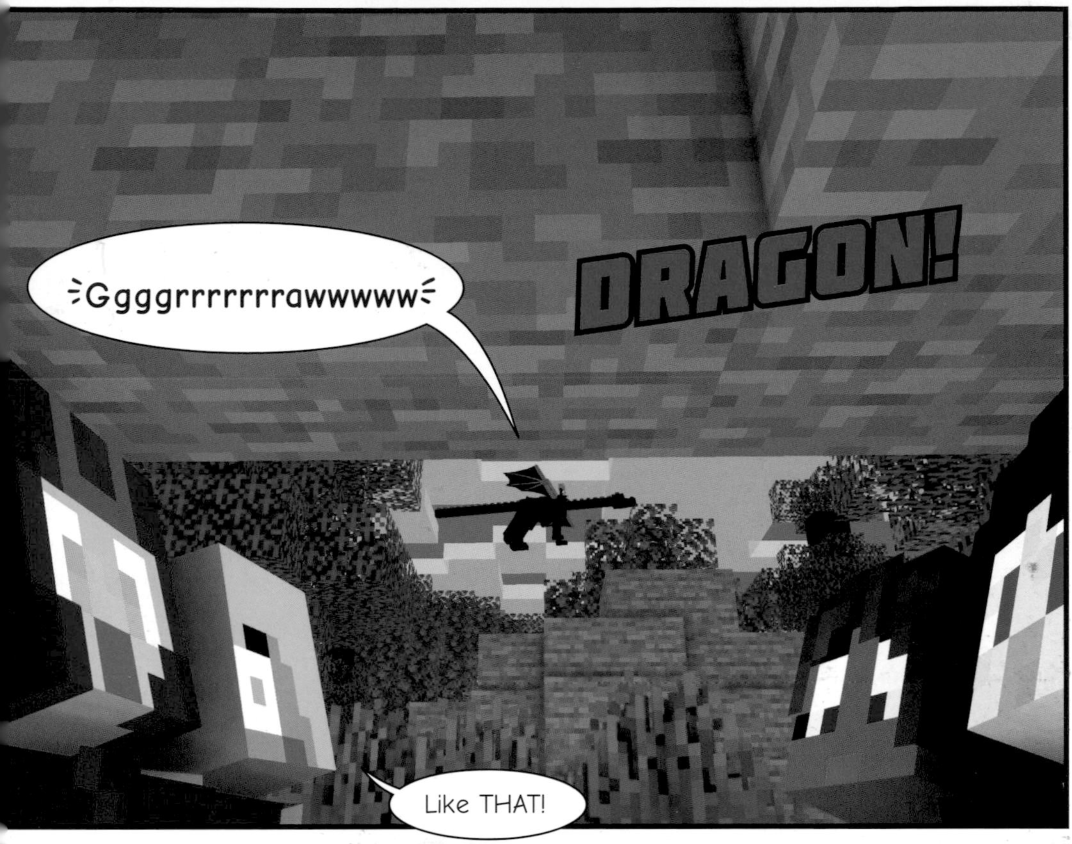
Ggggrrrrrrawwwww
DRAGON!
Like THAT!
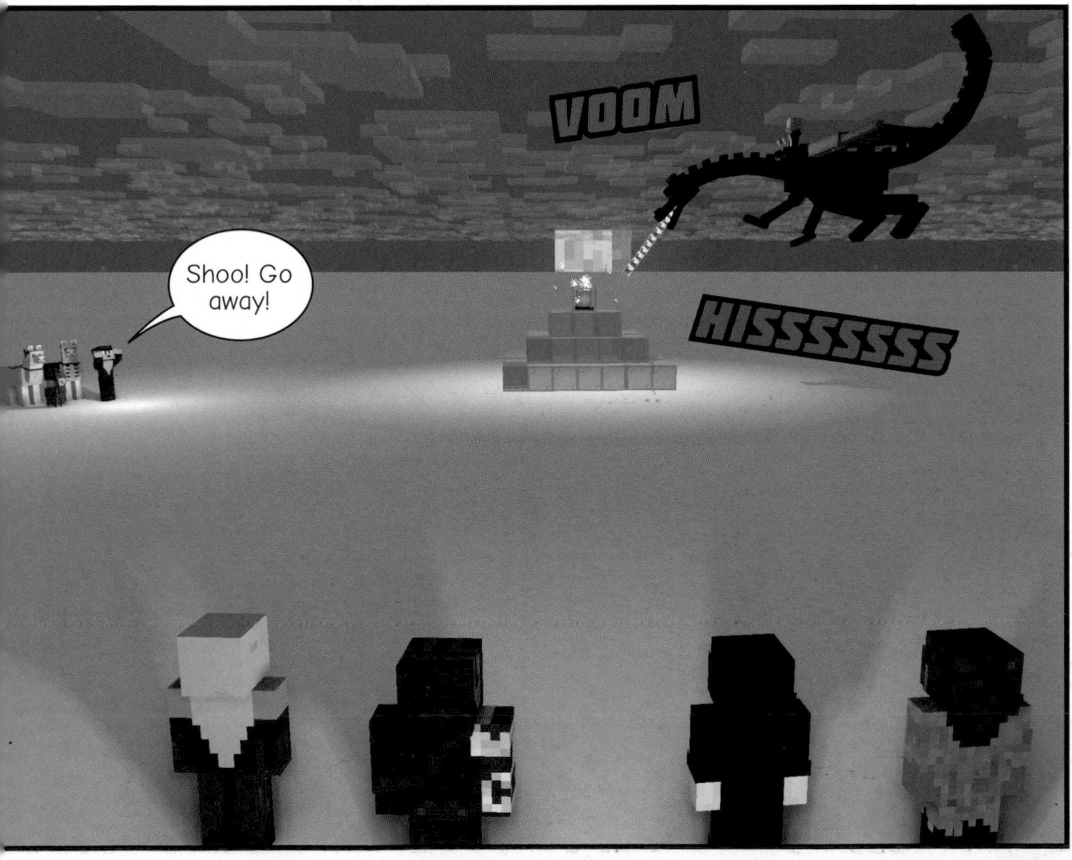
VOOM
Shoo! Go away!
HISSSSSSS

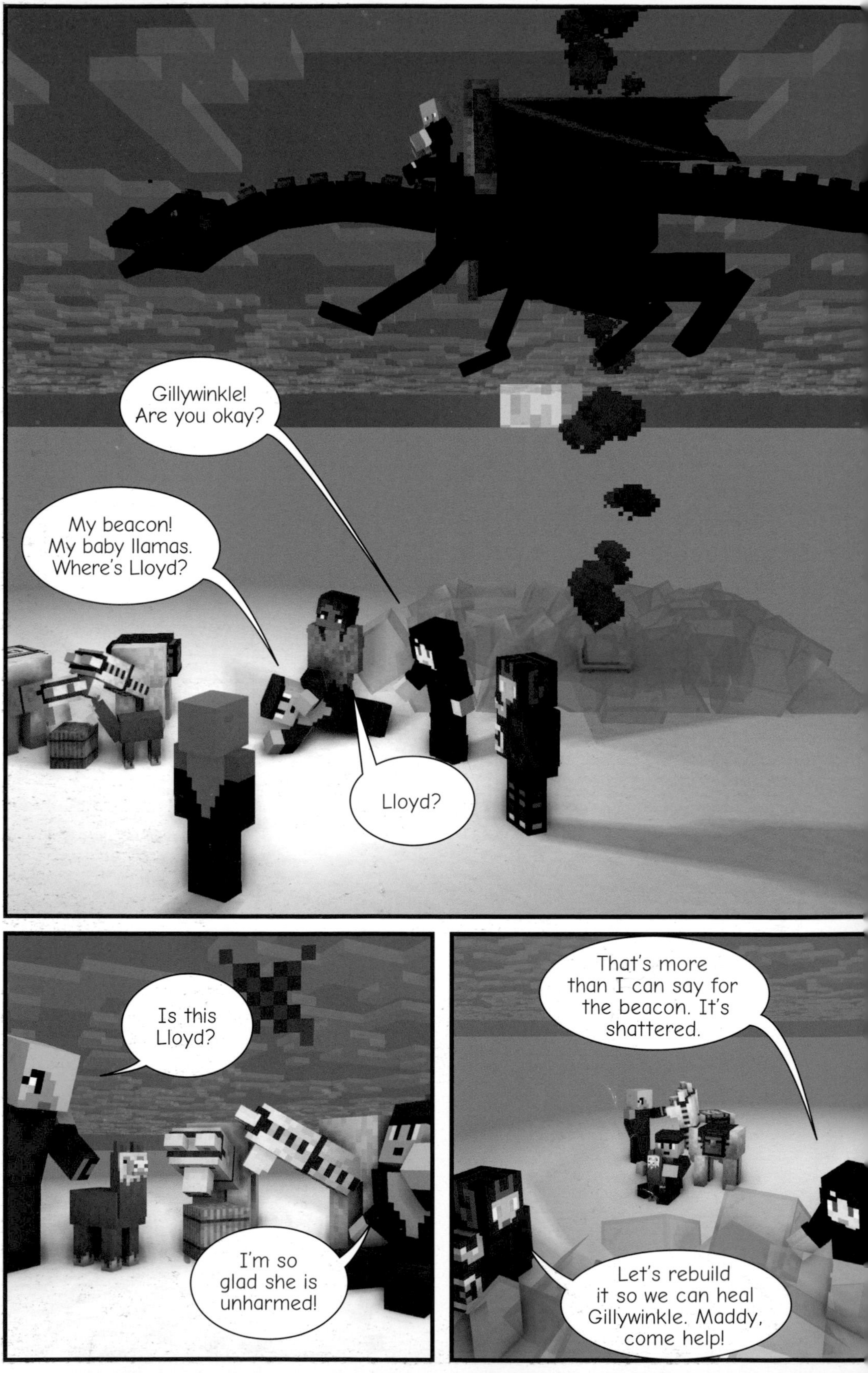
Gillywinkle! Are you okay?
My beacon! My baby llamas. Where's Lloyd?
Lloyd?
Is this Lloyd?
I'm so glad she is unharmed!
That's more than I can say for the beacon. It's shattered.
Let's rebuild it so we can heal Gillywinkle. Maddy, come help!

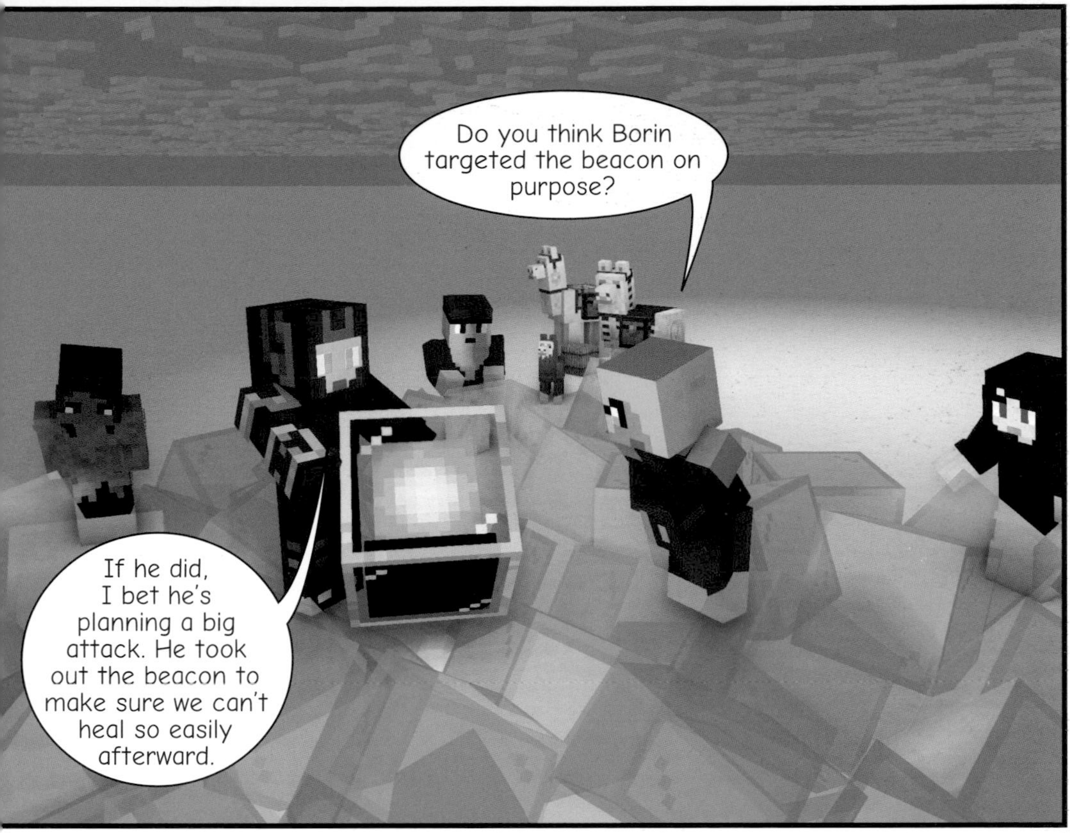
Do you think Borin targeted the beacon on purpose?
If he did, I bet he's planning a big attack. He took out the beacon to make sure we can't heal so easily afterward.

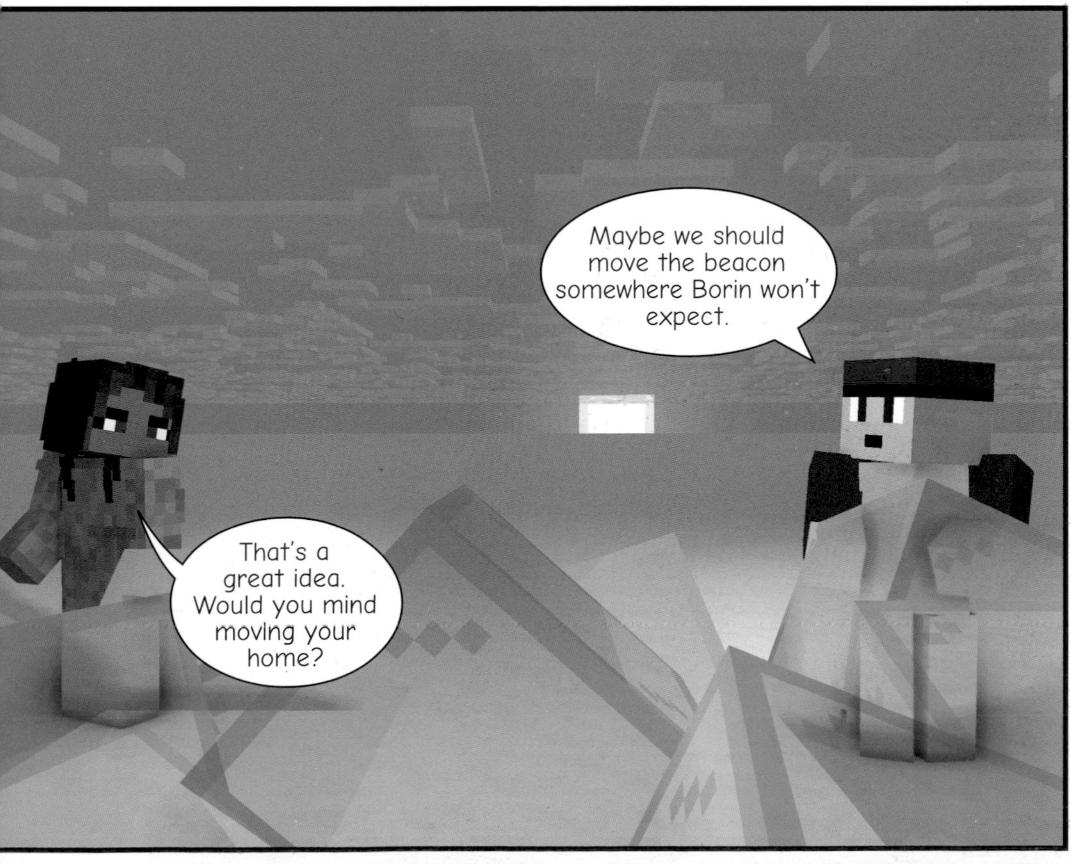
Maybe we should move the beacon somewhere Borin won't expect.
That's a great idea. Would you mind moving your home?

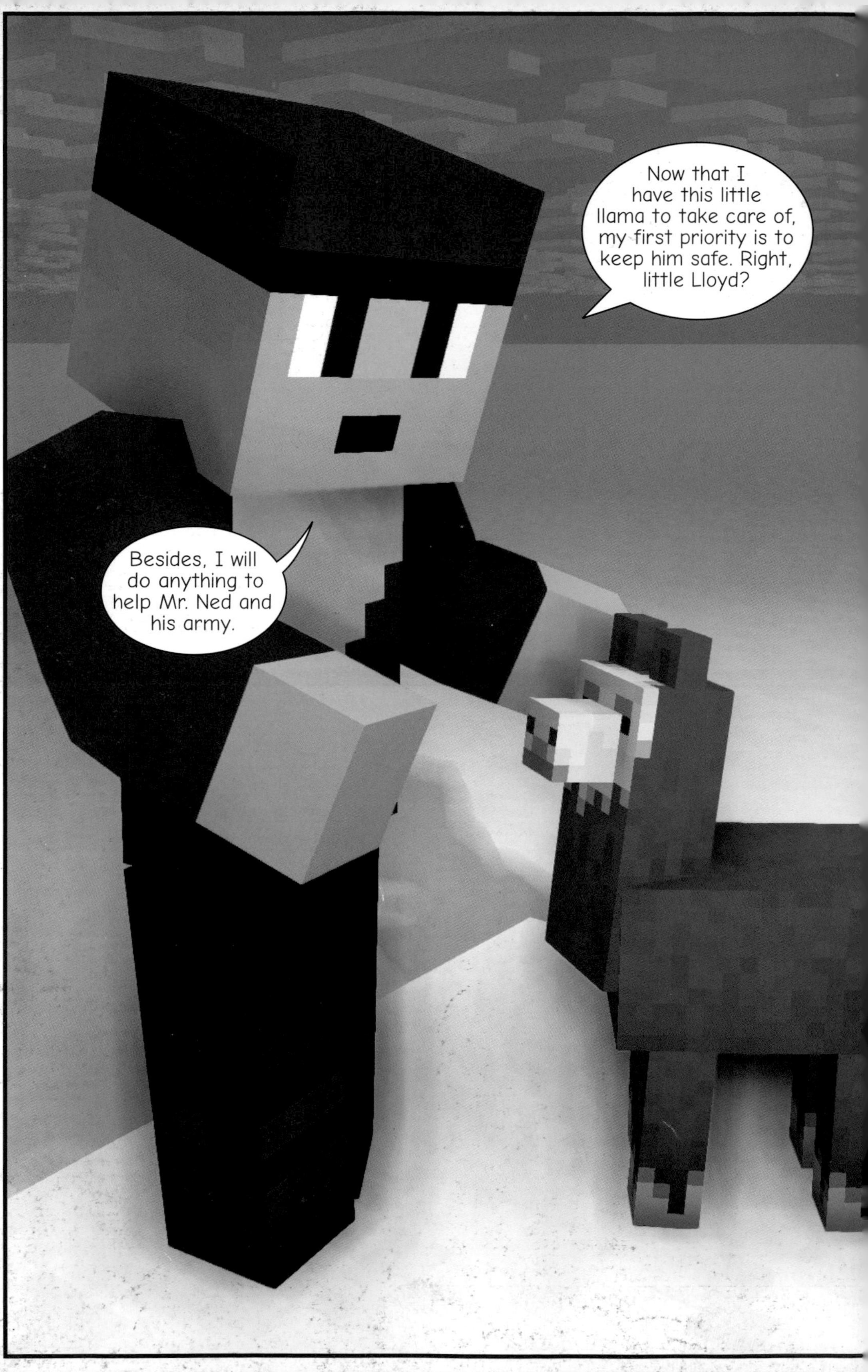
Now that I have this little llama to take care of, my first priority is to keep him safe. Right, little Lloyd?
Besides, I will do anything to help Mr. Ned and his army.

CHAPTER 5

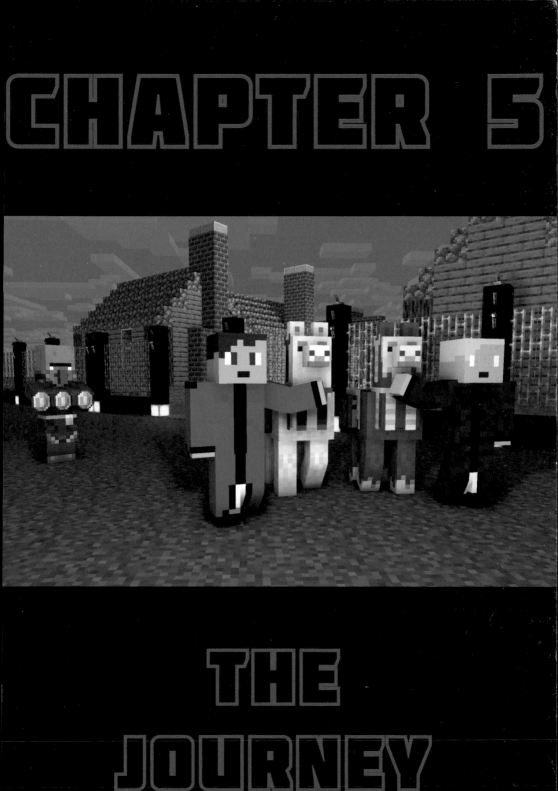

THE

JOURNEY

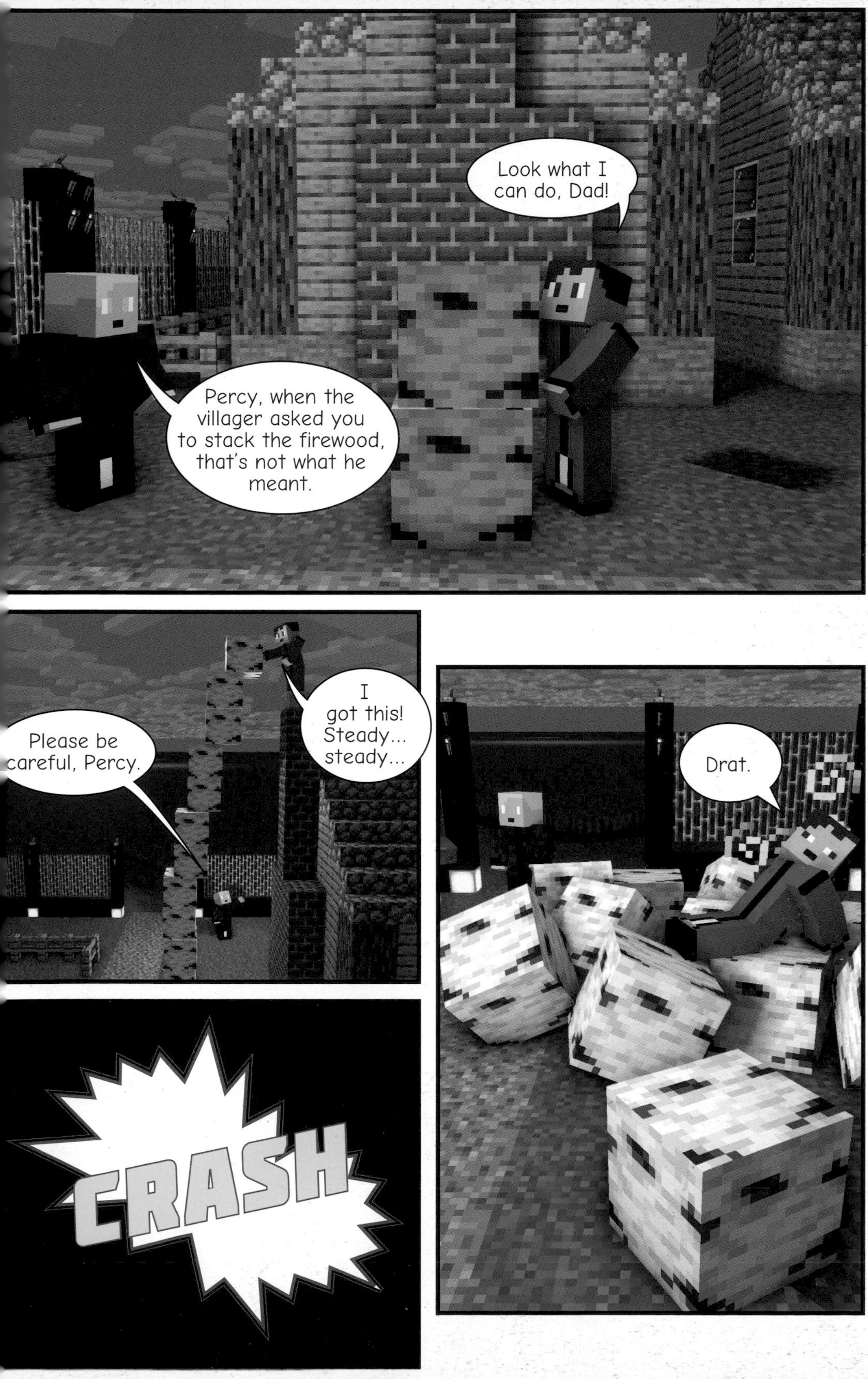
Look what I can do, Dad!
Percy, when the villager asked you to stack the firewood, that's not what he meant.
Please be careful, Percy.
I got this! Steady... steady...
CRASH
Drat.

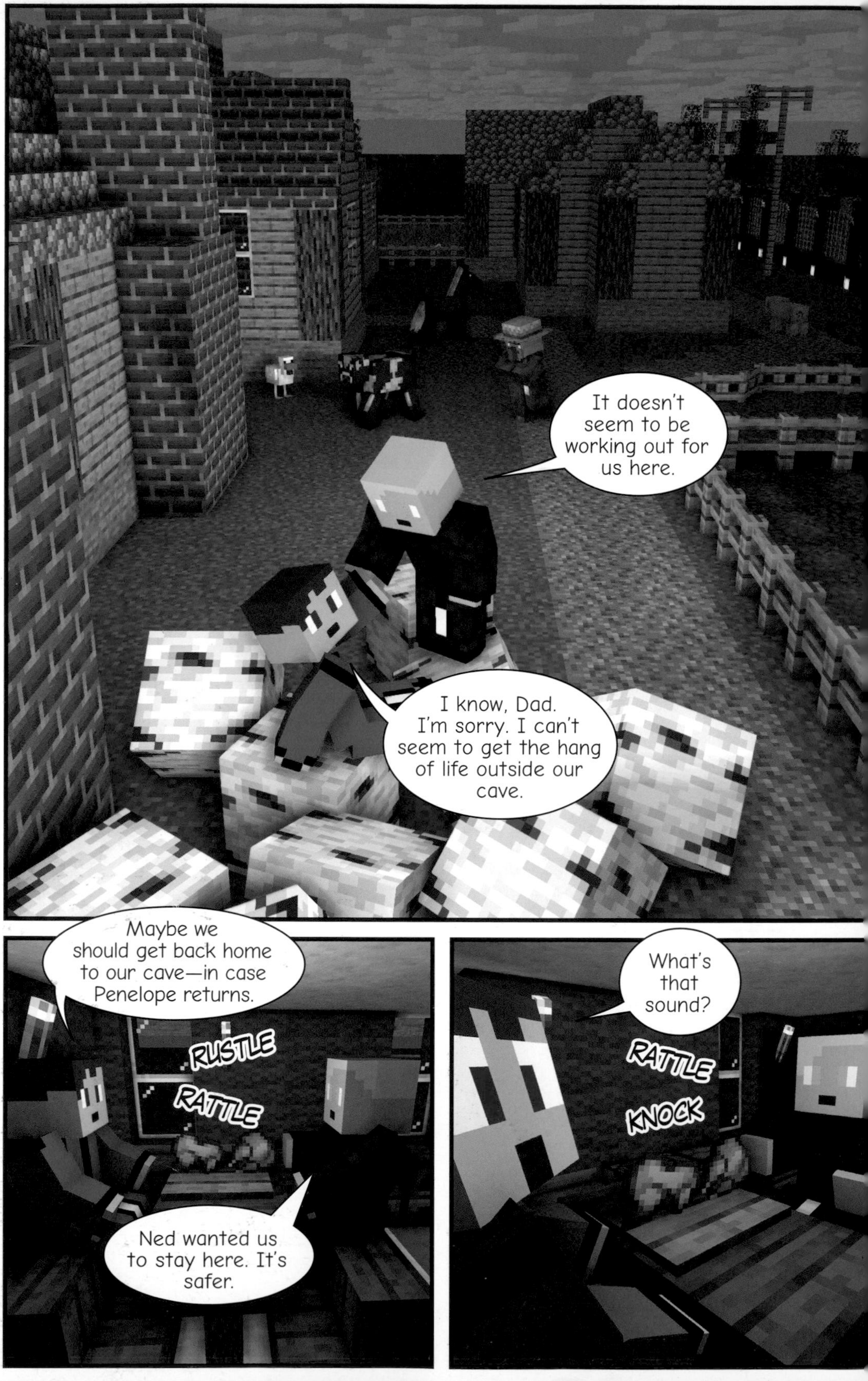
It doesn't seem to be working out for us here.
I know, Dad. I'm sorry. I can't seem to get the hang of life outside our cave.
Maybe we should get back home to our cave—in case Penelope returns.
RUSTLE
RATTLE
Ned wanted us to stay here. It's safer.
What's that sound?
RATTLE
KNOCK

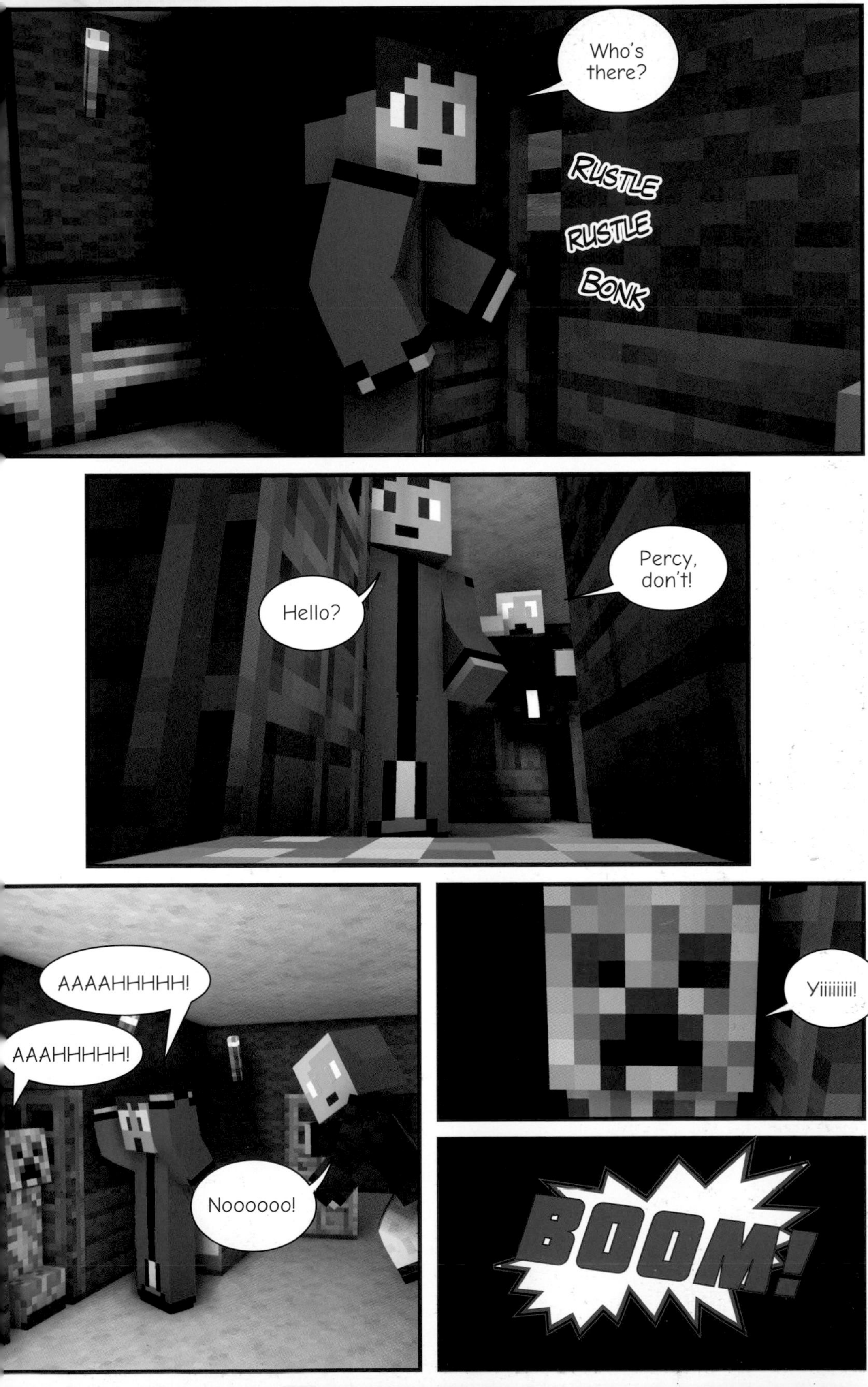

Who's there?
RUSTLE
RUSTLE
BONK
Percy, don't!
Hello?
AAAAHHHHH!
AAAHHHHH!
Noooooo!
Yiiiiiii!
BOOM!

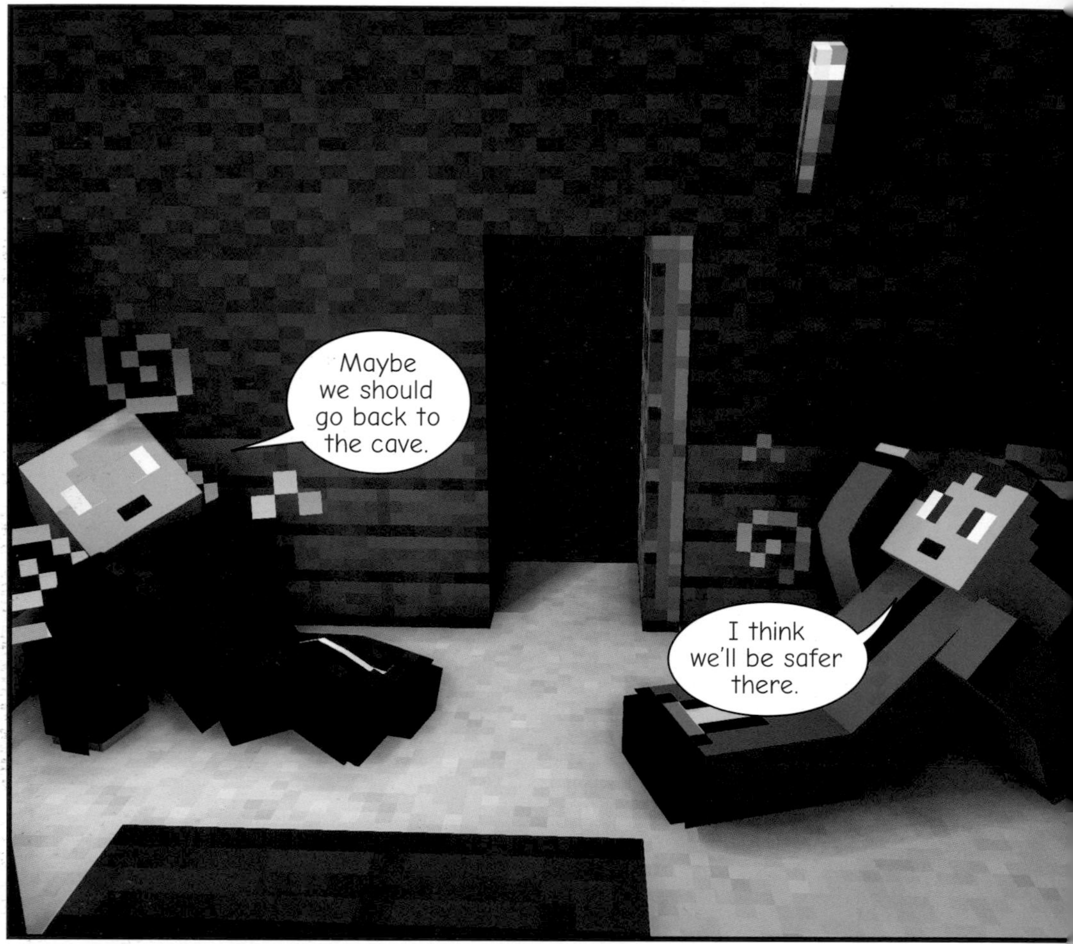
Maybe we should go back to the cave.
I think we'll be safer there.

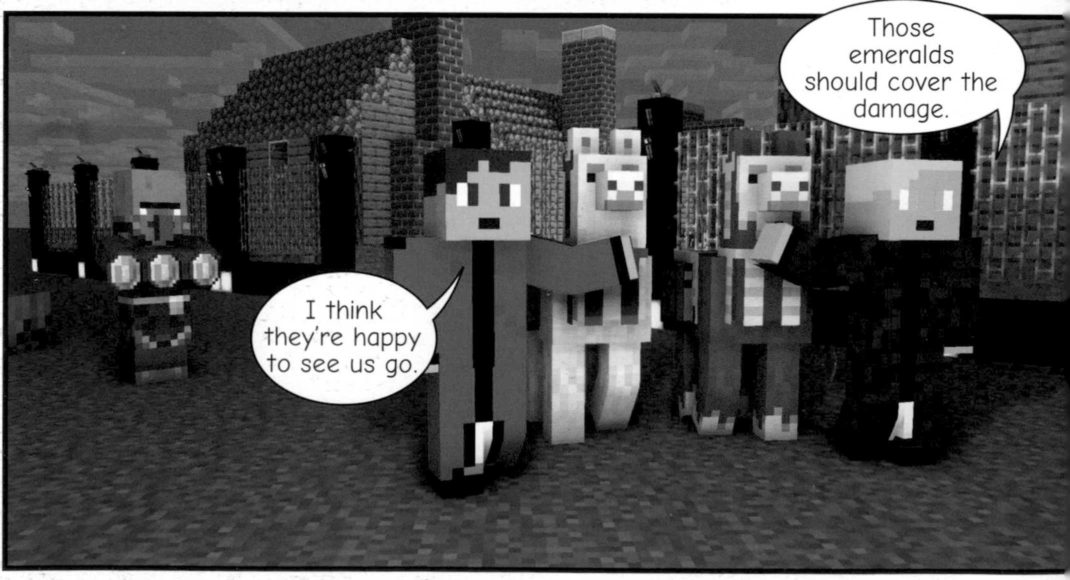
Those emeralds should cover the damage.
I think they're happy to see us go.

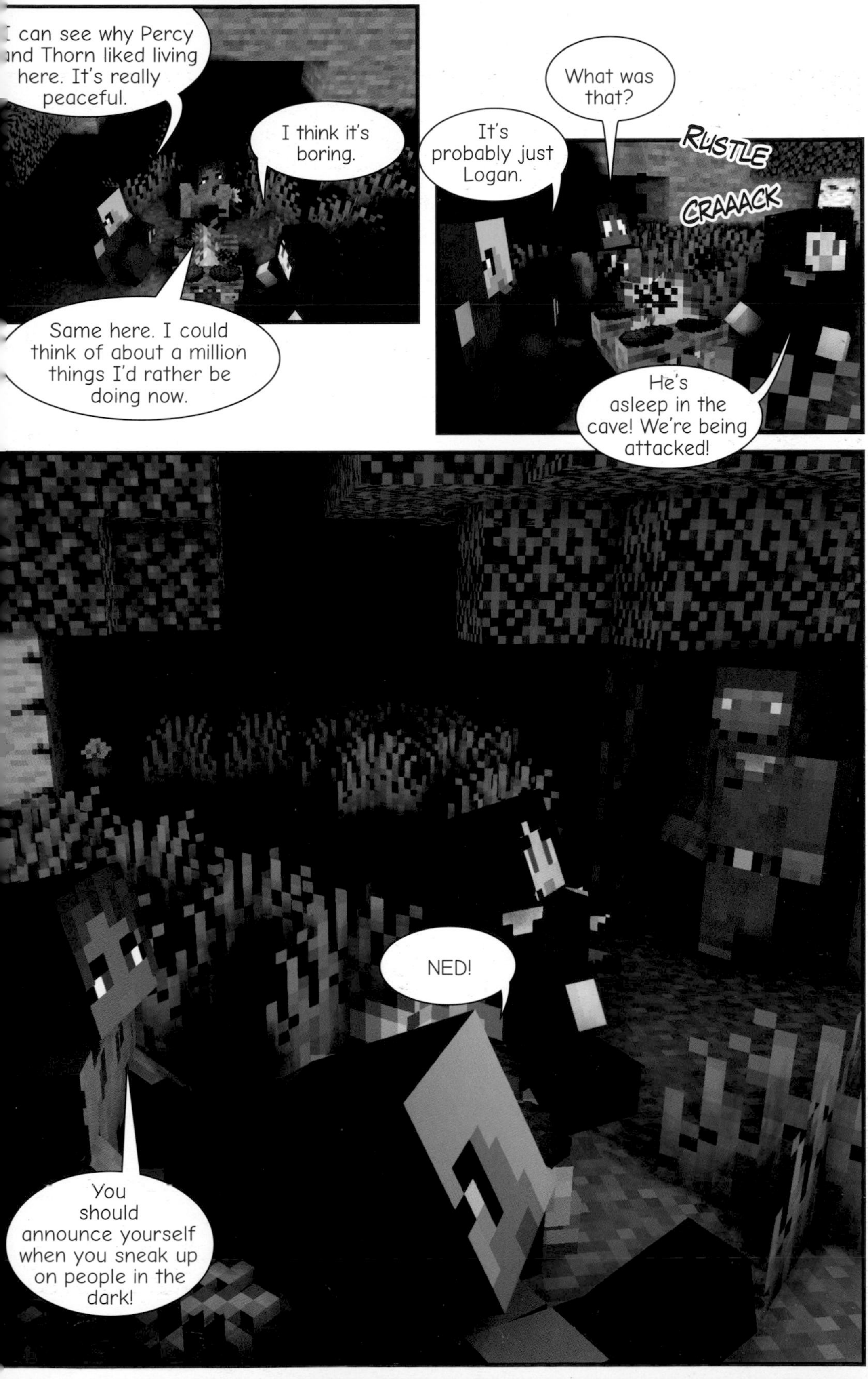
I can see why Percy and Thorn liked living here. It's really peaceful.
I think it's boring.
Same here. I could think of about a million things I'd rather be doing now.
What was that?
It's probably just Logan.
RUSTLE
CRAAACK
He's asleep in the cave! We're being attacked!
NED!
You should announce yourself when you sneak up on people in the dark!

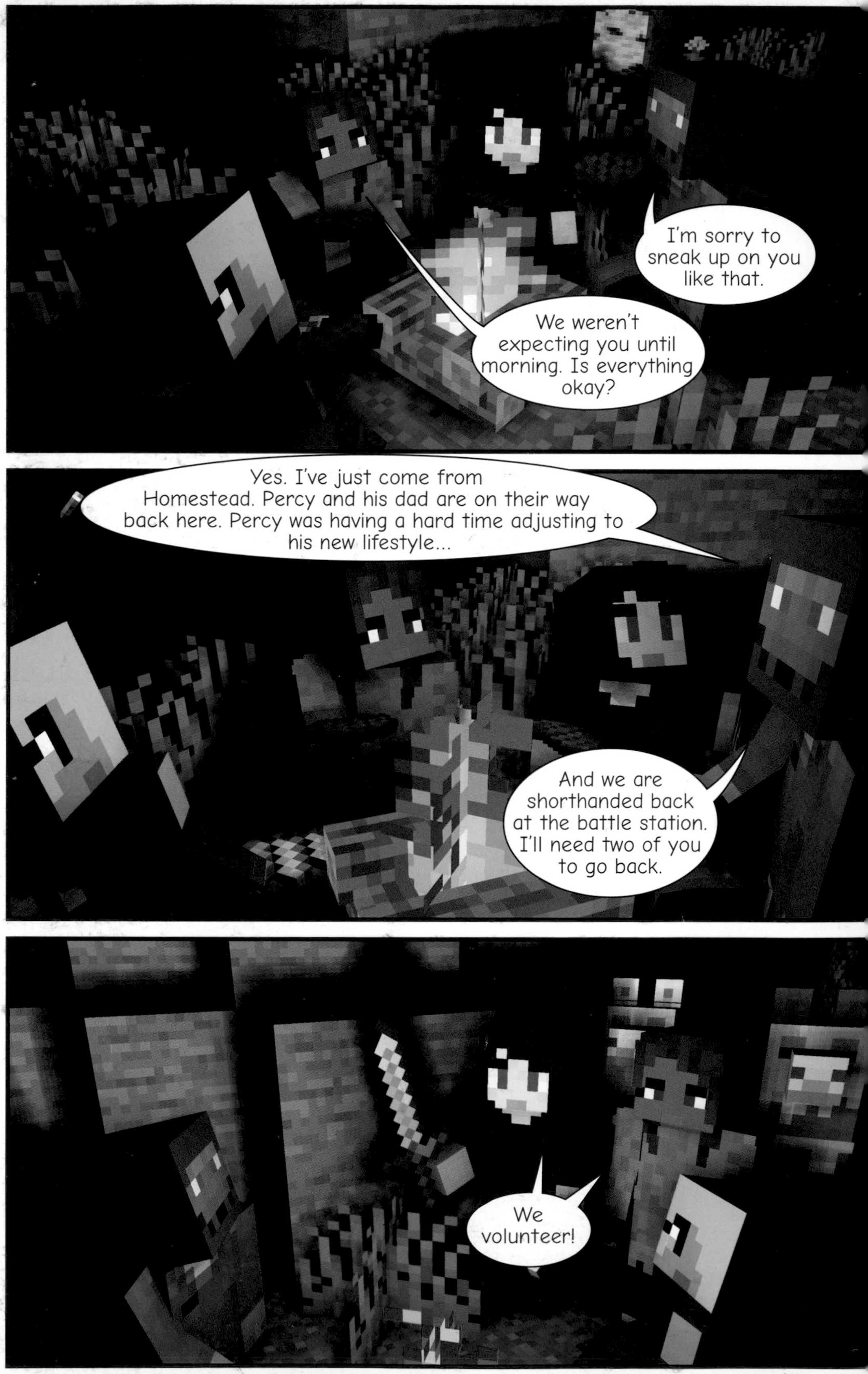
I'm sorry to sneak up on you like that.
We weren't expecting you until morning. Is everything okay?
Yes. I've just come from Homestead. Percy and his dad are on their way back here. Percy was having a hard time adjusting to his new lifestyle...
And we are shorthanded back at the battle station. I'll need two of you to go back.
We volunteer!

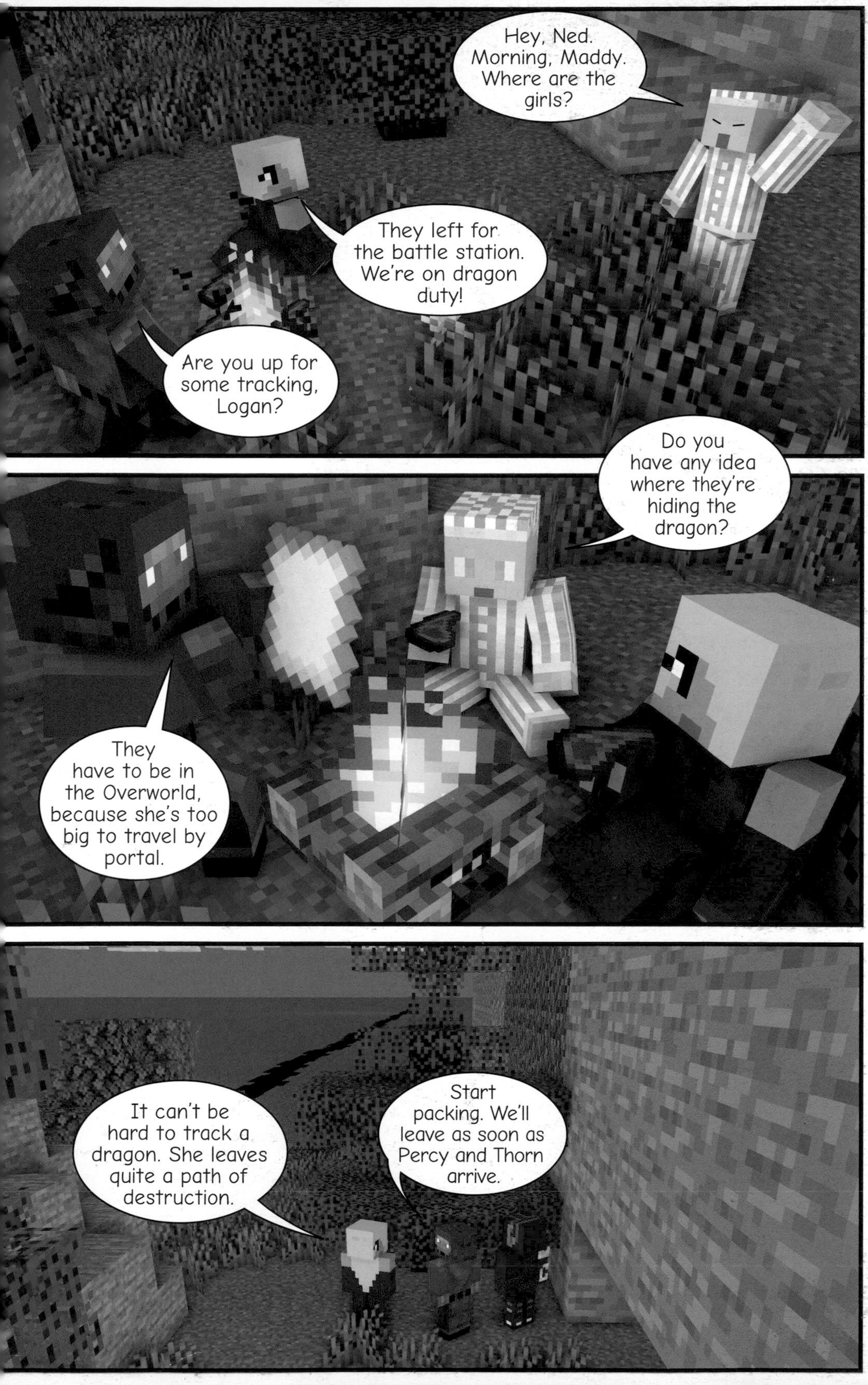
Hey, Ned. Morning, Maddy. Where are the girls?
They left for the battle station. We're on dragon duty!
Are you up for some tracking, Logan?
Do you have any idea where they're hiding the dragon?
They have to be in the Overworld, because she's too big to travel by portal.
It can't be hard to track a dragon. She leaves quite a path of destruction.
Start packing. We'll leave as soon as Percy and Thorn arrive.

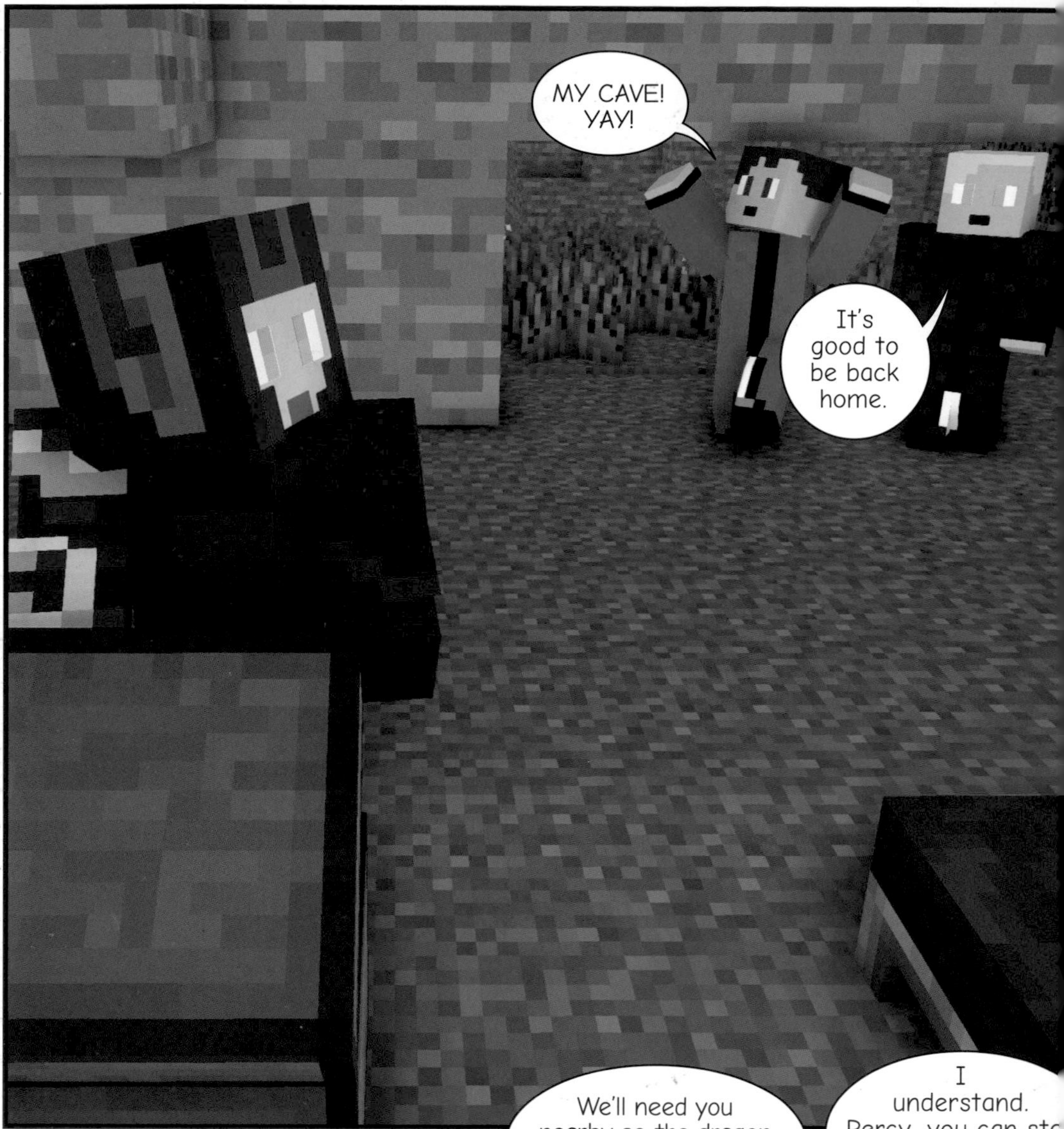
MY CAVE! YAY!
It's good to be back home.

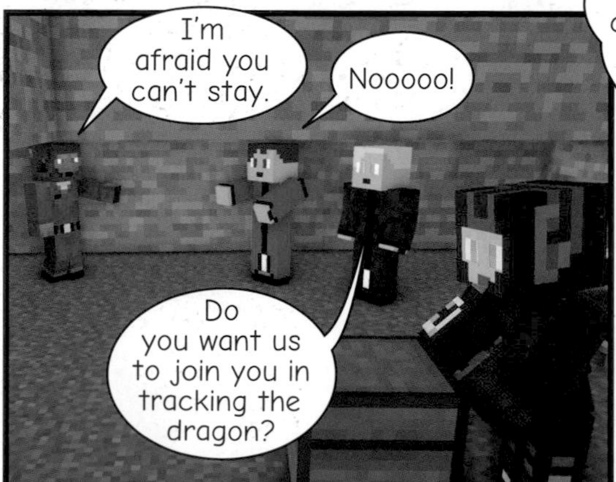
I'm afraid you can't stay.
Noooooo!
Do you want us to join you in tracking the dragon?

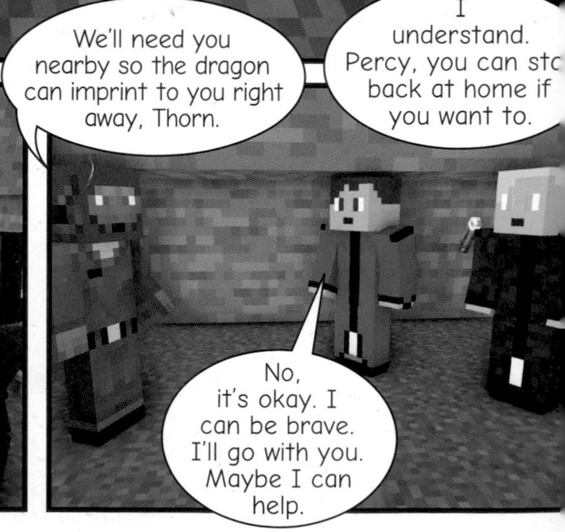
We'll need you nearby so the dragon can imprint to you right away, Thorn.
I understand. Percy, you can st
back at home if you want to.
No, it's okay. I can be brave. I'll go with you. Maybe I can help.

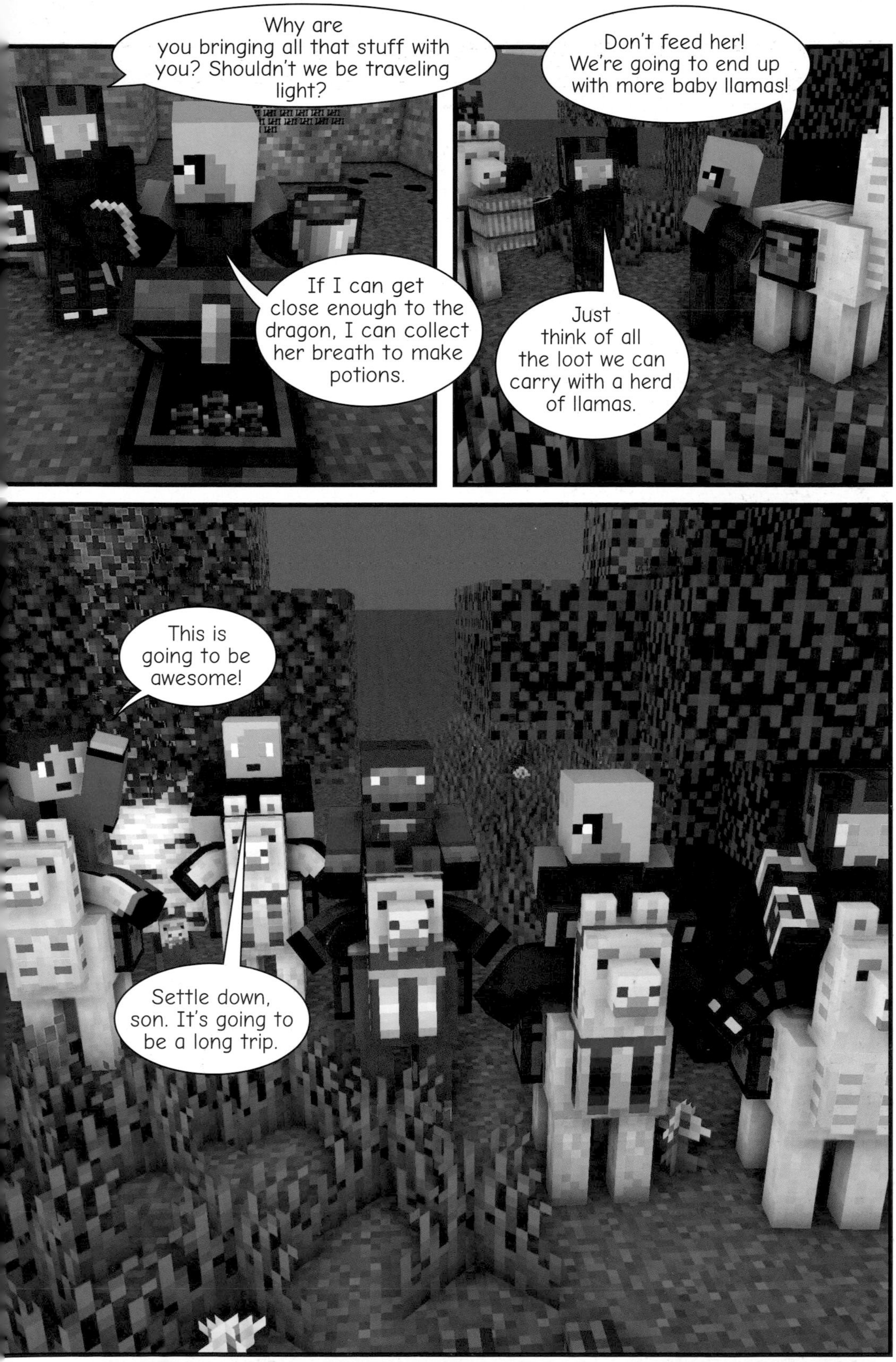
Why are you bringing all that stuff with you? Shouldn't we be traveling light?
If I can get close enough to the dragon, I can collect her breath to make potions.
Don't feed her! We're going to end up with more baby llamas!
Just think of all the loot we can carry with a herd of llamas.
This is going to be awesome!
Settle down, son. It's going to be a long trip.

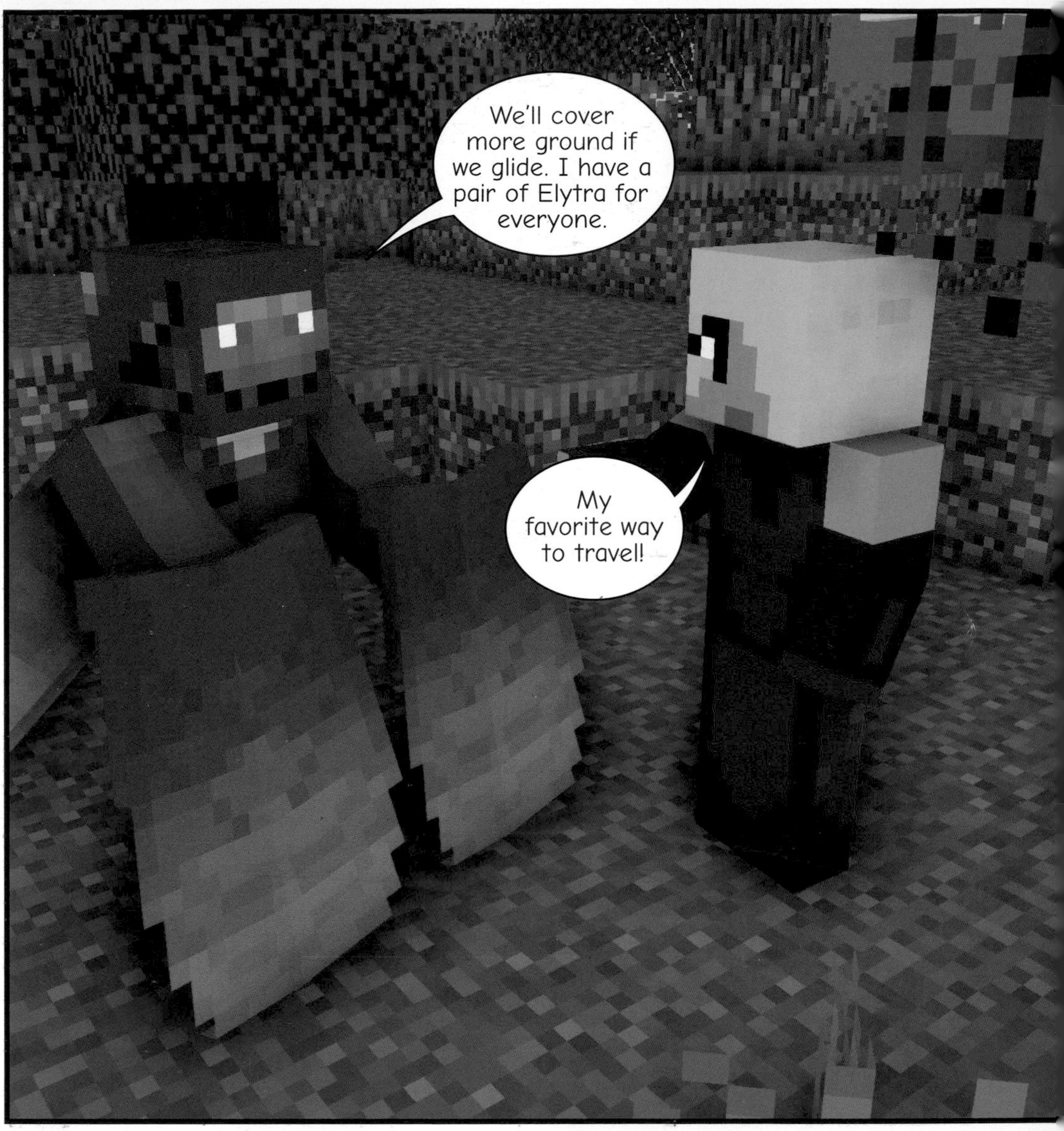
We'll cover more ground if we glide. I have a pair of Elytra for everyone.
My favorite way to travel!

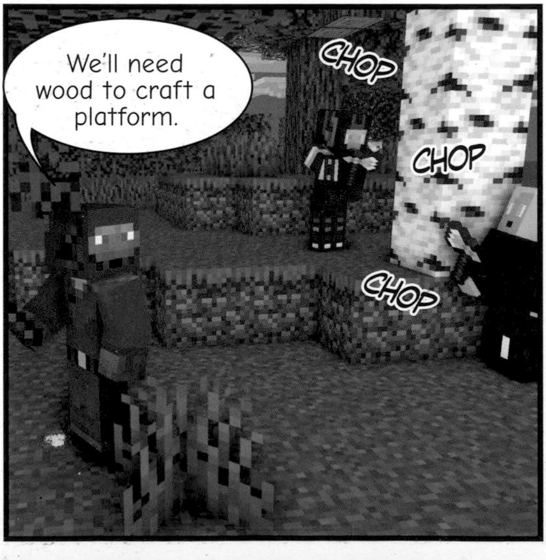
We'll need wood to craft a platform.
CHOP
CHOP
CHOP

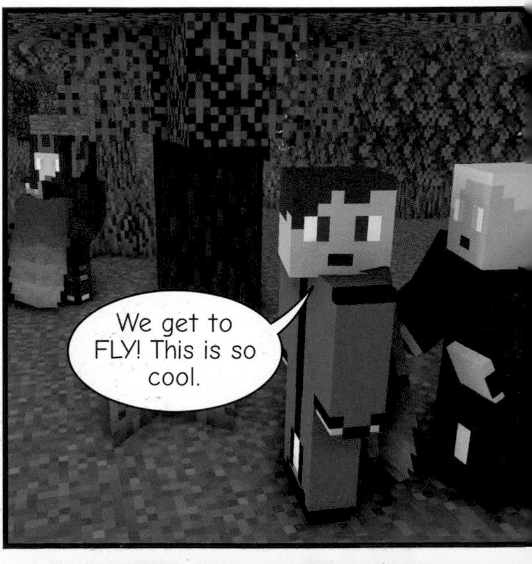
We get to FLY! This is so cool.

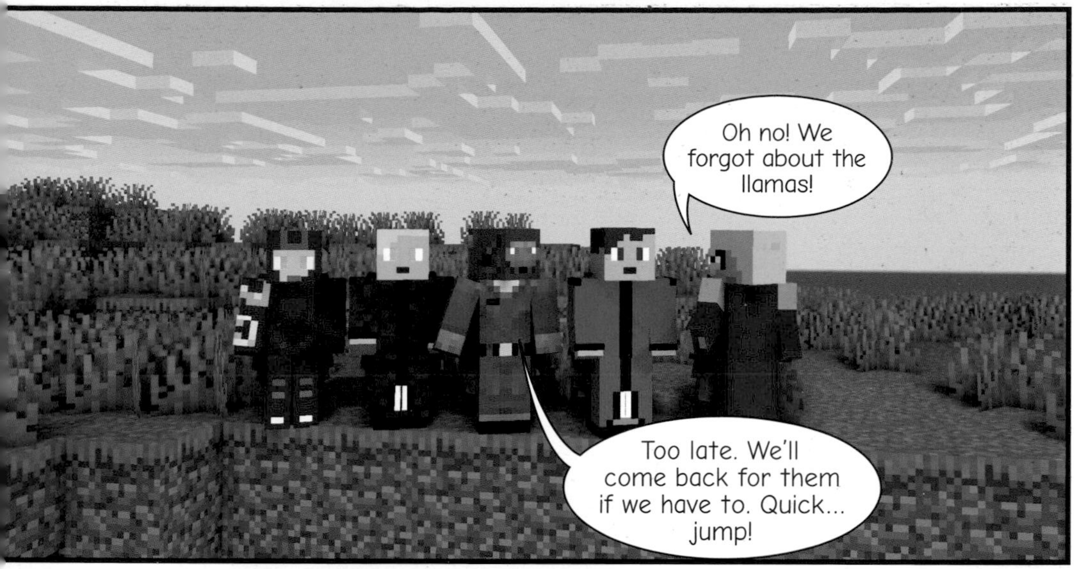
Oh no! We forgot about the llamas!
Too late. We'll come back for them if we have to. Quick... jump!

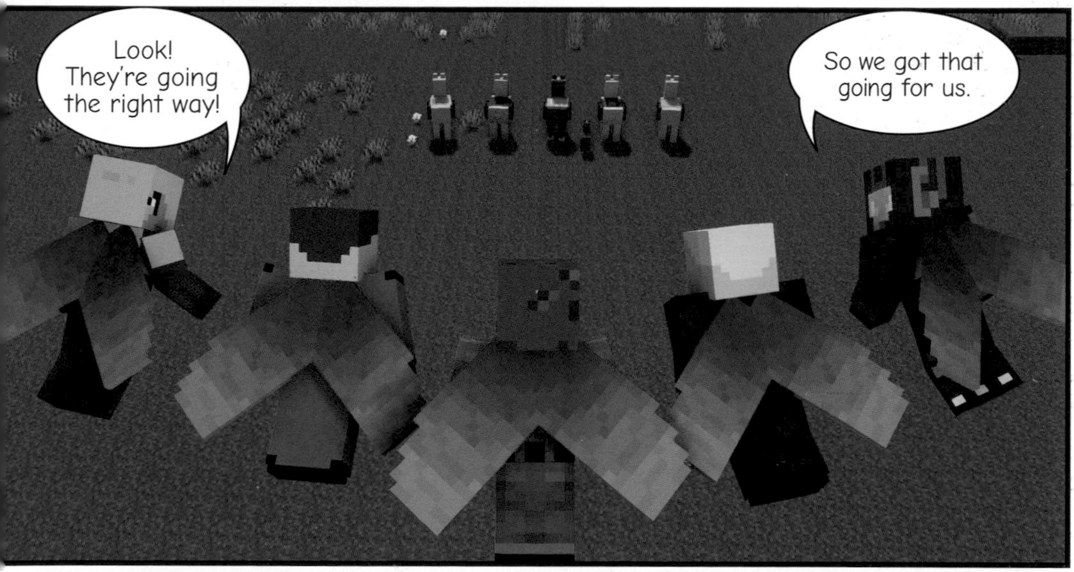
Look! They're going the right way!
So we got that going for us.

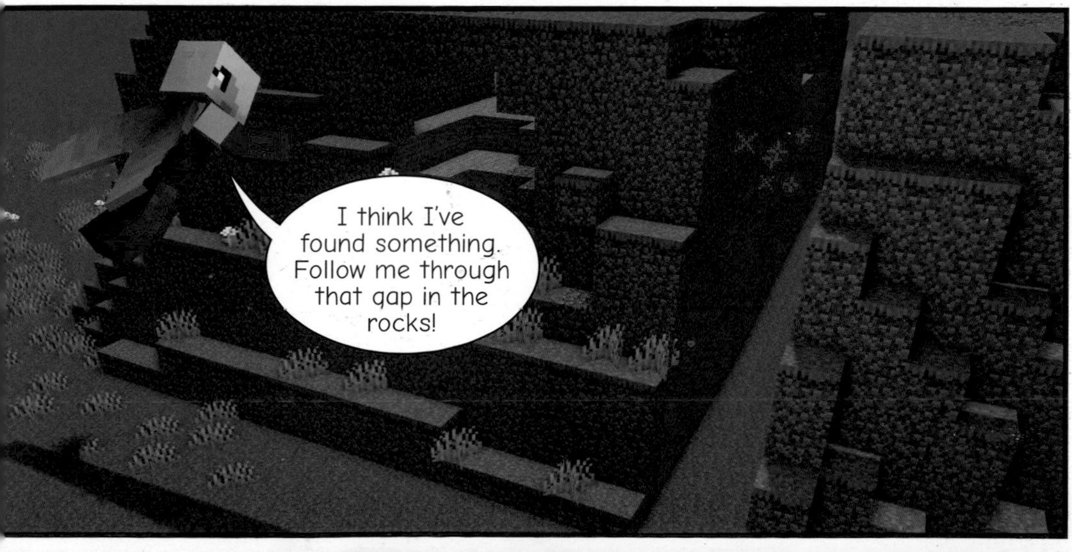
I think I've found something. Follow me through that gap in the rocks!

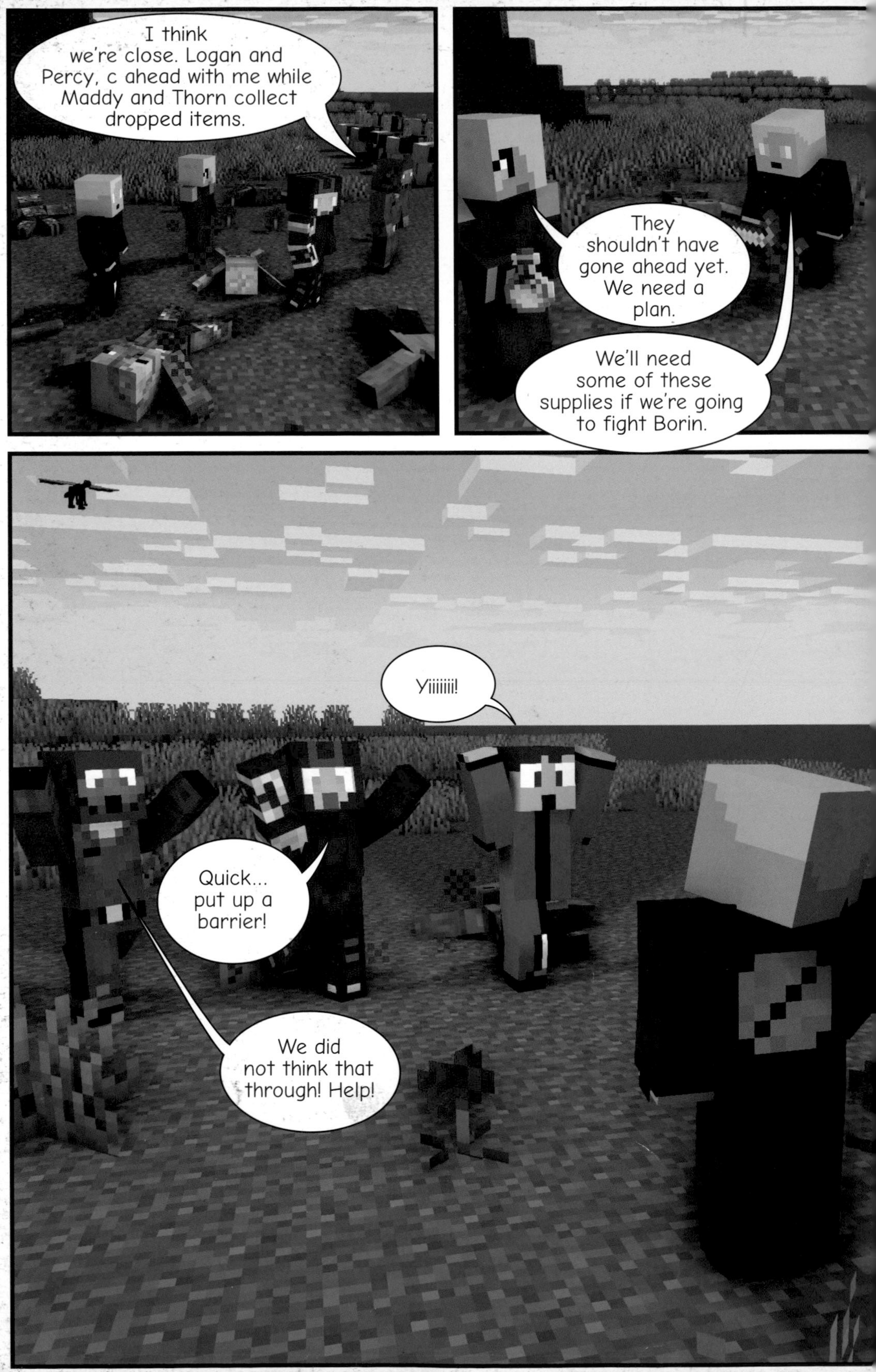
I think we're close. Logan and Percy, c ahead with me while Maddy and Thorn collect dropped items.
They shouldn't have gone ahead yet. We need a plan.
We'll need some of these supplies if we're going to fight Borin.
Yiiiiii!
Quick... put up a barrier!
We did not think that through! Help!

CHAPTER 6

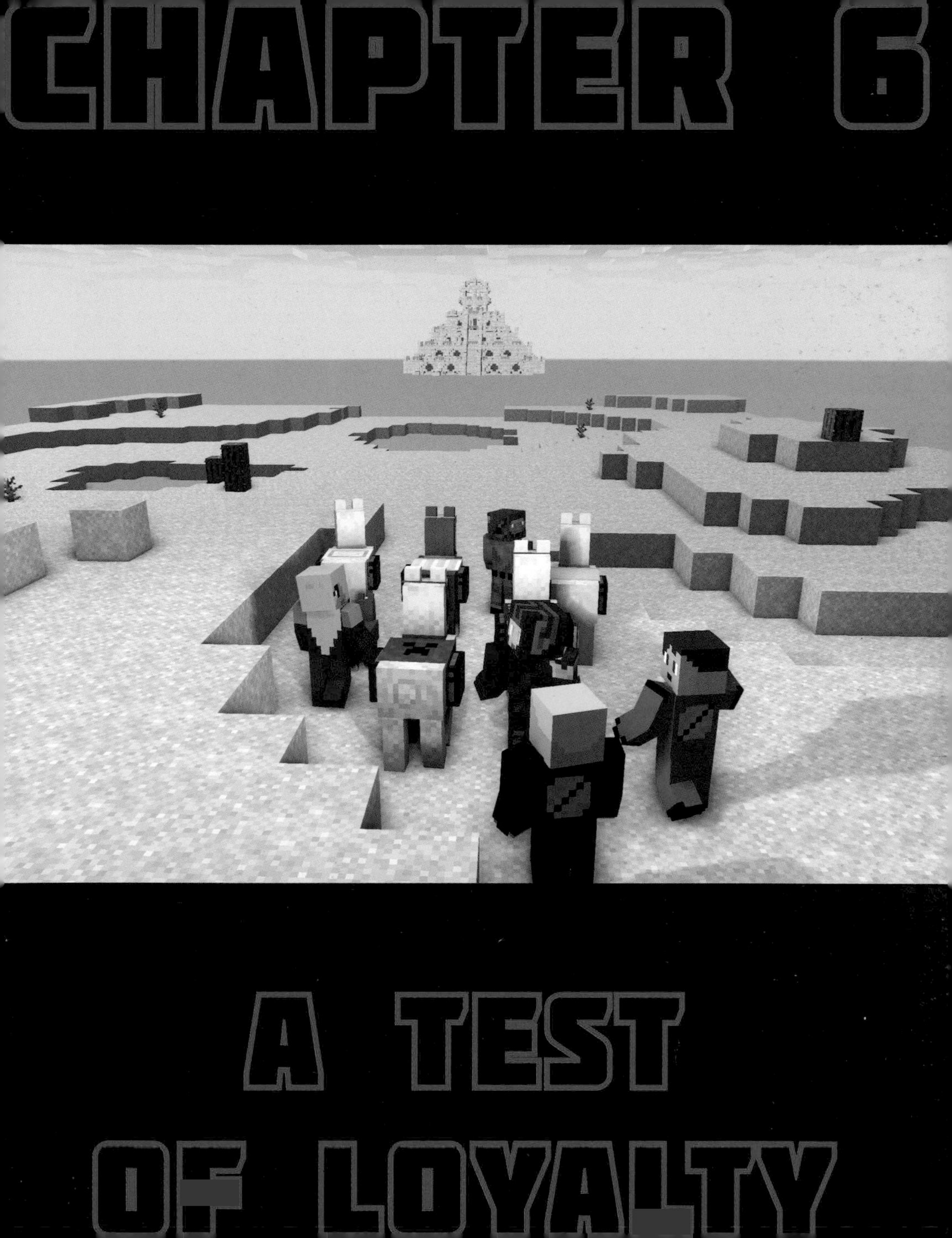

A TEST OF LOYALTY

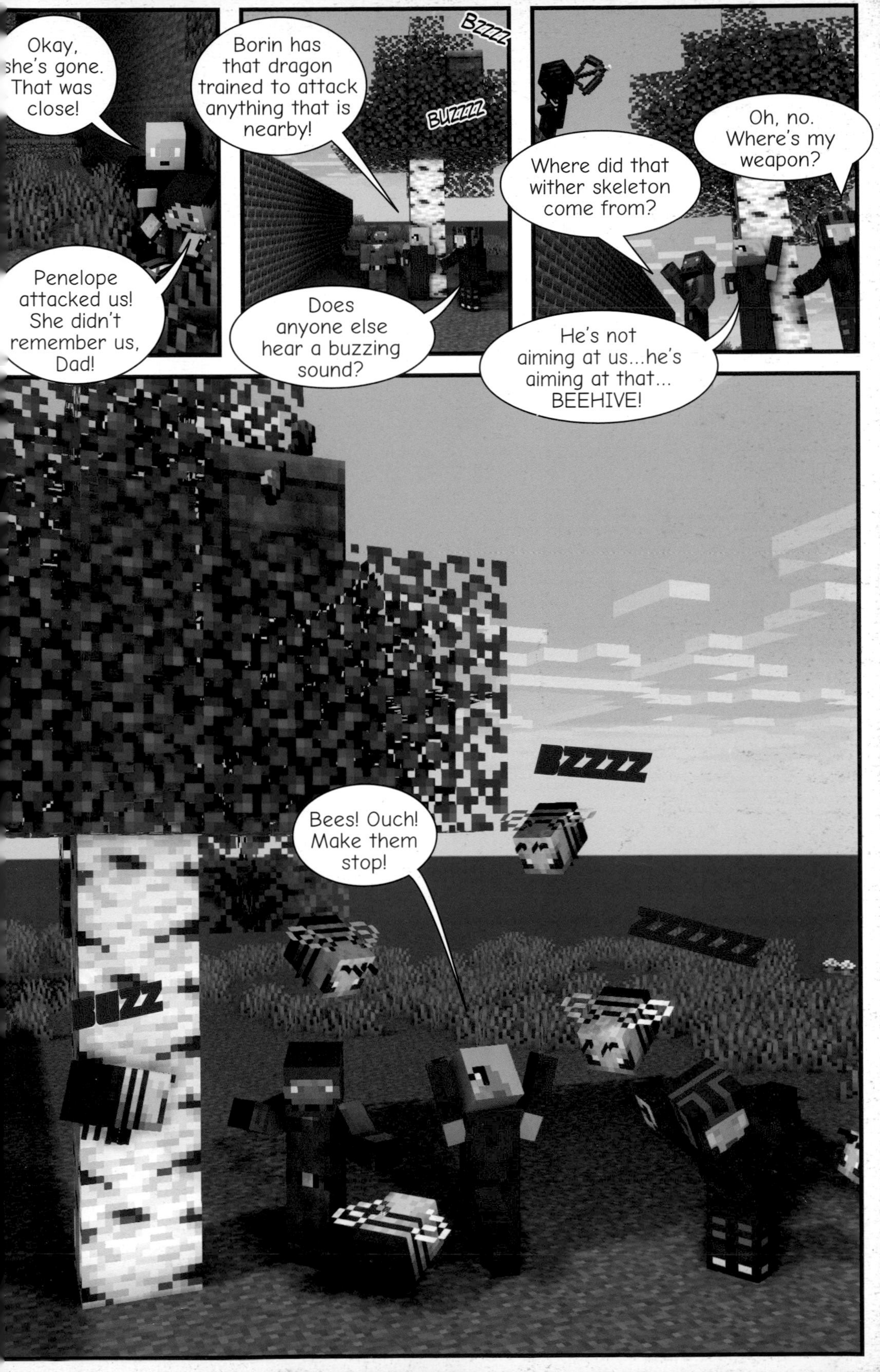
Okay, she's gone. That was close!
Penelope attacked us! She didn't remember us, Dad!
Bzzzz
Borin has that dragon trained to attack anything that is nearby!
Buzzzz
Does anyone else hear a buzzing sound?
Where did that wither skeleton come from?
Oh, no. Where's my weapon?
He's not aiming at us...he's aiming at that... BEEHIVE!
Bzzzz
Bees! Ouch! Make them stop!
Zzzzzz
Buzz

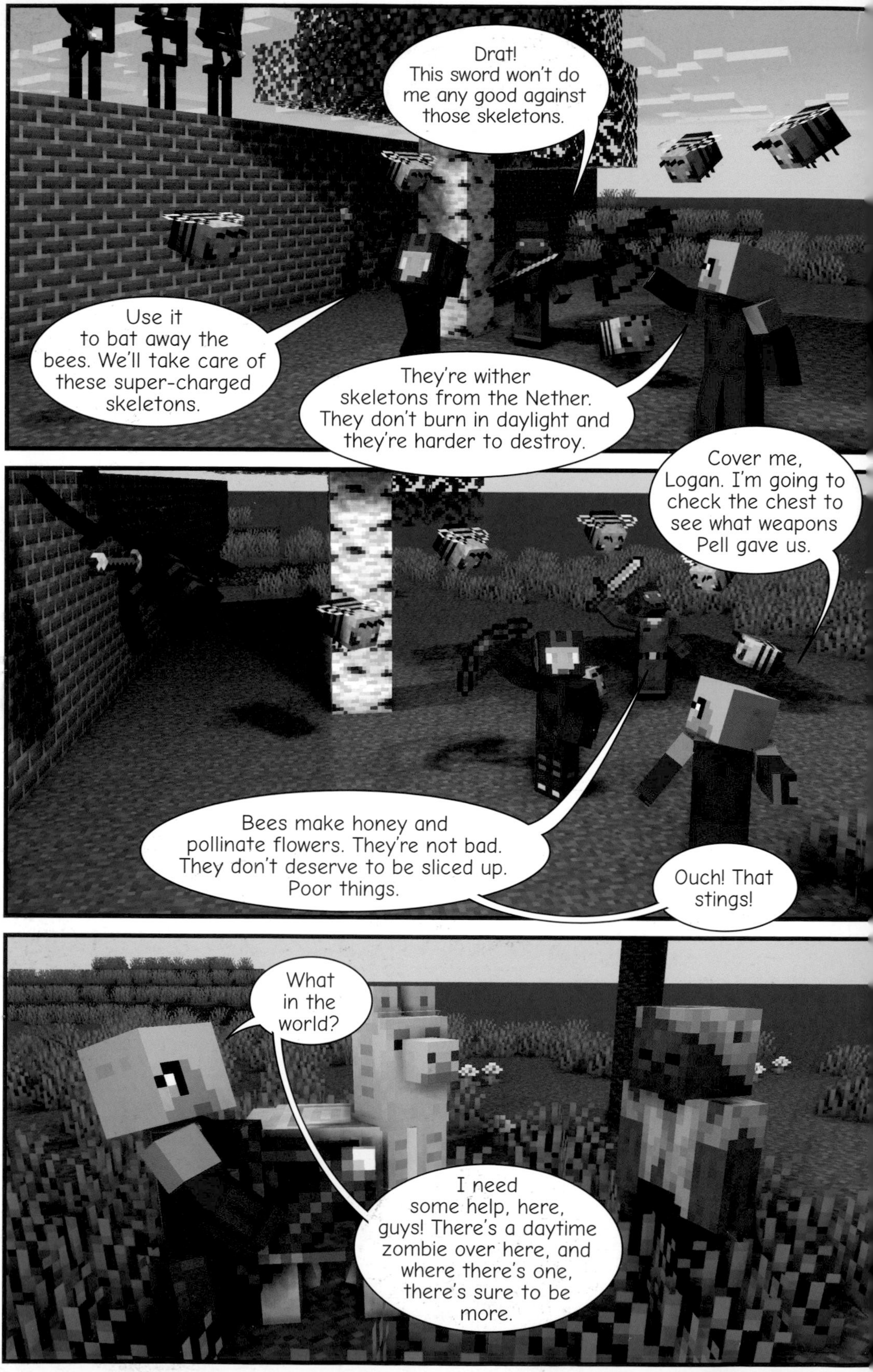
Drat! This sword won't do me any good against those skeletons.
Use it to bat away the bees. We'll take care of these super-charged skeletons.
They're wither skeletons from the Nether. They don't burn in daylight and they're harder to destroy.
Cover me, Logan. I'm going to check the chest to see what weapons Pell gave us.
Bees make honey and pollinate flowers. They're not bad. They don't deserve to be sliced up. Poor things.
Ouch! That stings!
What in the world?
I need some help, here, guys! There's a daytime zombie over here, and where there's one, there's sure to be more.

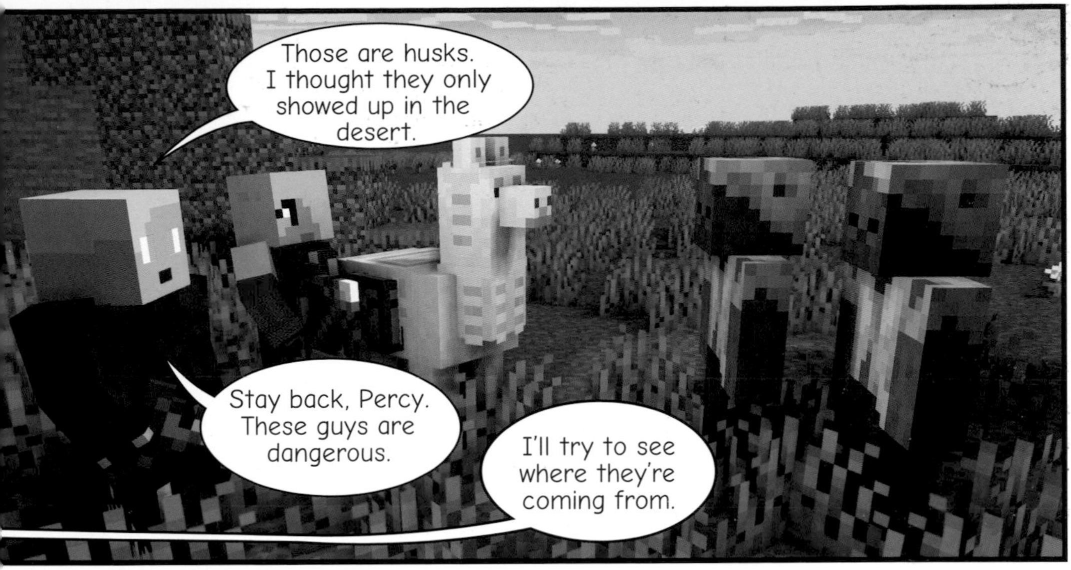
Those are husks. I thought they only showed up in the desert.
Stay back, Percy. These guys are dangerous.
I'll try to see where they're coming from.

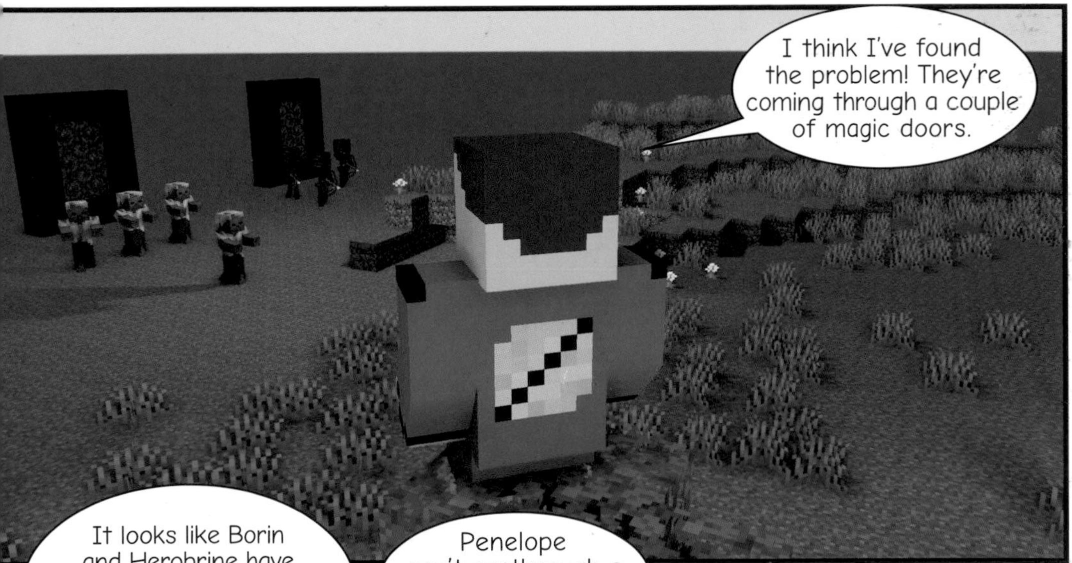
I think I've found the problem! They're coming through a couple of magic doors.

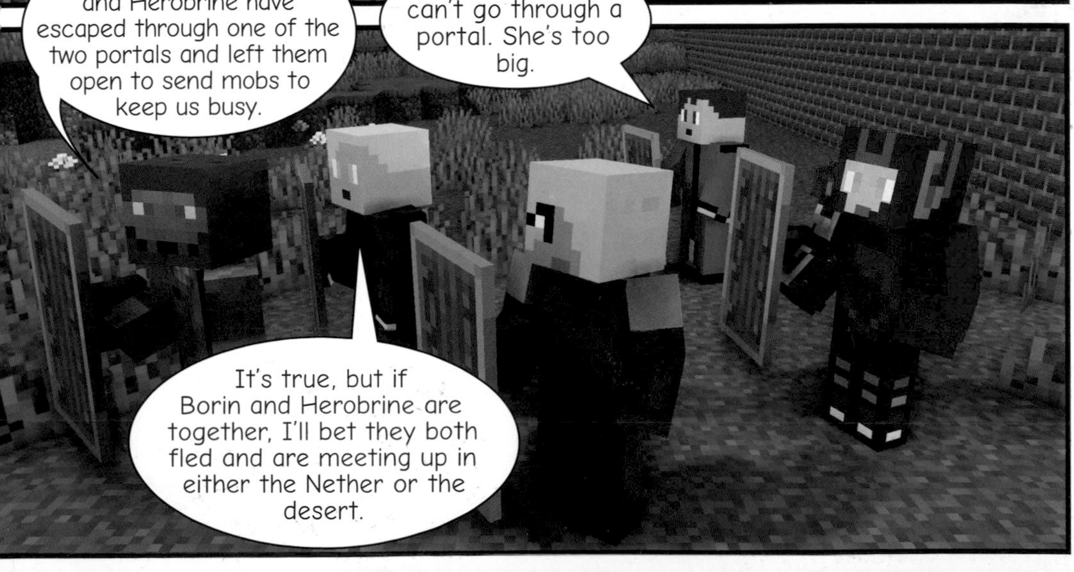
It looks like Borin and Herobrine have escaped through one of the two portals and left them open to send mobs to keep us busy.
Penelope can't go through a portal. She's too big.
It's true, but if Borin and Herobrine are together, I'll bet they both fled and are meeting up in either the Nether or the desert.

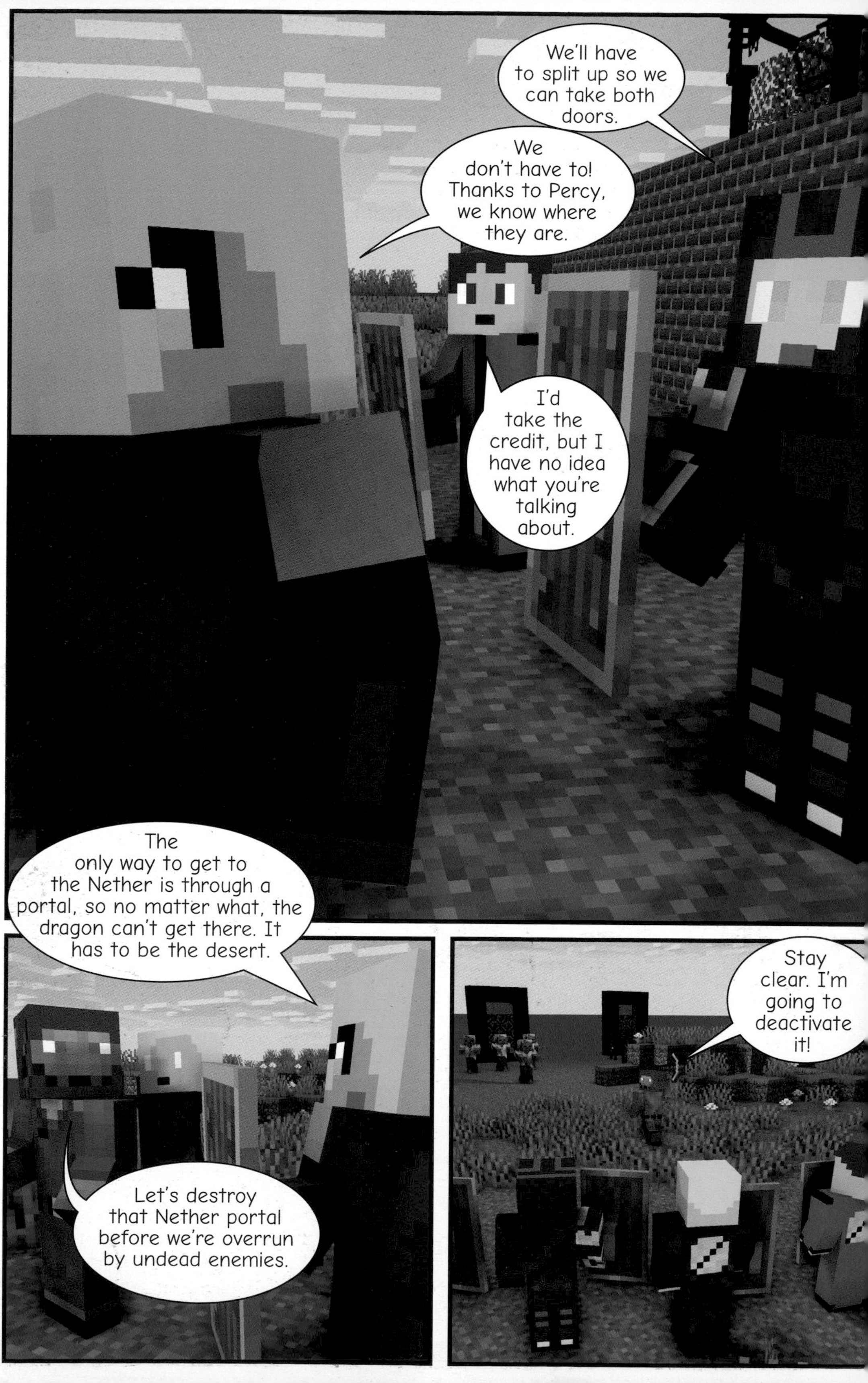
We'll have to split up so we can take both doors.
We don't have to! Thanks to Percy, we know where they are.
I'd take the credit, but I have no idea what you're talking about.
The only way to get to the Nether is through a portal, so no matter what, the dragon can't get there. It has to be the desert.
Let's destroy that Nether portal before we're overrun by undead enemies.
Stay clear. I'm going to deactivate it!

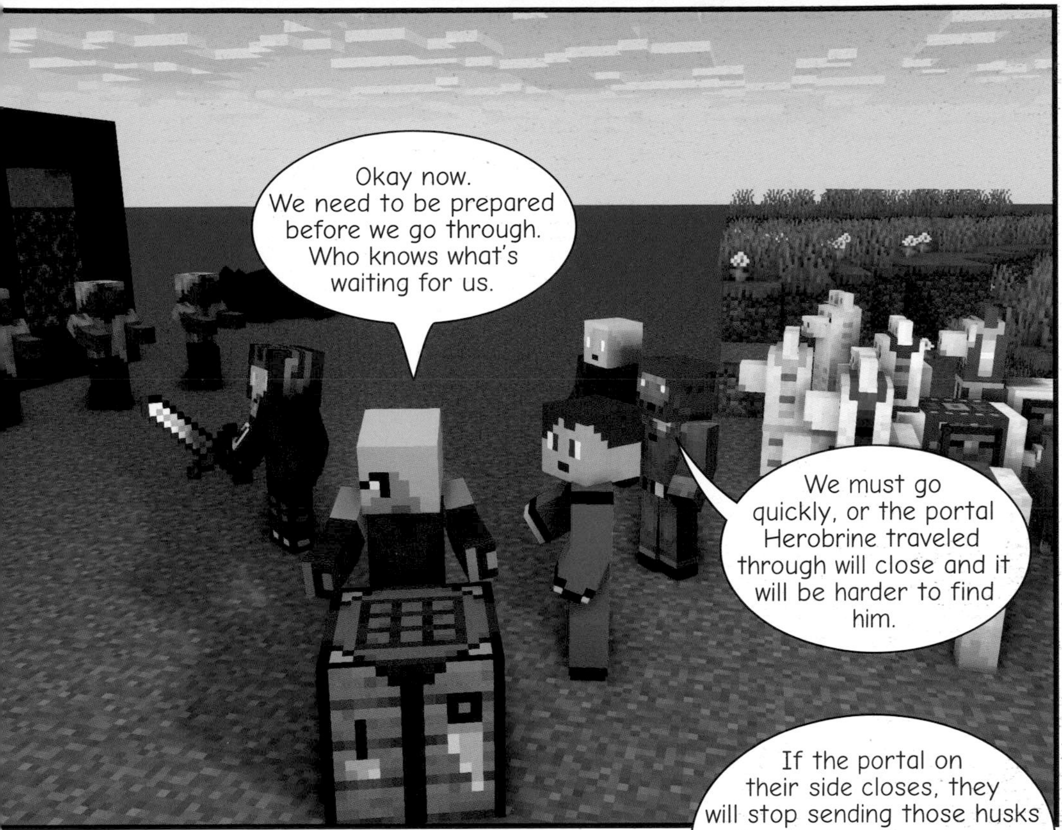
Okay now. We need to be prepared before we go through. Who knows what's waiting for us.
We must go quickly, or the portal Herobrine traveled through will close and it will be harder to find him.

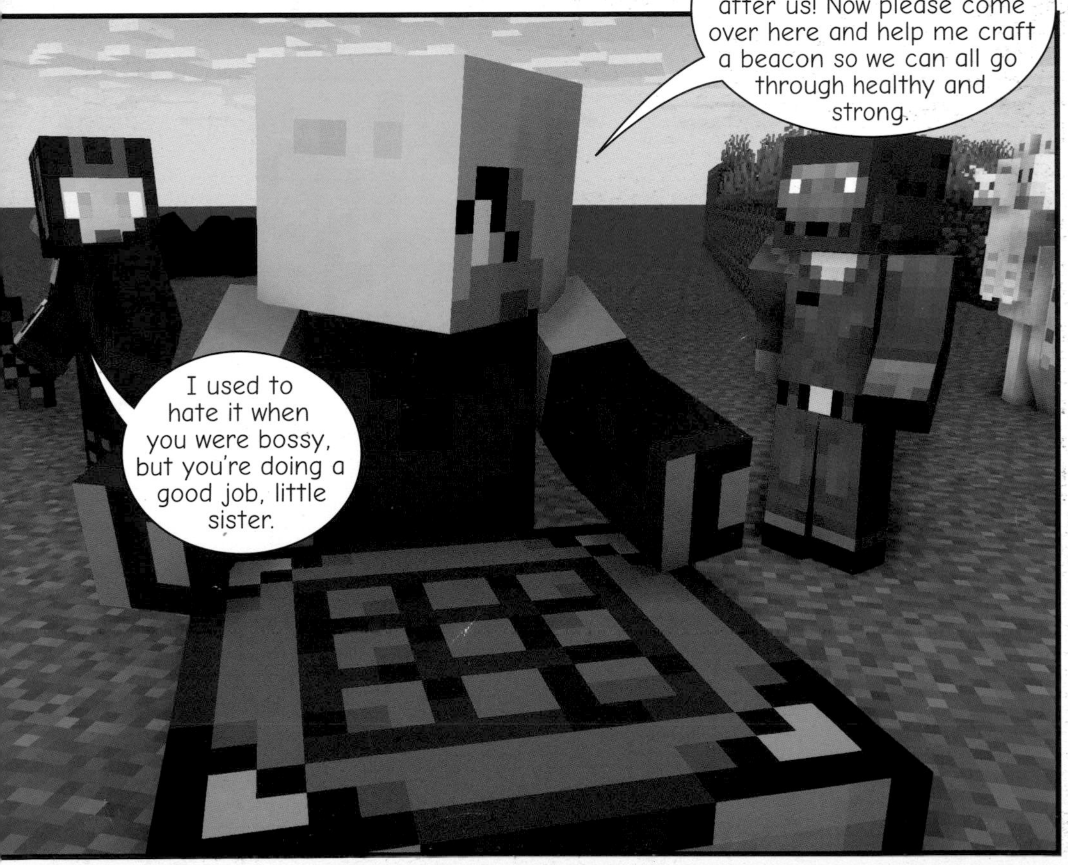
If the portal on their side closes, they will stop sending those husks after us! Now please come over here and help me craft a beacon so we can all go through healthy and strong.
I used to hate it when you were bossy, but you're doing a good job, little sister.

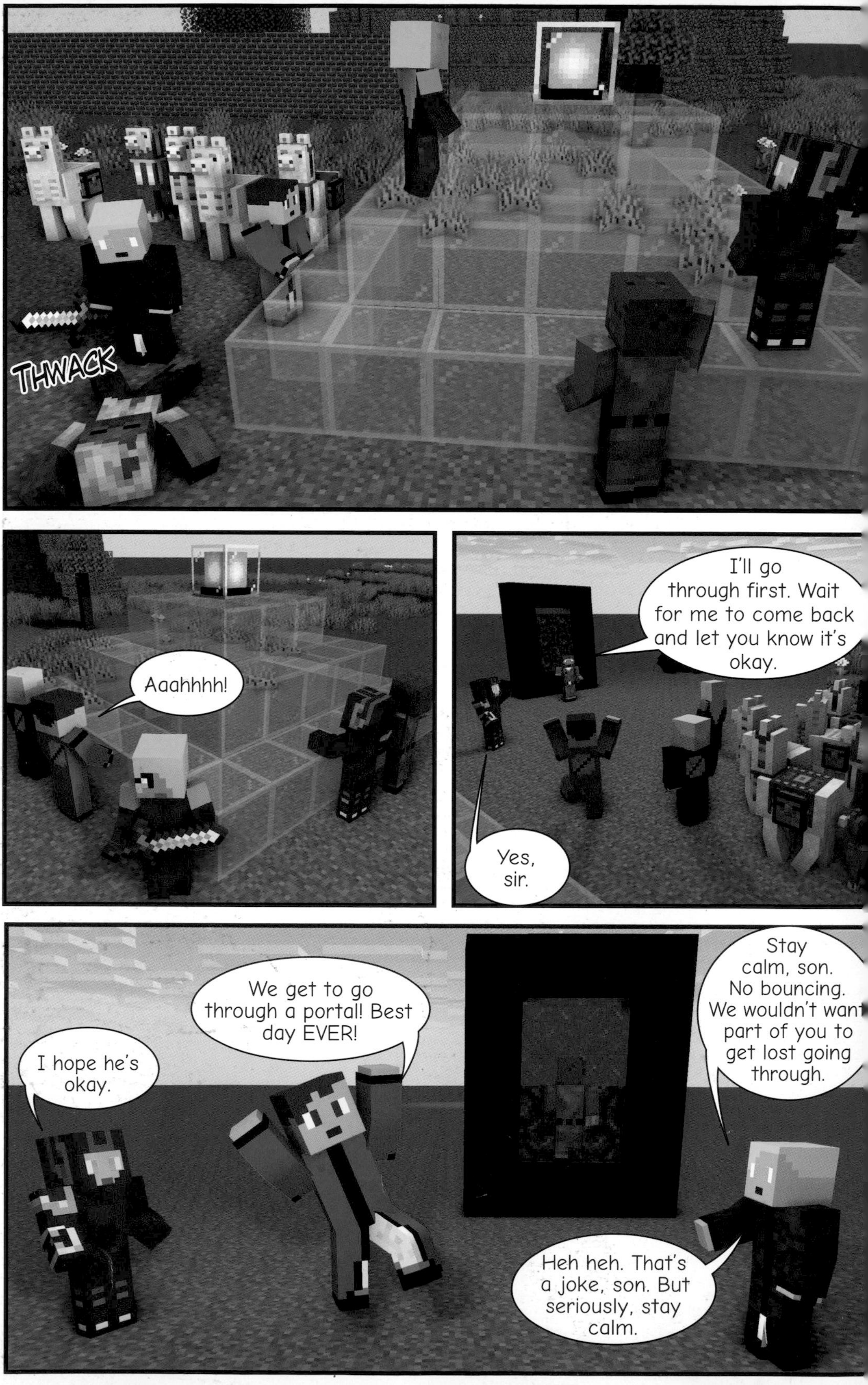
THWACK
Aaahhhh!
I'll go through first. Wait for me to come back and let you know it's okay.
Yes, sir.
I hope he's okay.
We get to go through a portal! Best day EVER!
Stay calm, son. No bouncing. We wouldn't want part of you to get lost going through.
Heh heh. That's a joke, son. But seriously, stay calm.

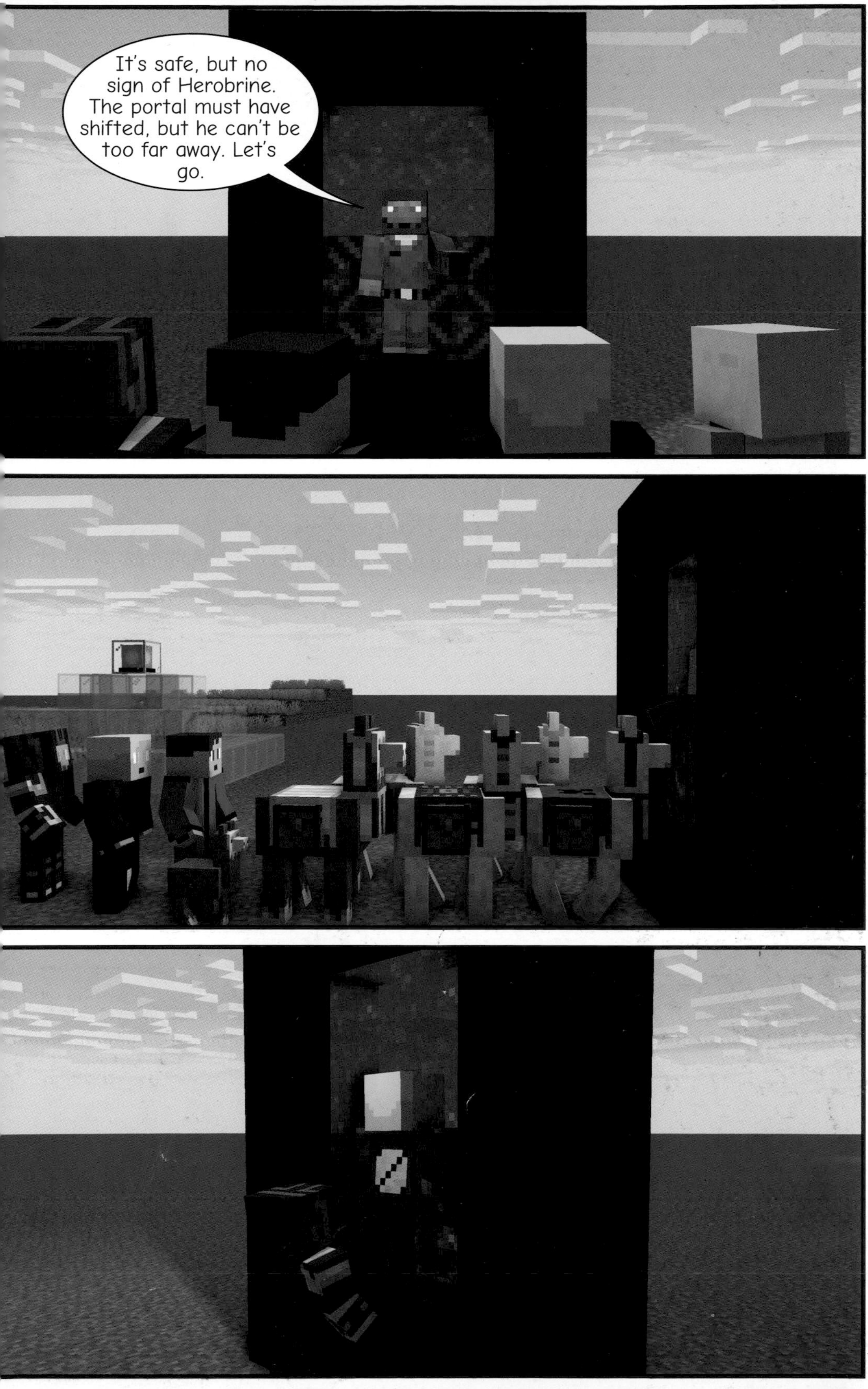
It's safe, but no sign of Herobrine. The portal must have shifted, but he can't be too far away. Let's go.

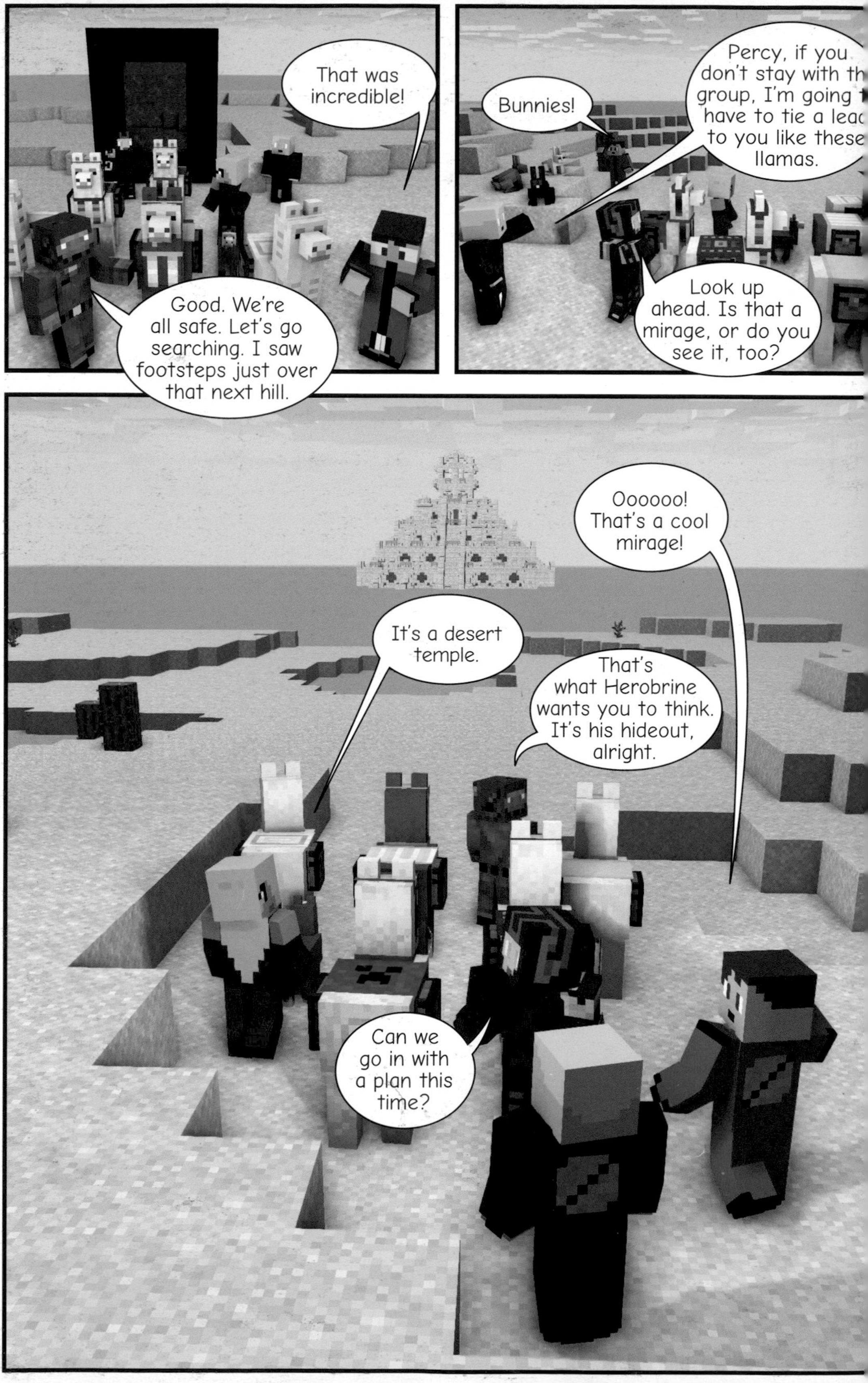

That was incredible!
Good. We're all safe. Let's go searching. I saw footsteps just over that next hill.
Bunnies!
Percy, if you don't stay with th group, I'm going have to tie a lea to you like these llamas.
Look up ahead. Is that a mirage, or do you see it, too?
Oooooo! That's a cool mirage!
It's a desert temple.
That's what Herobrine wants you to think. It's his hideout, alright.
Can we go in with a plan this time?

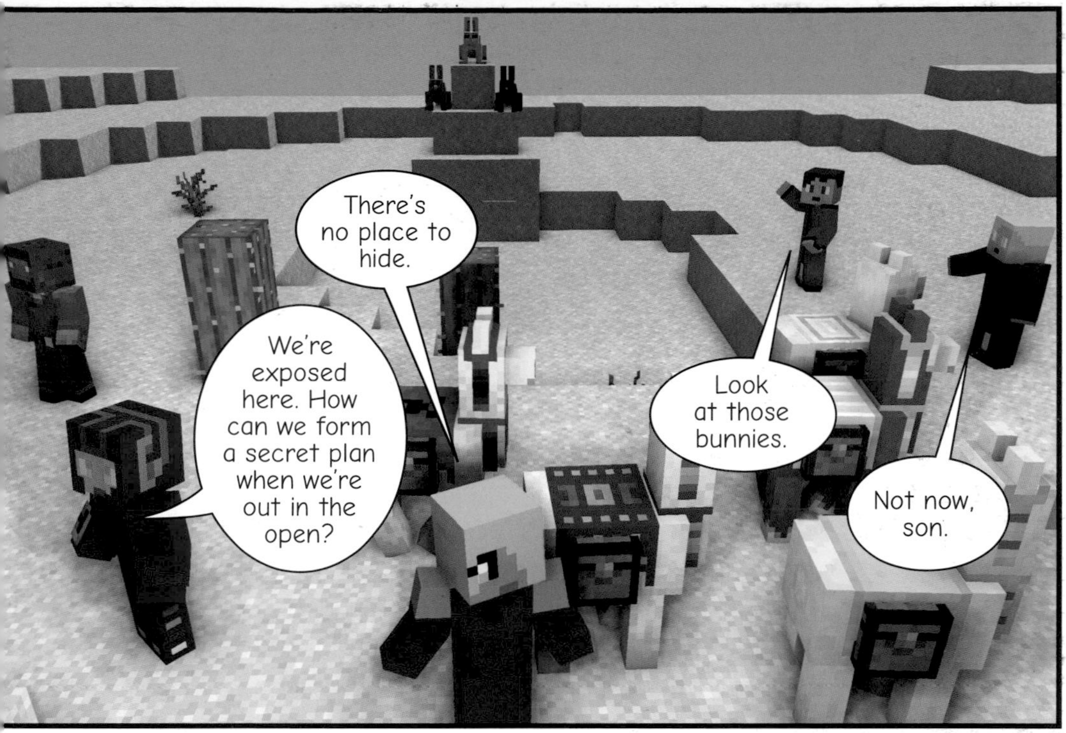
We're exposed here. How can we form a secret plan when we're out in the open?
There's no place to hide.
Look at those bunnies.
Not now, son.

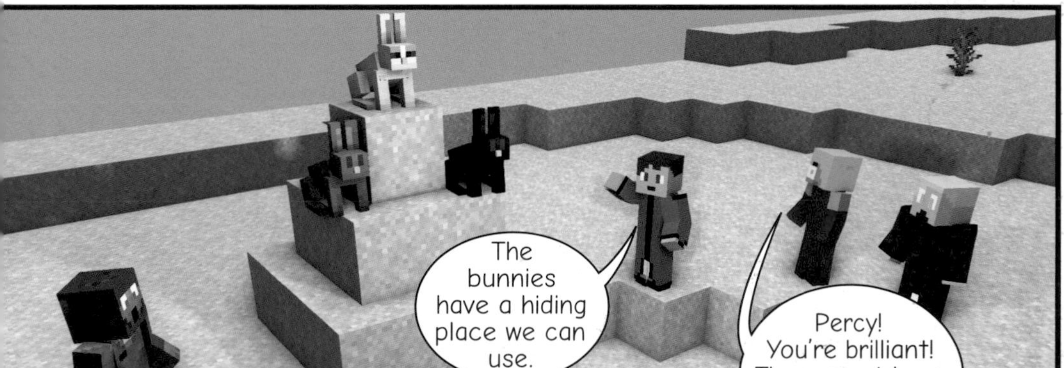
The bunnies have a hiding place we can use.
Percy! You're brilliant! There must be a cave down there. Let's dig!

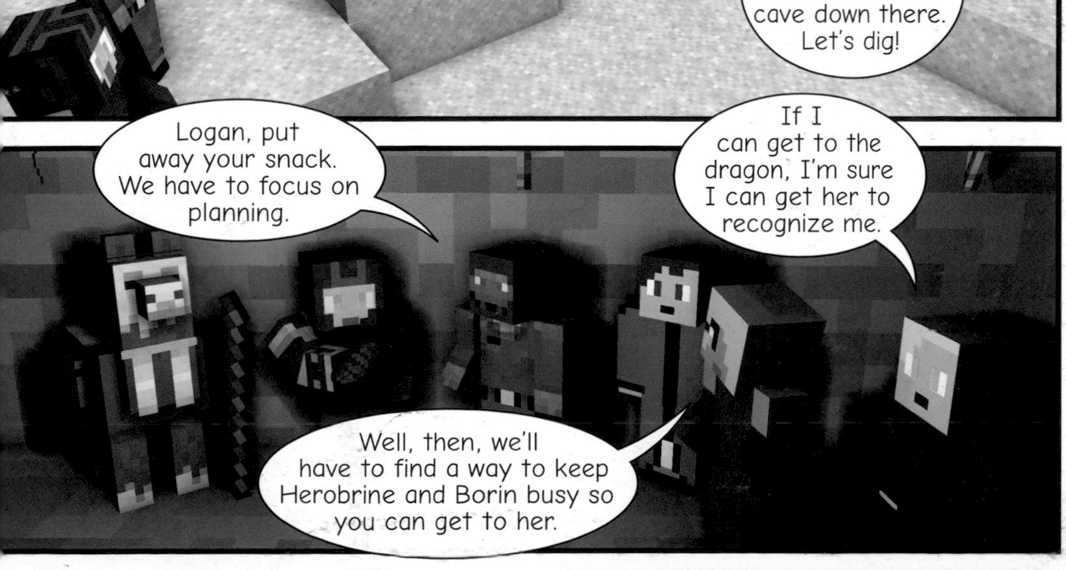
Logan, put away your snack. We have to focus on planning.
If I can get to the dragon, I'm sure I can get her to recognize me.
Well, then, we'll have to find a way to keep Herobrine and Borin busy so you can get to her.

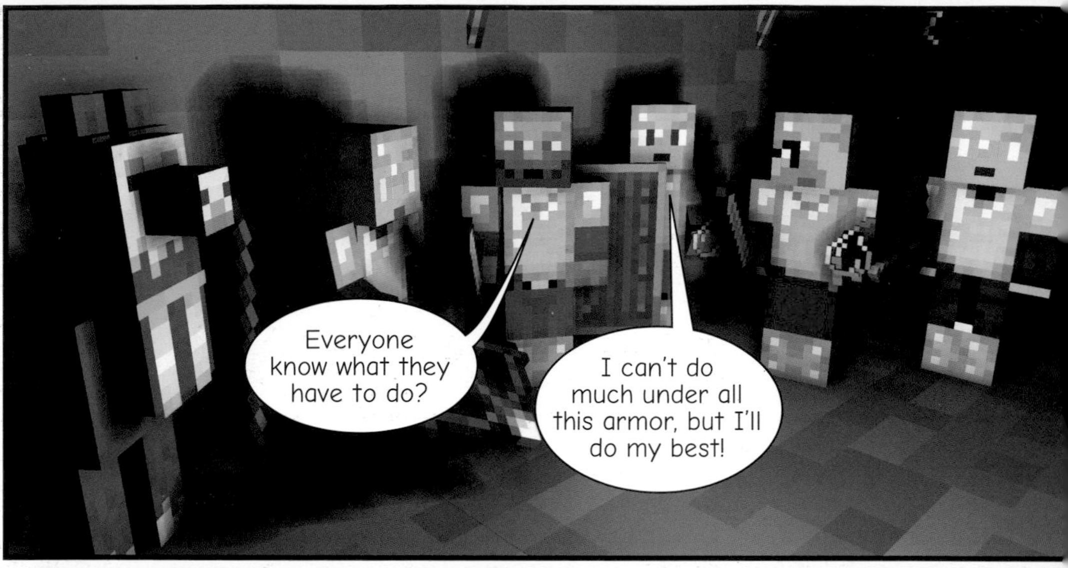
Everyone know what they have to do?
I can't do much under all this armor, but I'll do my best!

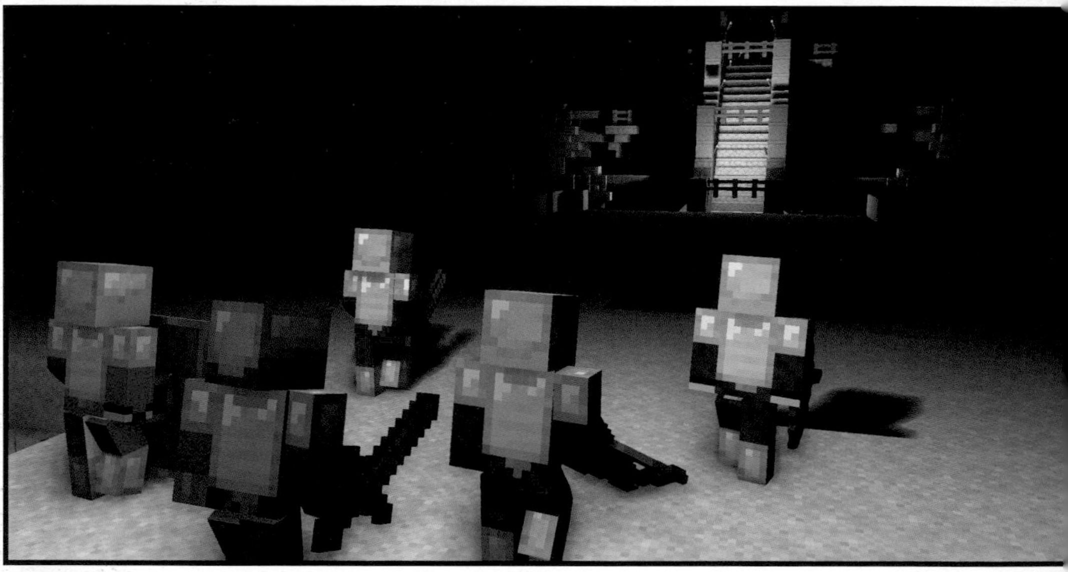

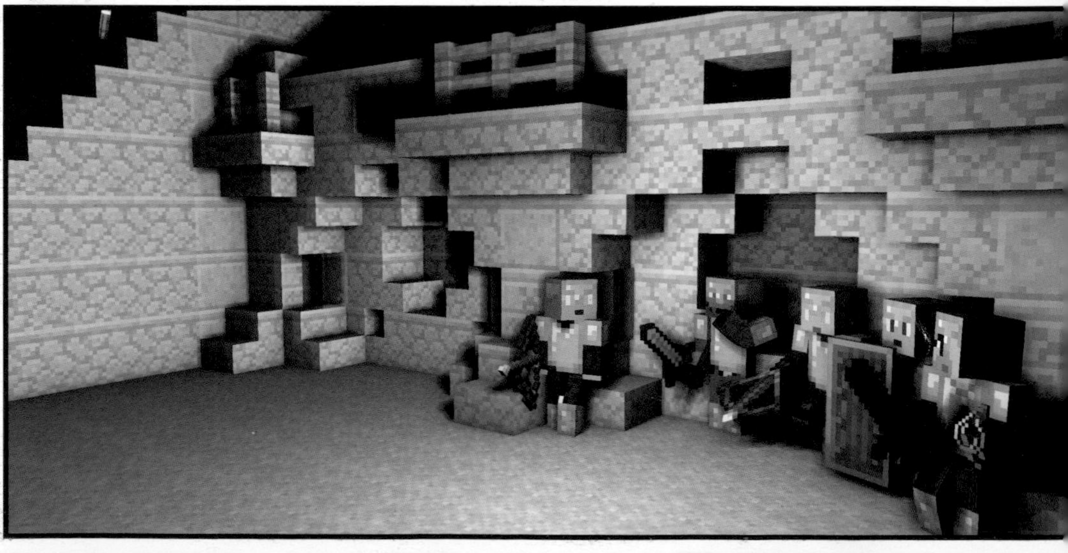

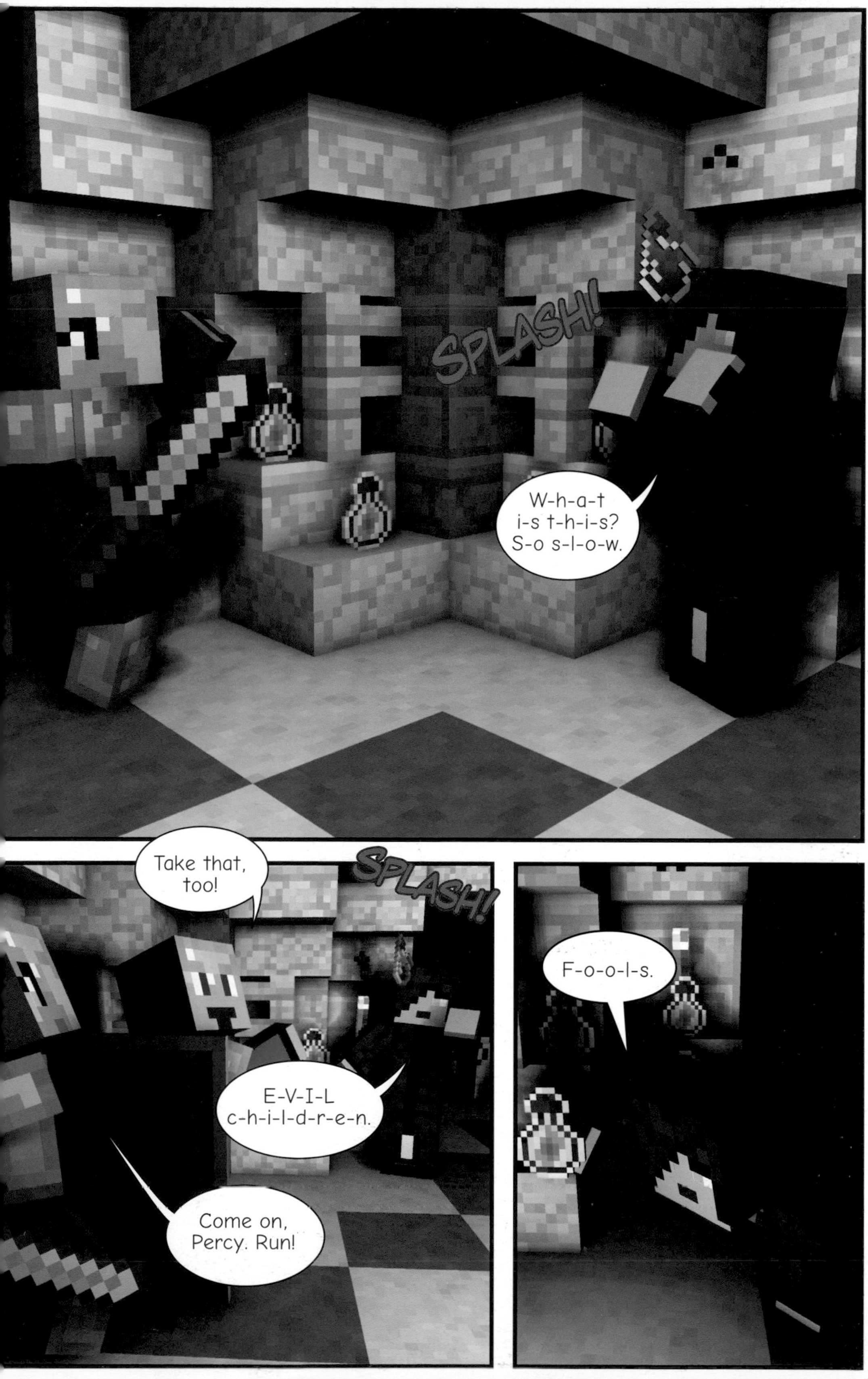
SPLASH!
W-h-a-t i-s t-h-i-s? S-o s-l-o-w.
Take that, too!
SPLASH!
E-V-I-L c-h-i-l-d-r-e-n.
Come on, Percy. Run!
F-o-o-l-s.

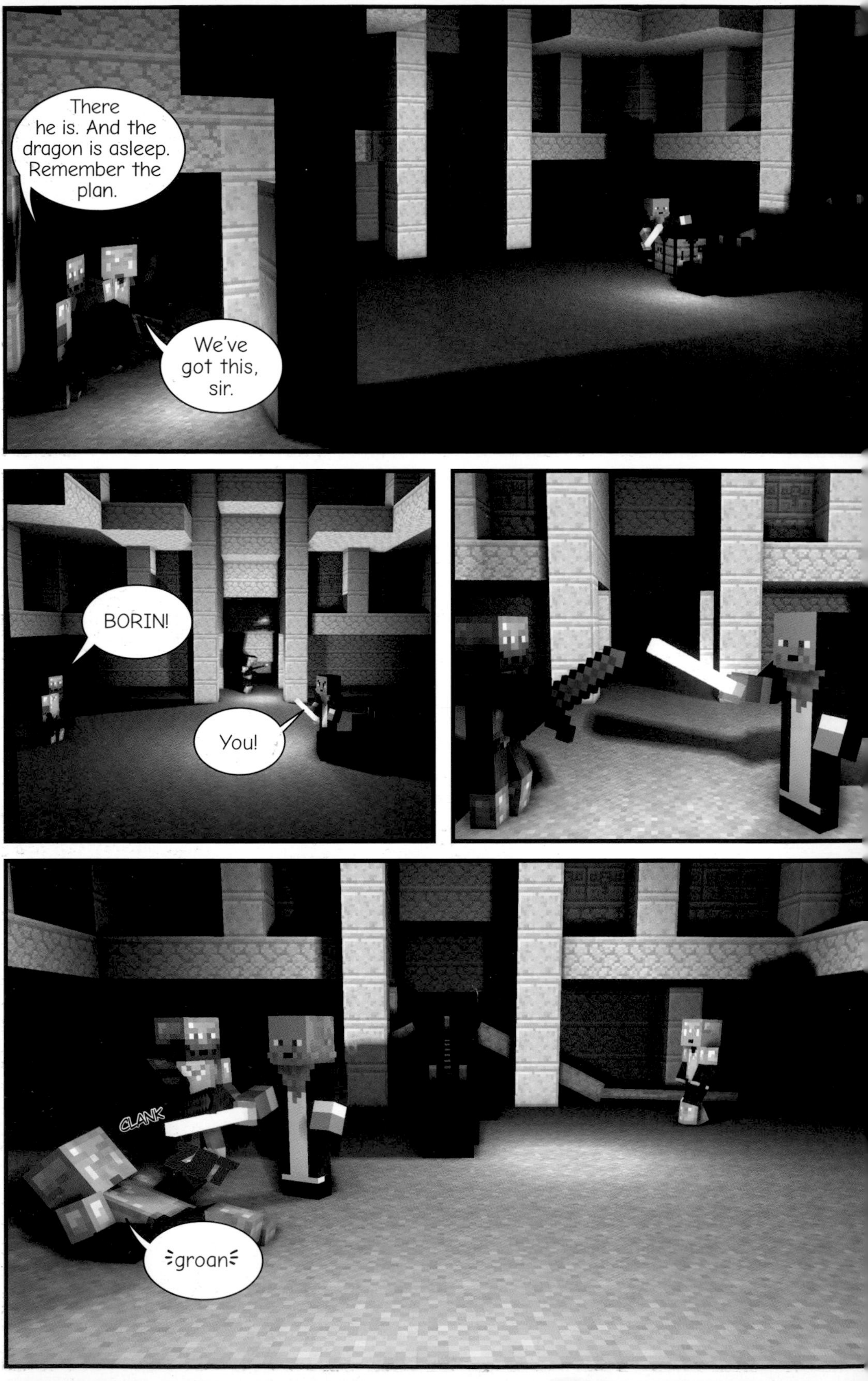
There he is. And the dragon is asleep. Remember the plan.
We've got this, sir.
BORIN!
You!
CLANK
groan

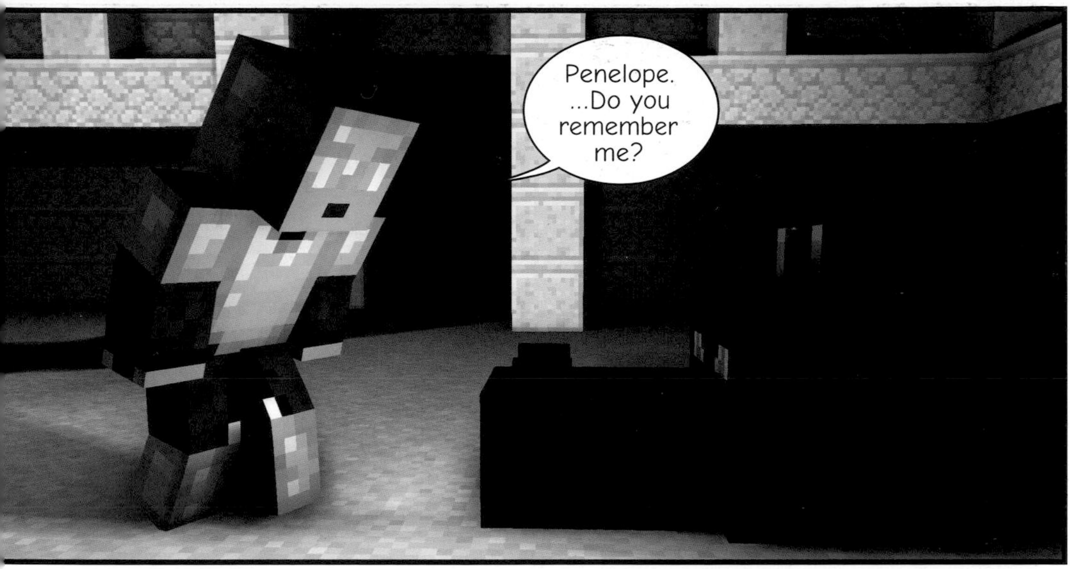
Penelope. ...Do you remember me?

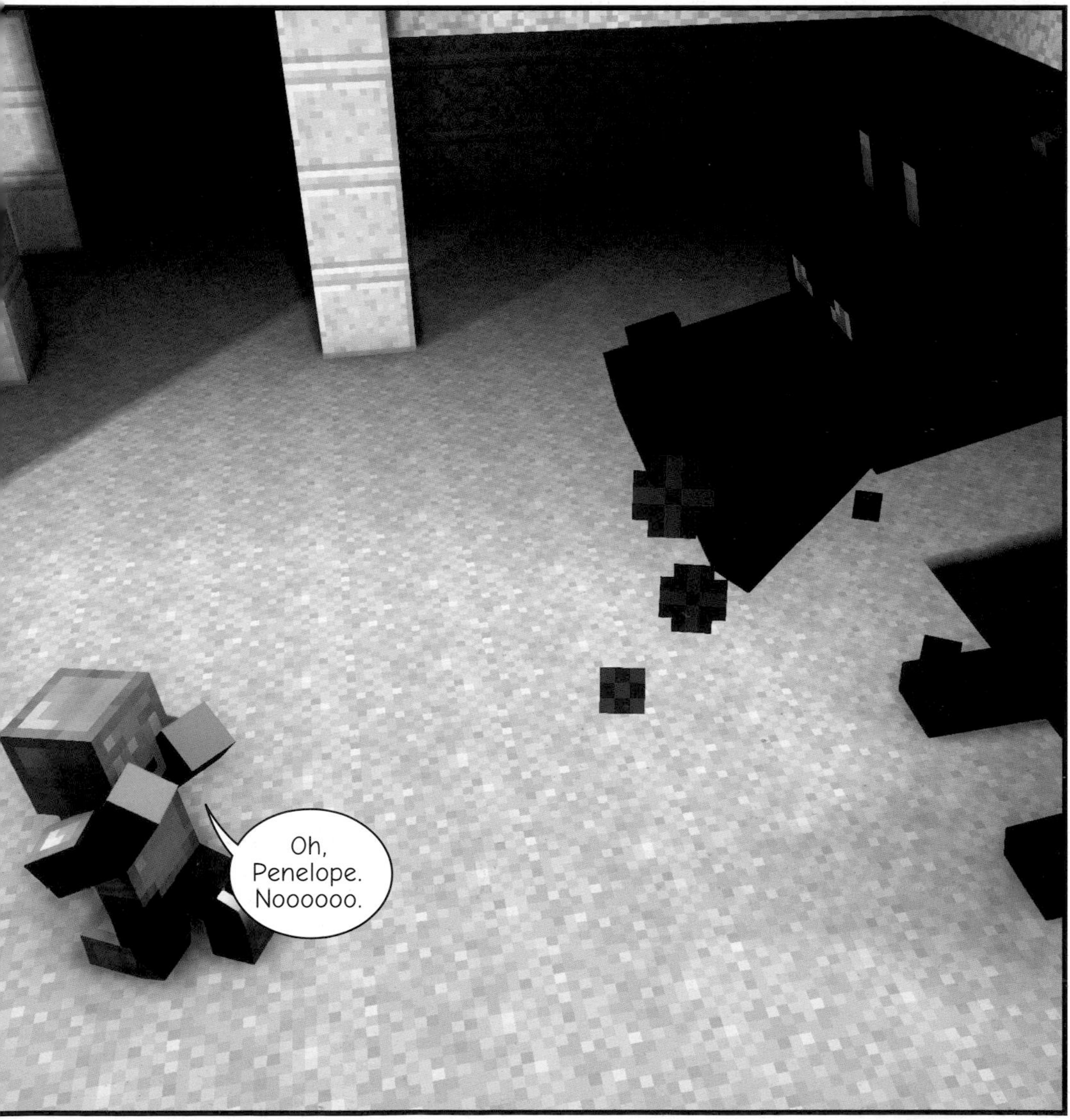
Oh, Penelope. Noooooo.

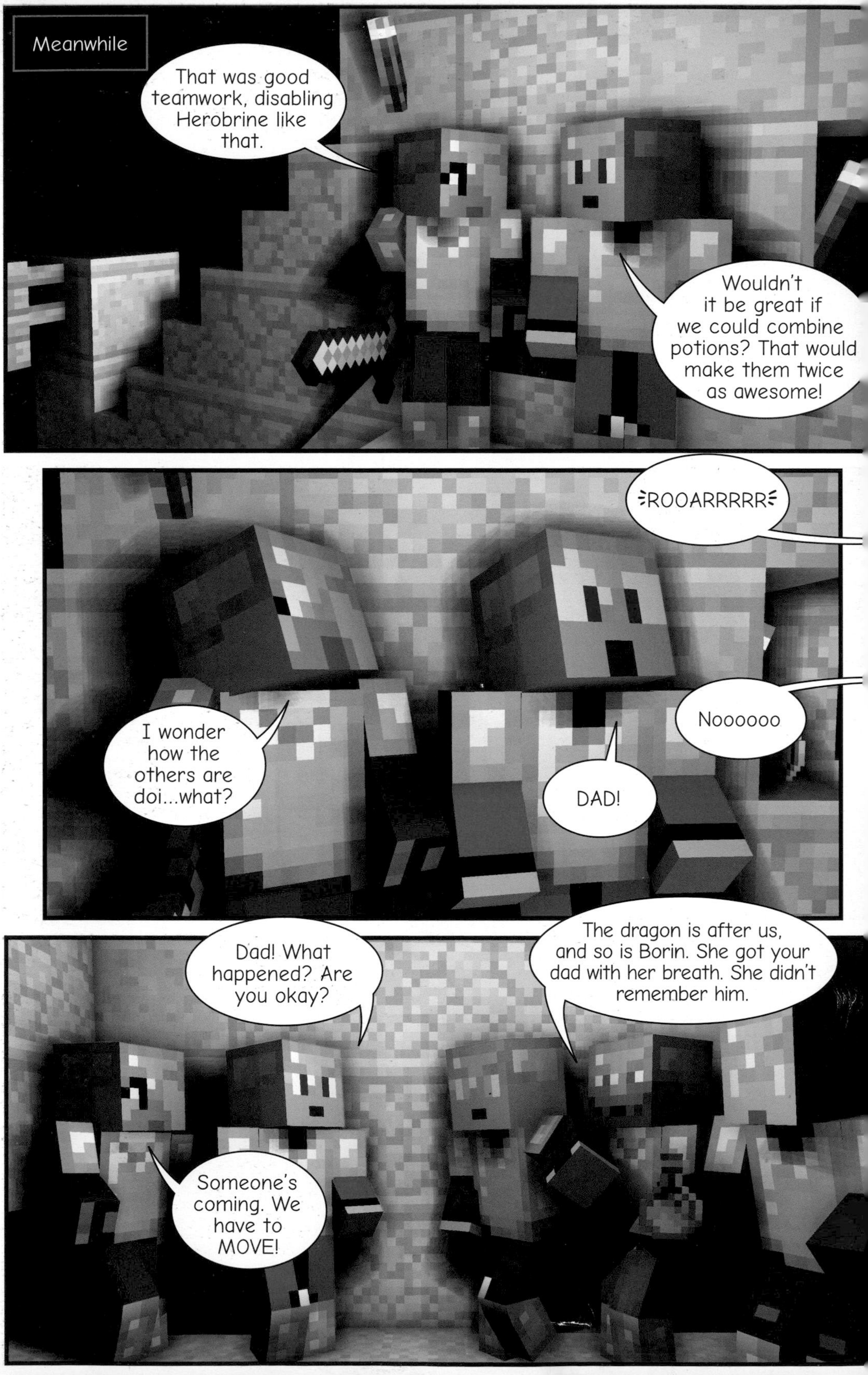

Meanwhile
That was good teamwork, disabling Herobrine like that.
Wouldn't it be great if we could combine potions? That would make them twice as awesome!
ROOARRRRR
I wonder how the others are doi...what?
DAD!
Noooooo
Dad! What happened? Are you okay?
The dragon is after us, and so is Borin. She got your dad with her breath. She didn't remember him.
Someone's coming. We have to MOVE!

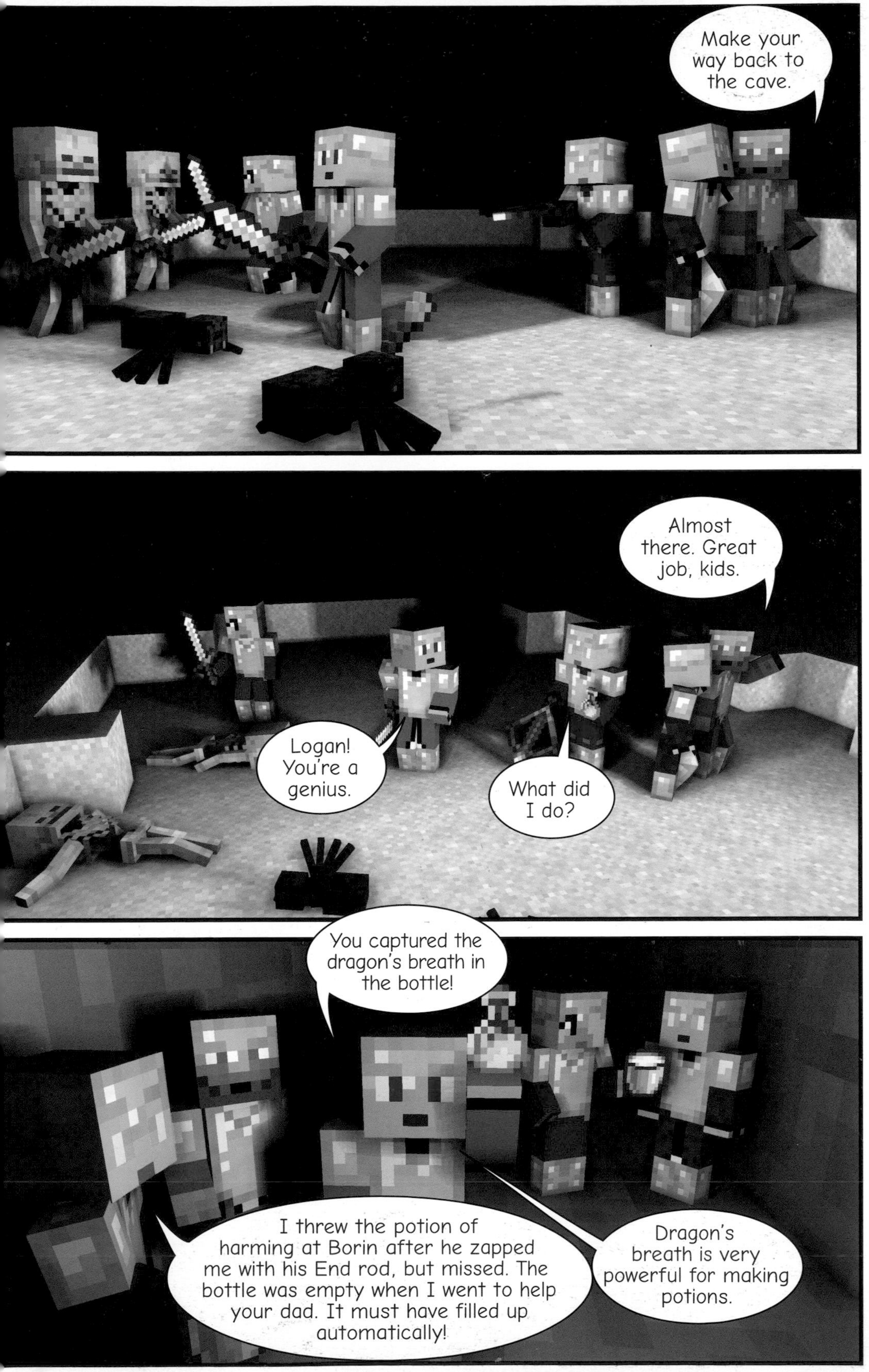

Make your way back to the cave.
Almost there. Great job, kids.
Logan! You're a genius.
What did I do?
You captured the dragon's breath in the bottle!
I threw the potion of harming at Borin after he zapped me with his End rod, but missed. The bottle was empty when I went to help your dad. It must have filled up automatically!
Dragon's breath is very powerful for making potions.

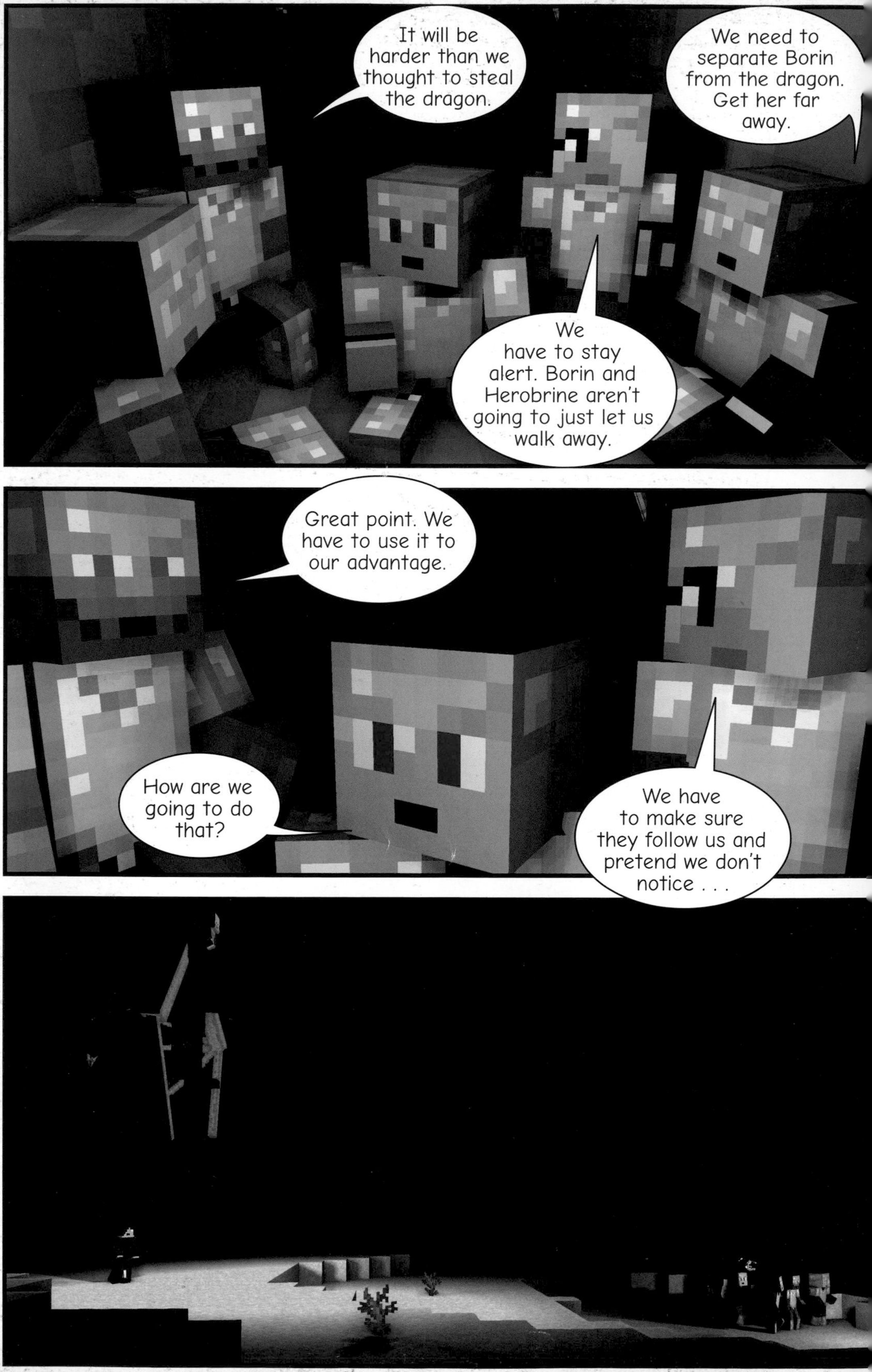
It will be harder than we thought to steal the dragon.
We need to separate Borin from the dragon. Get her far away.
We have to stay alert. Borin and Herobrine aren't going to just let us walk away.
Great point. We have to use it to our advantage.
How are we going to do that?
We have to make sure they follow us and pretend we don't notice . . .

CHAPTER 7

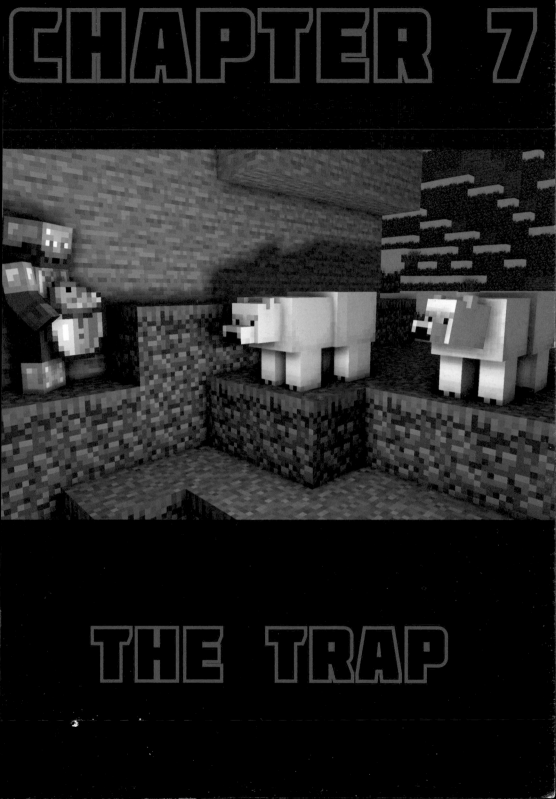

THE TRAP

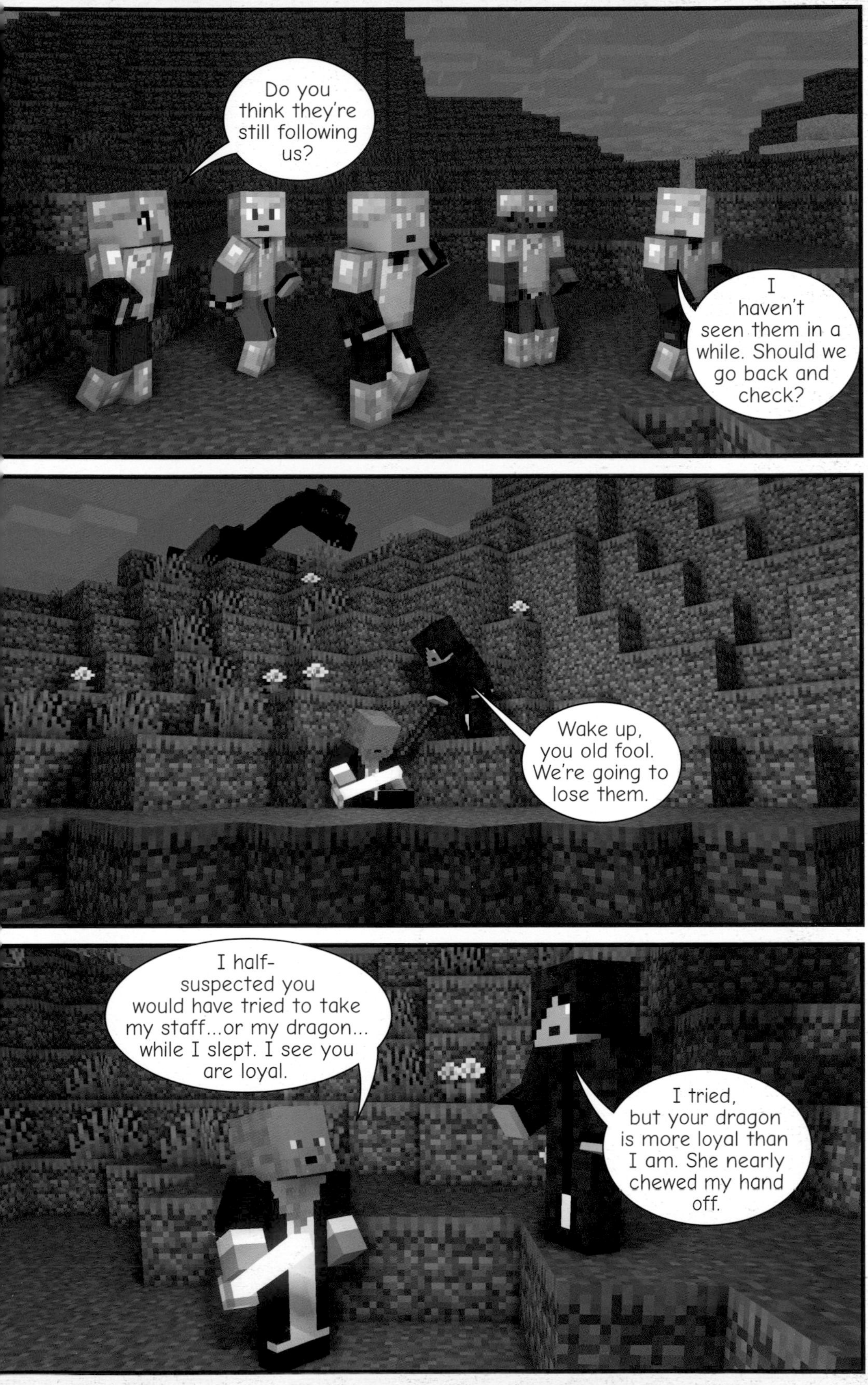
Do you think they're still following us?
I haven't seen them in a while. Should we go back and check?
Wake up, you old fool. We're going to lose them.
I half-suspected you would have tried to take my staff...or my dragon... while I slept. I see you are loyal.
I tried, but your dragon is more loyal than I am. She nearly chewed my hand off.

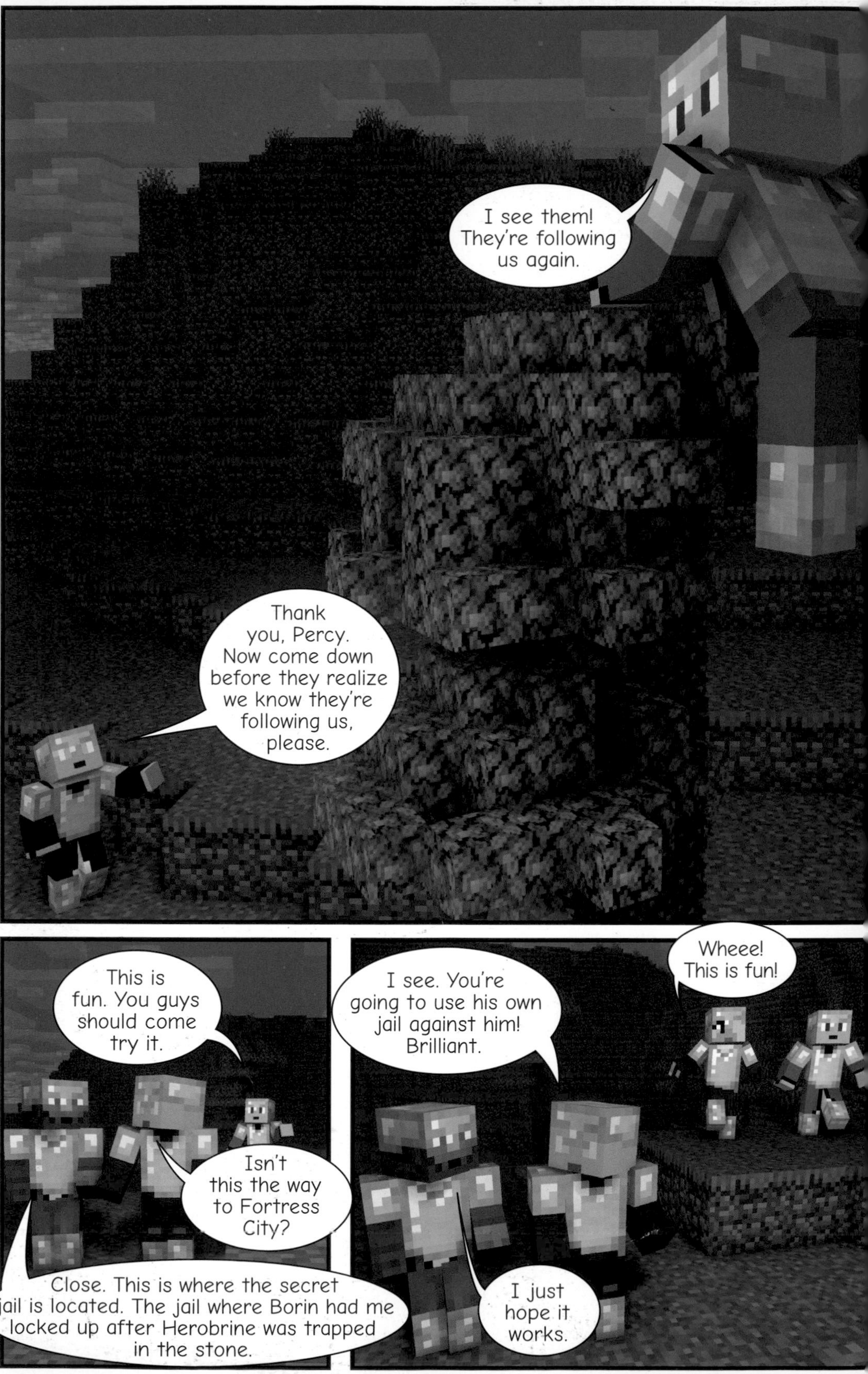

I see them! They're following us again.
Thank you, Percy. Now come down before they realize we know they're following us, please.
This is fun. You guys should come try it.
Isn't this the way to Fortress City?
Close. This is where the secret jail is located. The jail where Borin had me locked up after Herobrine was trapped in the stone.
Wheee! This is fun!
I see. You're going to use his own jail against him! Brilliant.
I just hope it works.

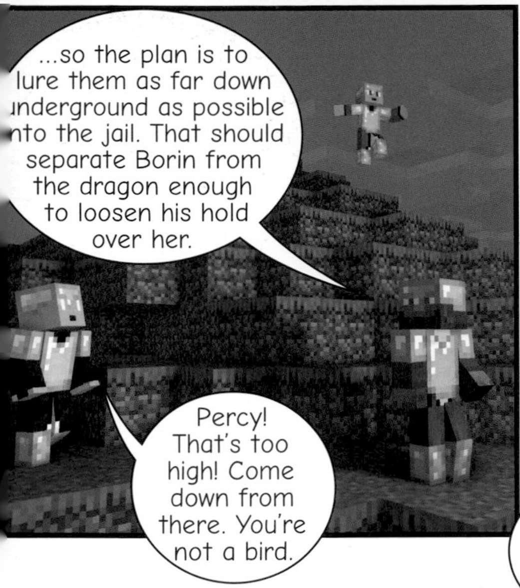
...so the plan is to lure them as far down underground as possible into the jail. That should separate Borin from the dragon enough to loosen his hold over her.
Percy! That's too high! Come down from there. You're not a bird.

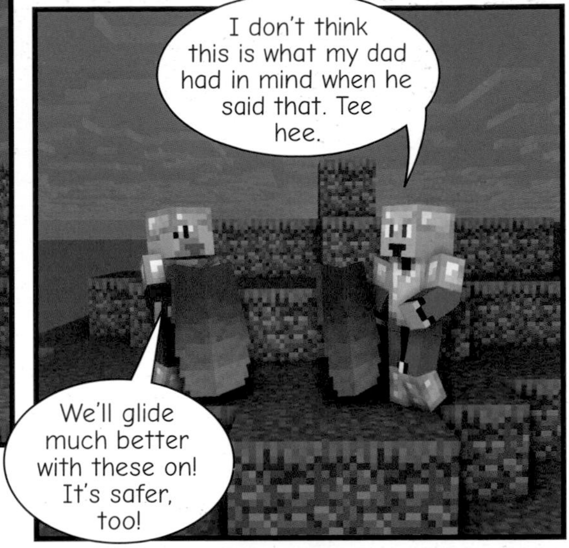
I don't think this is what my dad had in mind when he said that. Tee hee.
We'll glide much better with these on! It's safer, too!

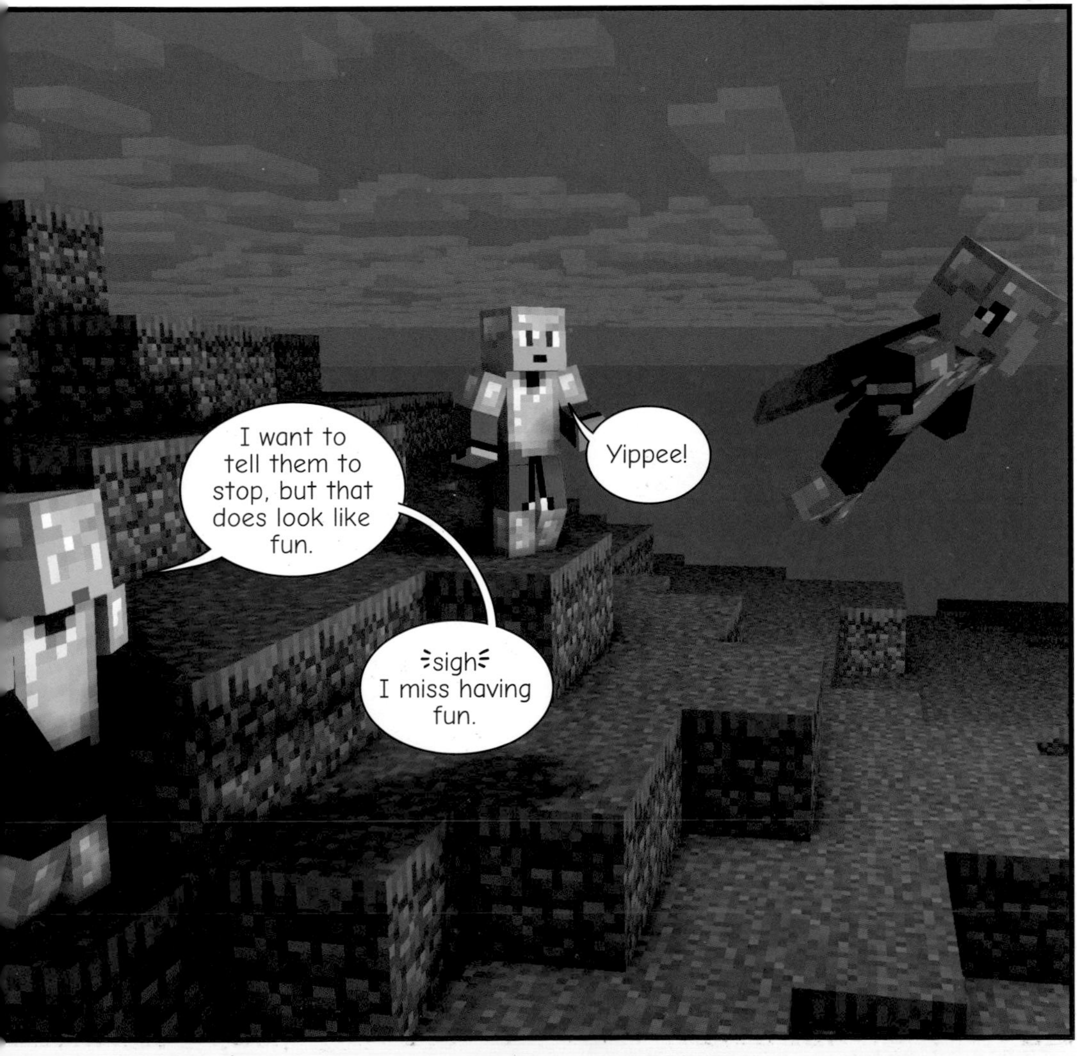
I want to tell them to stop, but that does look like fun.
Yippee!
sigh
I miss having fun.

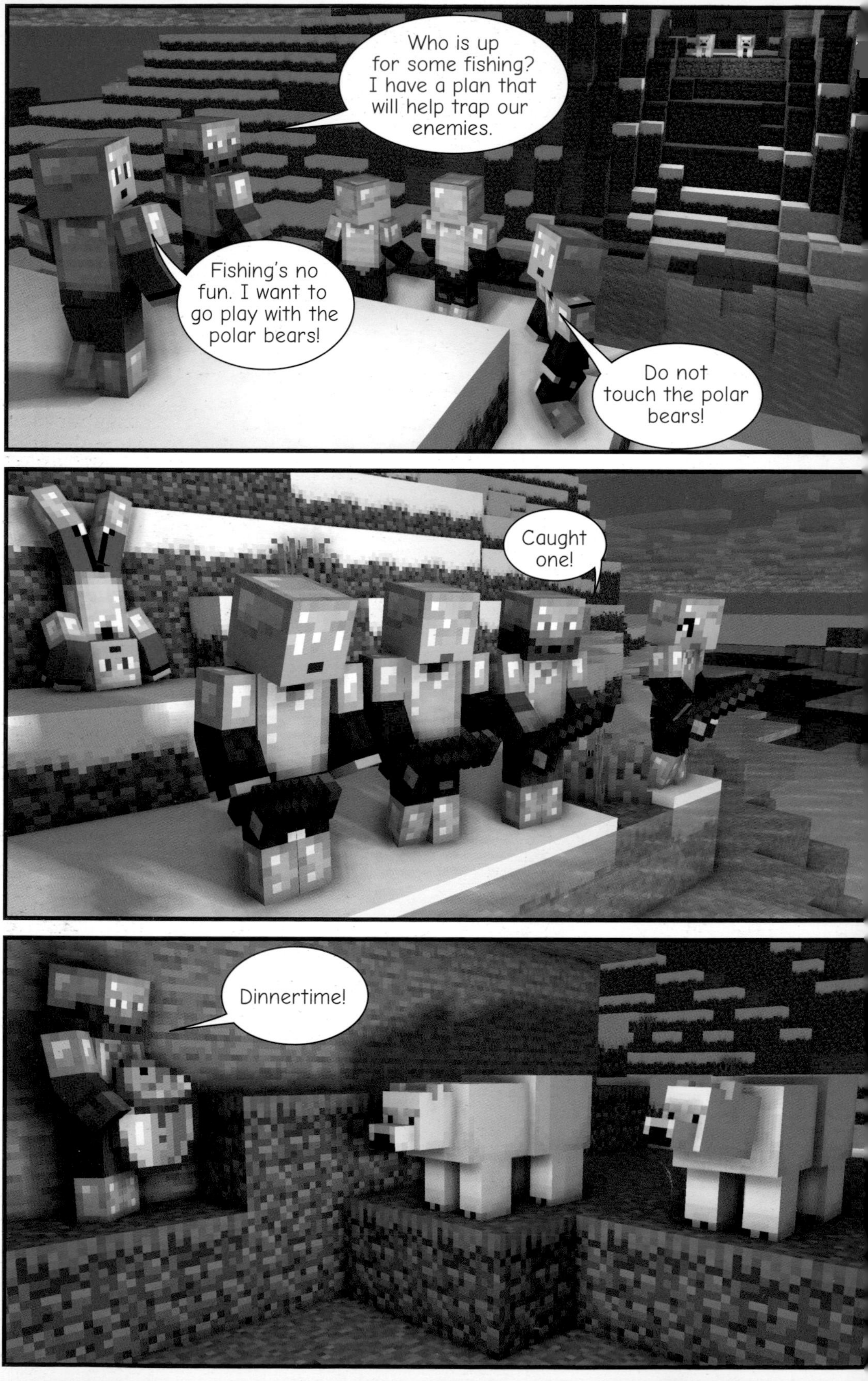
Who is up for some fishing? I have a plan that will help trap our enemies.
Fishing's no fun. I want to go play with the polar bears!
Do not touch the polar bears!
Caught one!
Dinnertime!

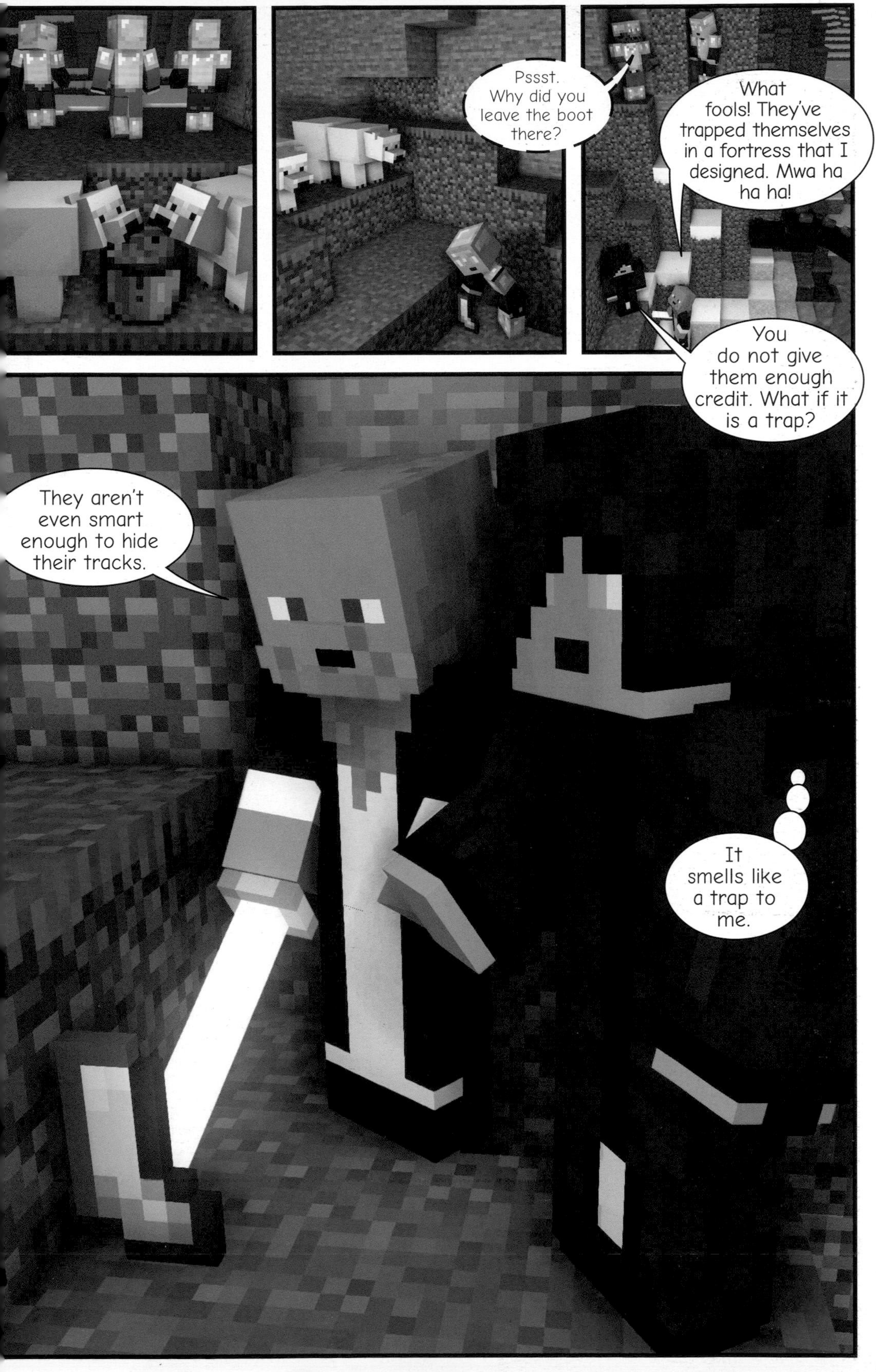
Pssst. Why did you leave the boot there?
What fools! They've trapped themselves in a fortress that I designed. Mwa ha ha ha!
You do not give them enough credit. What if it is a trap?
They aren't even smart enough to hide their tracks.
It smells like a trap to me.

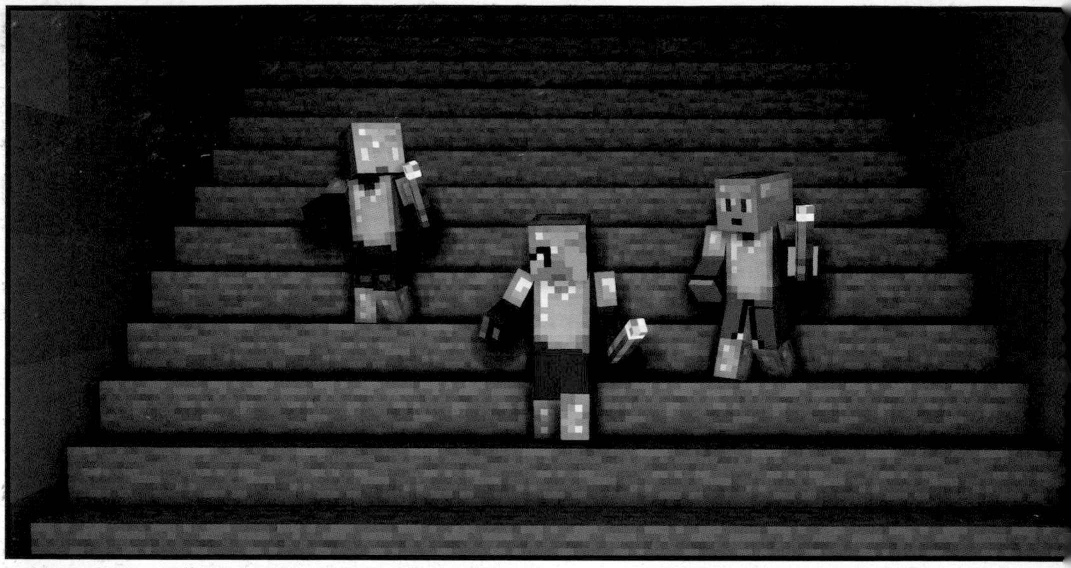

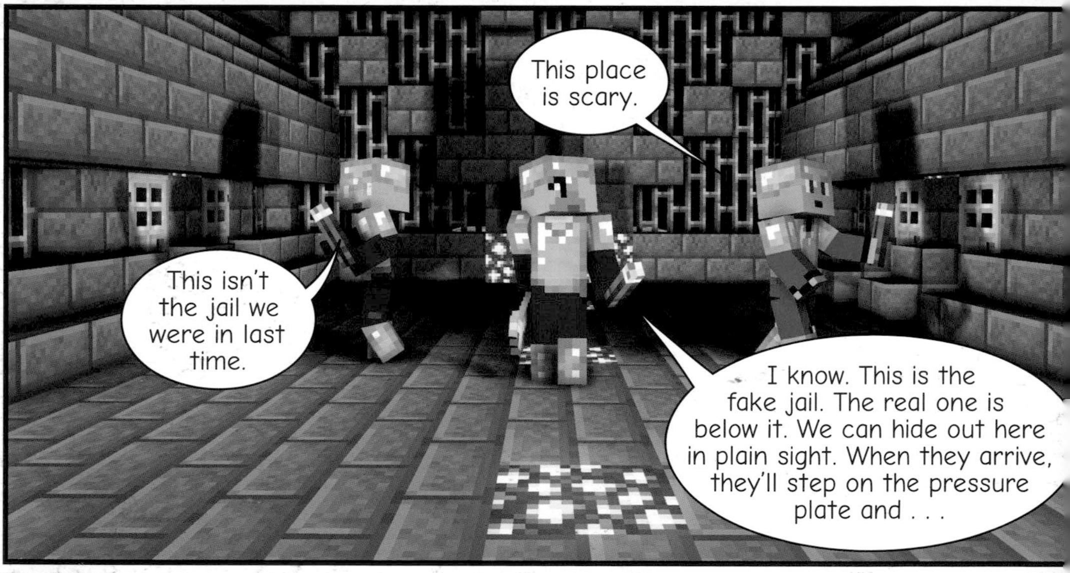
This place is scary.
This isn't the jail we were in last time.
I know. This is the fake jail. The real one is below it. We can hide out here in plain sight. When they arrive, they'll step on the pressure plate and . . .

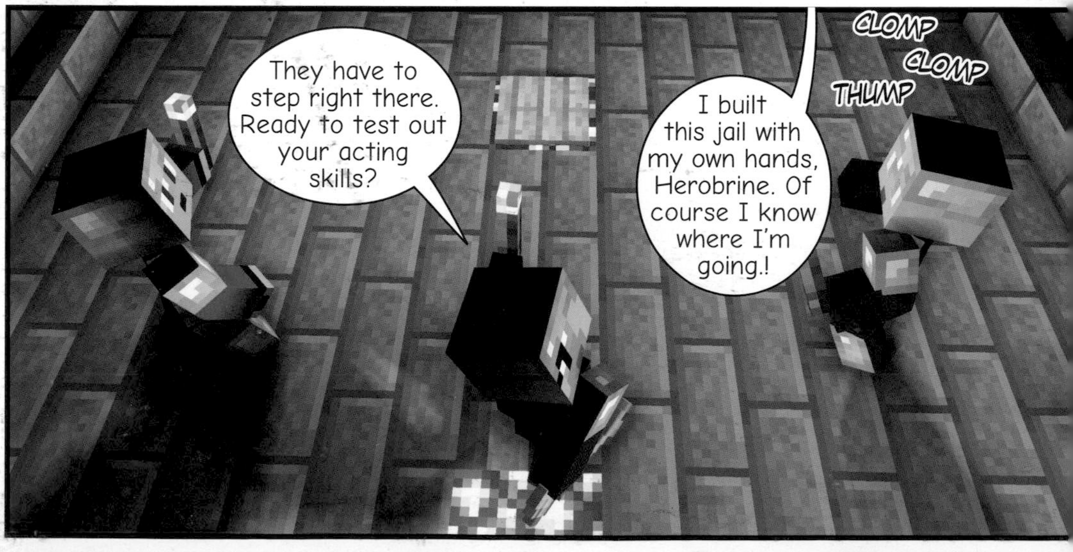
They have to step right there. Ready to test out your acting skills?
I built this jail with my own hands, Herobrine. Of course I know where I'm going.!
CLOMP
CLOMP
THUMP

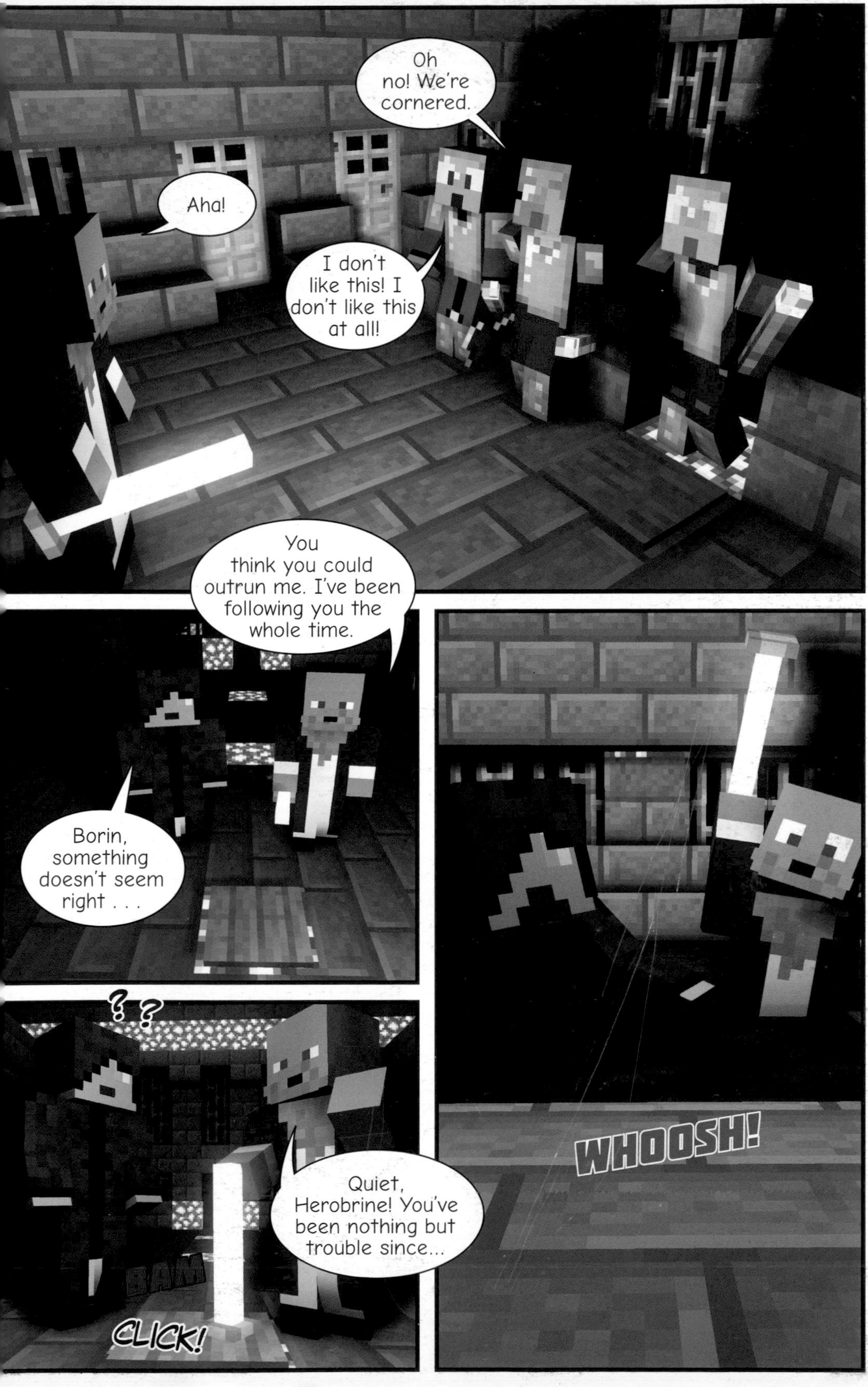
Aha!
Oh no! We're cornered.
I don't like this! I don't like this at all!
You think you could outrun me. I've been following you the whole time.
Borin, something doesn't seem right . . .
? ?
Quiet, Herobrine! You've been nothing but trouble since...
CLICK!
WHOOSH!

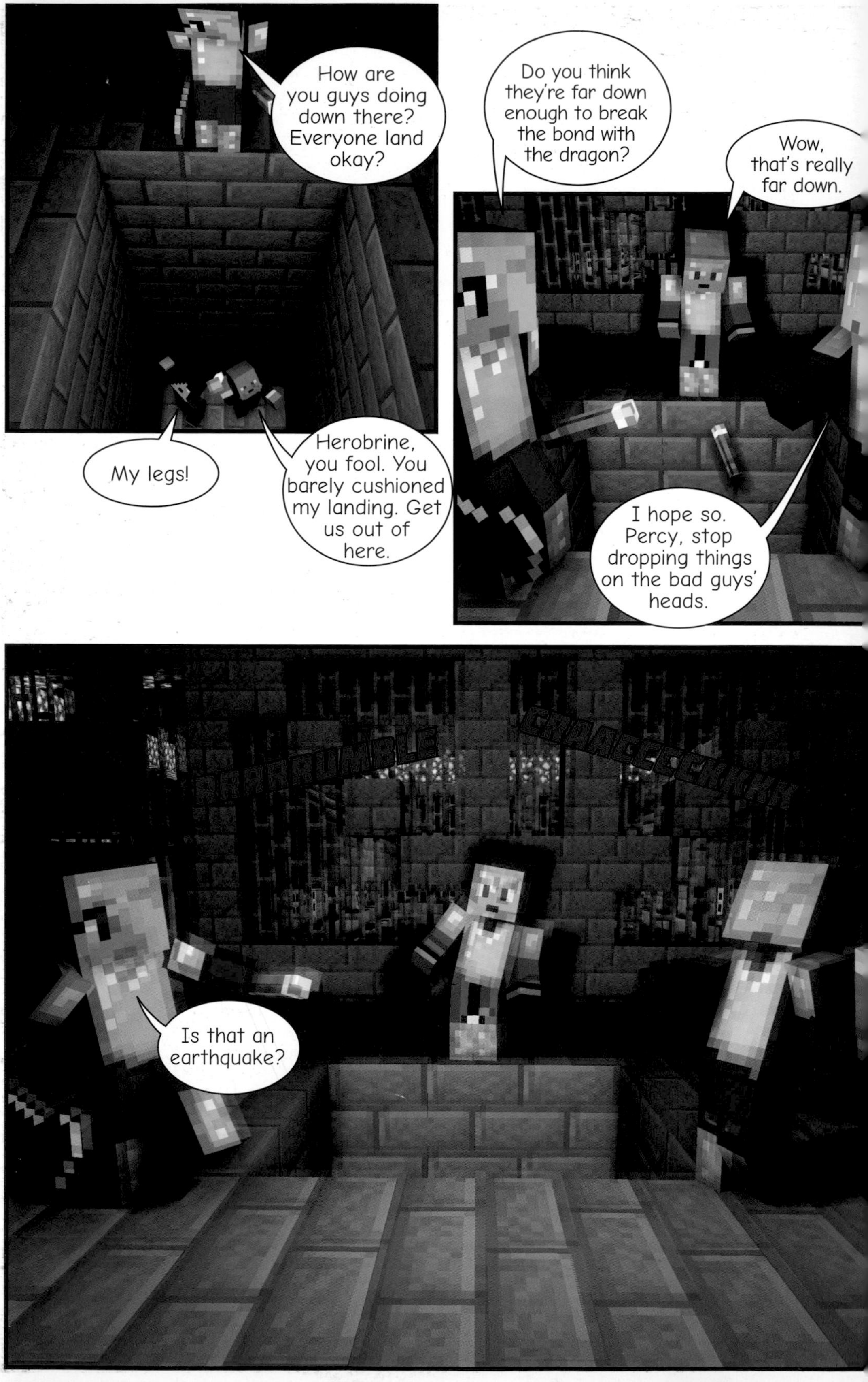
How are you guys doing down there? Everyone land okay?
My legs!
Herobrine, you fool. You barely cushioned my landing. Get us out of here.
Do you think they're far down enough to break the bond with the dragon?
Wow, that's really far down.
I hope so. Percy, stop dropping things on the bad guys' heads.
Is that an earthquake?

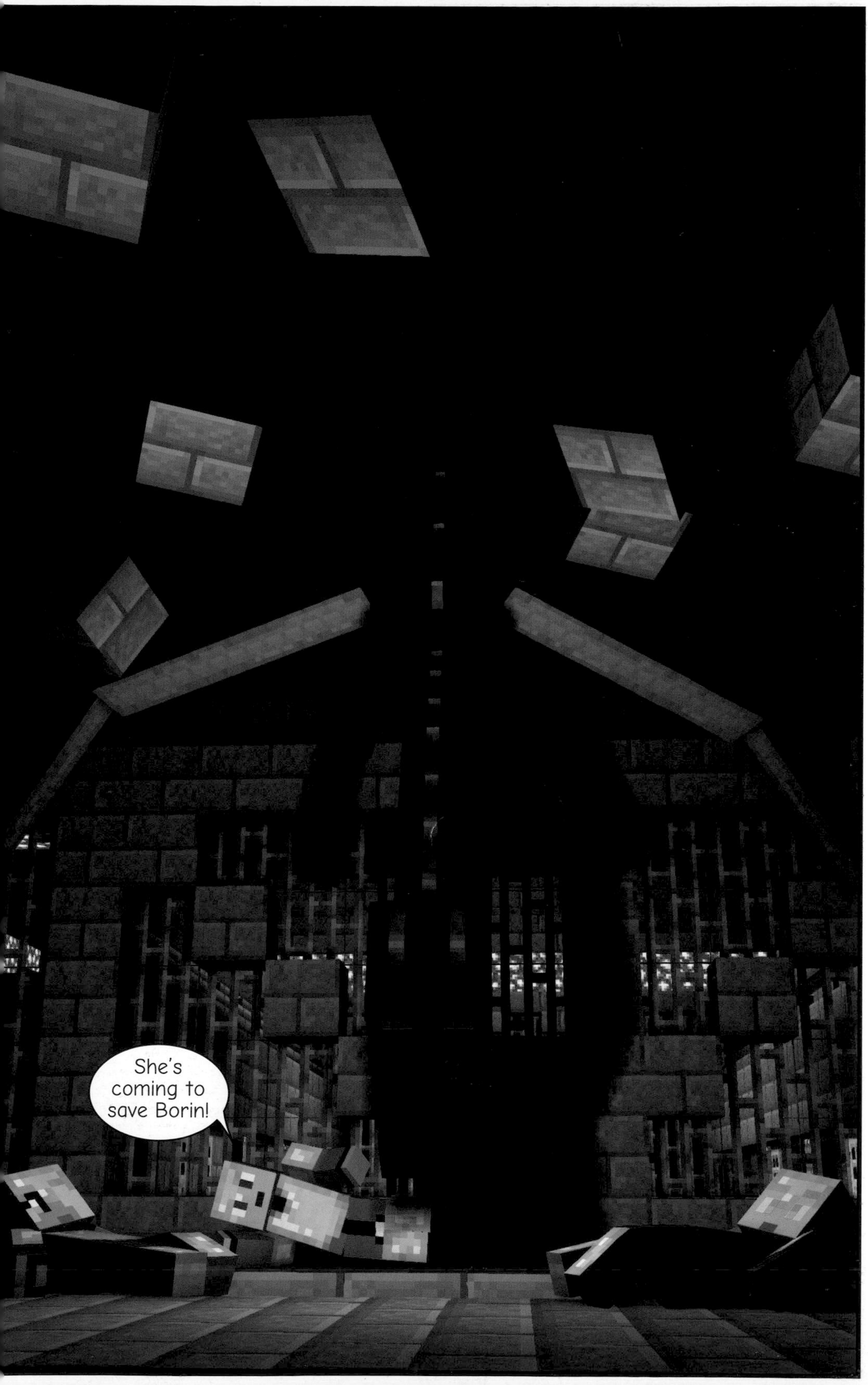
She's coming to save Borin!

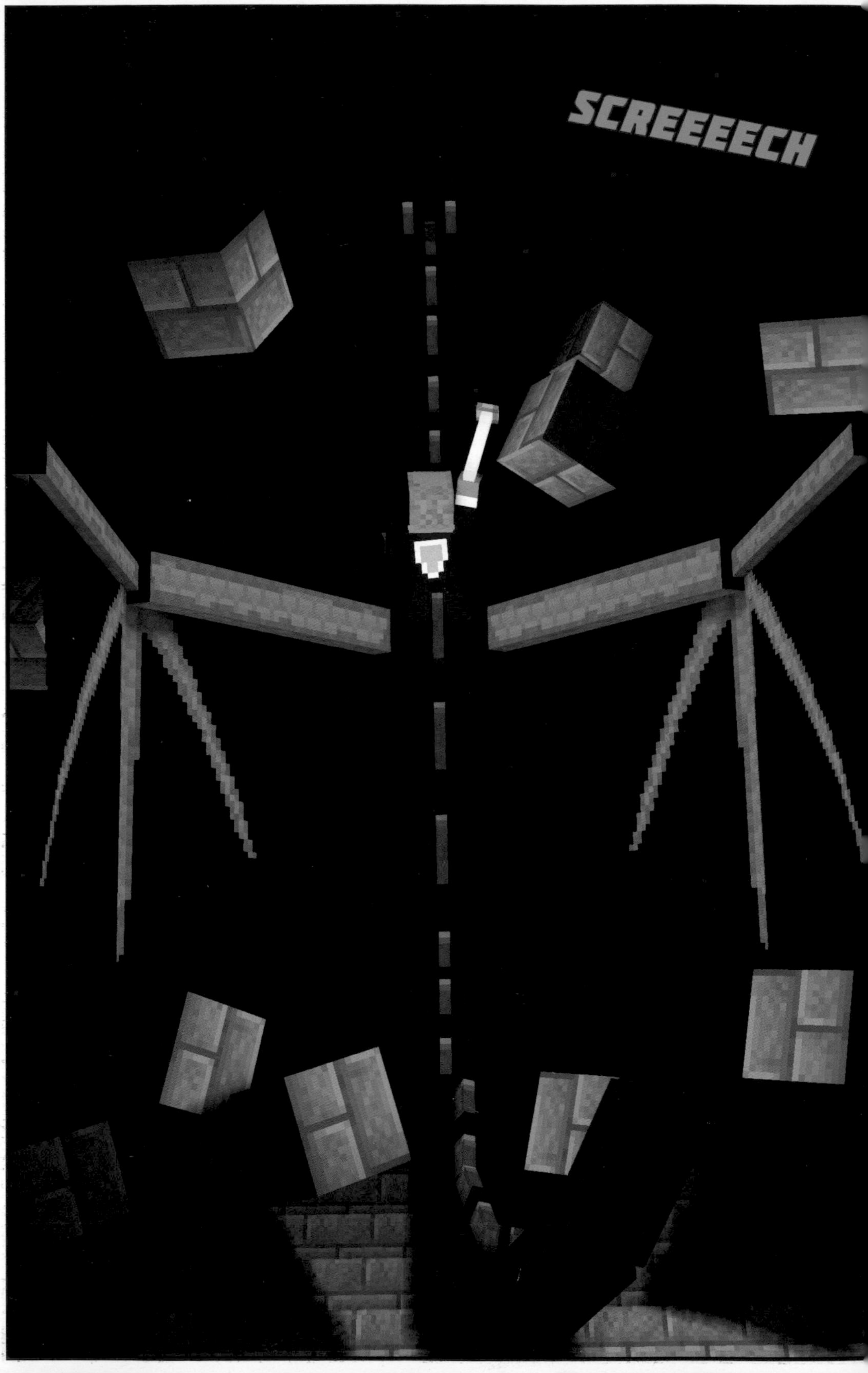
SCREEEEECH

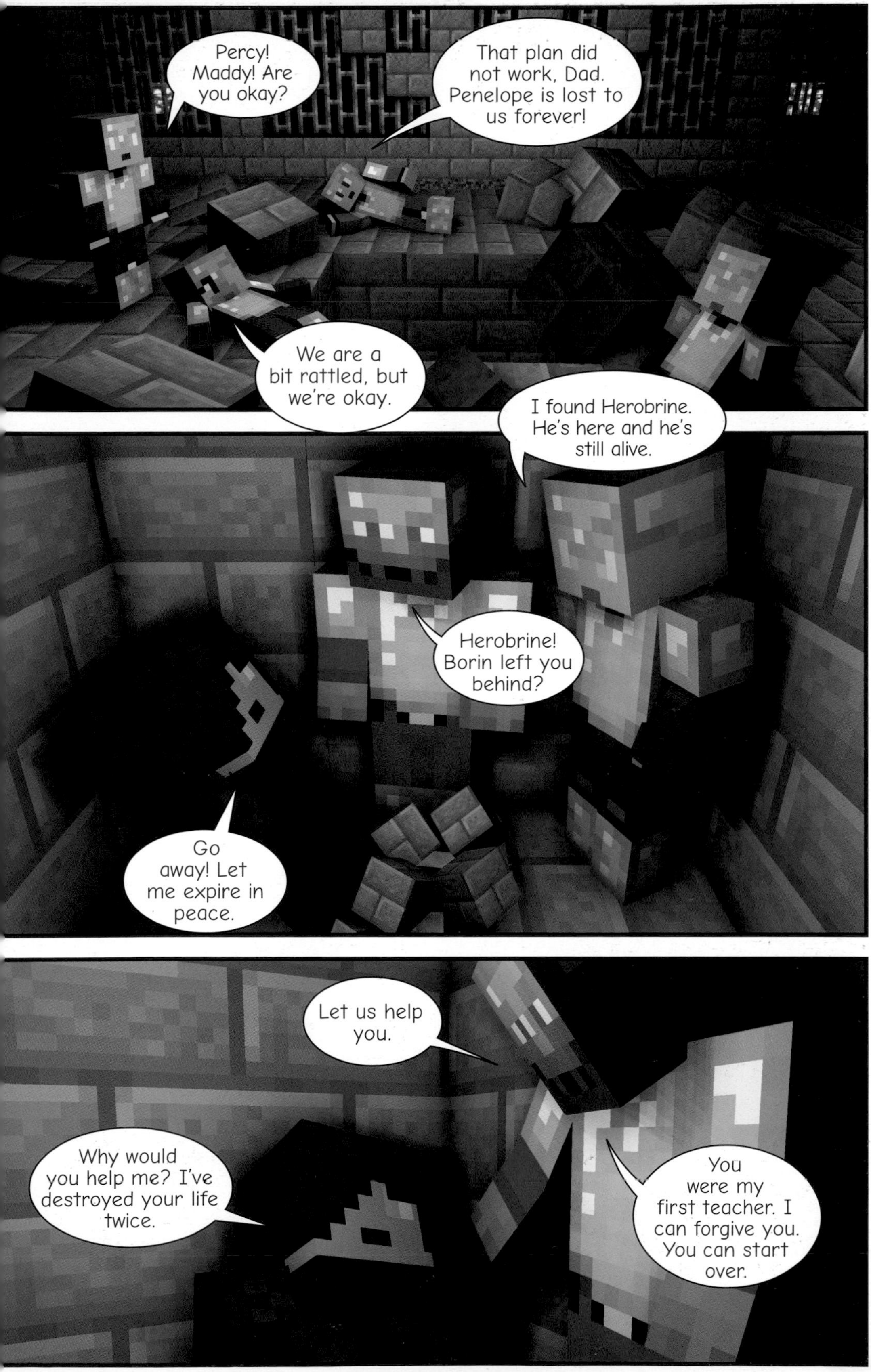
Percy! Maddy! Are you okay?
That plan did not work, Dad. Penelope is lost to us forever!
We are a bit rattled, but we're okay.
I found Herobrine. He's here and he's still alive.
Herobrine! Borin left you behind?
Go away! Let me expire in peace.
Let us help you.
Why would you help me? I've destroyed your life twice.
You were my first teacher. I can forgive you. You can start over.

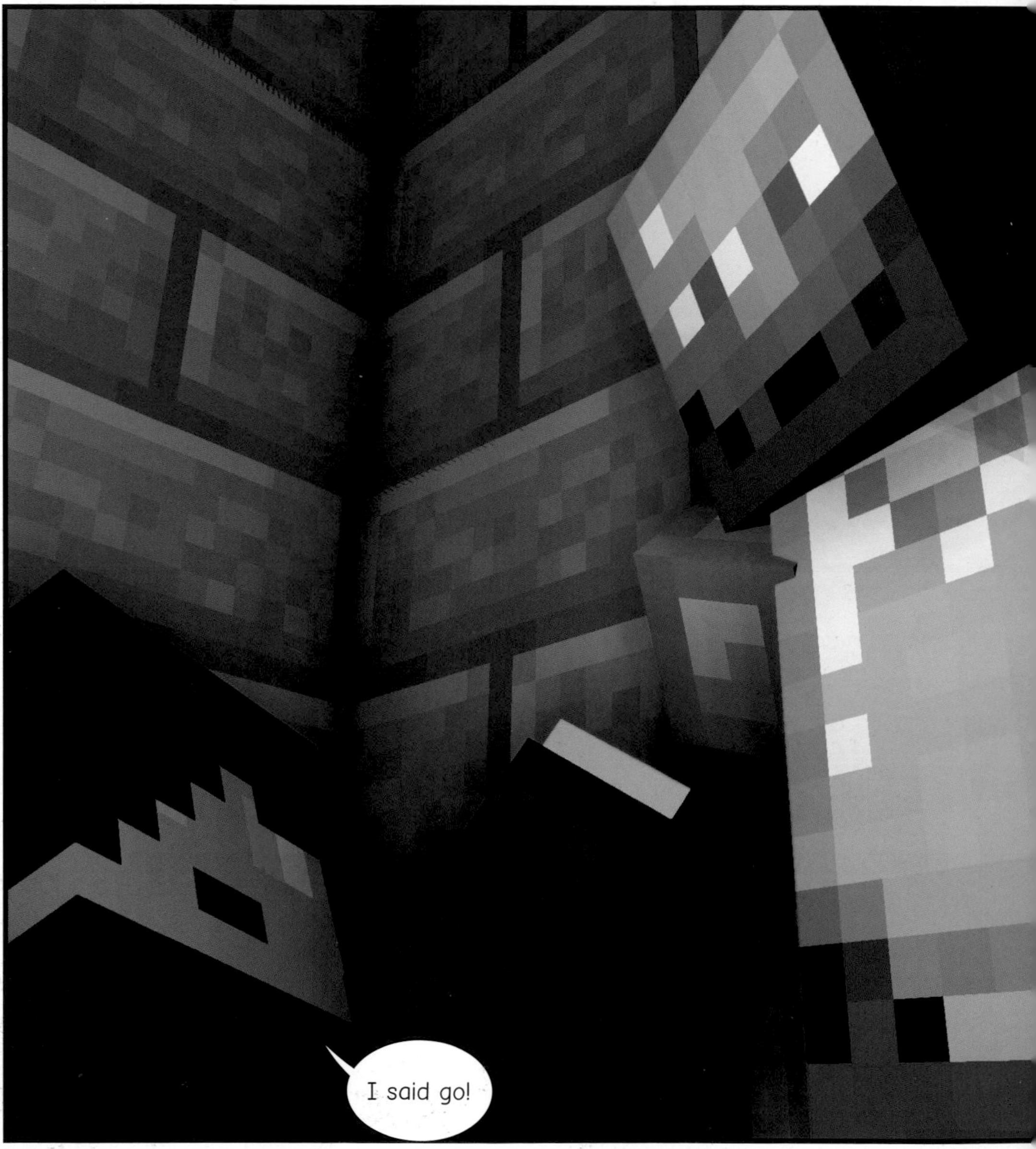
I said go!

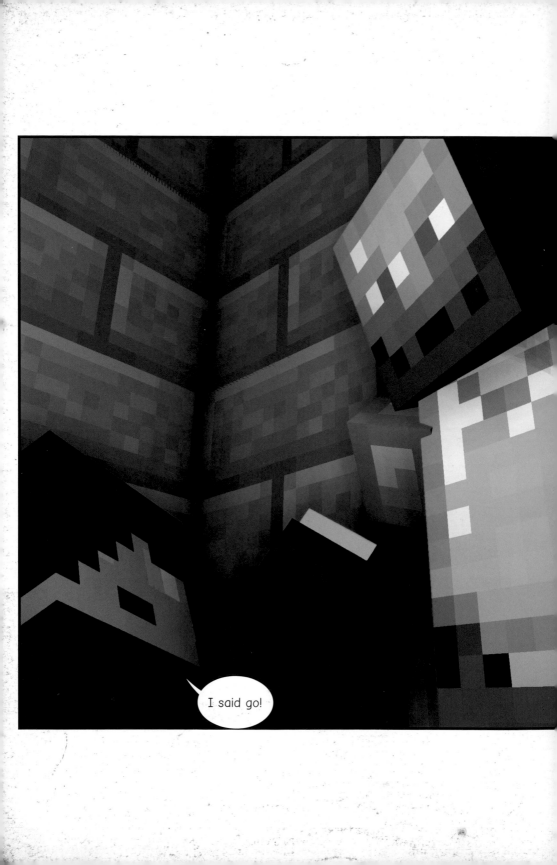

CHAPTER 8

FRENEMIES

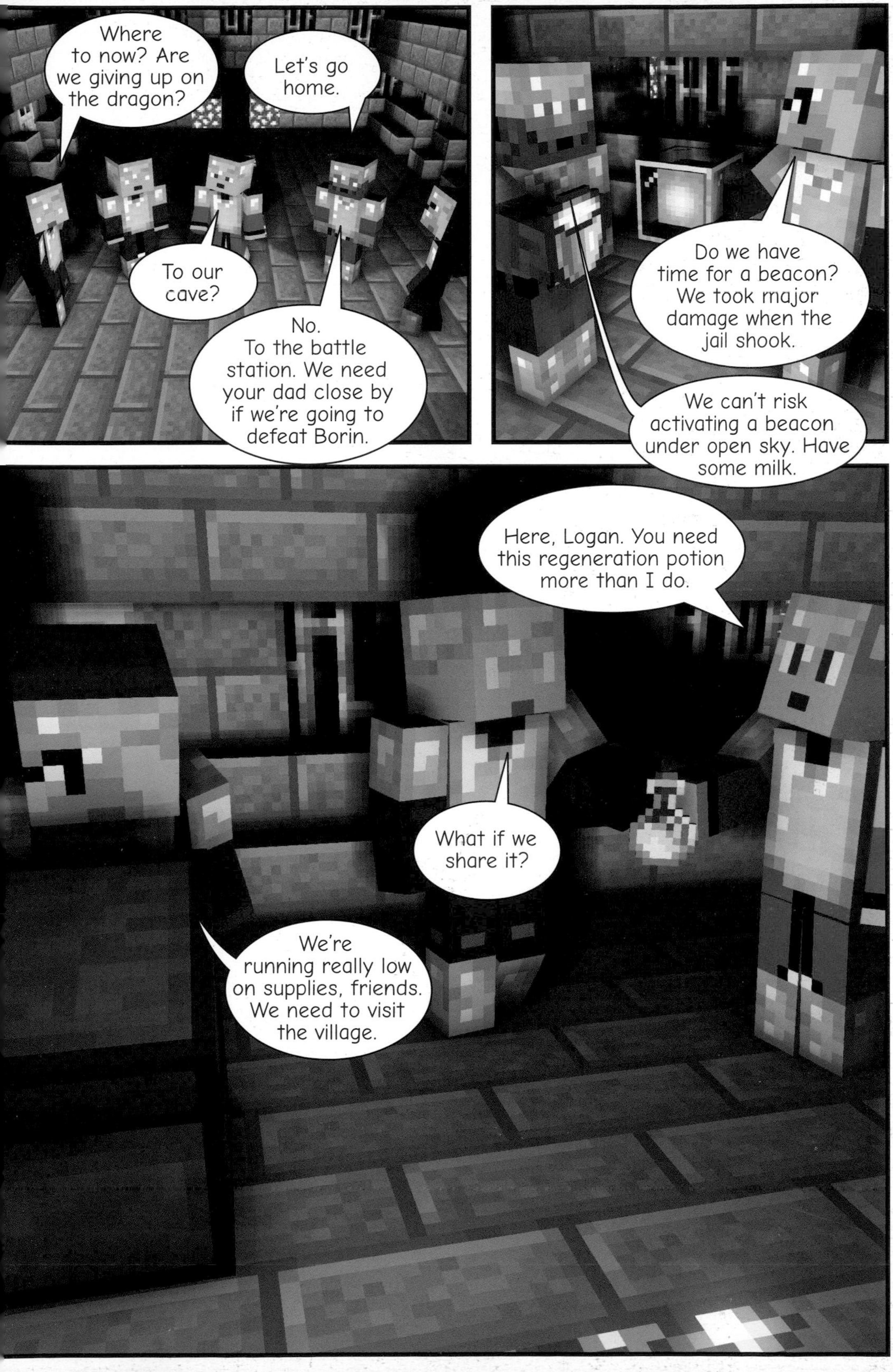
Where to now? Are we giving up on the dragon?
Let's go home.
To our cave?
No. To the battle station. We need your dad close by if we're going to defeat Borin.
Do we have time for a beacon? We took major damage when the jail shook.
We can't risk activating a beacon under open sky. Have some milk.
Here, Logan. You need this regeneration potion more than I do.
What if we share it?
We're running really low on supplies, friends. We need to visit the village.

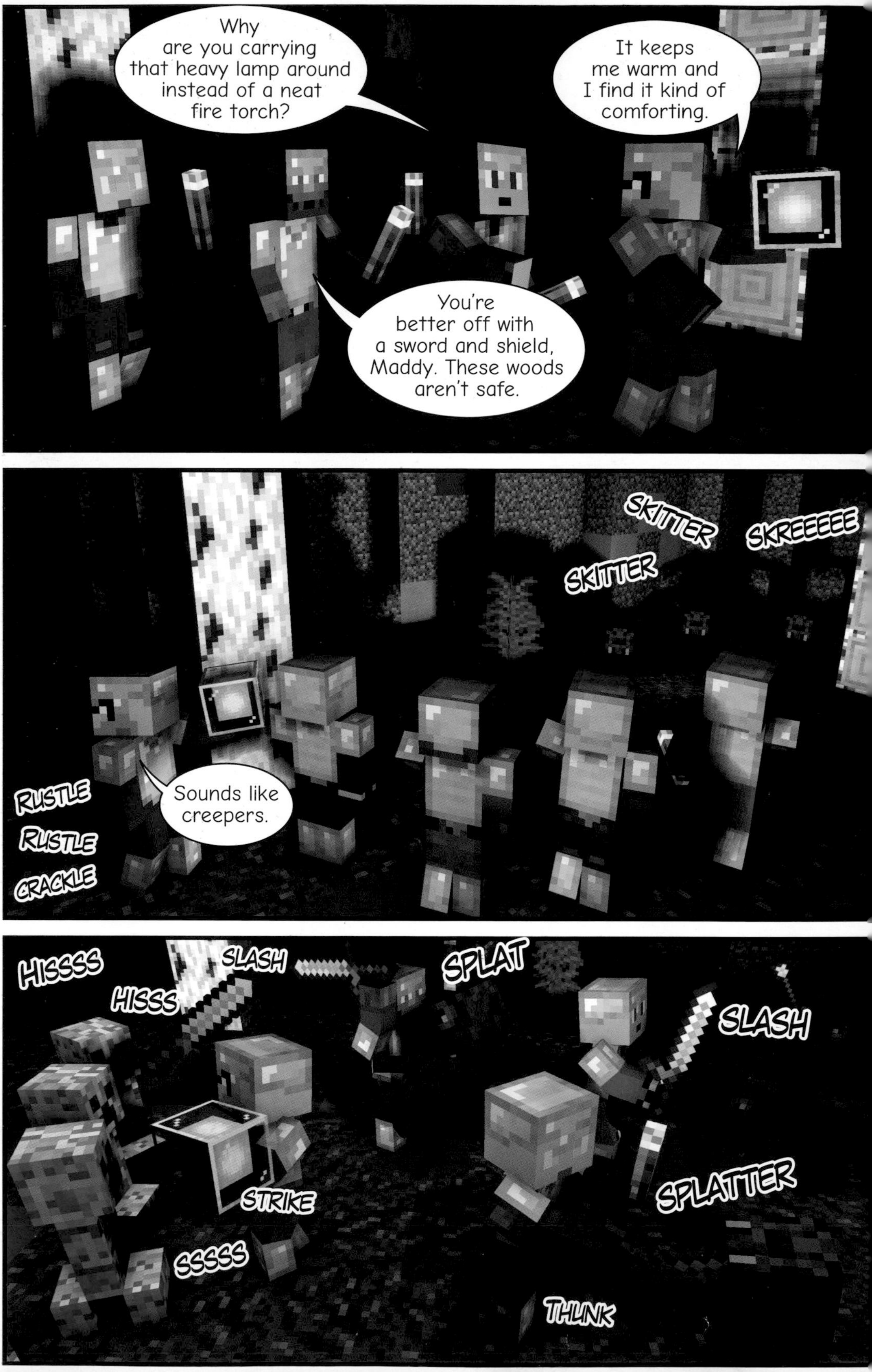
Why are you carrying that heavy lamp around instead of a neat fire torch?
It keeps me warm and I find it kind of comforting.
You're better off with a sword and shield, Maddy. These woods aren't safe.
SKITTER
SKREEEEEE
SKITTER
Sounds like creepers.
RUSTLE
RUSTLE
CRACKLE
HISSSS
SLASH
HISSS
SPLAT
SLASH
STRIKE
SPLATTER
SSSSS
THUNK

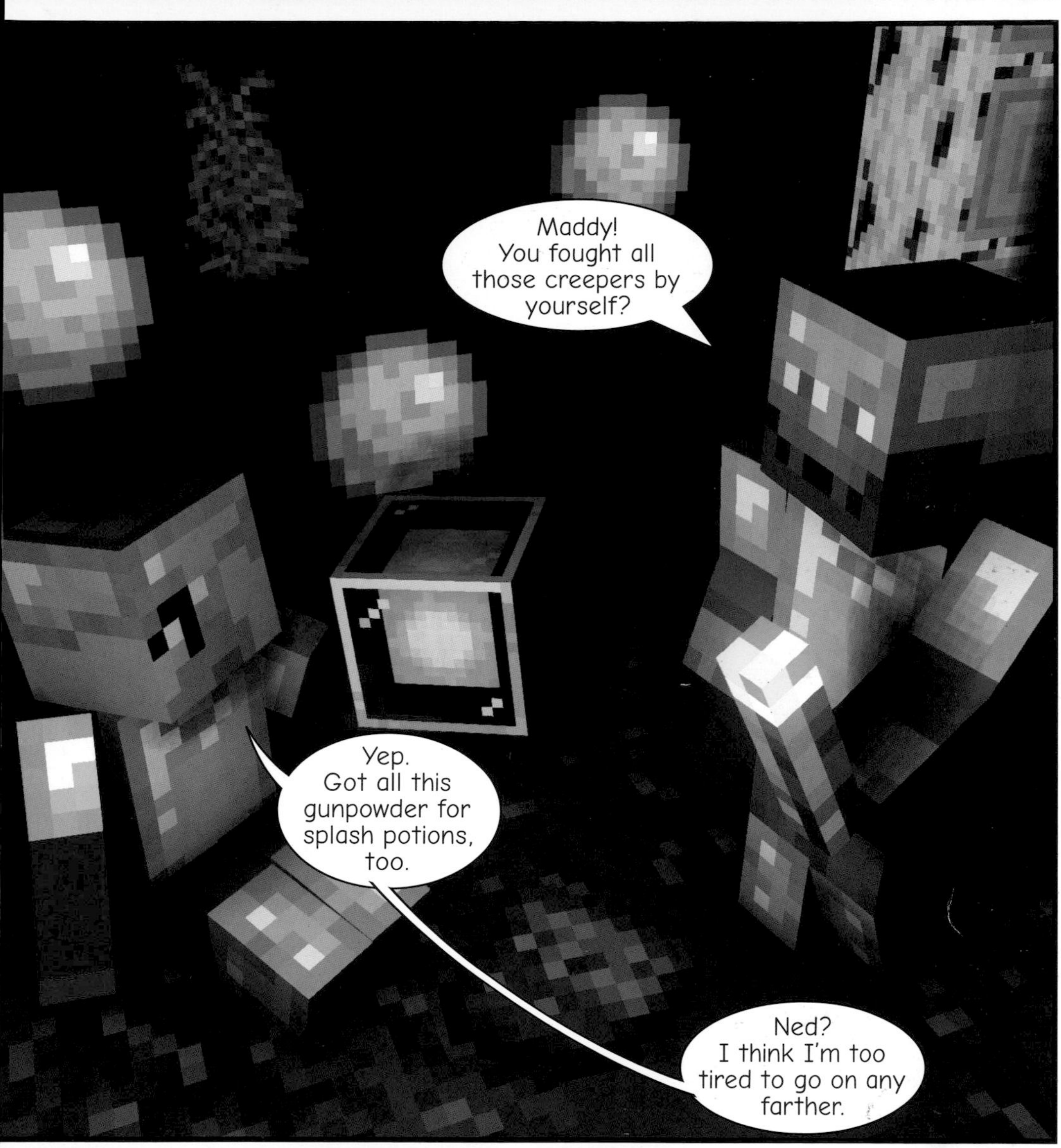
Maddy!
You fought all those creepers by yourself?
Yep.
Got all this gunpowder for splash potions, too.
Ned?
I think I'm too tired to go on any farther.

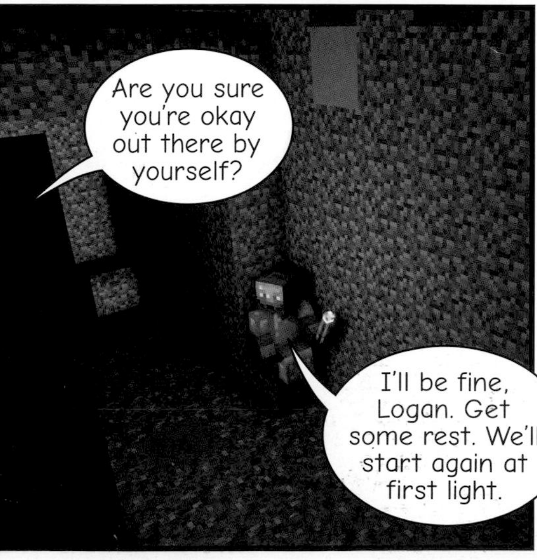
Are you sure you're okay out there by yourself?
I'll be fine, Logan. Get some rest. We'll start again at first light.

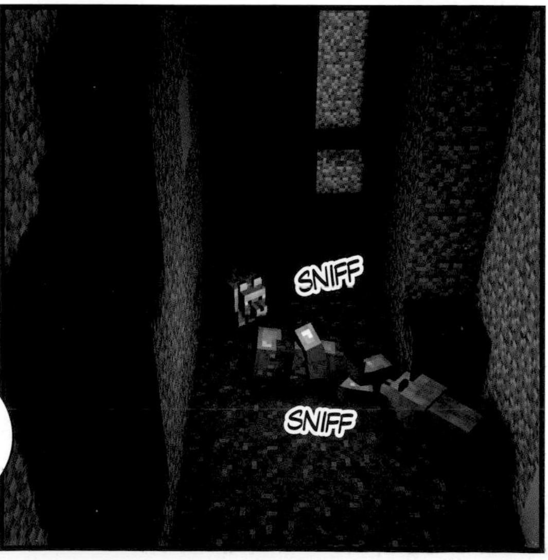
SNIFF
SNIFF

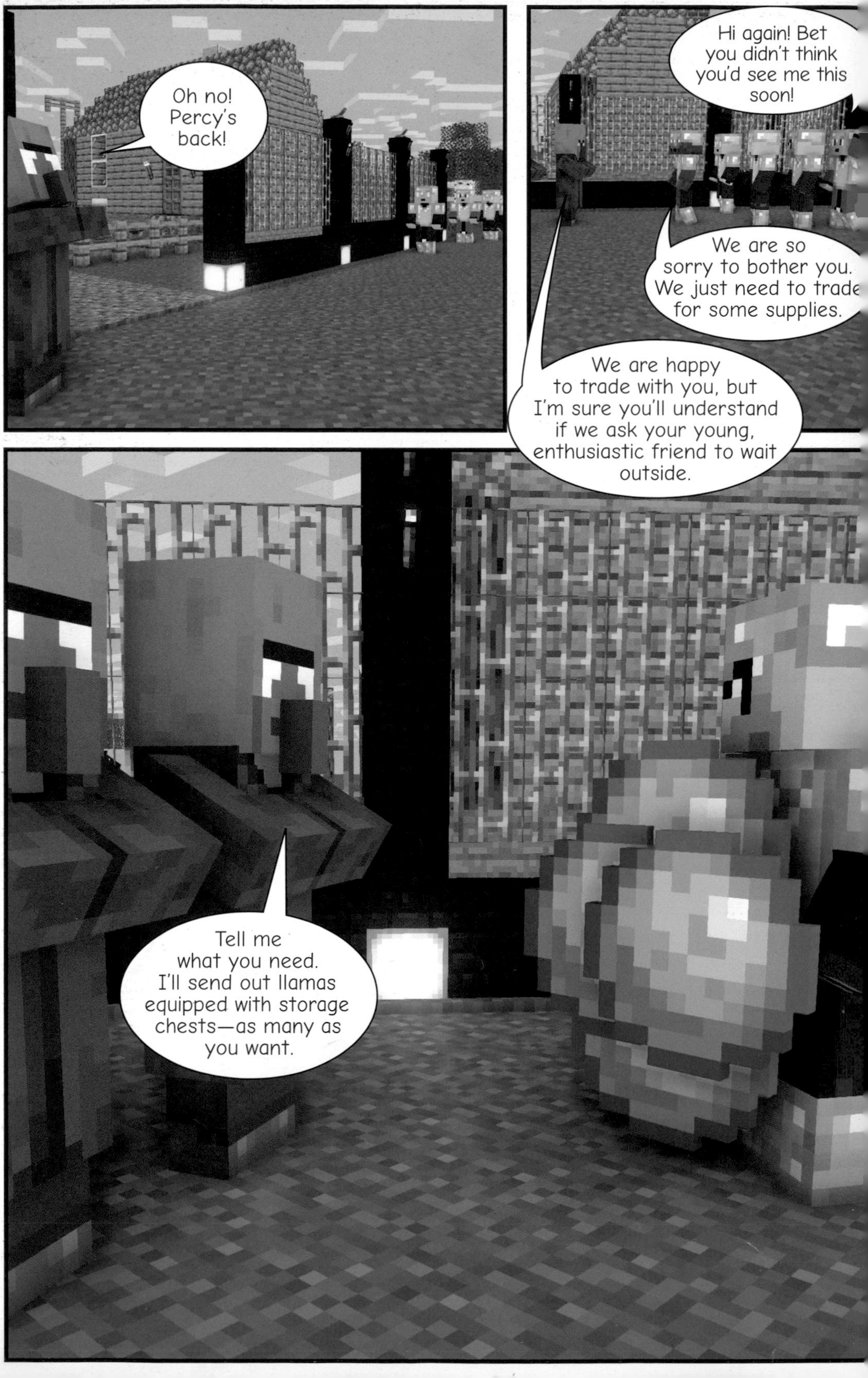

Oh no! Percy's back!
Hi again! Bet you didn't think you'd see me this soon!
We are so sorry to bother you. We just need to trade for some supplies.
We are happy to trade with you, but I'm sure you'll understand if we ask your young, enthusiastic friend to wait outside.
Tell me what you need. I'll send out llamas equipped with storage chests—as many as you want.

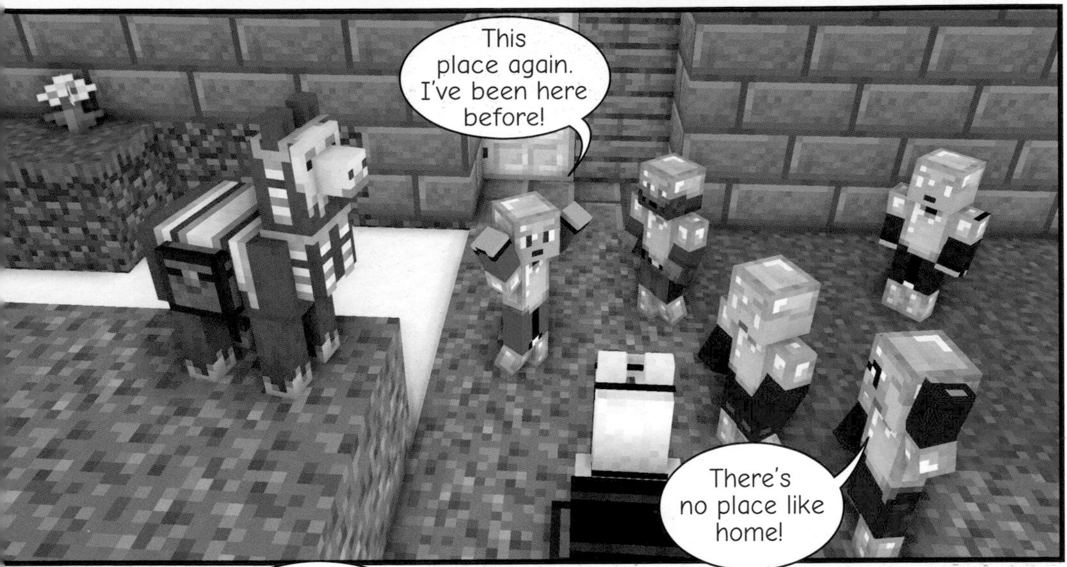
This place again. I've been here before!
There's no place like home!

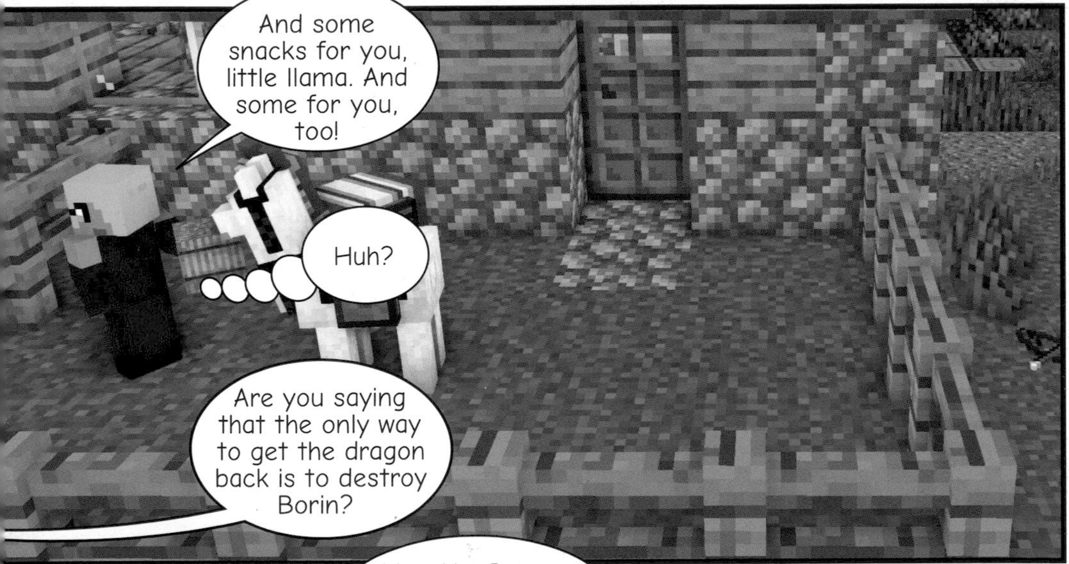
And some snacks for you, little llama. And some for you, too!
Huh?
Are you saying that the only way to get the dragon back is to destroy Borin?

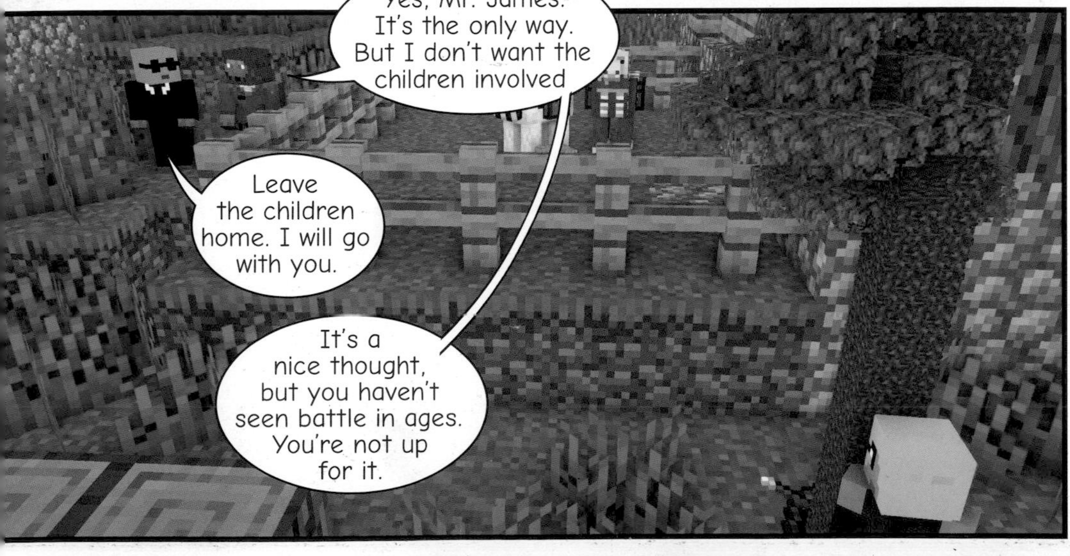
Yes, Mr. James. It's the only way. But I don't want the children involved
Leave the children home. I will go with you.
It's a nice thought, but you haven't seen battle in ages. You're not up for it.

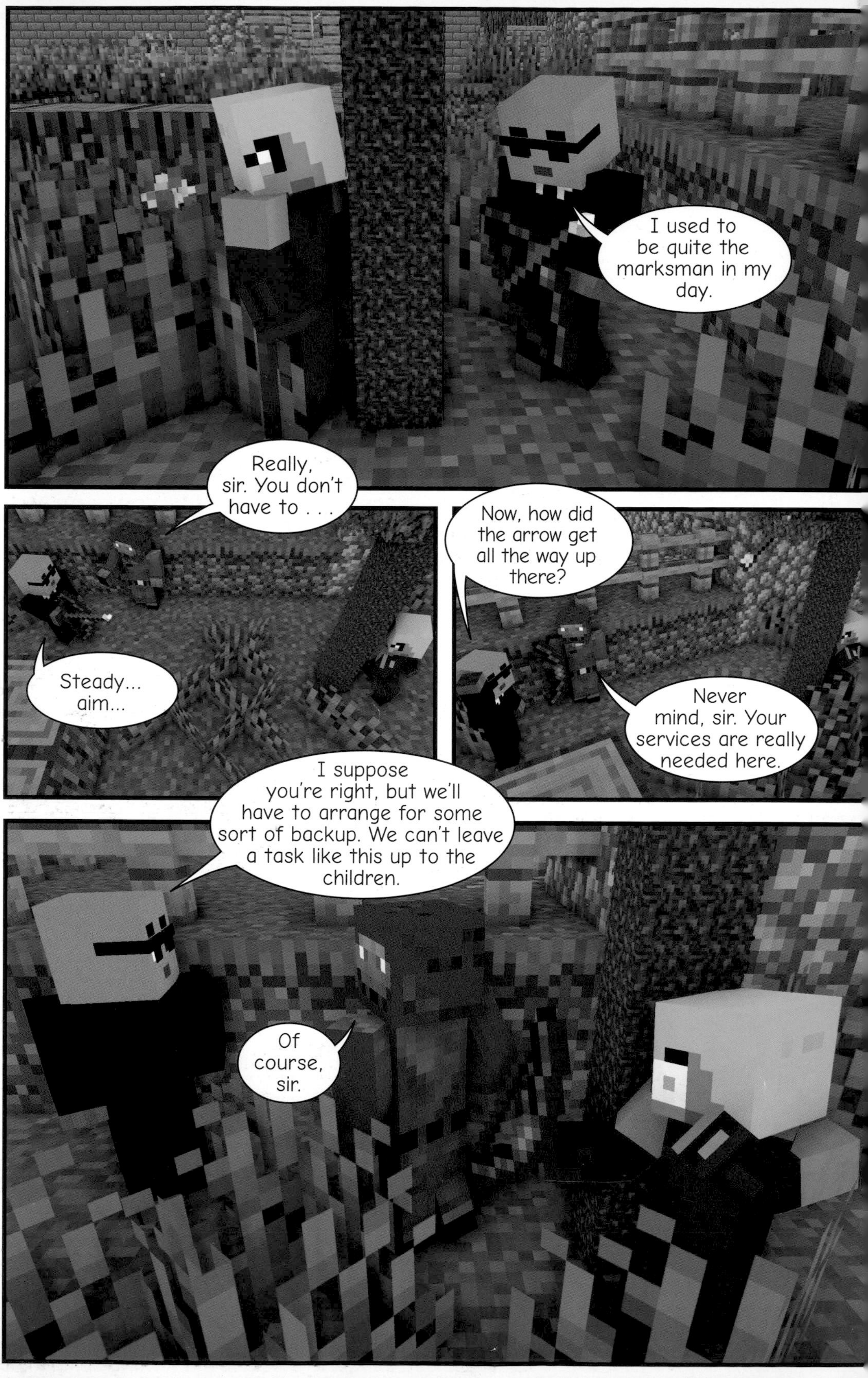
I used to be quite the marksman in my day.
Really, sir. You don't have to . . .
Steady... aim...
Now, how did the arrow get all the way up there?
Never mind, sir. Your services are really needed here.
I suppose you're right, but we'll have to arrange for some sort of backup. We can't leave a task like this up to the children.
Of course, sir.

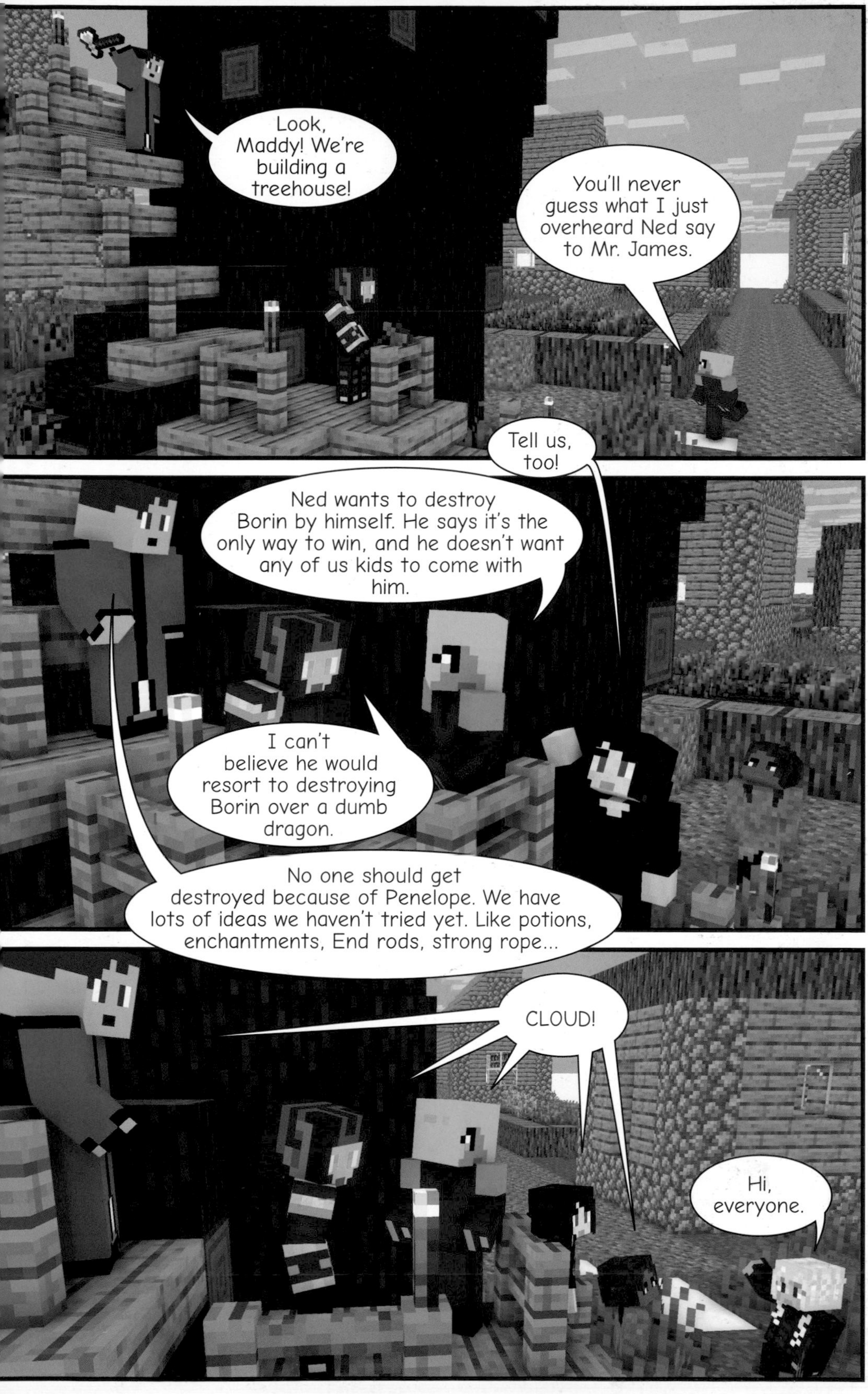

Look, Maddy! We're building a treehouse!
You'll never guess what I just overheard Ned say to Mr. James.
Tell us, too!
Ned wants to destroy Borin by himself. He says it's the only way to win, and he doesn't want any of us kids to come with him.
I can't believe he would resort to destroying Borin over a dumb dragon.
No one should get destroyed because of Penelope. We have lots of ideas we haven't tried yet. Like potions, enchantments, End rods, strong rope...
CLOUD!
Hi, everyone.

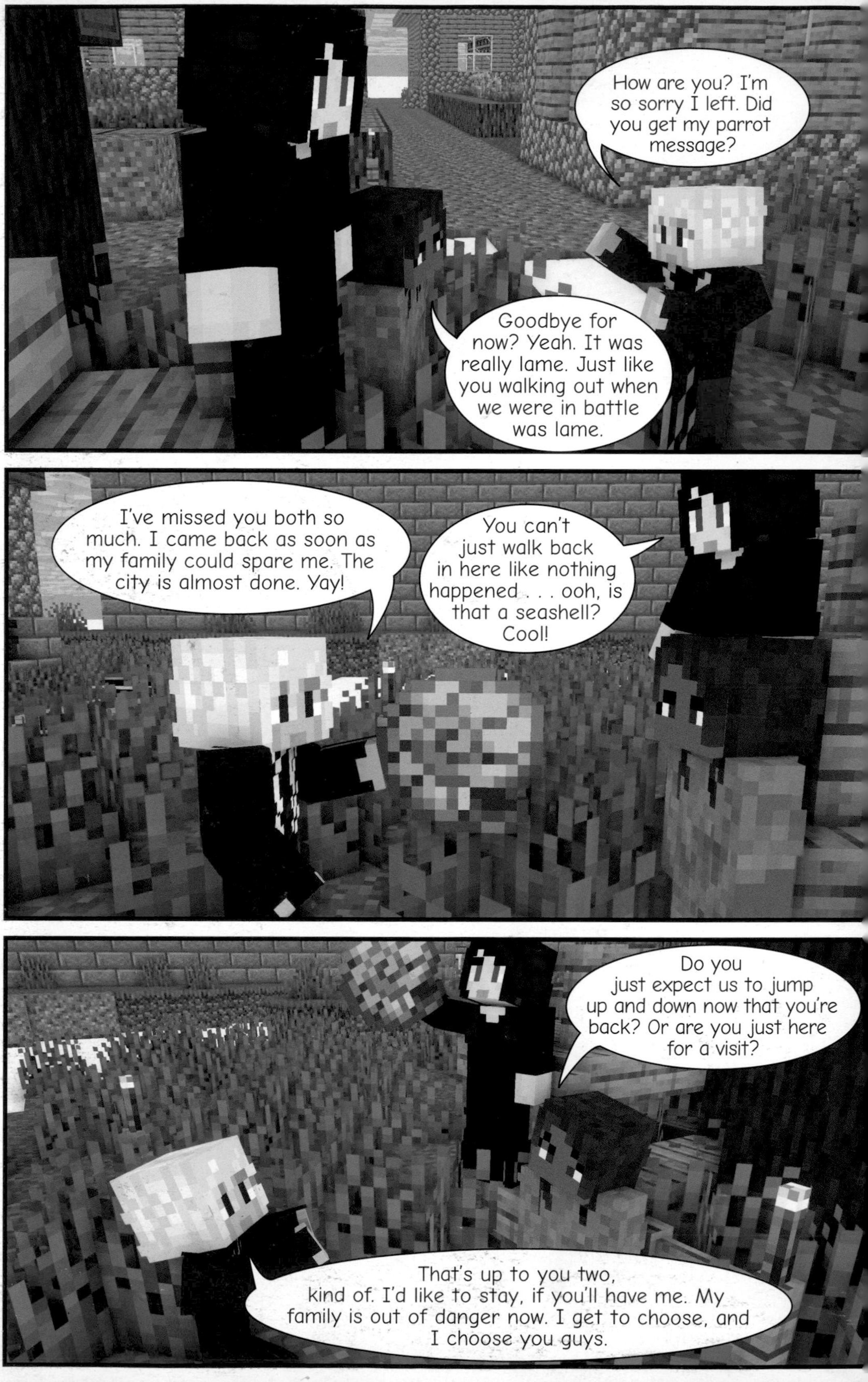
How are you? I'm so sorry I left. Did you get my parrot message?
Goodbye for now? Yeah. It was really lame. Just like you walking out when we were in battle was lame.
I've missed you both so much. I came back as soon as my family could spare me. The city is almost done. Yay!
You can't just walk back in here like nothing happened . . . ooh, is that a seashell? Cool!
Do you just expect us to jump up and down now that you're back? Or are you just here for a visit?
That's up to you two, kind of. I'd like to stay, if you'll have me. My family is out of danger now. I get to choose, and I choose you guys.

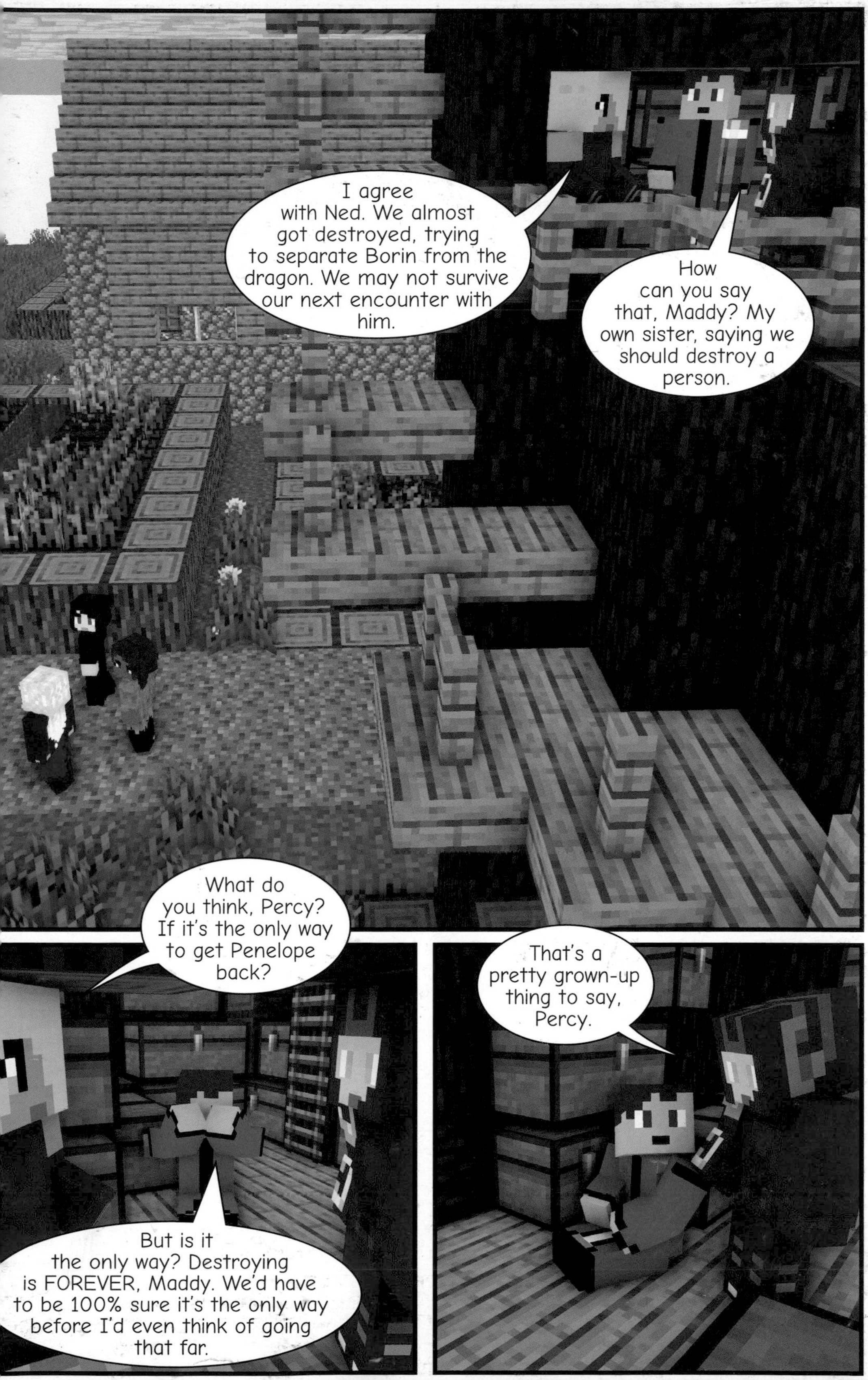
I agree with Ned. We almost got destroyed, trying to separate Borin from the dragon. We may not survive our next encounter with him.
How can you say that, Maddy? My own sister, saying we should destroy a person.
What do you think, Percy? If it's the only way to get Penelope back?
But is it the only way? Destroying is FOREVER, Maddy. We'd have to be 100% sure it's the only way before I'd even think of going that far.
That's a pretty grown-up thing to say, Percy.

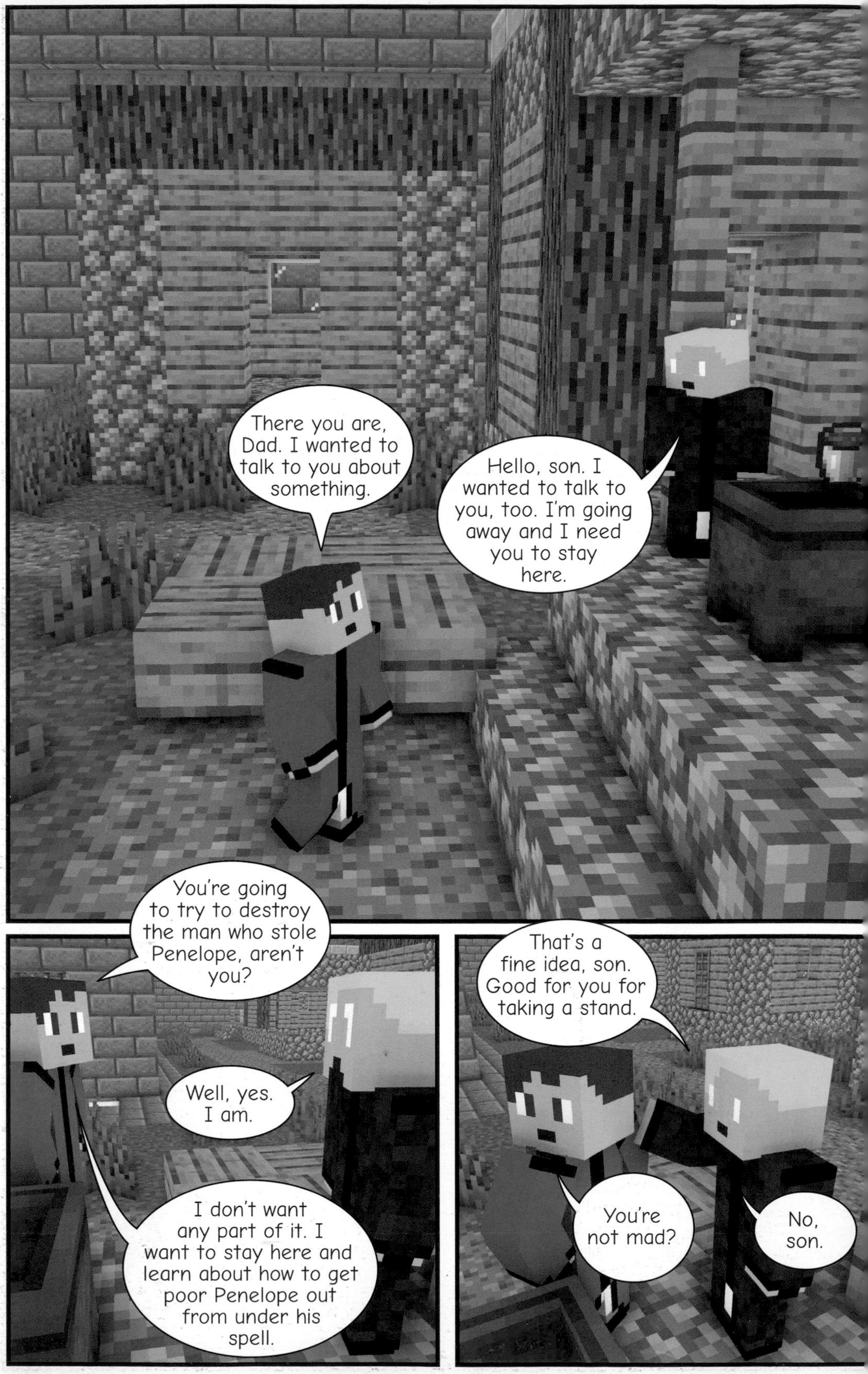

There you are, Dad. I wanted to talk to you about something.
Hello, son. I wanted to talk to you, too. I'm going away and I need you to stay here.
You're going to try to destroy the man who stole Penelope, aren't you?
Well, yes. I am.
I don't want any part of it. I want to stay here and learn about how to get poor Penelope out from under his spell.
That's a fine idea, son. Good for you for taking a stand.
You're not mad?
No, son.

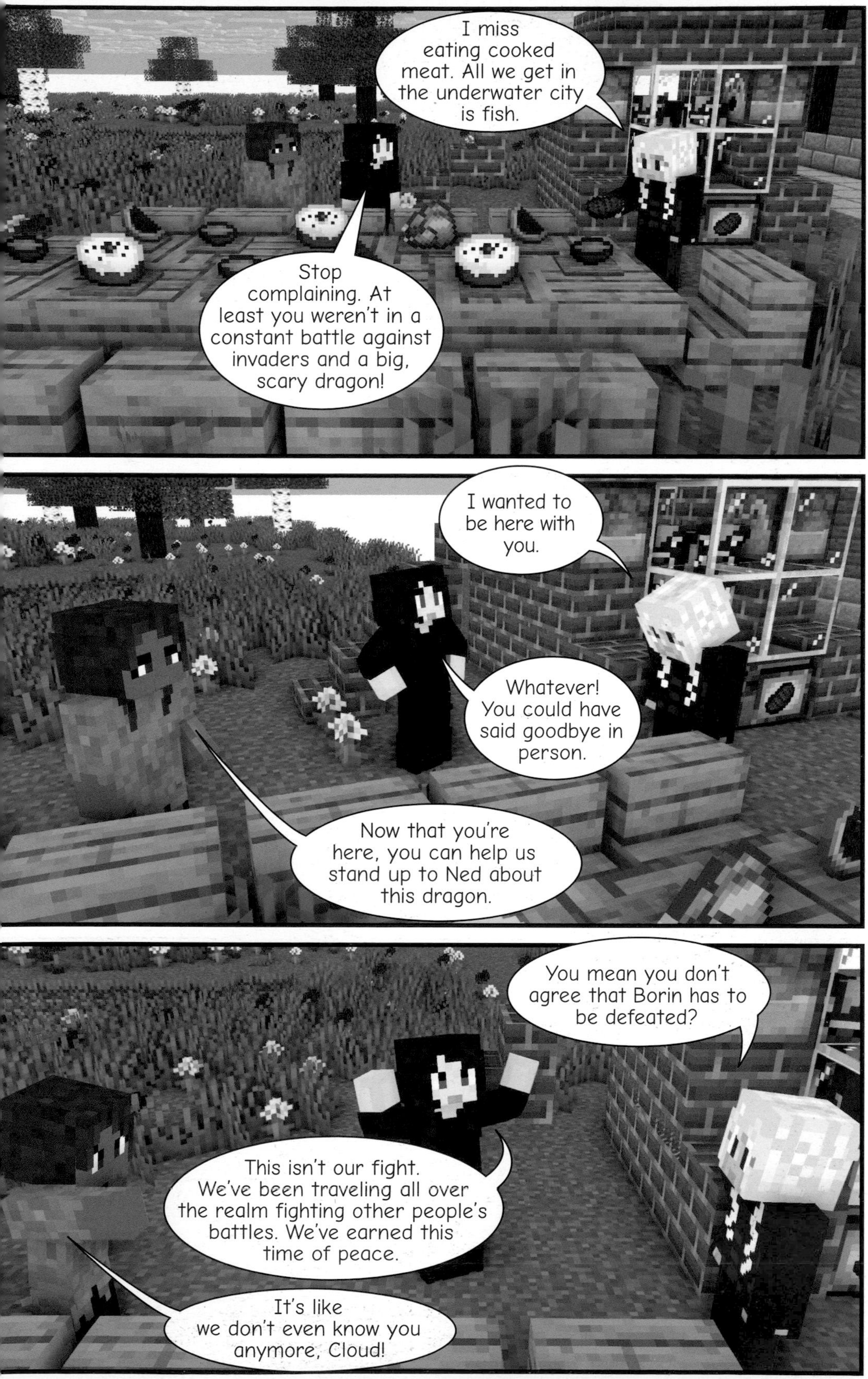

I miss eating cooked meat. All we get in the underwater city is fish.
Stop complaining. At least you weren't in a constant battle against invaders and a big, scary dragon!
I wanted to be here with you.
Whatever! You could have said goodbye in person.
Now that you're here, you can help us stand up to Ned about this dragon.
You mean you don't agree that Borin has to be defeated?
This isn't our fight. We've been traveling all over the realm fighting other people's battles. We've earned this time of peace.
It's like we don't even know you anymore, Cloud!

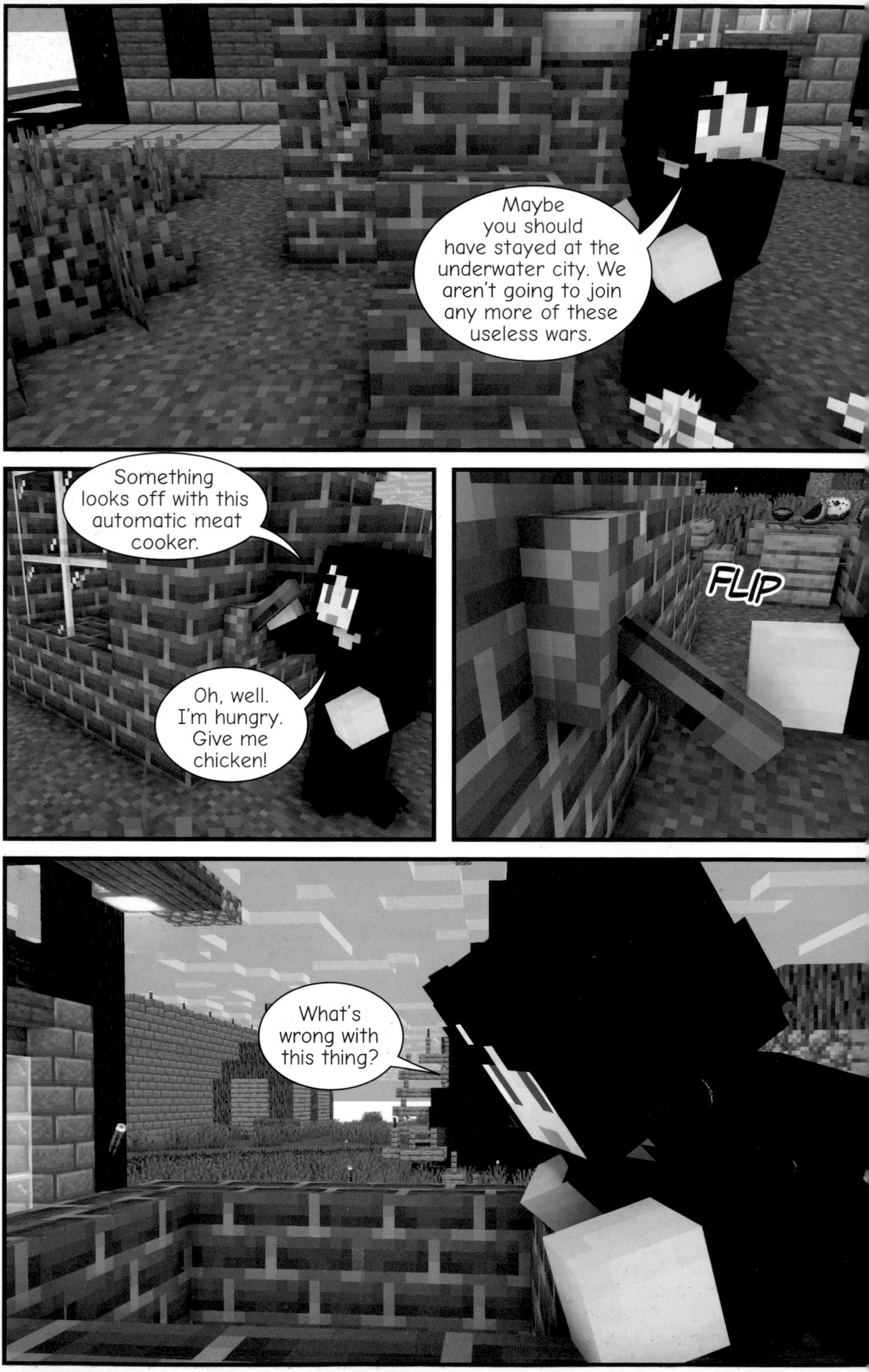
Maybe you should have stayed at the underwater city. We aren't going to join any more of these useless wars.
Something looks off with this automatic meat cooker.
Oh, well. I'm hungry. Give me chicken!
FLIP
What's wrong with this thing?

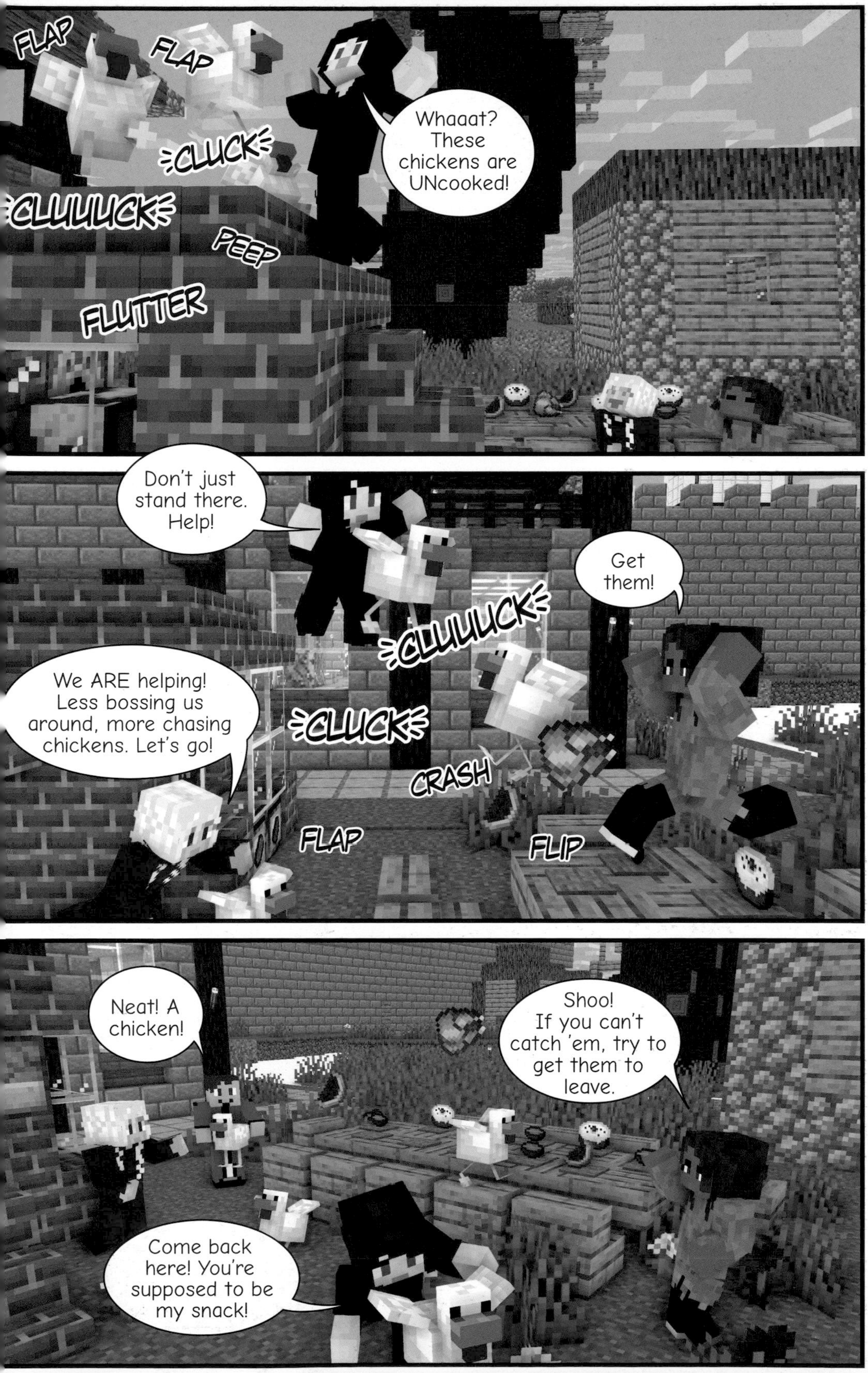
FLAP
FLAP
Whaaat? These chickens are UNcooked!
CLUCK
CLUUUCK
PEEP
FLUTTER
Don't just stand there. Help!
Get them!
CLUUUCK
We ARE helping! Less bossing us around, more chasing chickens. Let's go!
CLUCK
CRASH
FLAP
FLIP
Neat! A chicken!
Shoo! If you can't catch 'em, try to get them to leave.
Come back here! You're supposed to be my snack!

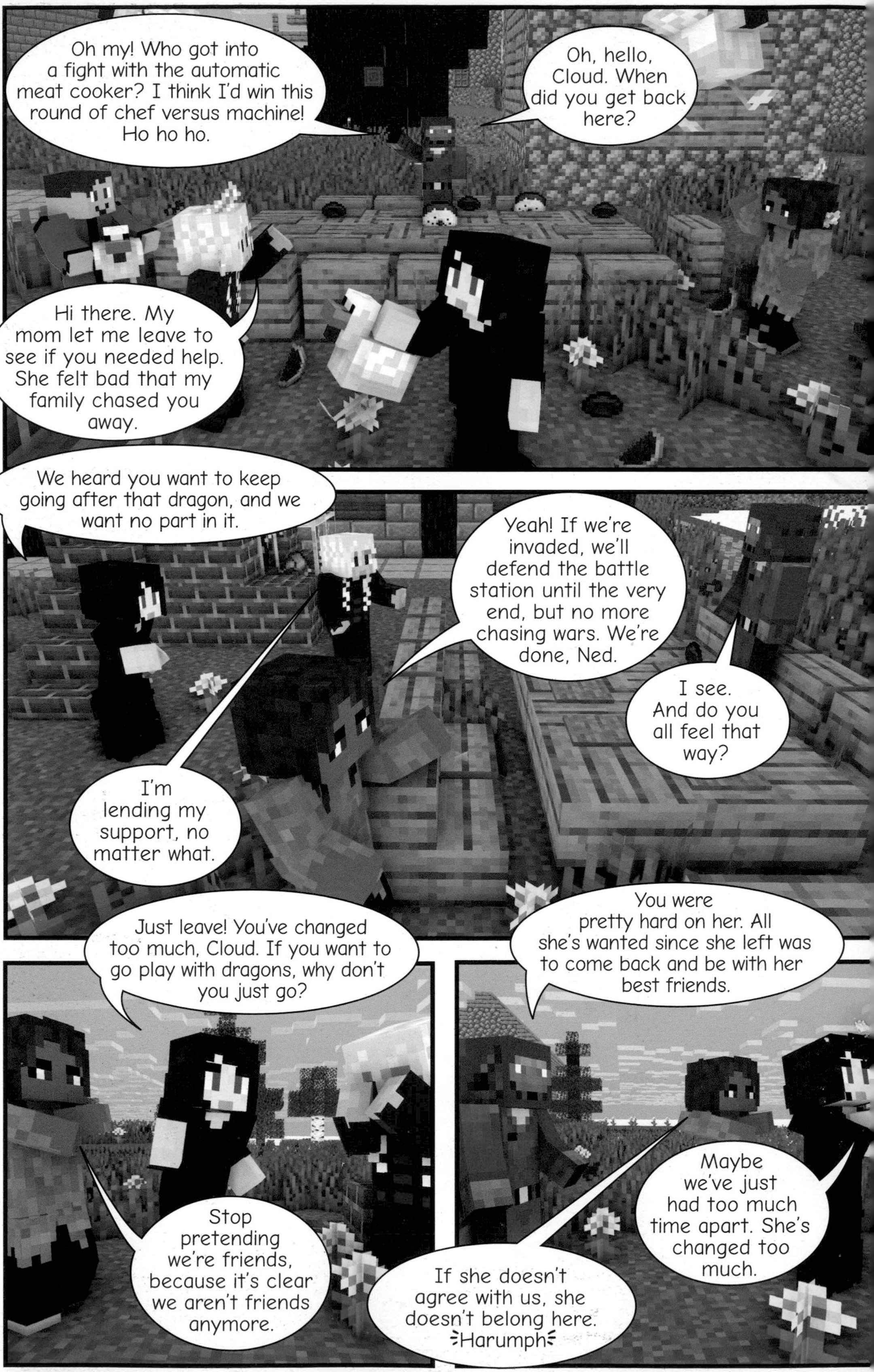
Oh my! Who got into a fight with the automatic meat cooker? I think I'd win this round of chef versus machine! Ho ho ho.
Oh, hello, Cloud. When did you get back here?
Hi there. My mom let me leave to see if you needed help. She felt bad that my family chased you away.
We heard you want to keep going after that dragon, and we want no part in it.
Yeah! If we're invaded, we'll defend the battle station until the very end, but no more chasing wars. We're done, Ned.
I see. And do you all feel that way?
I'm lending my support, no matter what.
Just leave! You've changed too much, Cloud. If you want to go play with dragons, why don't you just go?
Stop pretending we're friends, because it's clear we aren't friends anymore.
You were pretty hard on her. All she's wanted since she left was to come back and be with her best friends.
Maybe we've just had too much time apart. She's changed too much.
If she doesn't agree with us, she doesn't belong here.
Harumph

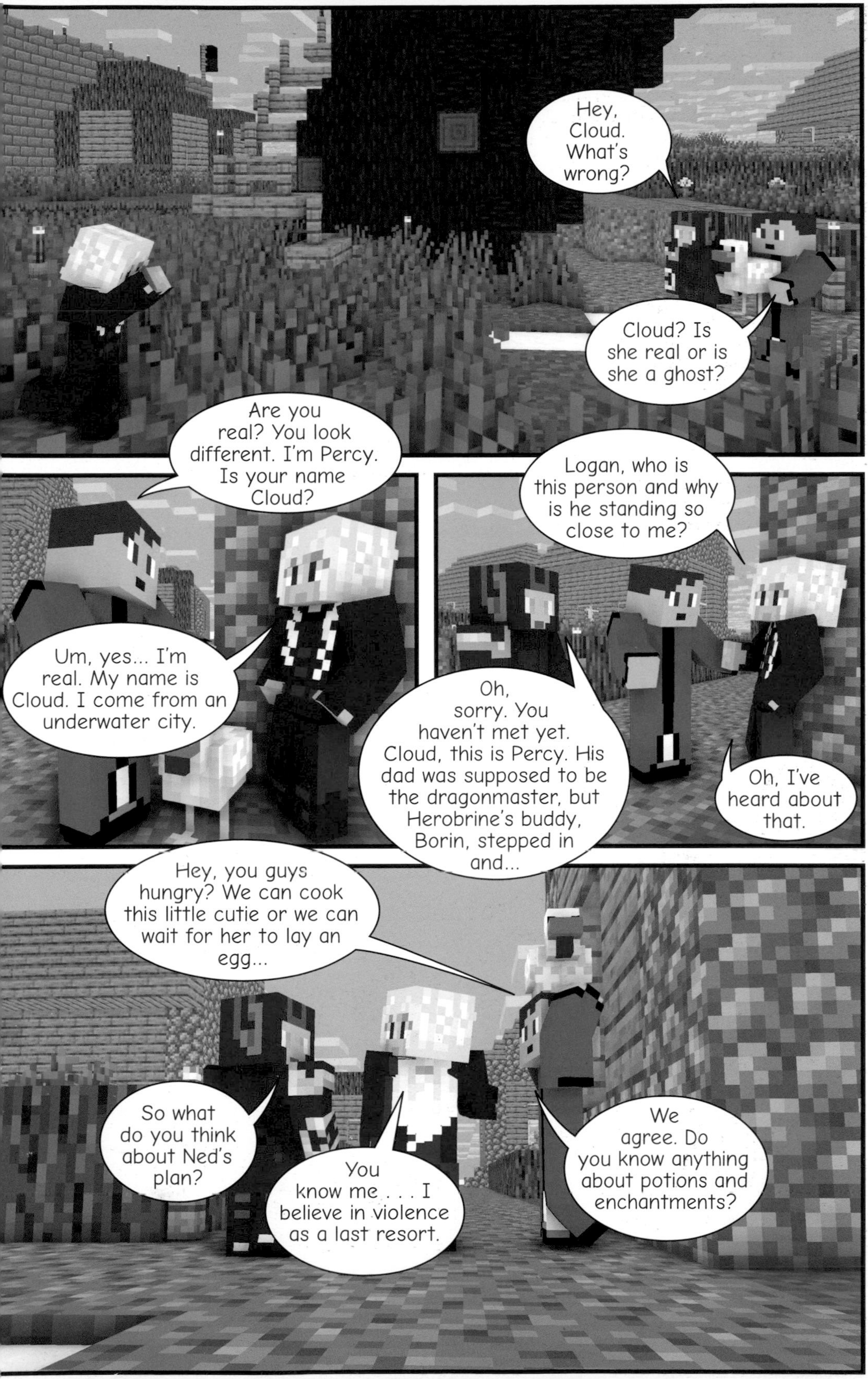

Hey, Cloud. What's wrong?
Cloud? Is she real or is she a ghost?
Are you real? You look different. I'm Percy. Is your name Cloud?
Um, yes... I'm real. My name is Cloud. I come from an underwater city.
Logan, who is this person and why is he standing so close to me?
Oh, sorry. You haven't met yet. Cloud, this is Percy. His dad was supposed to be the dragonmaster, but Herobrine's buddy, Borin, stepped in and...
Oh, I've heard about that.
Hey, you guys hungry? We can cook this little cutie or we can wait for her to lay an egg...
So what do you think about Ned's plan?
You know me . . . I believe in violence as a last resort.
We agree. Do you know anything about potions and enchantments?

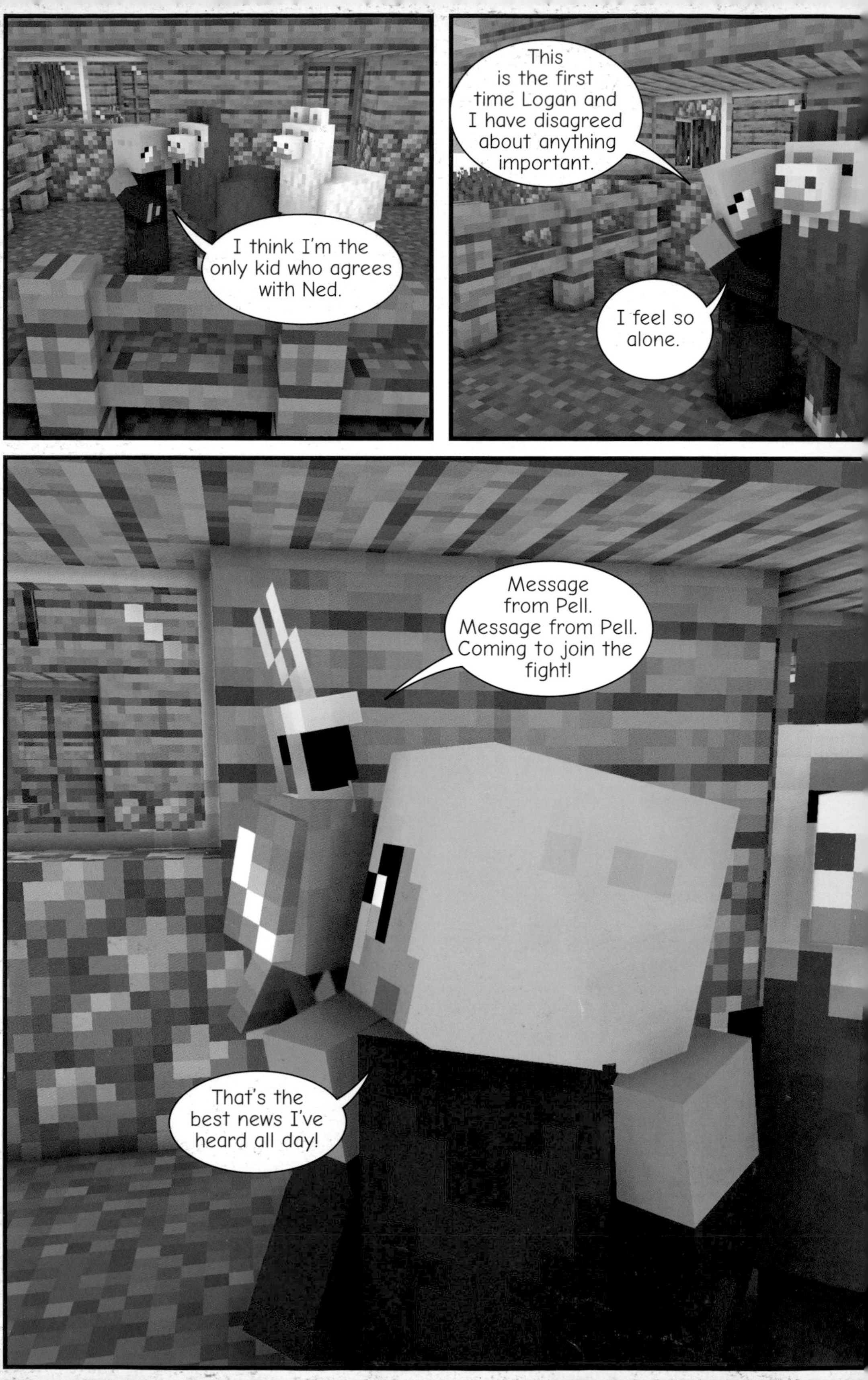
I think I'm the only kid who agrees with Ned.
This is the first time Logan and I have disagreed about anything important.
I feel so alone.
Message from Pell. Message from Pell. Coming to join the fight!
That's the best news I've heard all day!

CHAPTER 9

JOURNEY'S END

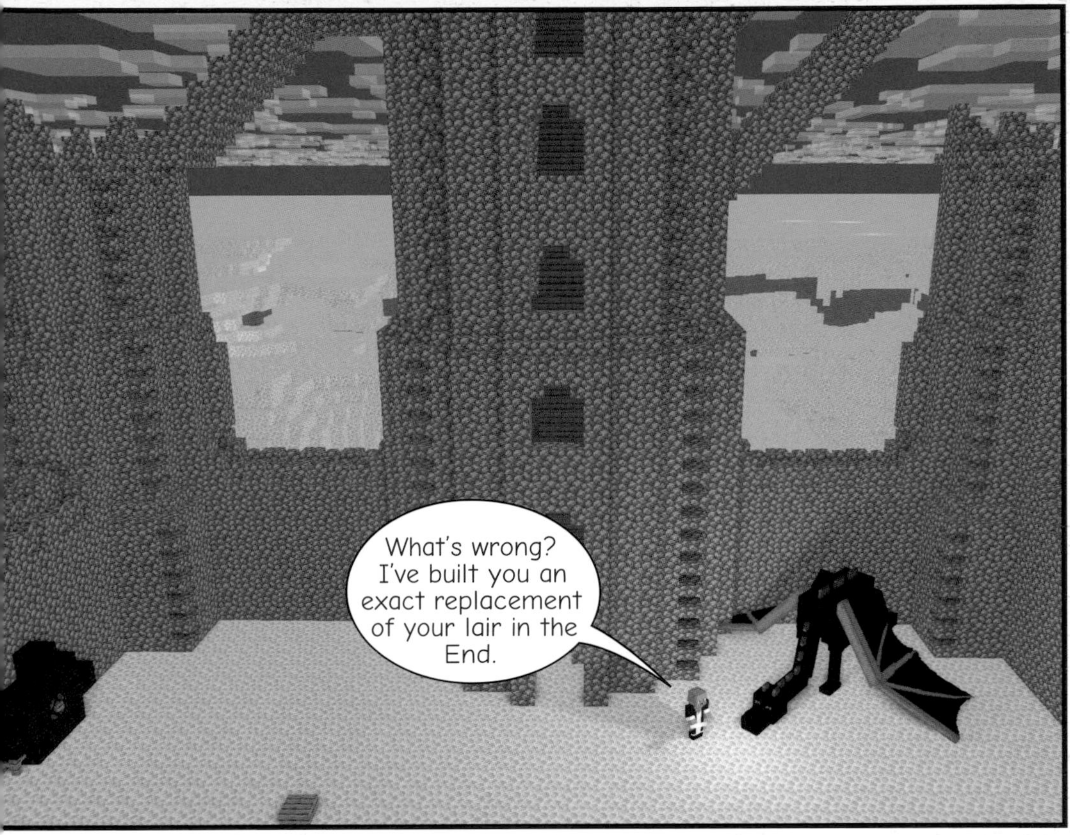
What's wrong? I've built you an exact replacement of your lair in the End.

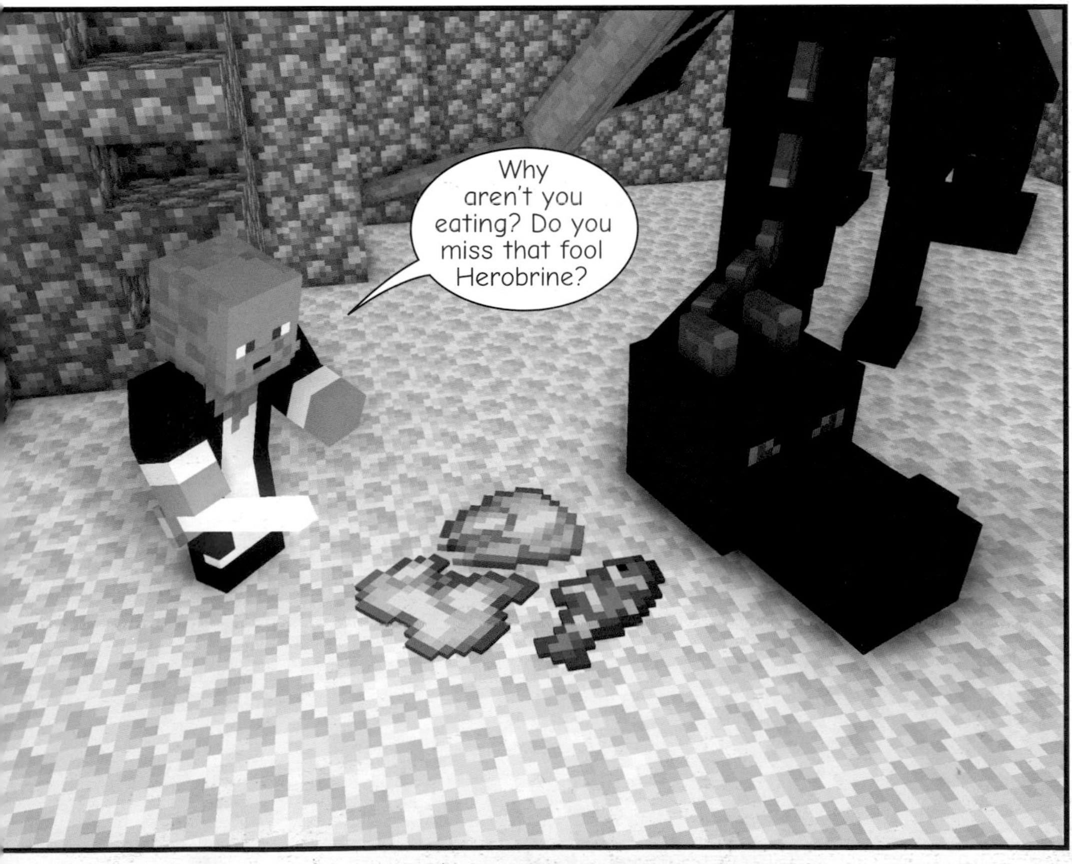
Why aren't you eating? Do you miss that fool Herobrine?

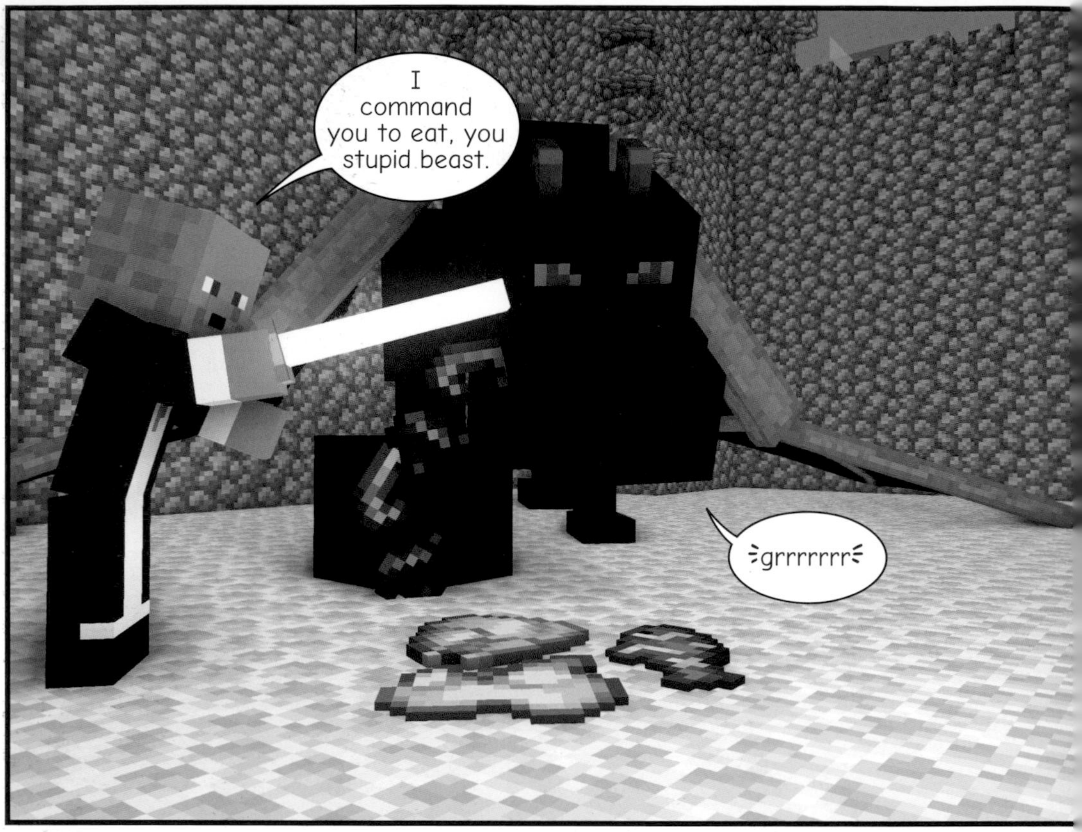
I command you to eat, you stupid beast.
grrrrrrr

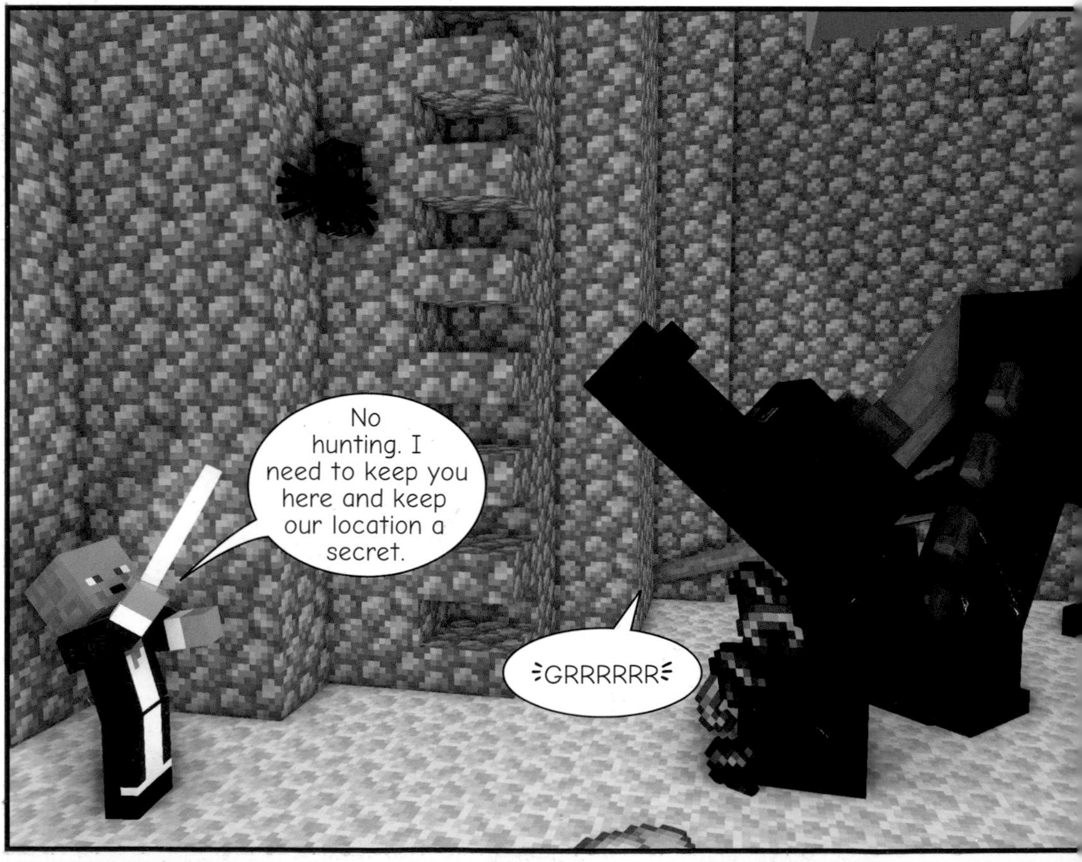
No hunting. I need to keep you here and keep our location a secret.
GRRRRRR

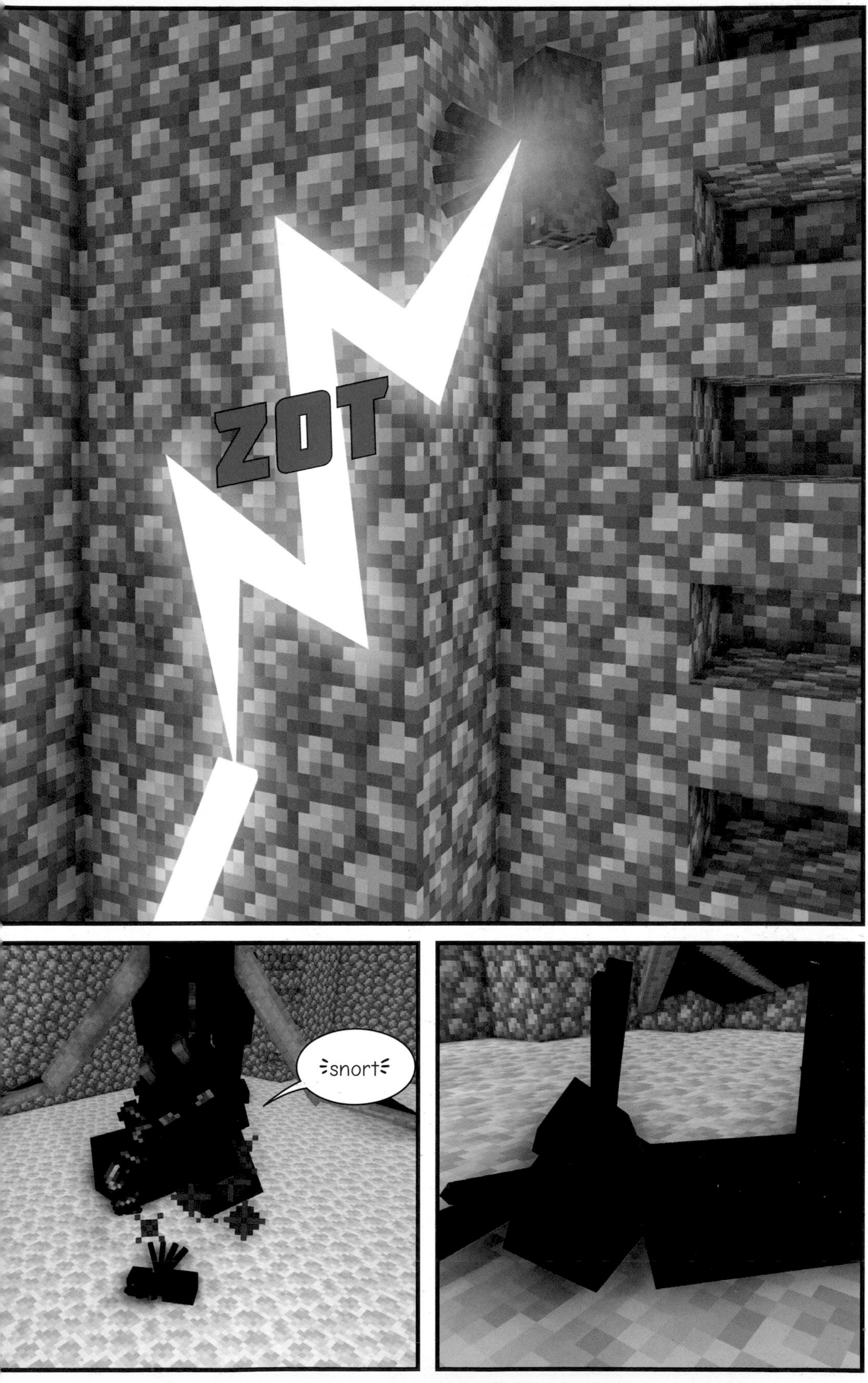
ZOT
snort

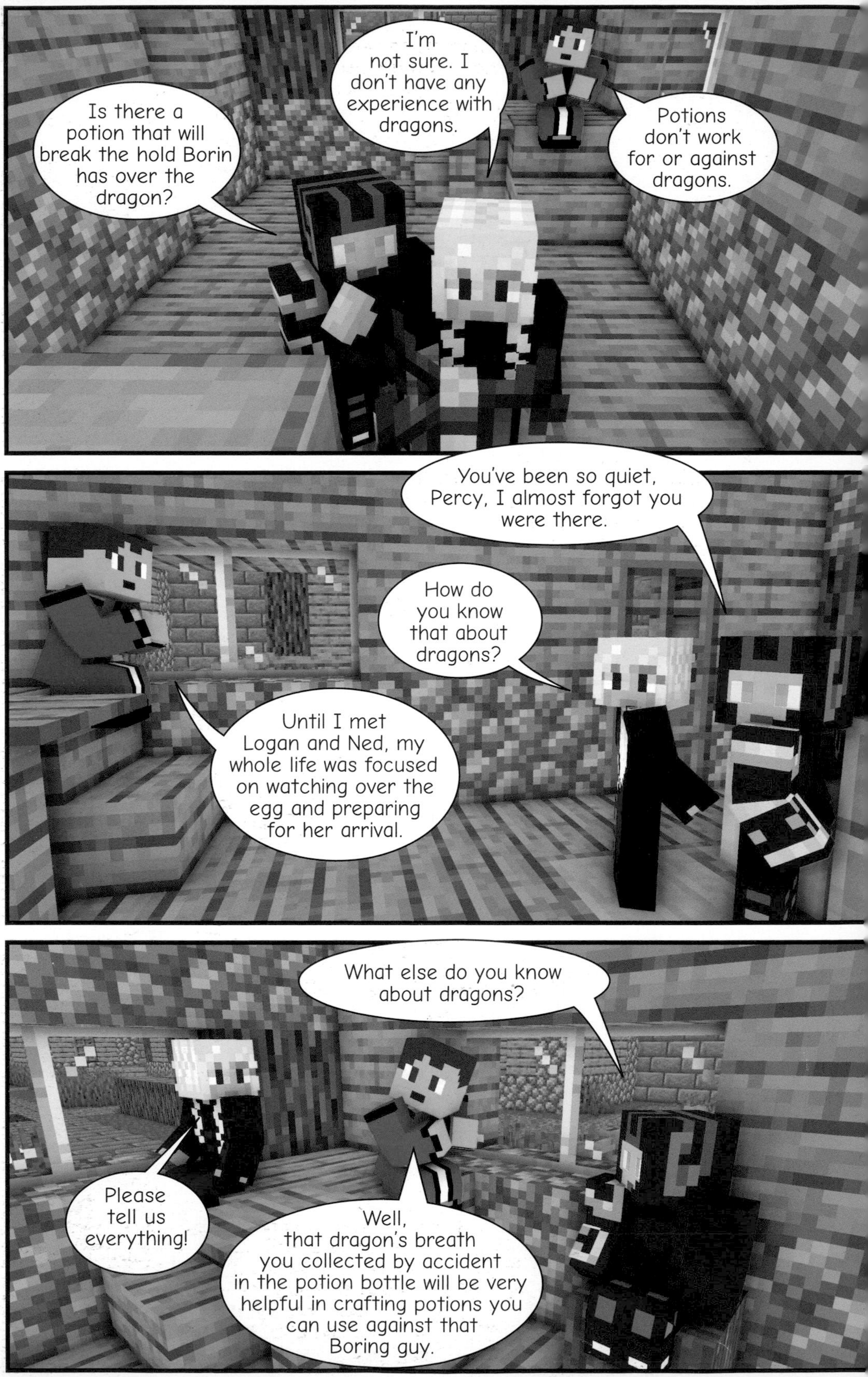
Is there a potion that will break the hold Borin has over the dragon?
I'm not sure. I don't have any experience with dragons.
Potions don't work for or against dragons.
You've been so quiet, Percy, I almost forgot you were there.
How do you know that about dragons?
Until I met Logan and Ned, my whole life was focused on watching over the egg and preparing for her arrival.
What else do you know about dragons?
Please tell us everything!
Well, that dragon's breath you collected by accident in the potion bottle will be very helpful in crafting potions you can use against that Boring guy.

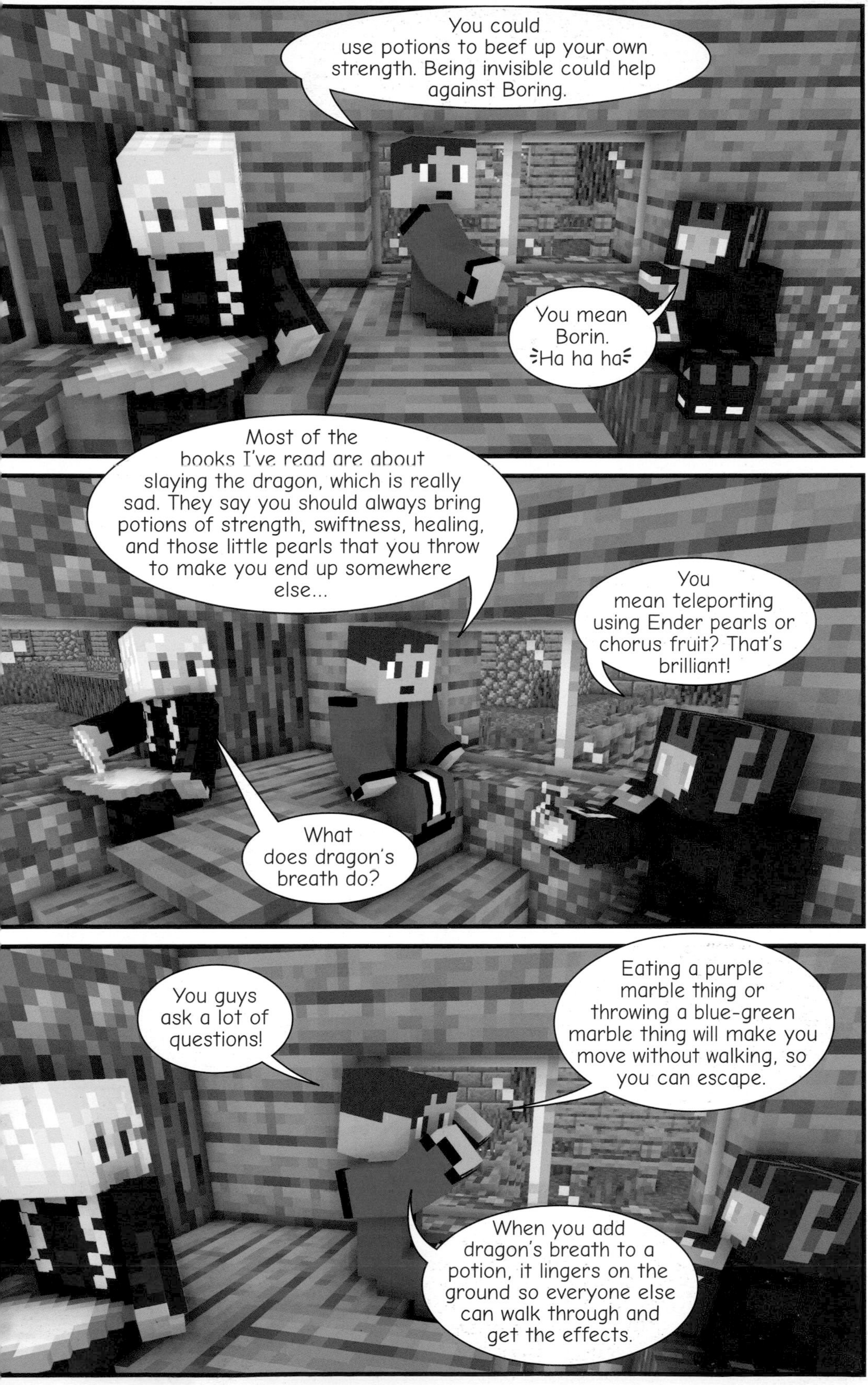
You could use potions to beef up your own strength. Being invisible could help against Boring.
You mean Borin. Ha ha ha
Most of the books I've read are about slaying the dragon, which is really sad. They say you should always bring potions of strength, swiftness, healing, and those little pearls that you throw to make you end up somewhere else...
You mean teleporting using Ender pearls or chorus fruit? That's brilliant!
What does dragon's breath do?
You guys ask a lot of questions!
Eating a purple marble thing or throwing a blue-green marble thing will make you move without walking, so you can escape.
When you add dragon's breath to a potion, it lingers on the ground so everyone else can walk through and get the effects.

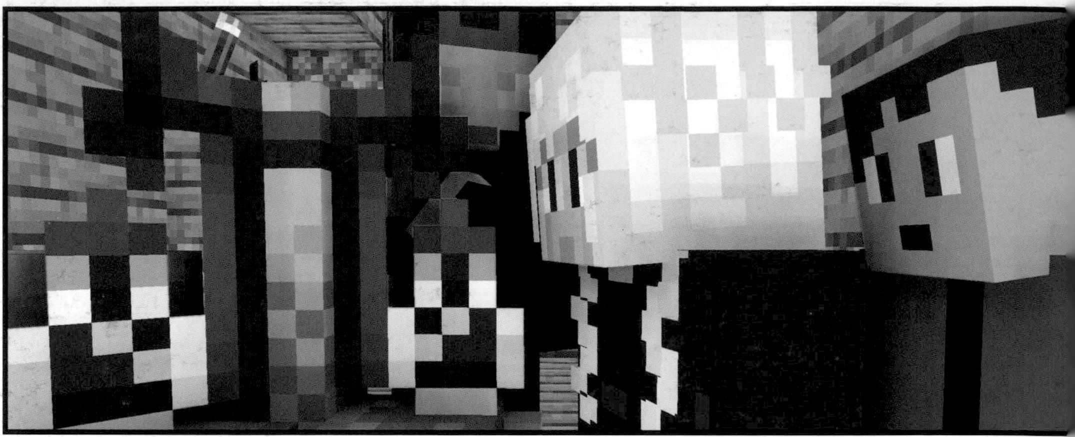

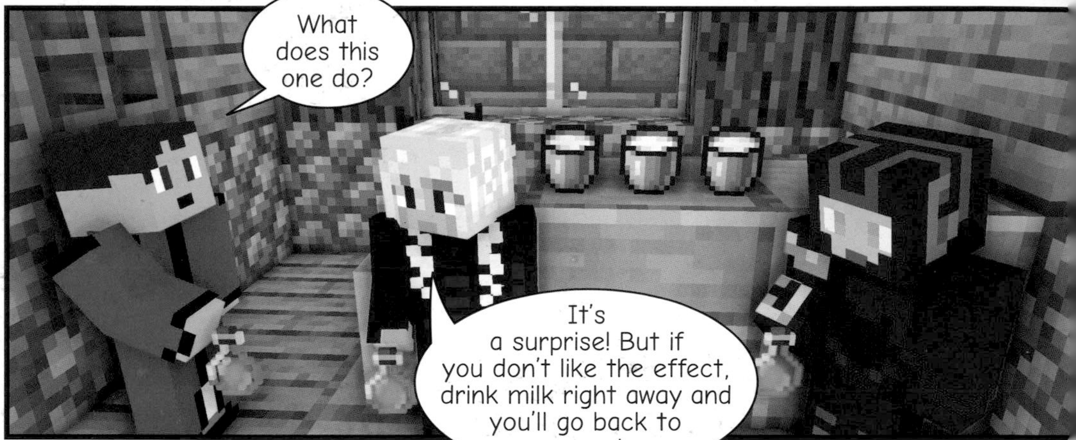
What does this one do?
It's a surprise! But if you don't like the effect, drink milk right away and you'll go back to normal.

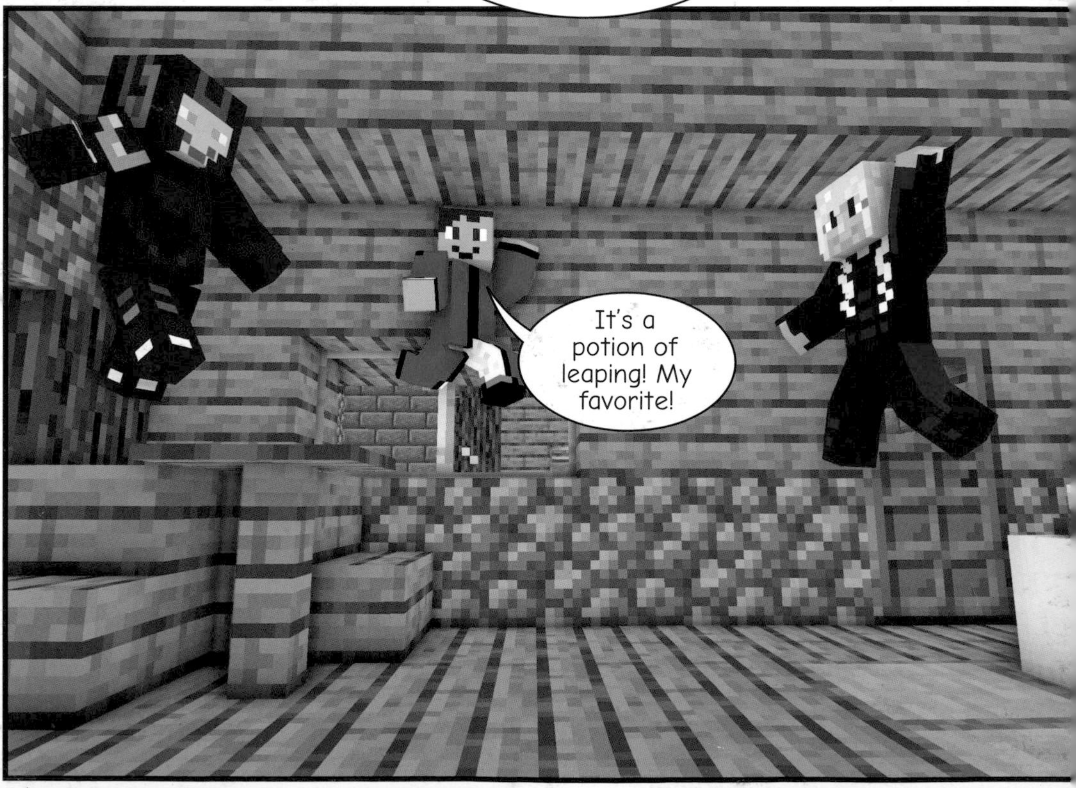
It's a potion of leaping! My favorite!

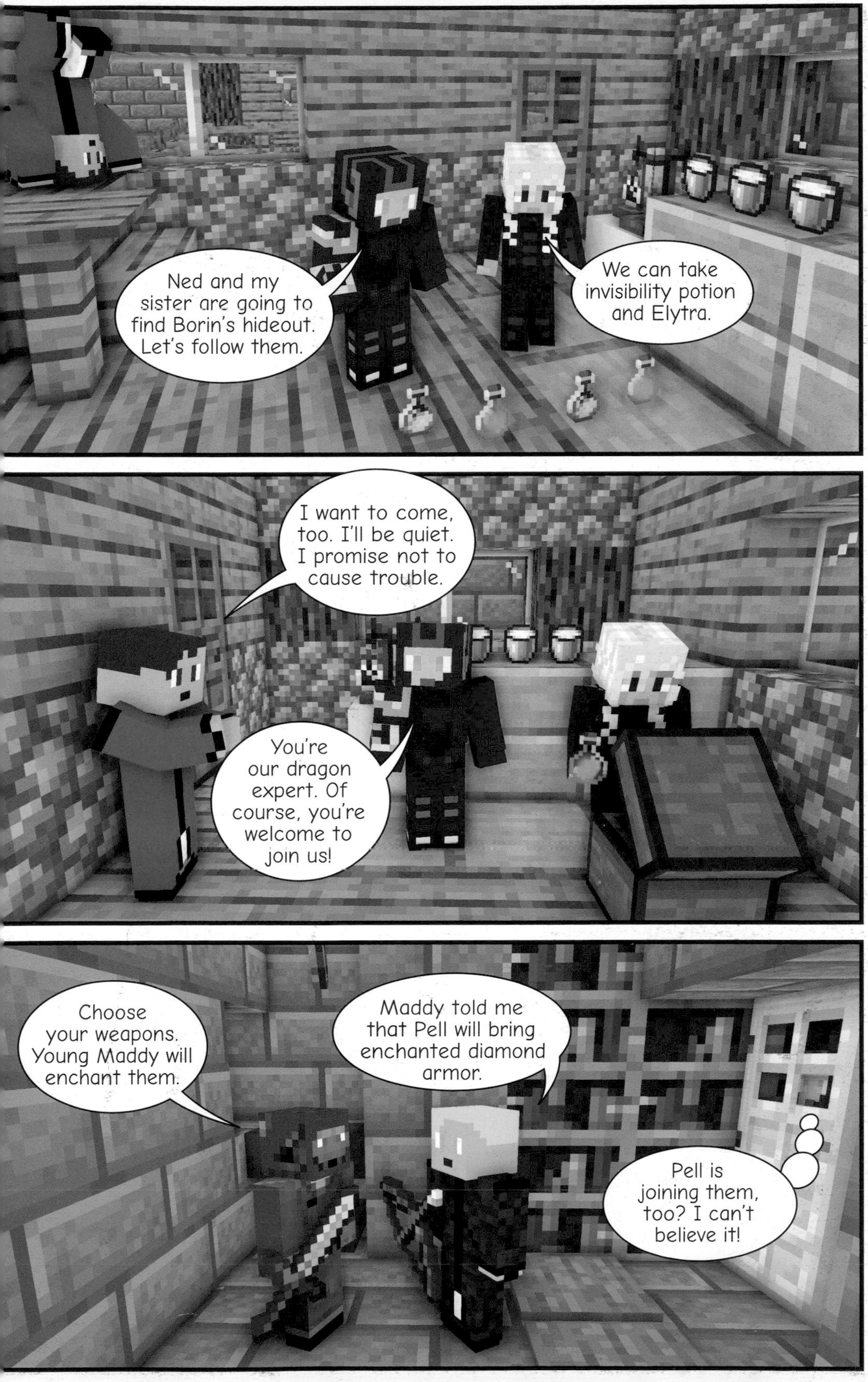

Ned and my sister are going to find Borin's hideout. Let's follow them.
We can take invisibility potion and Elytra.
I want to come, too. I'll be quiet. I promise not to cause trouble.
You're our dragon expert. Of course, you're welcome to join us!
Choose your weapons. Young Maddy will enchant them.
Maddy told me that Pell will bring enchanted diamond armor.
Pell is joining them, too? I can't believe it!

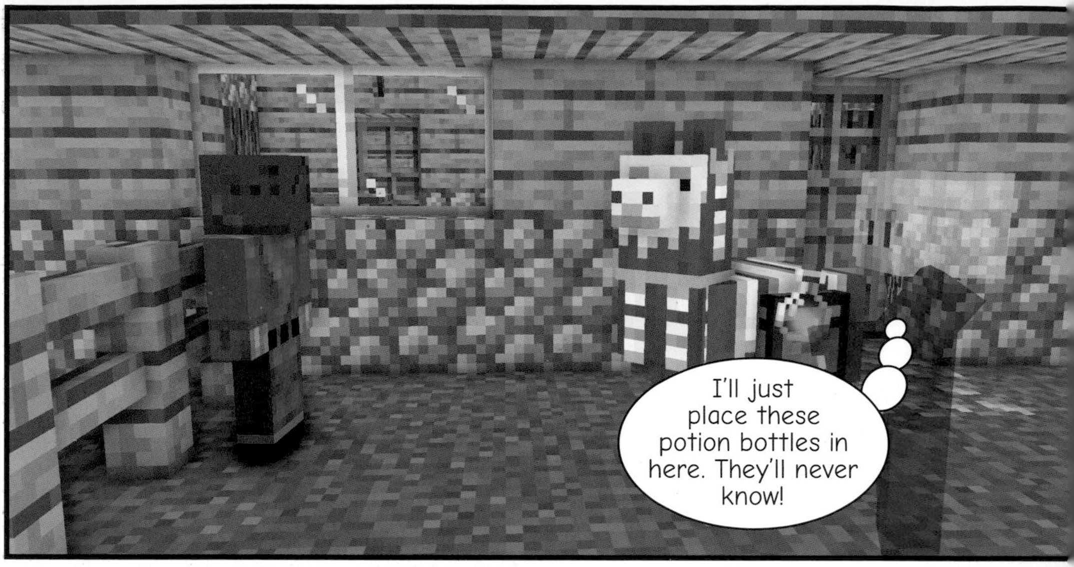
I'll just place these potion bottles in here. They'll never know!

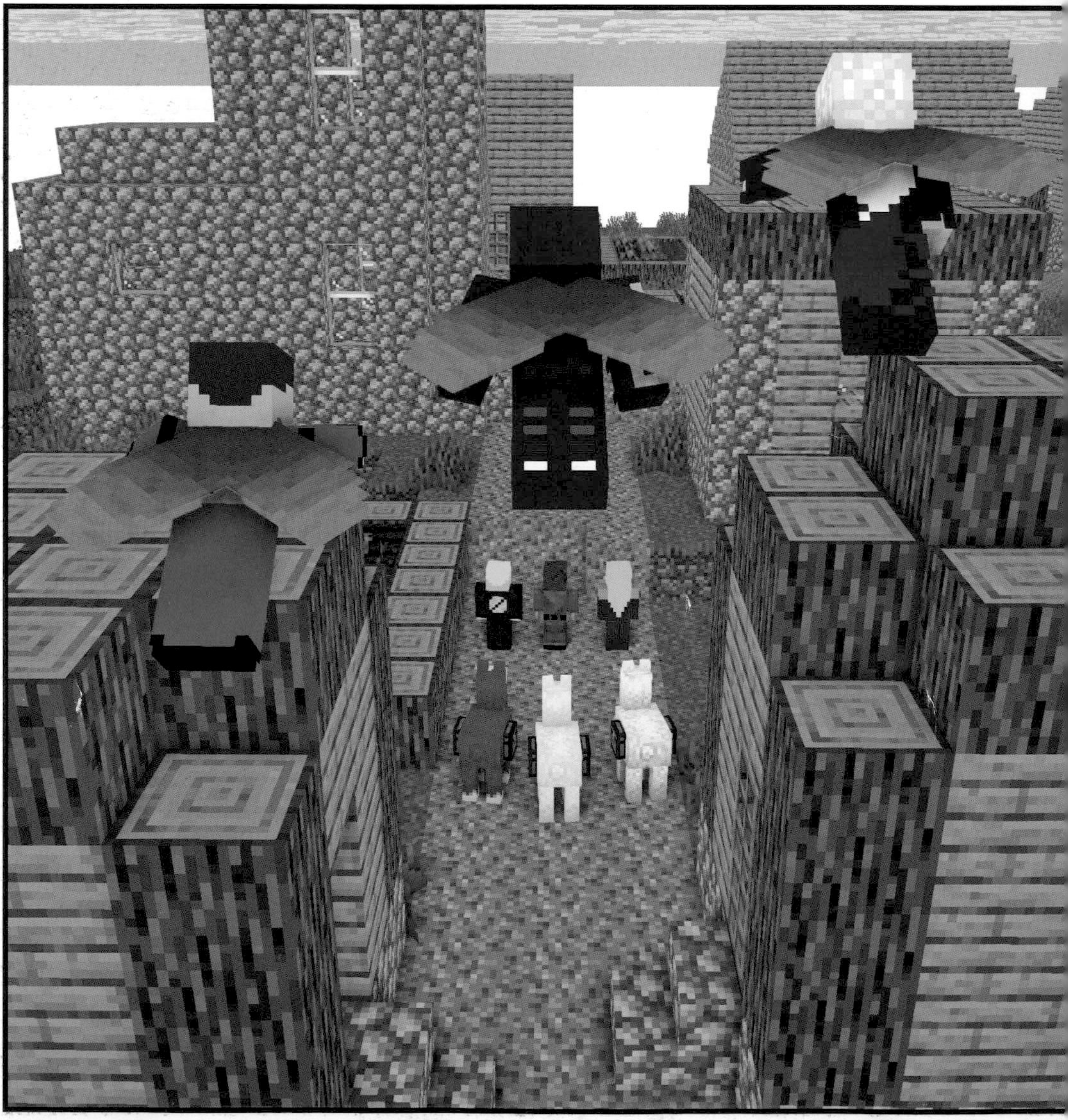

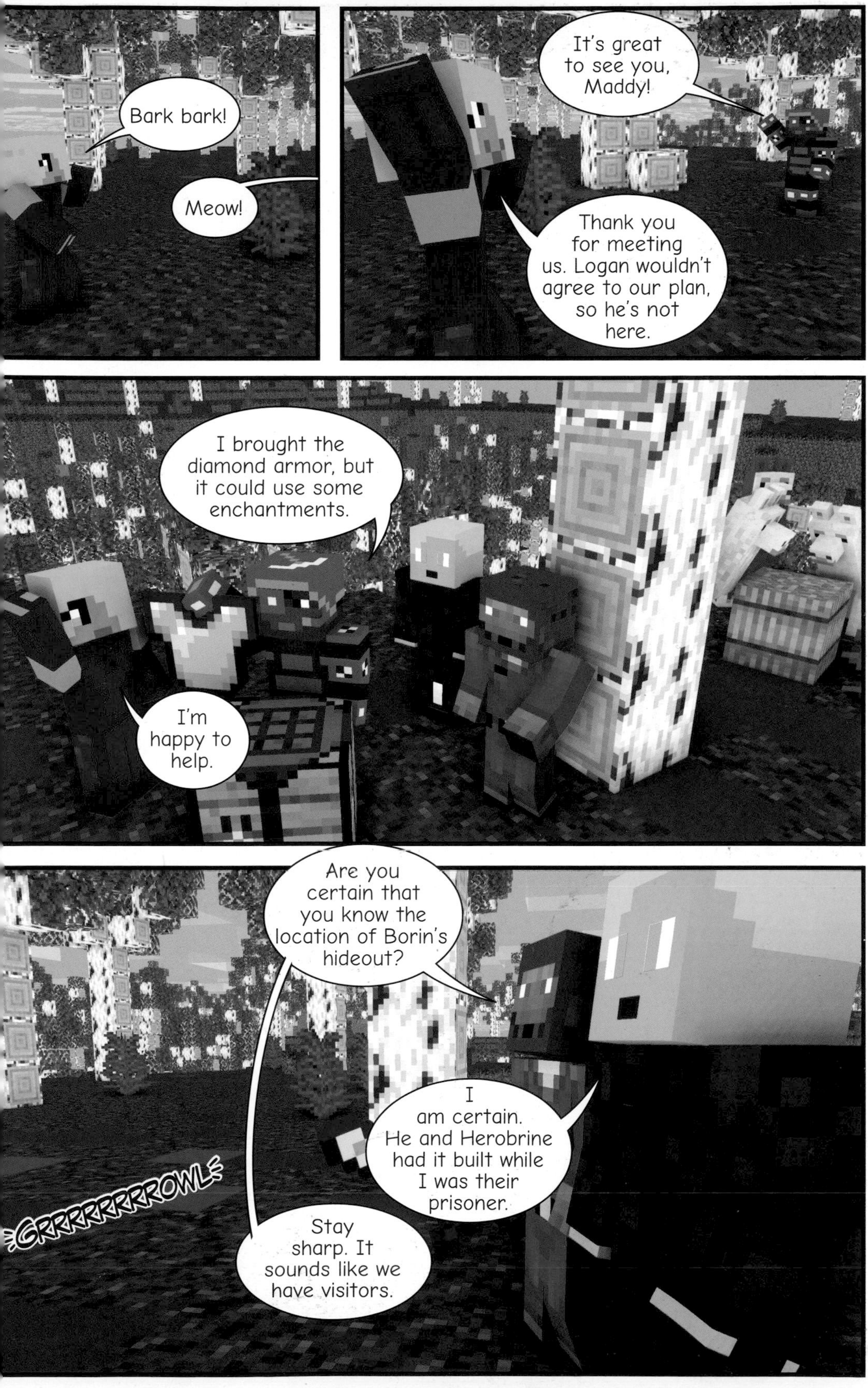
Bark bark!
Meow!
It's great to see you, Maddy!
Thank you for meeting us. Logan wouldn't agree to our plan, so he's not here.
I brought the diamond armor, but it could use some enchantments.
I'm happy to help.
Are you certain that you know the location of Borin's hideout?
I am certain. He and Herobrine had it built while I was their prisoner.
GRRRRRRRROWL
Stay sharp. It sounds like we have visitors.

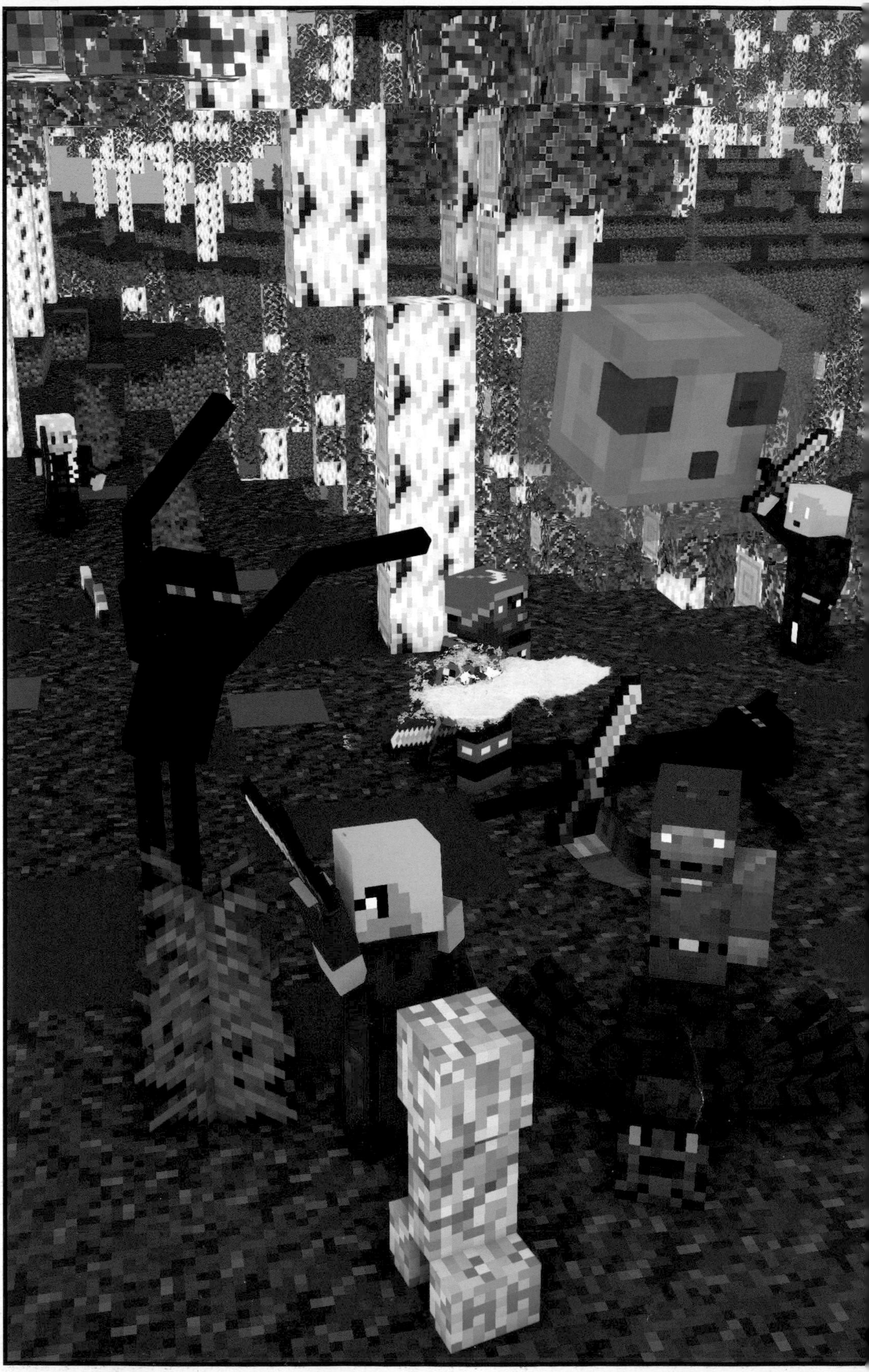

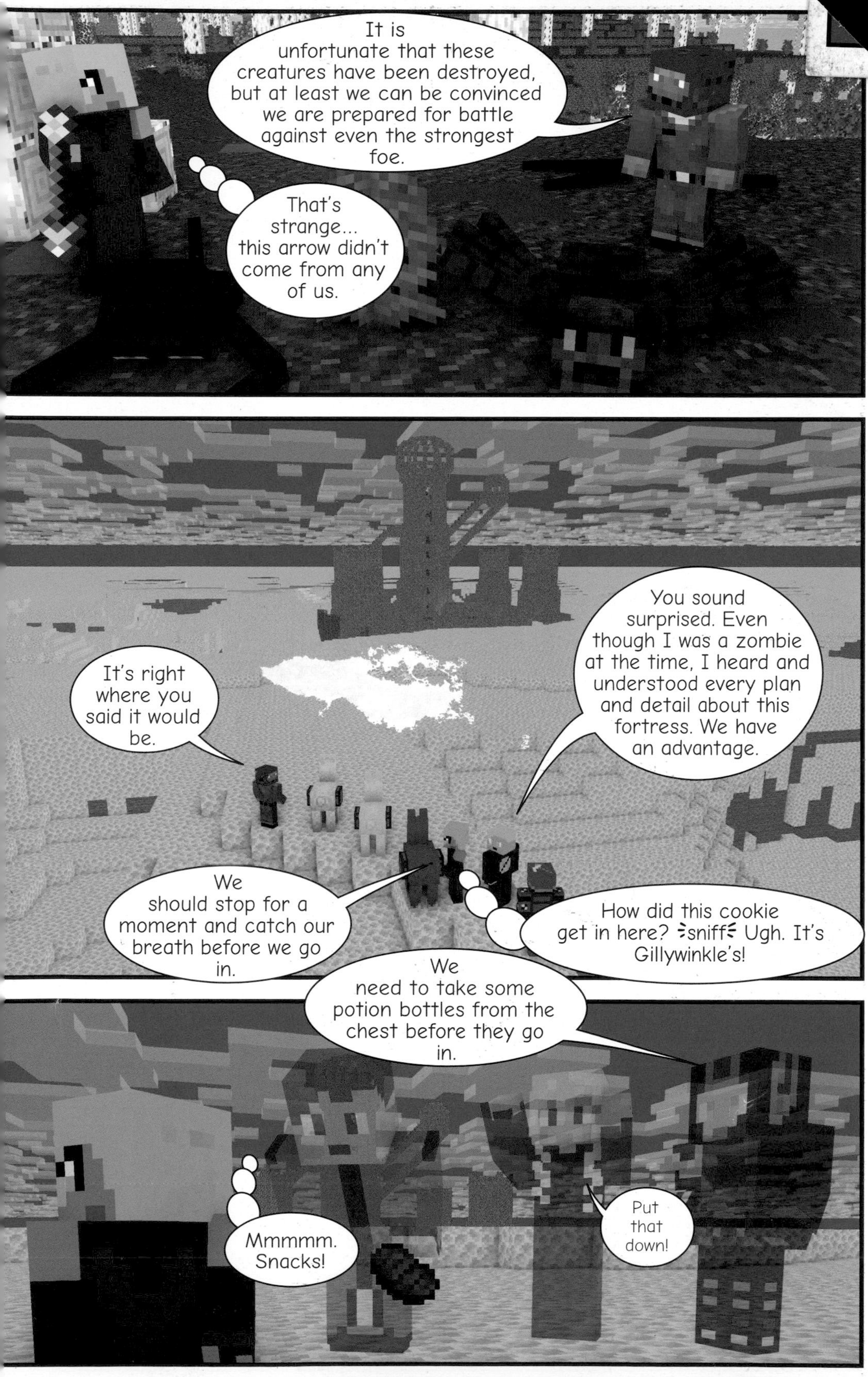
It is unfortunate that these creatures have been destroyed, but at least we can be convinced we are prepared for battle against even the strongest foe.
That's strange... this arrow didn't come from any of us.
It's right where you said it would be.
You sound surprised. Even though I was a zombie at the time, I heard and understood every plan and detail about this fortress. We have an advantage.
We should stop for a moment and catch our breath before we go in.
How did this cookie get in here? sniff Ugh. It's Gillywinkle's!
We need to take some potion bottles from the chest before they go in.
Mmmmm. Snacks!
Put that down!

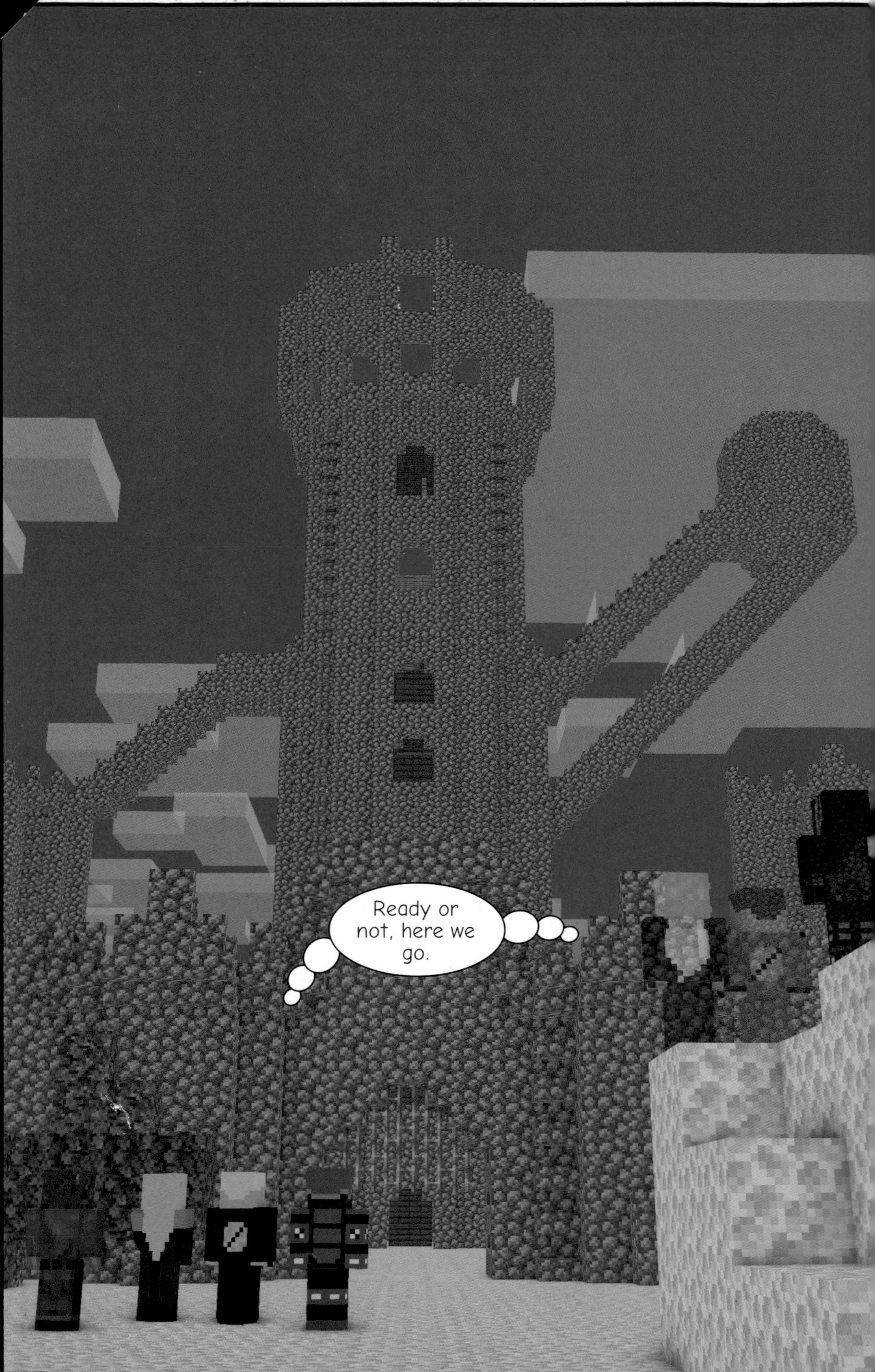
Ready or not, here we go.

CHAPTER 10

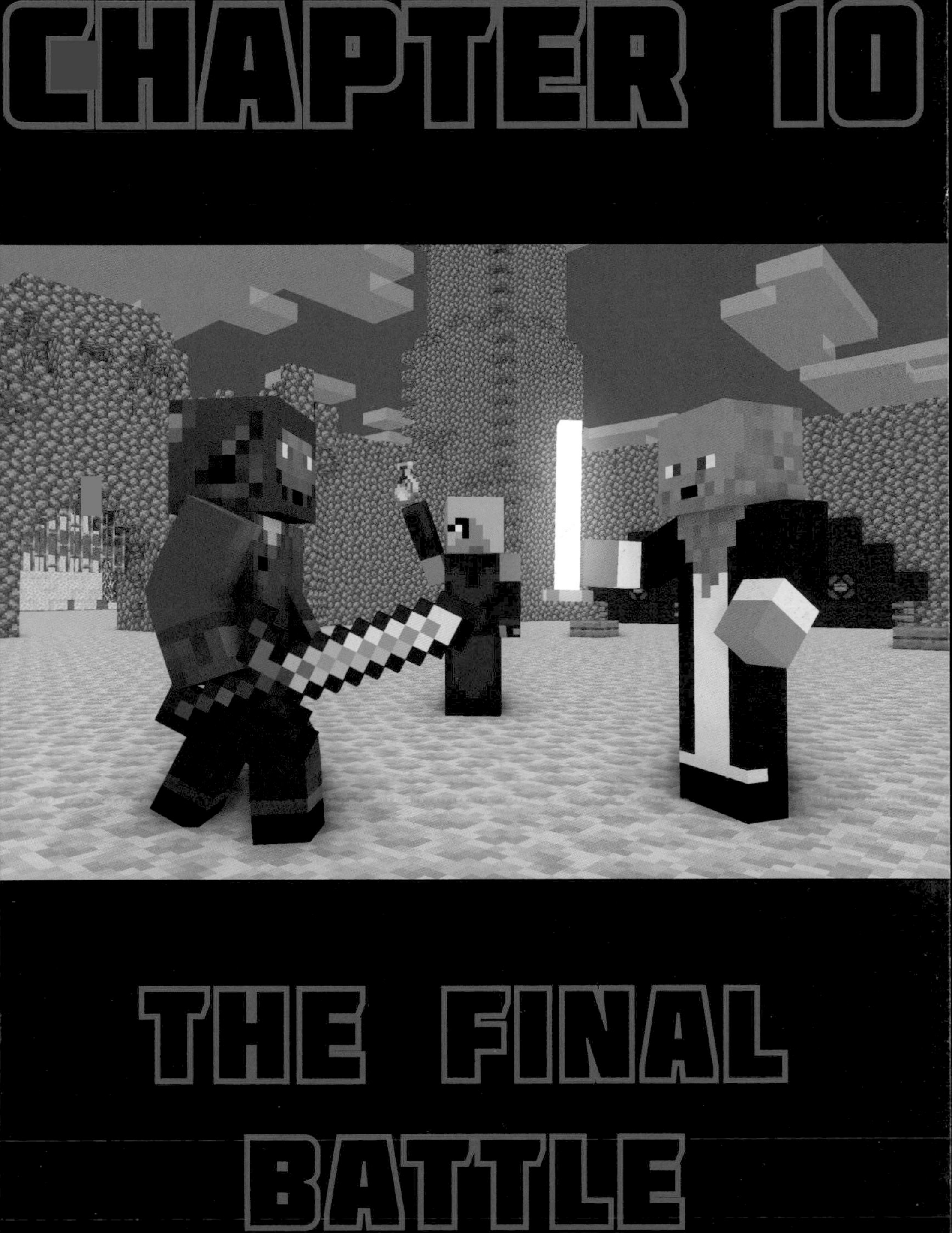

THE FINAL BATTLE

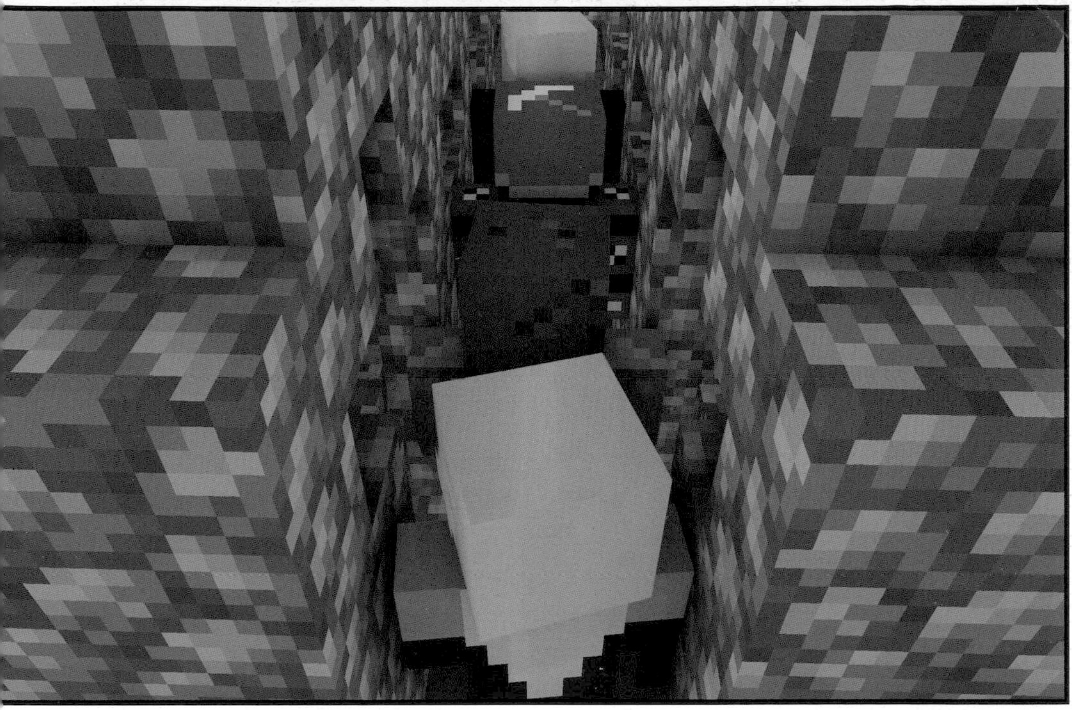

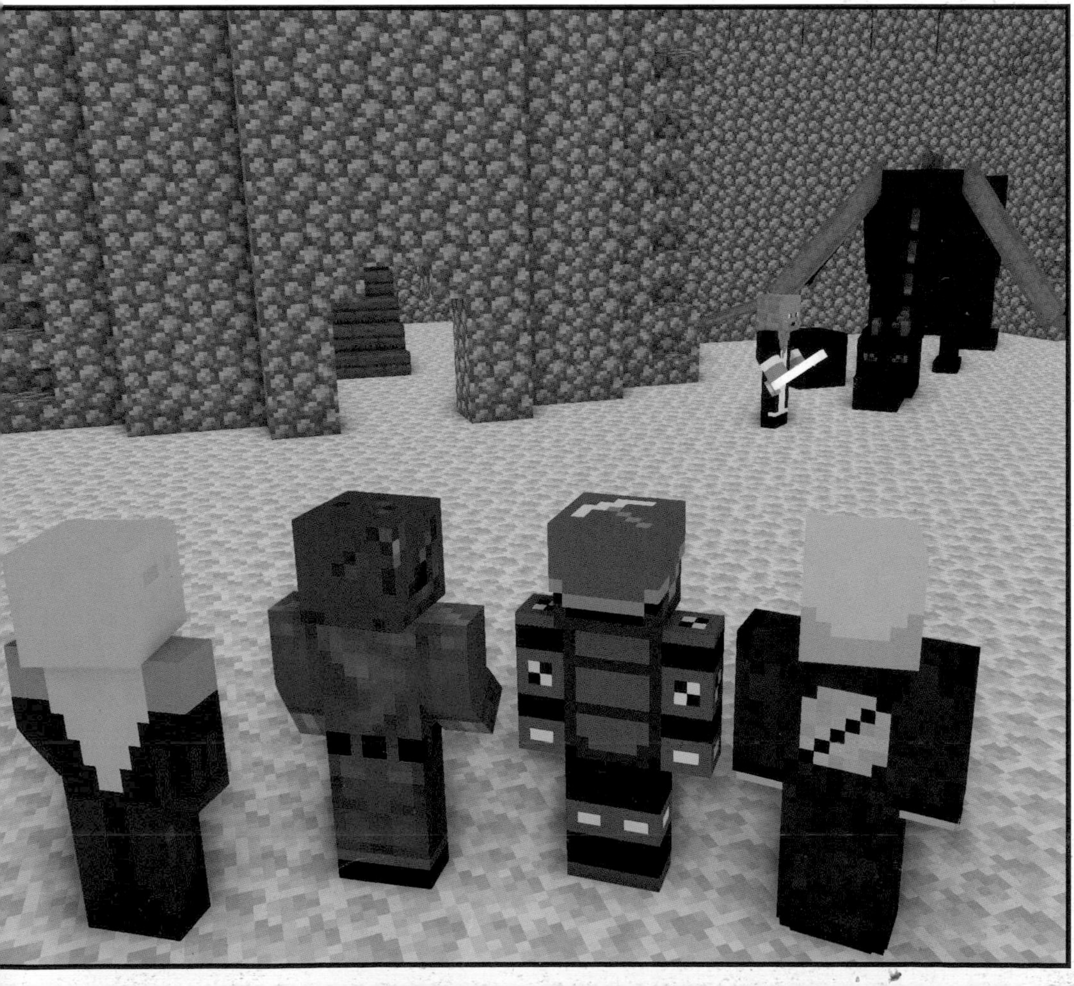

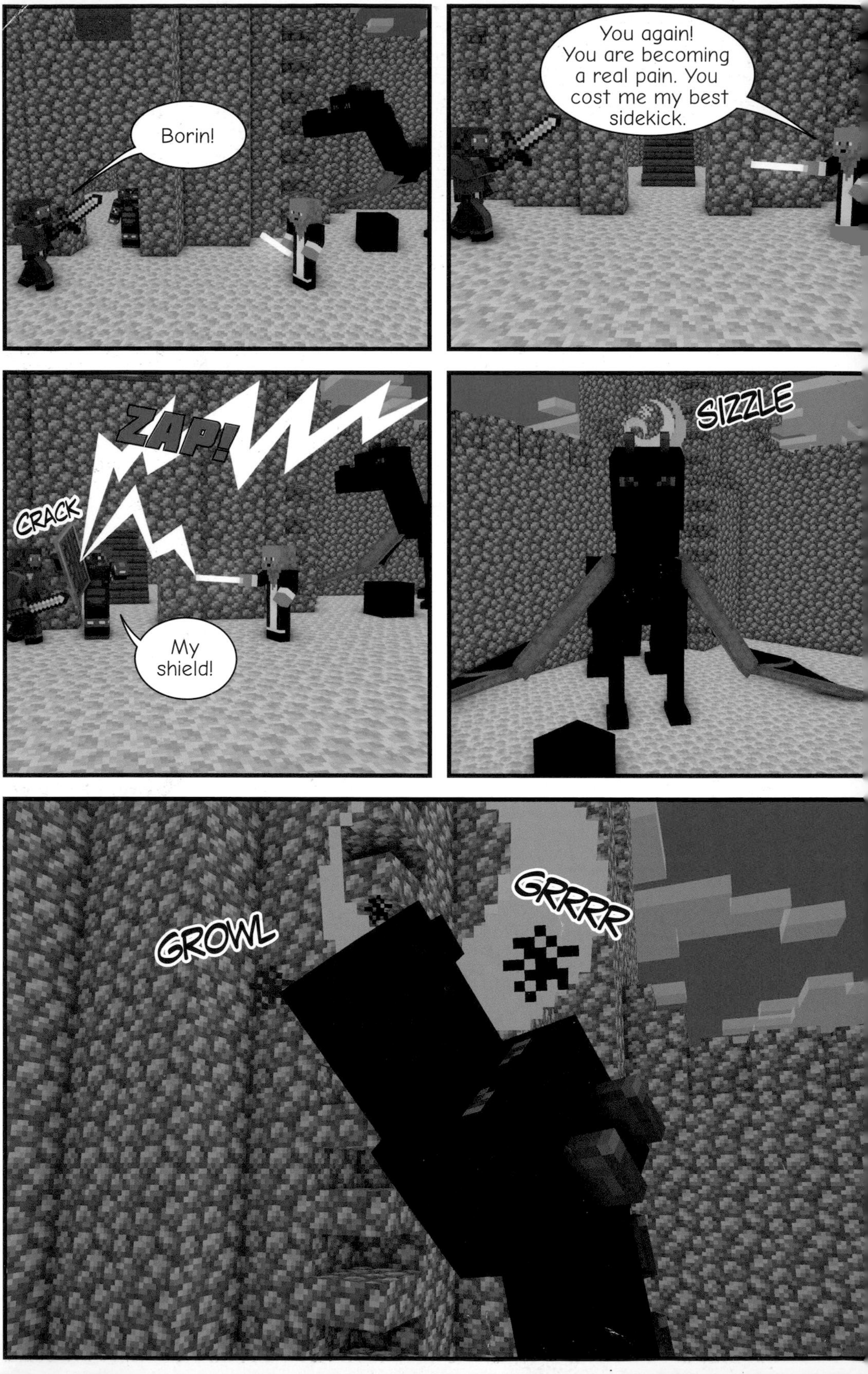
Borin!
You again! You are becoming a real pain. You cost me my best sidekick.
ZAP!
CRACK
My shield!
SIZZLE
GROWL
GRRRR

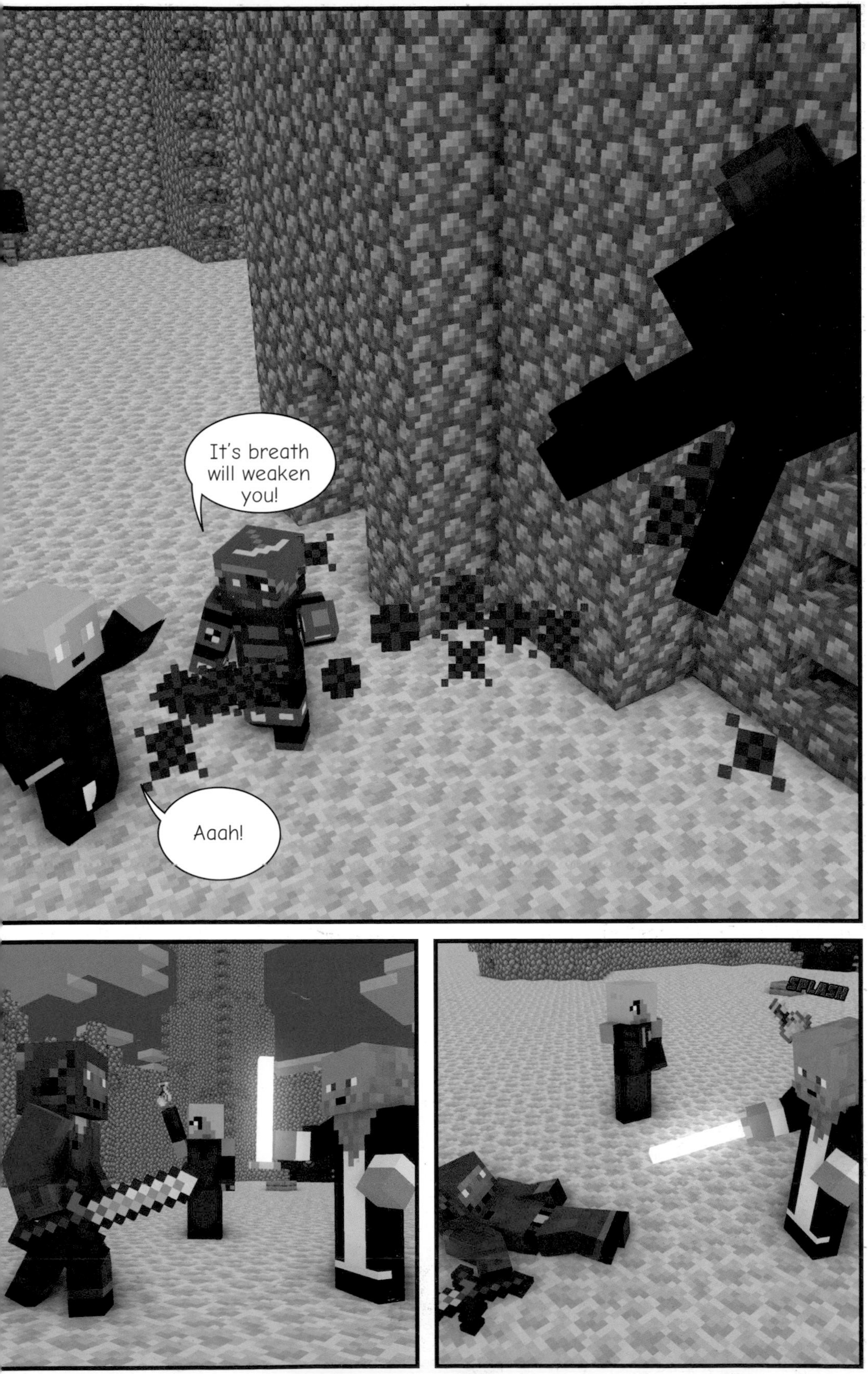
It's breath will weaken you!
Aaah!
SPLASH

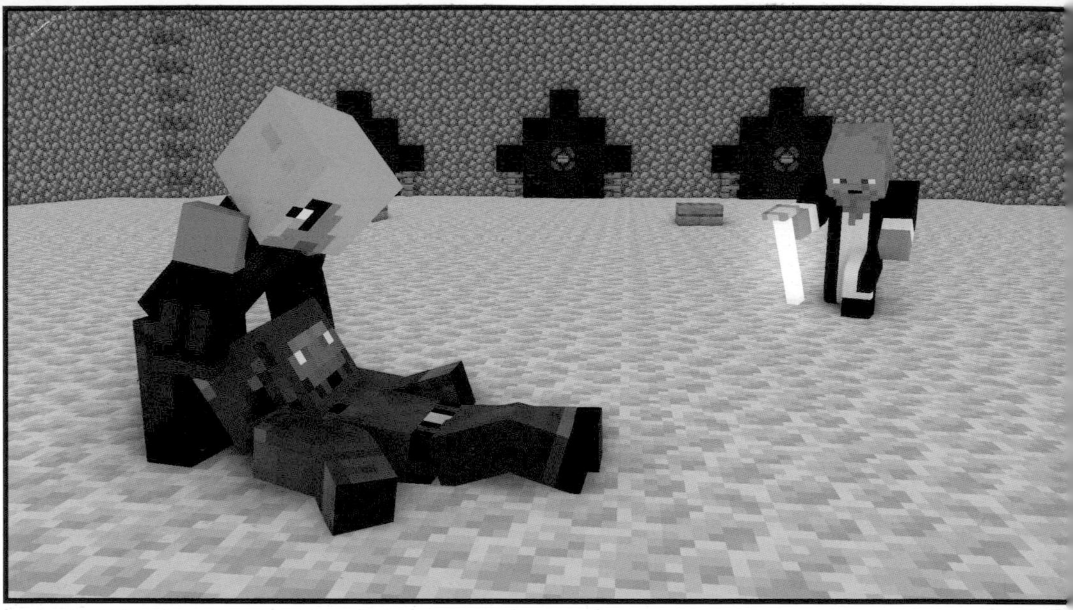

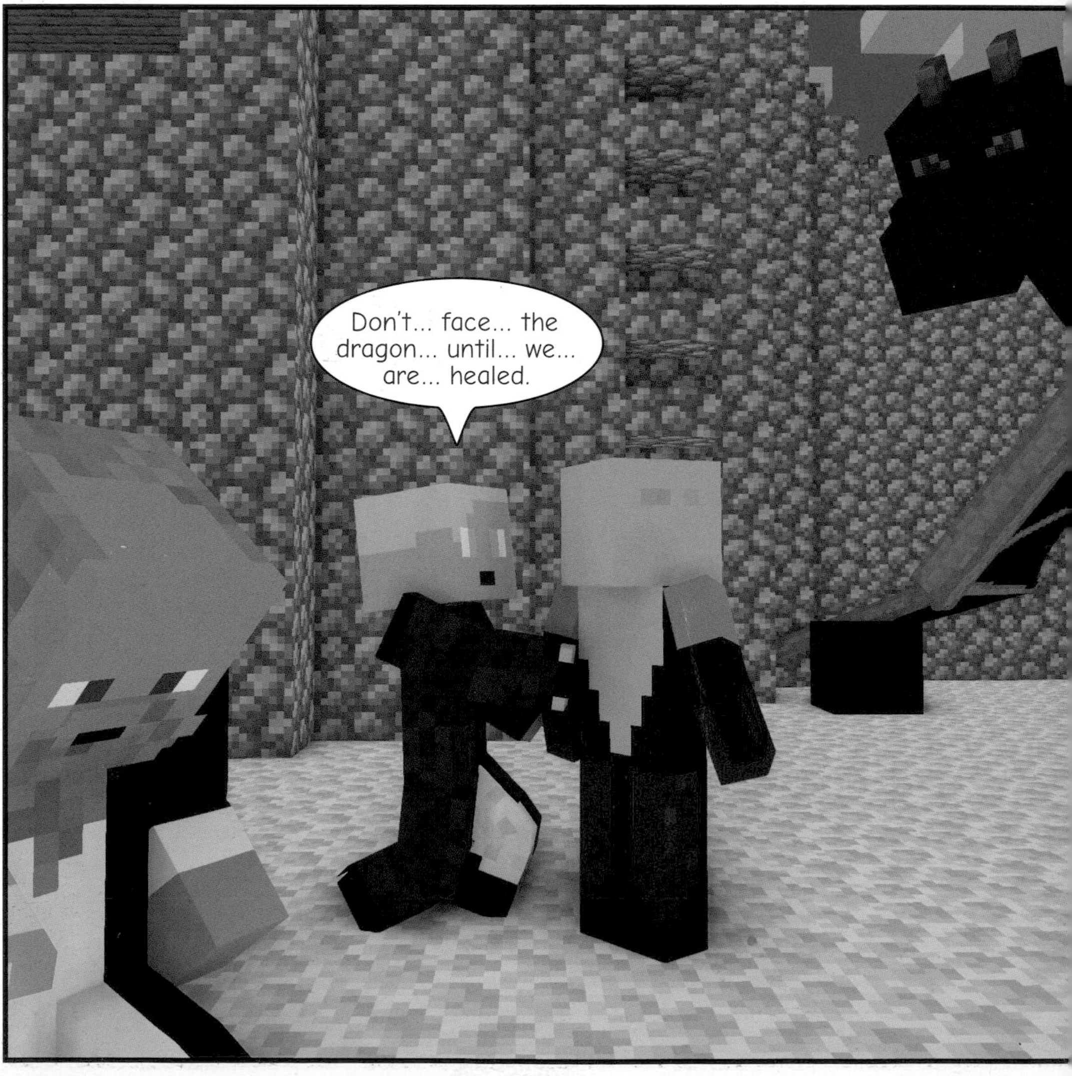
Don't... face... the dragon... until... we... are... healed.

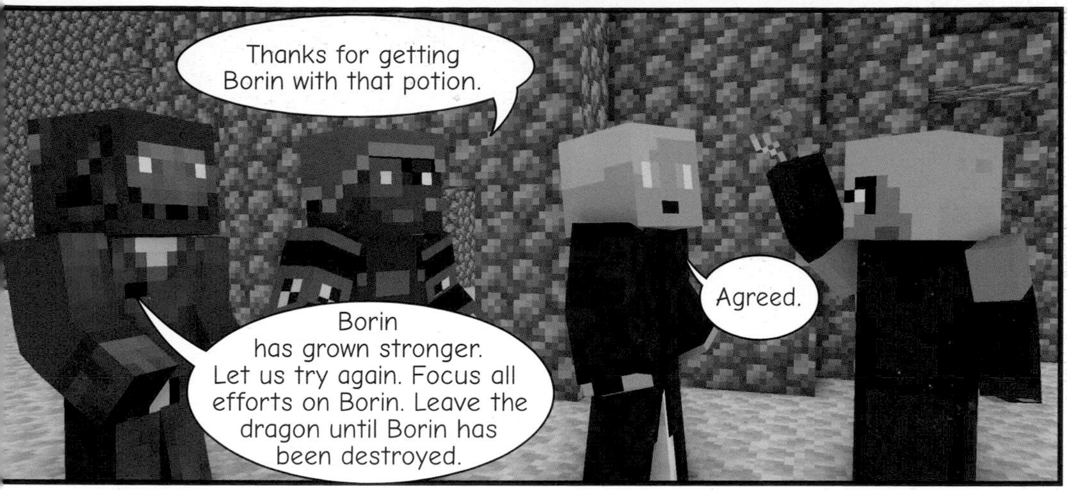
Thanks for getting Borin with that potion.
Borin has grown stronger. Let us try again. Focus all efforts on Borin. Leave the dragon until Borin has been destroyed.
Agreed.

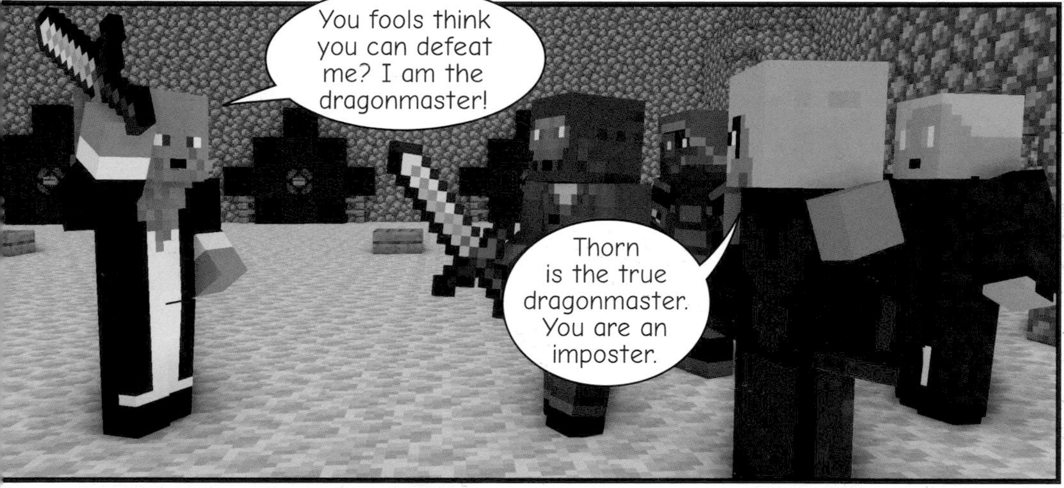
You fools think you can defeat me? I am the dragonmaster!
Thorn is the true dragonmaster. You are an imposter.

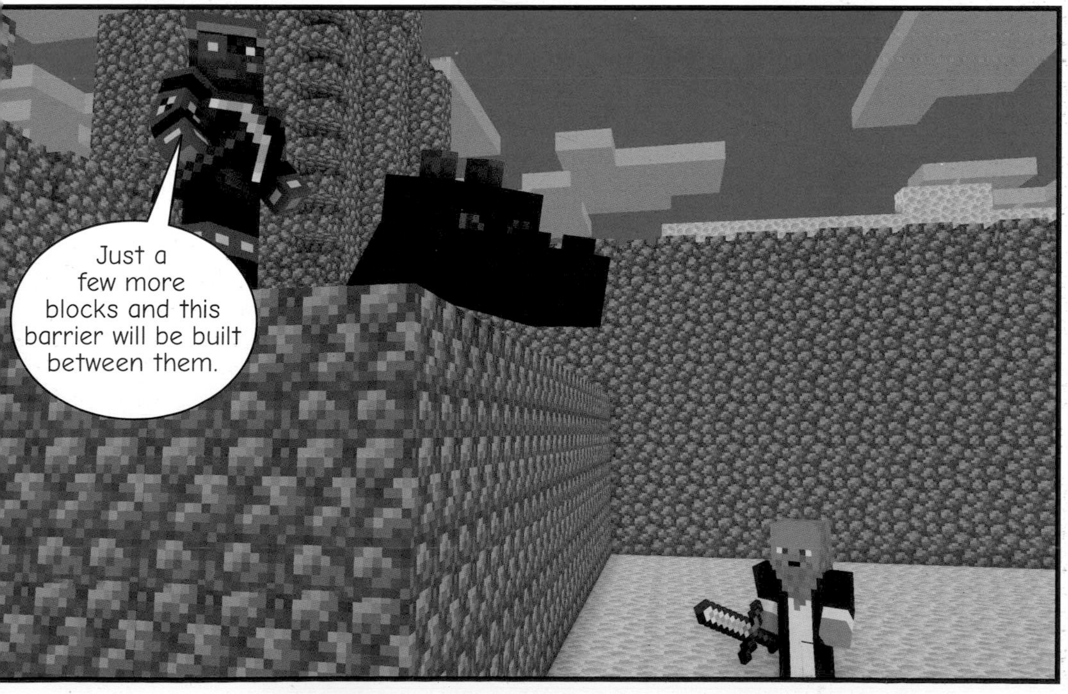
Just a few more blocks and this barrier will be built between them.

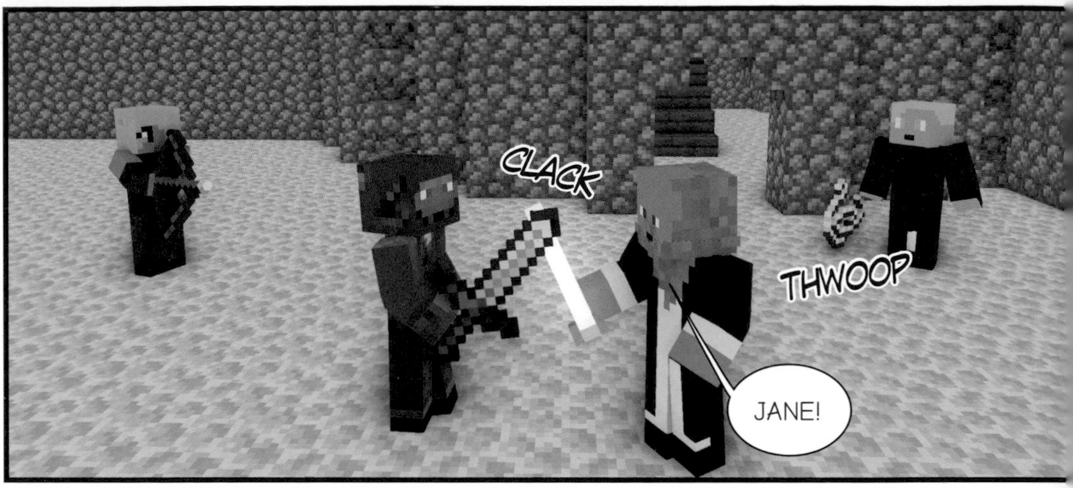
CLACK
THWOOP
JANE!
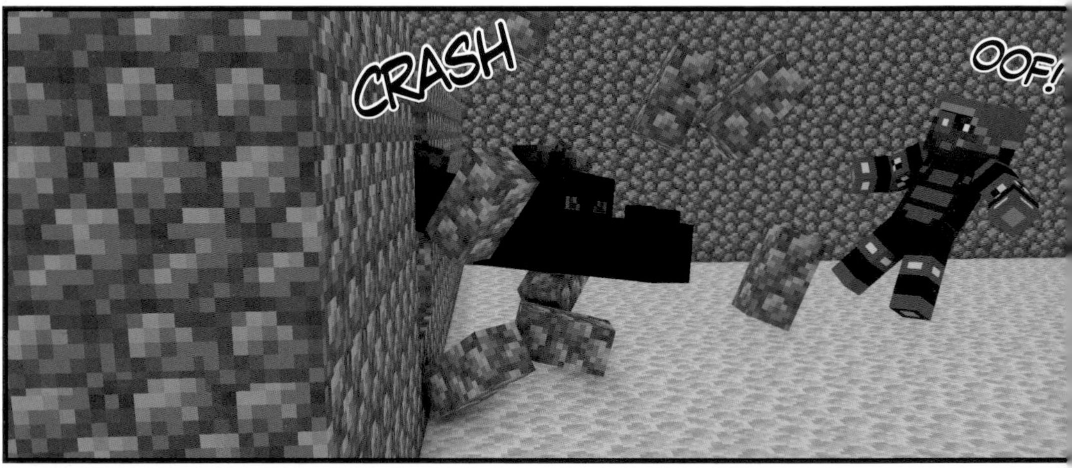
CRASH
OOF!
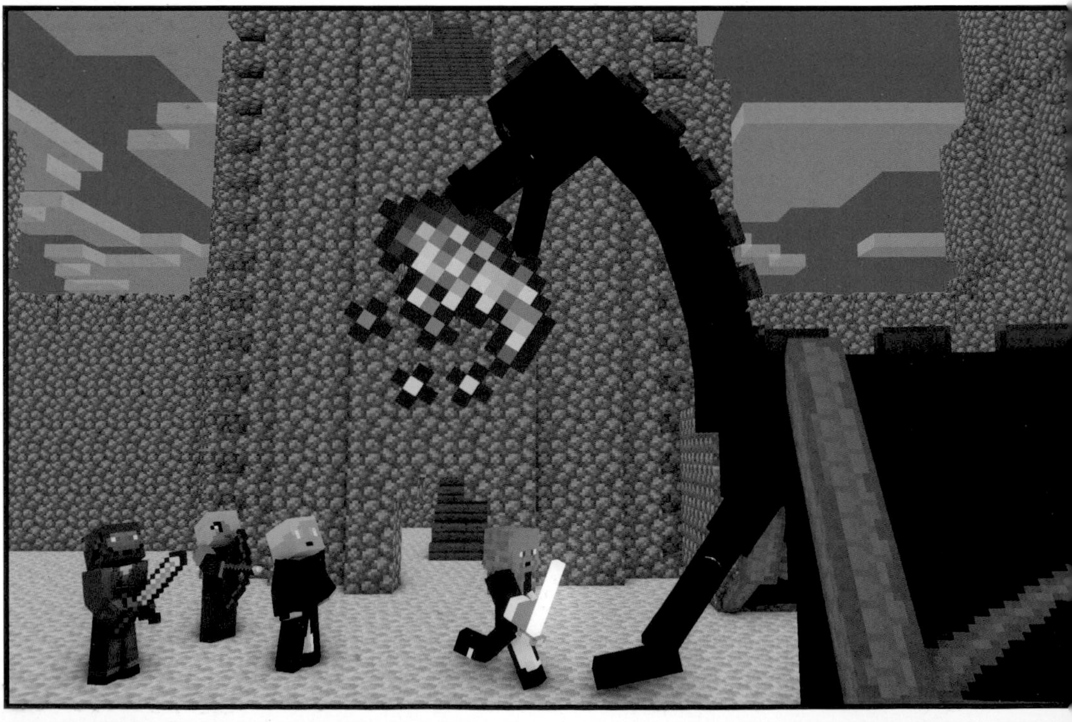

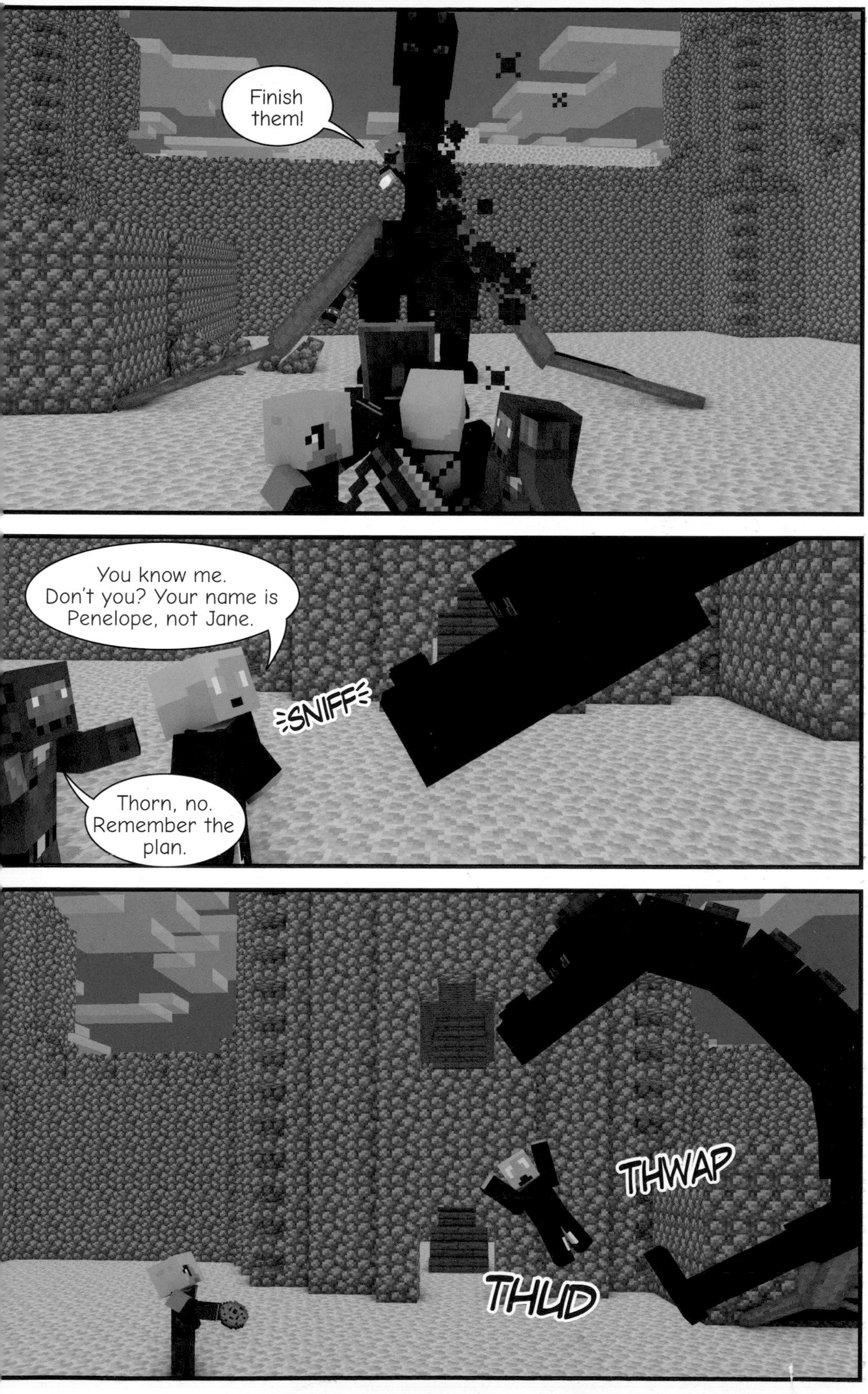
Finish them!
You know me. Don't you? Your name is Penelope, not Jane.
SNIFF
Thorn, no. Remember the plan.
THWAP
THUD

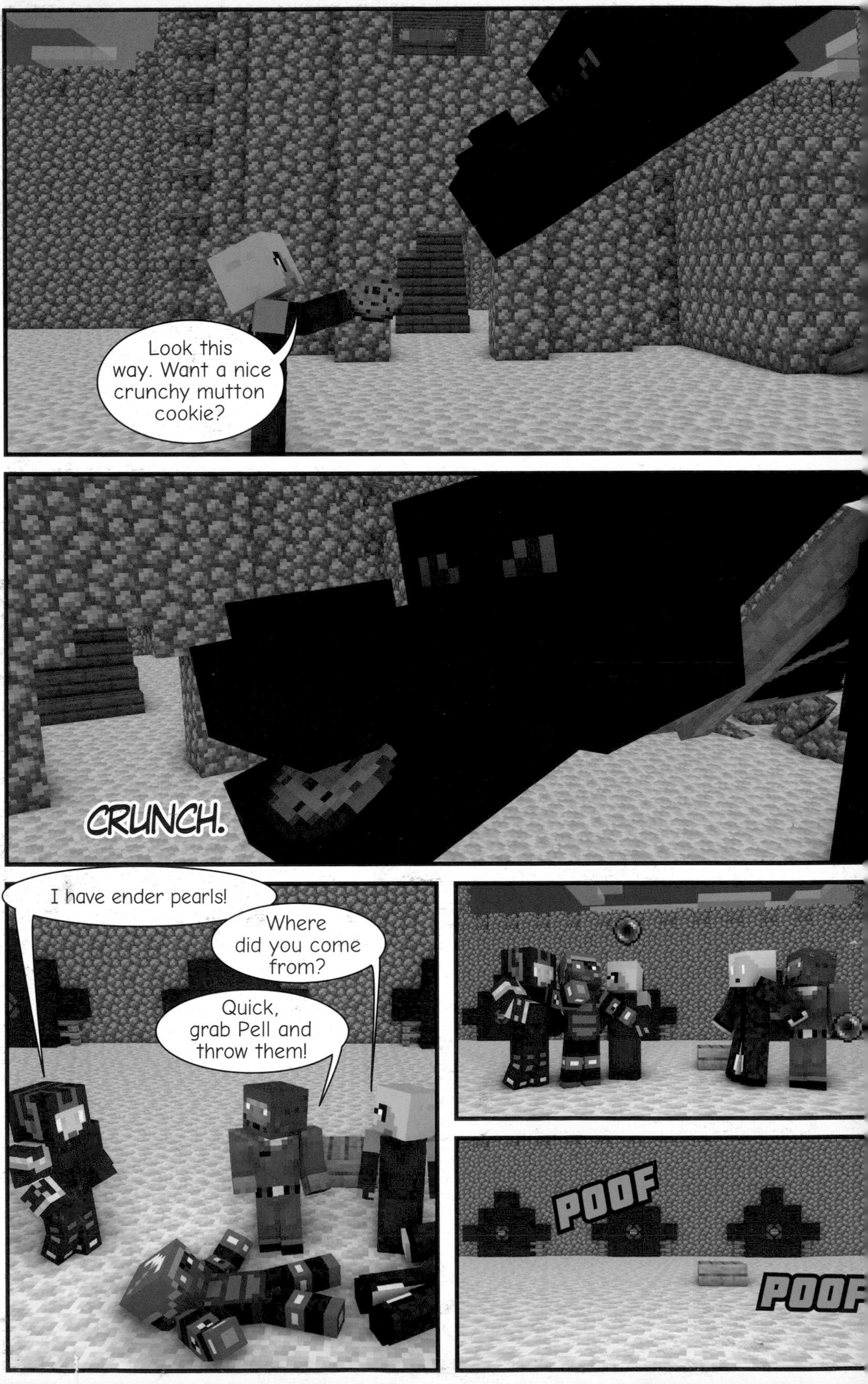
Look this way. Want a nice crunchy mutton cookie?
CRUNCH.
I have ender pearls!
Where did you come from?
Quick, grab Pell and throw them!
POOF
POOF

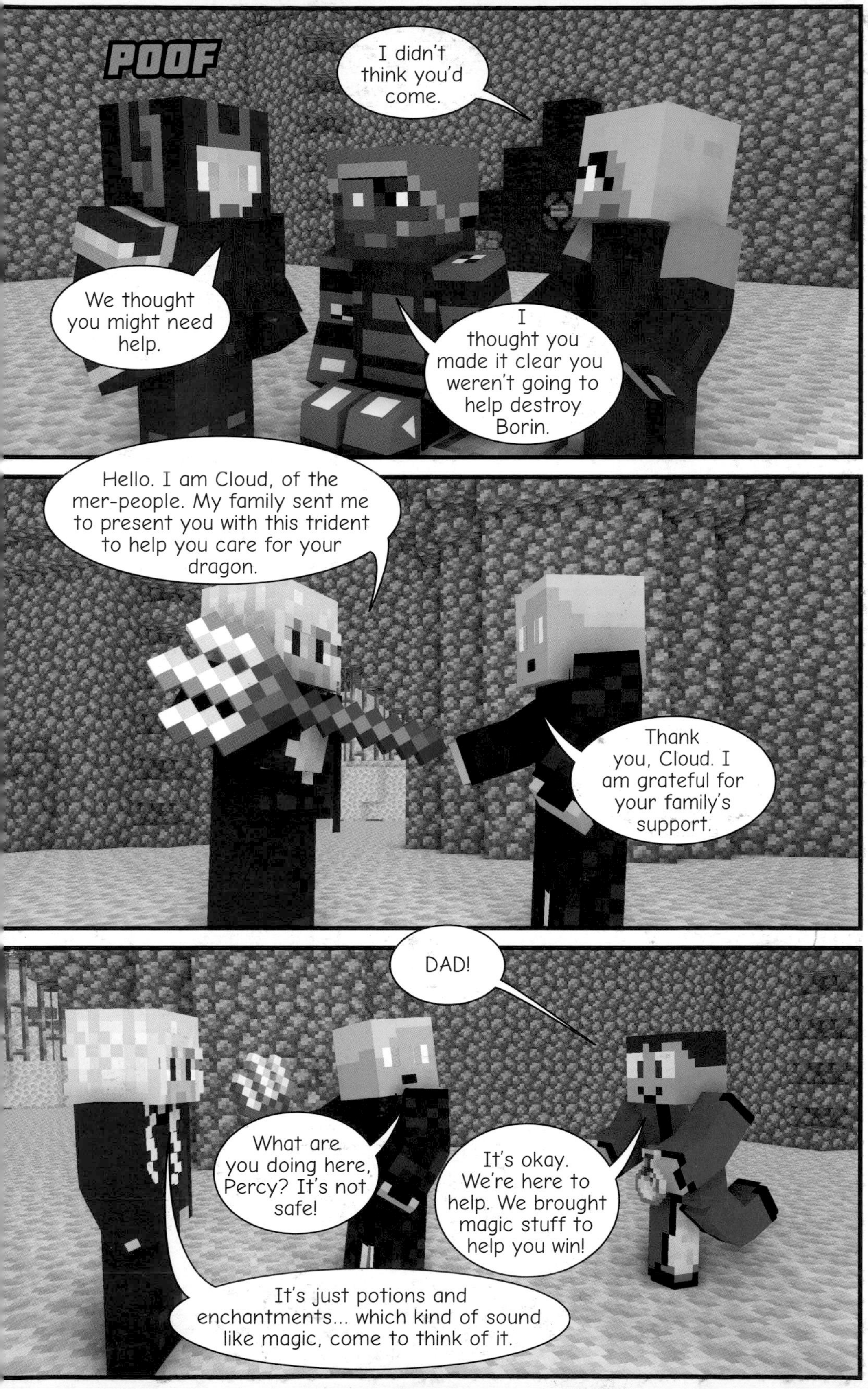
POOF
I didn't think you'd come.
We thought you might need help.
I thought you made it clear you weren't going to help destroy Borin.
Hello. I am Cloud, of the mer-people. My family sent me to present you with this trident to help you care for your dragon.
Thank you, Cloud. I am grateful for your family's support.
DAD!
What are you doing here, Percy? It's not safe!
It's okay. We're here to help. We brought magic stuff to help you win!
It's just potions and enchantments... which kind of sound like magic, come to think of it.

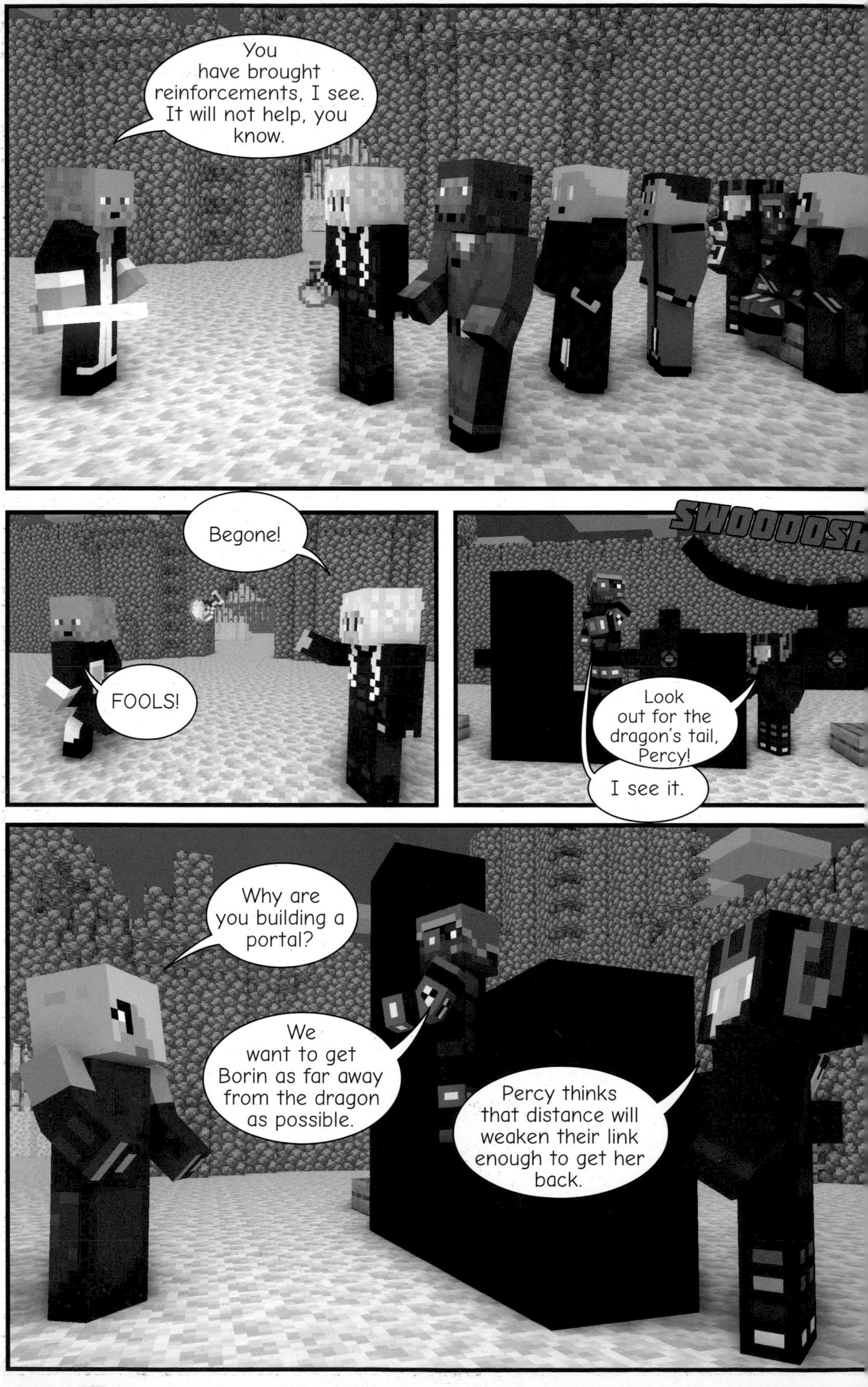

You have brought reinforcements, I see. It will not help, you know.
Begone!
FOOLS!
SWOOOOSH
Look out for the dragon's tail, Percy!
I see it.
Why are you building a portal?
We want to get Borin as far away from the dragon as possible.
Percy thinks that distance will weaken their link enough to get her back.

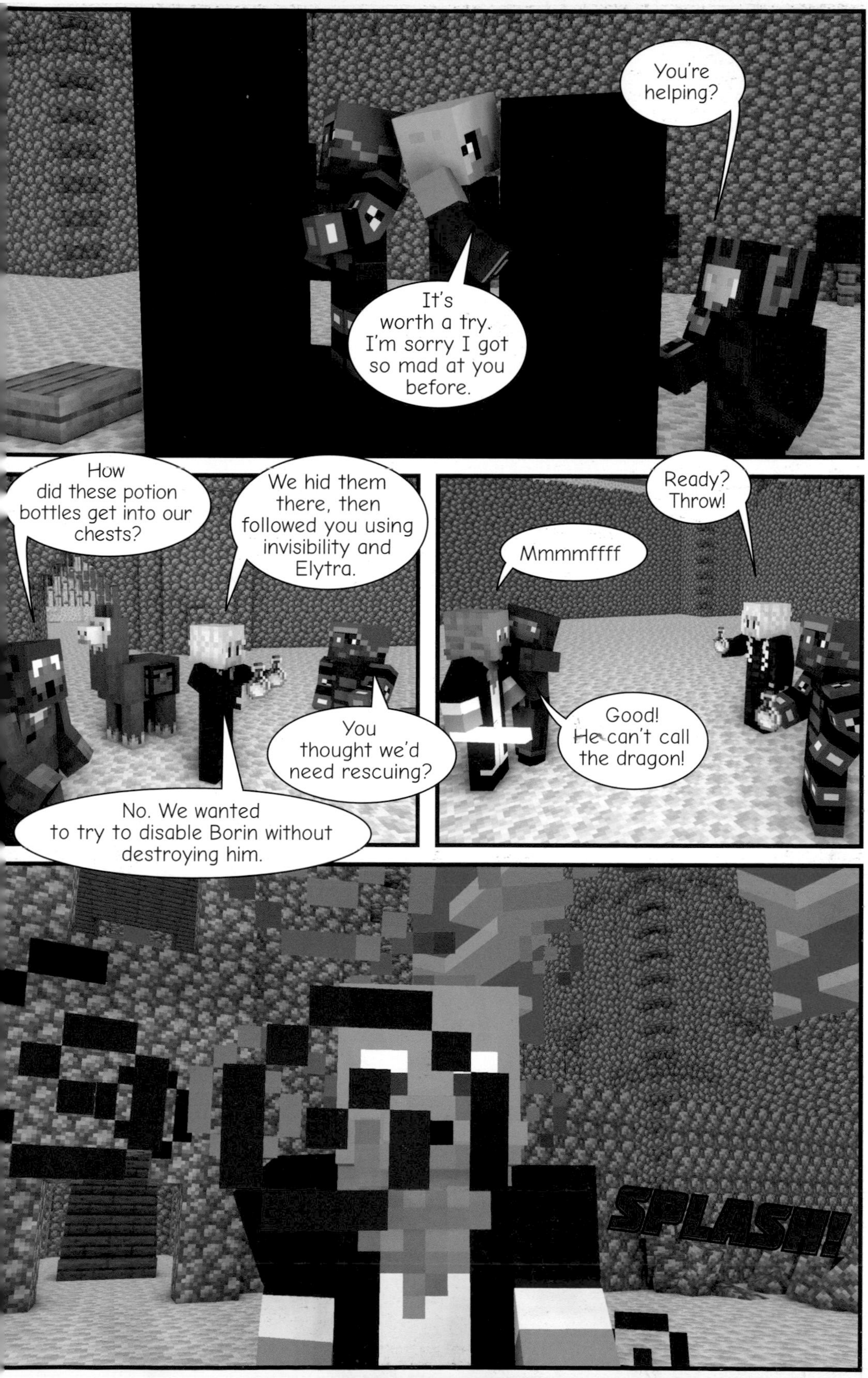
You're helping?
It's worth a try. I'm sorry I got so mad at you before.
How did these potion bottles get into our chests?
We hid them there, then followed you using invisibility and Elytra.
You thought we'd need rescuing?
No. We wanted to try to disable Borin without destroying him.
Ready? Throw!
Mmmmffff
Good! He can't call the dragon!
SPLASH!

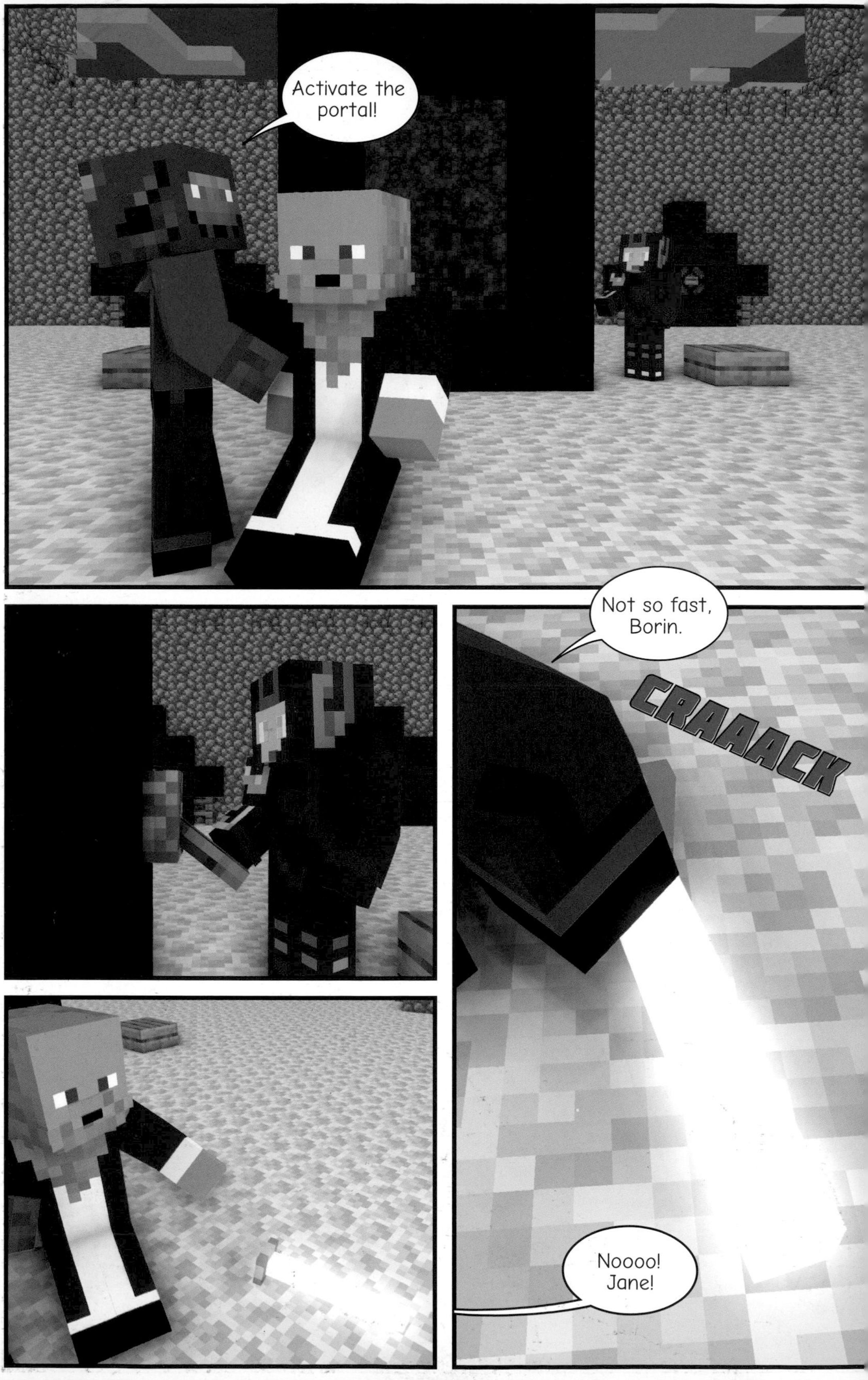
Activate the portal!
Not so fast, Borin.
CRAAACK
Noooo! Jane!

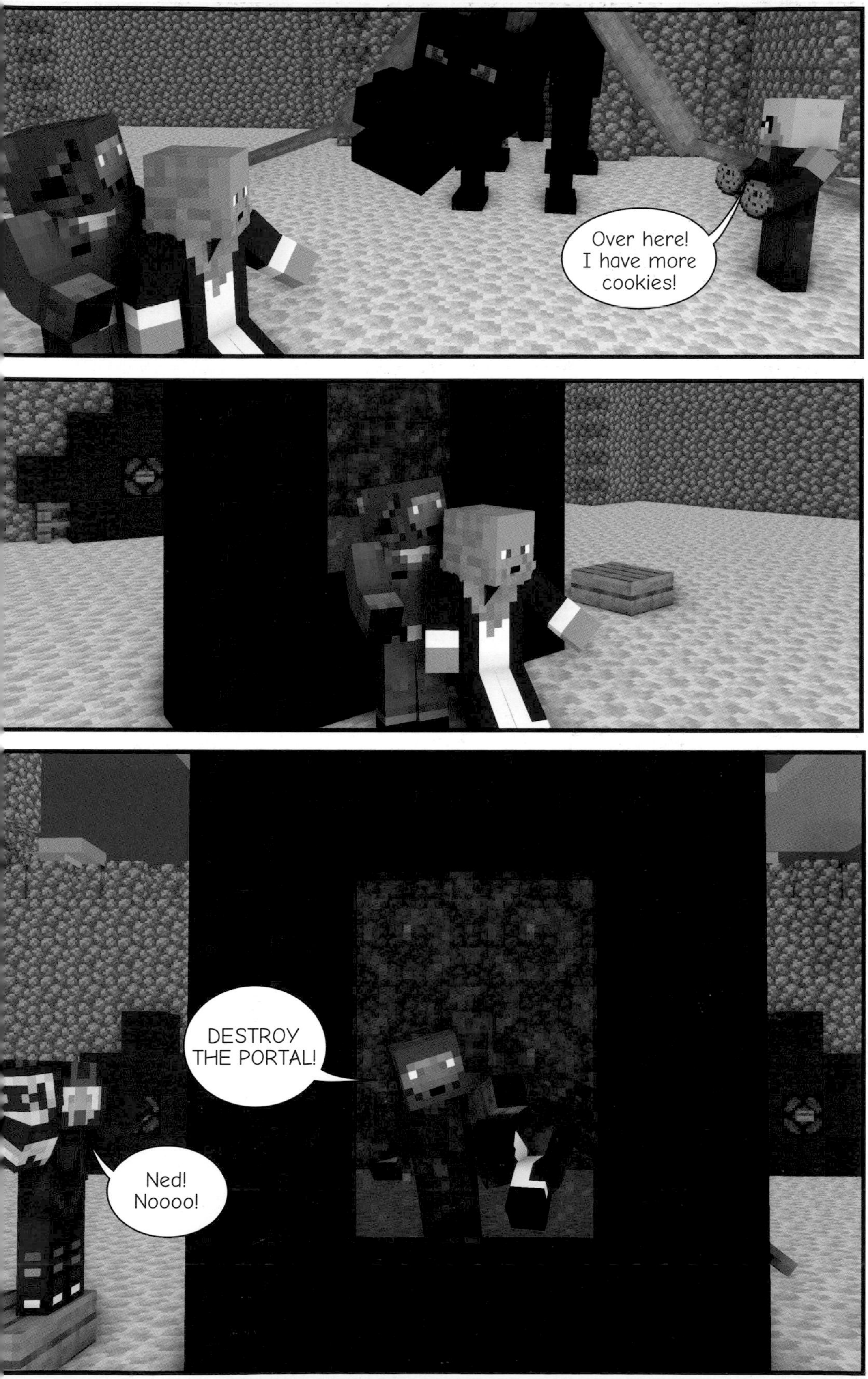
Over here! I have more cookies!
DESTROY THE PORTAL!
Ned! Noooo!

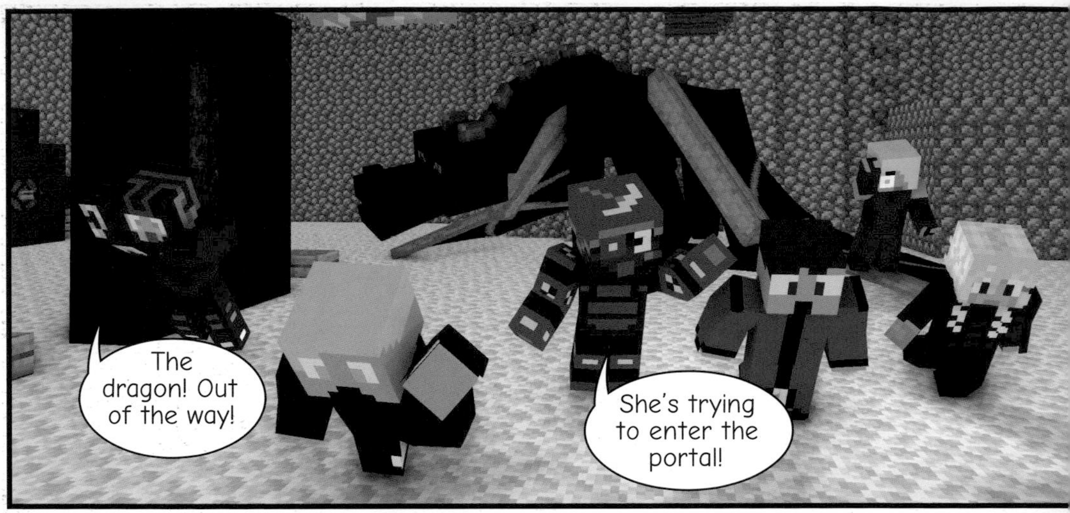
The dragon! Out of the way!
She's trying to enter the portal!

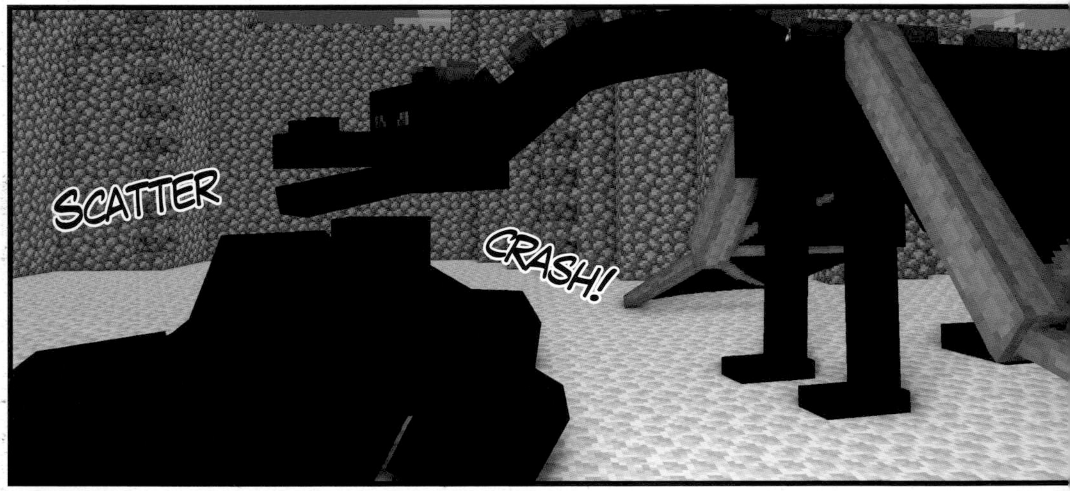
SCATTER
CRASH!

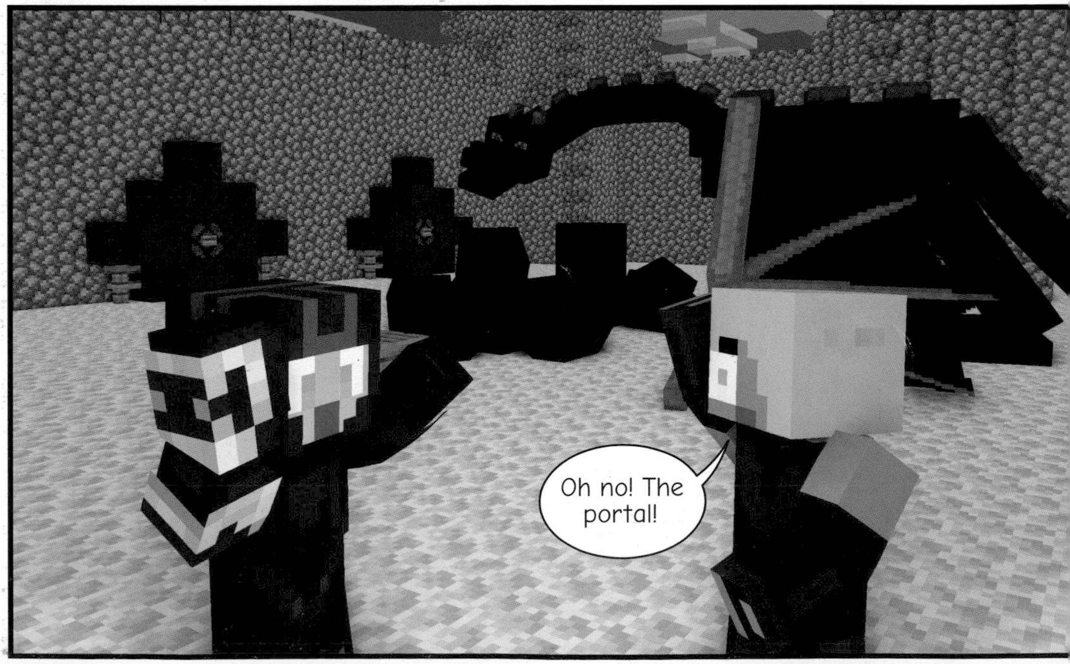
Oh no! The portal!

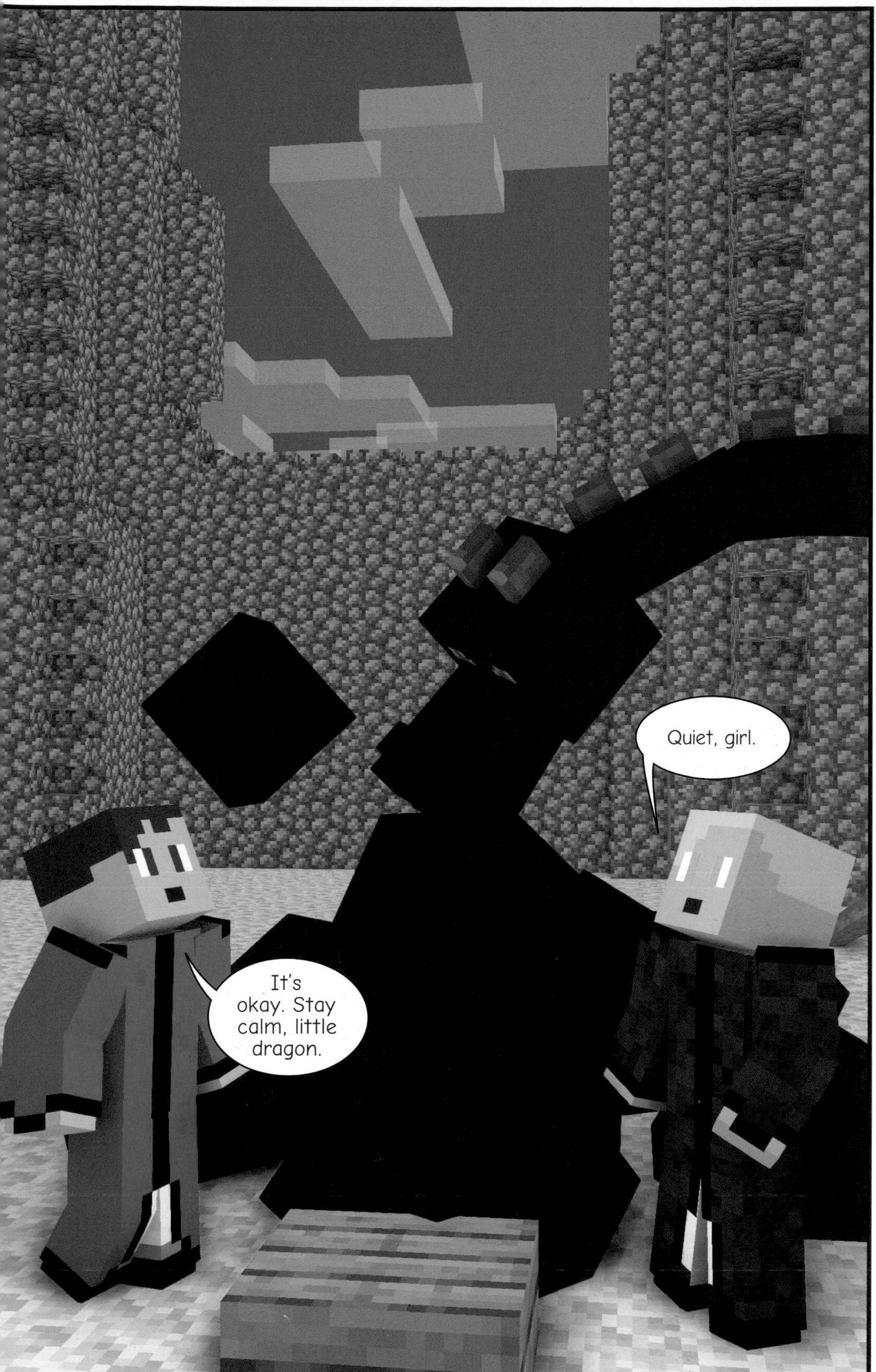
Quiet, girl.
It's okay. Stay calm, little dragon.

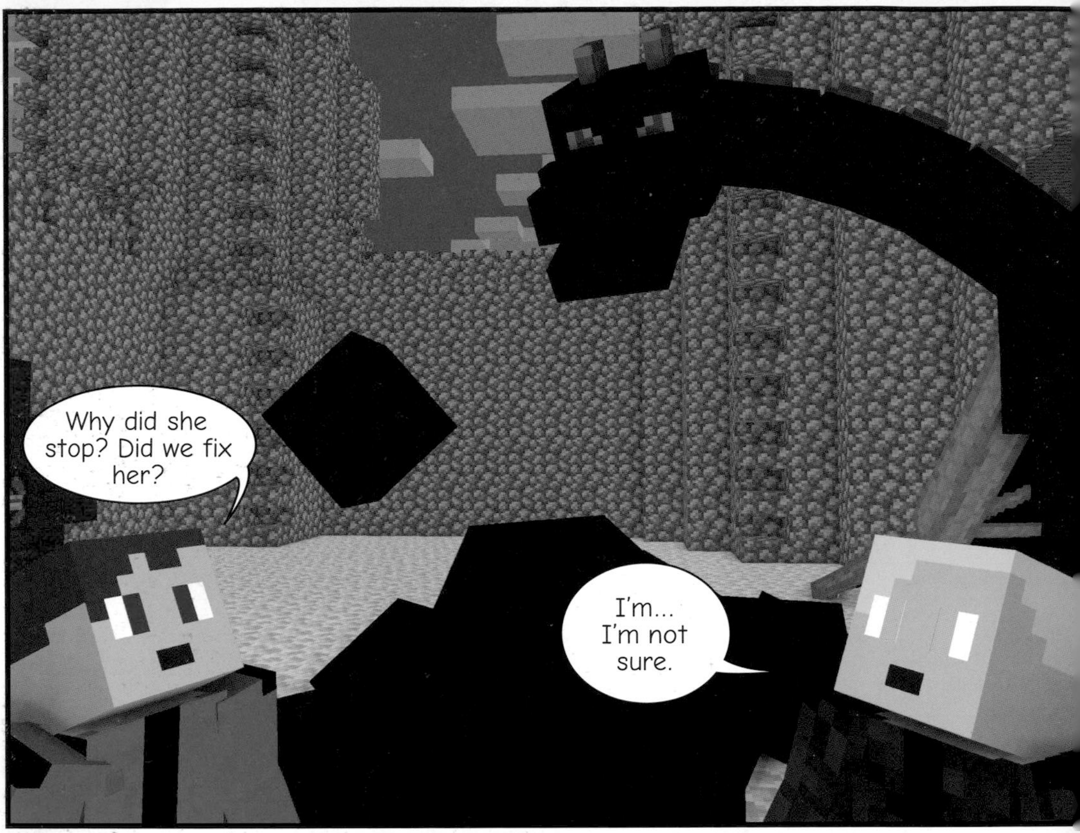
Why did she stop? Did we fix her?
I'm... I'm not sure.

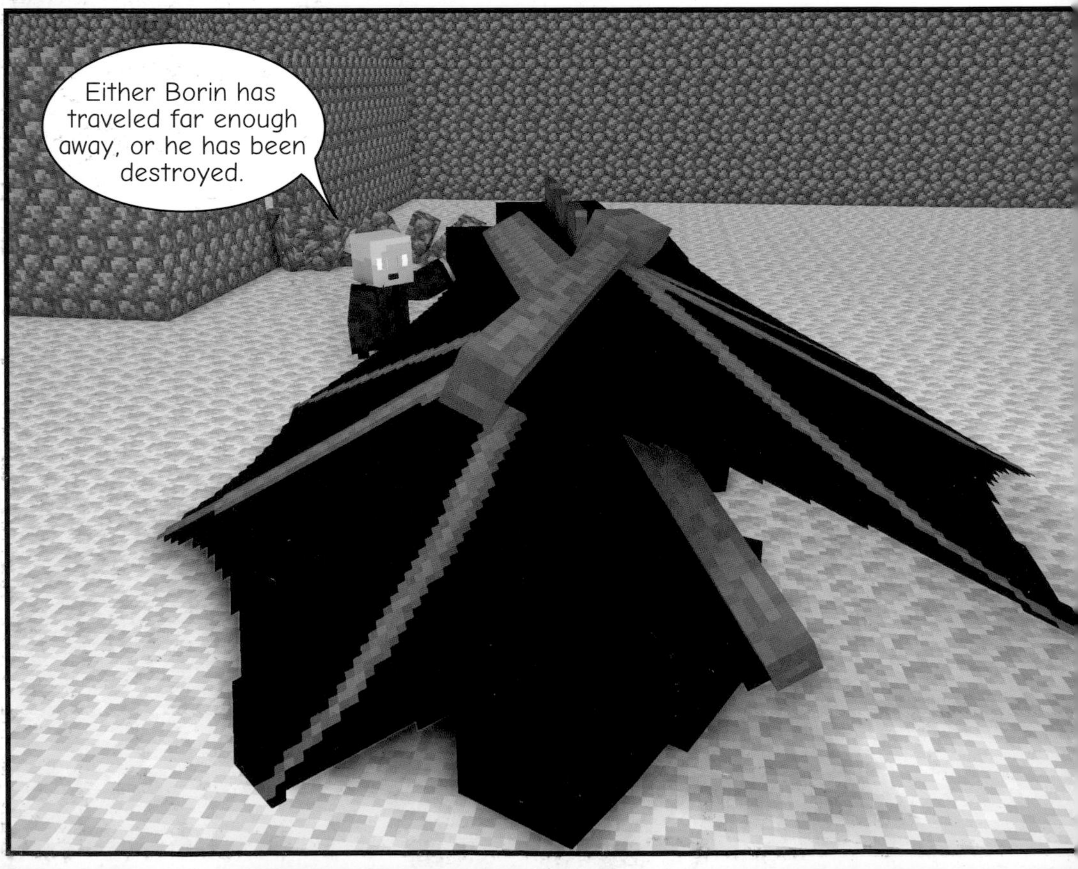
Either Borin has traveled far enough away, or he has been destroyed.

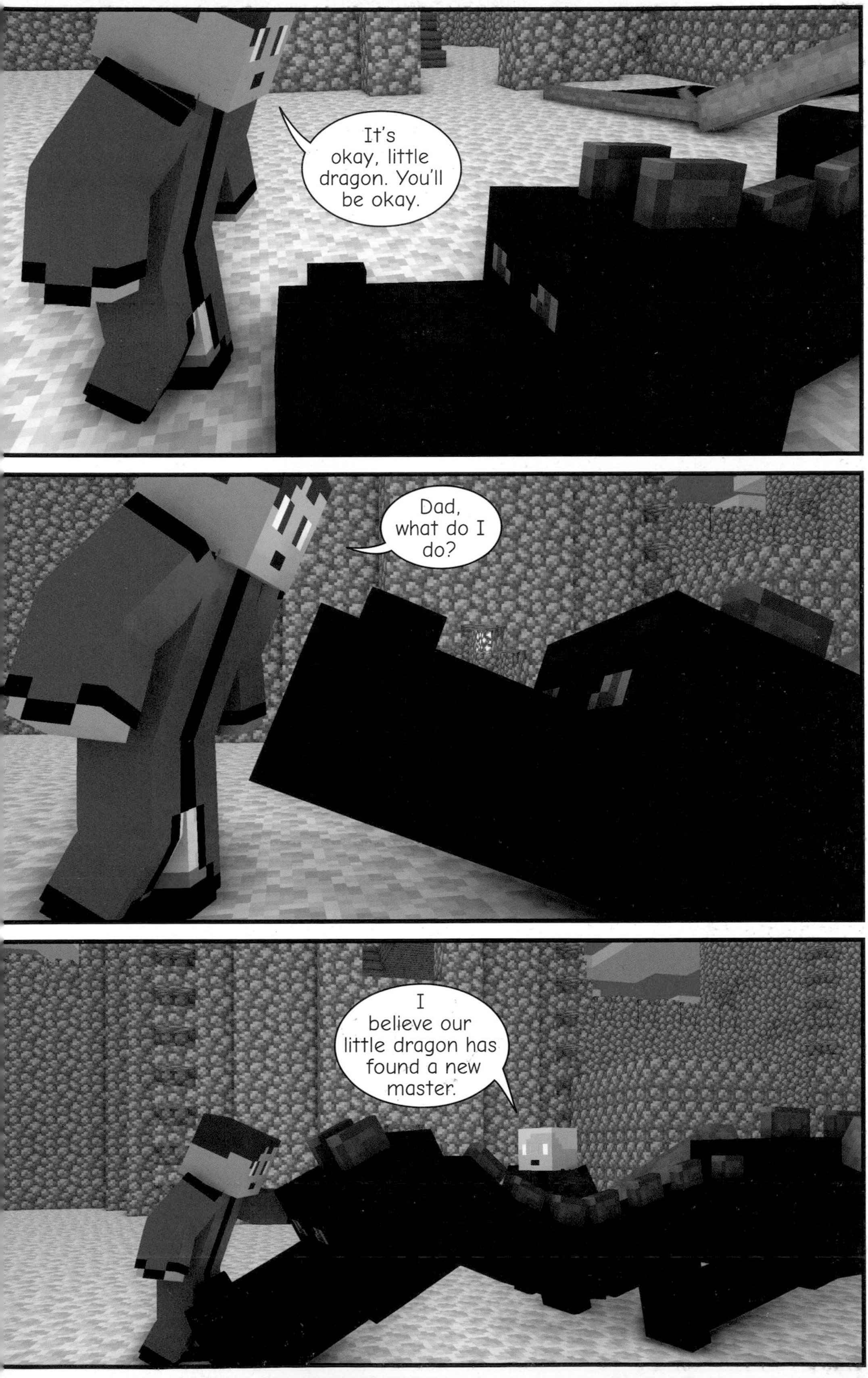
It's okay, little dragon. You'll be okay.
Dad, what do I do?
I believe our little dragon has found a new master.

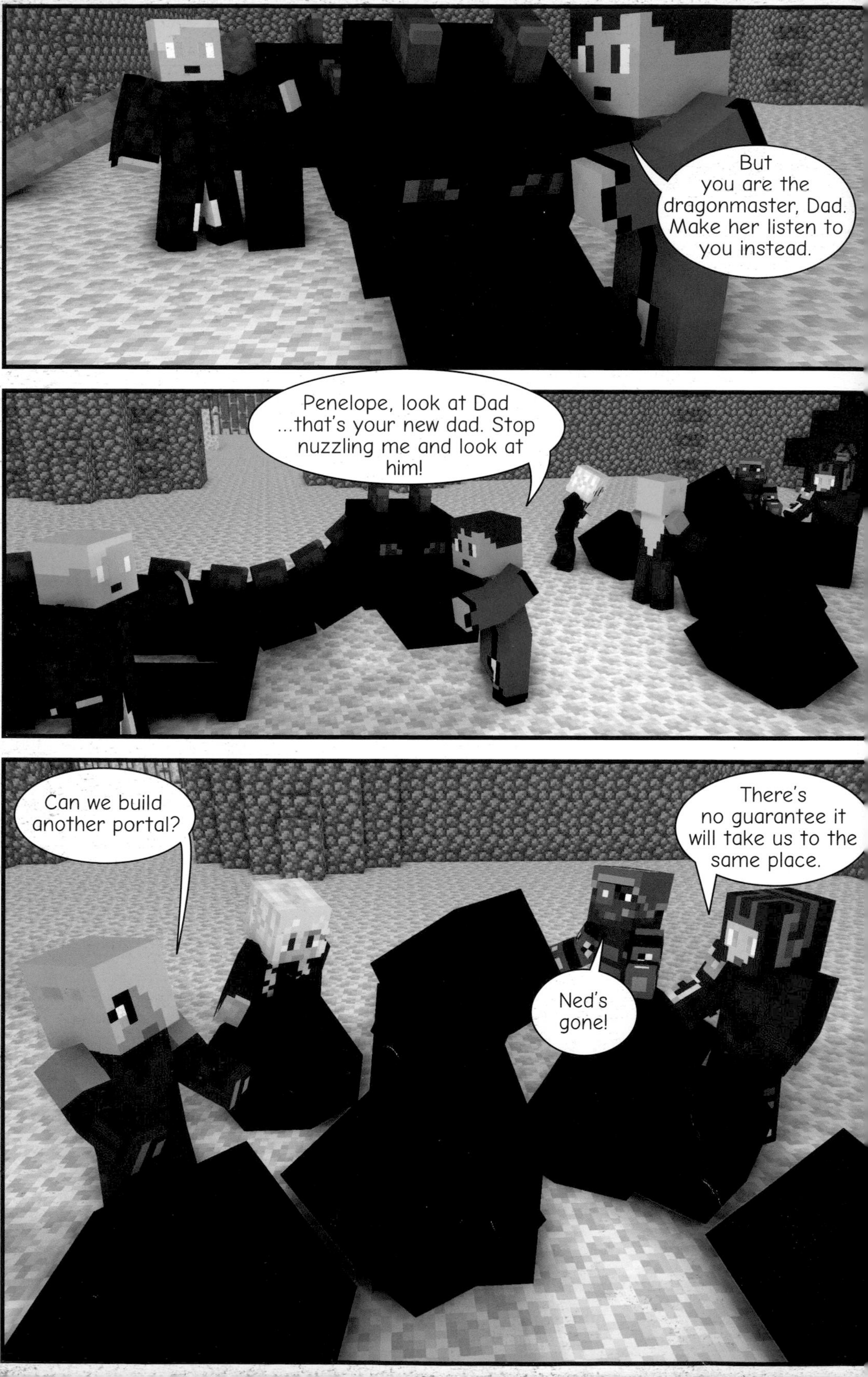
But you are the dragonmaster, Dad. Make her listen to you instead.
Penelope, look at Dad ...that's your new dad. Stop nuzzling me and look at him!
Can we build another portal?
There's no guarantee it will take us to the same place.
Ned's gone!

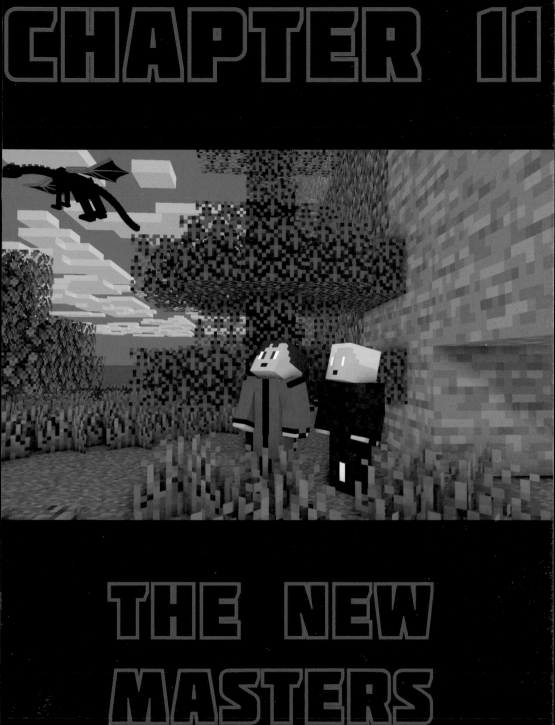

CHAPTER 11

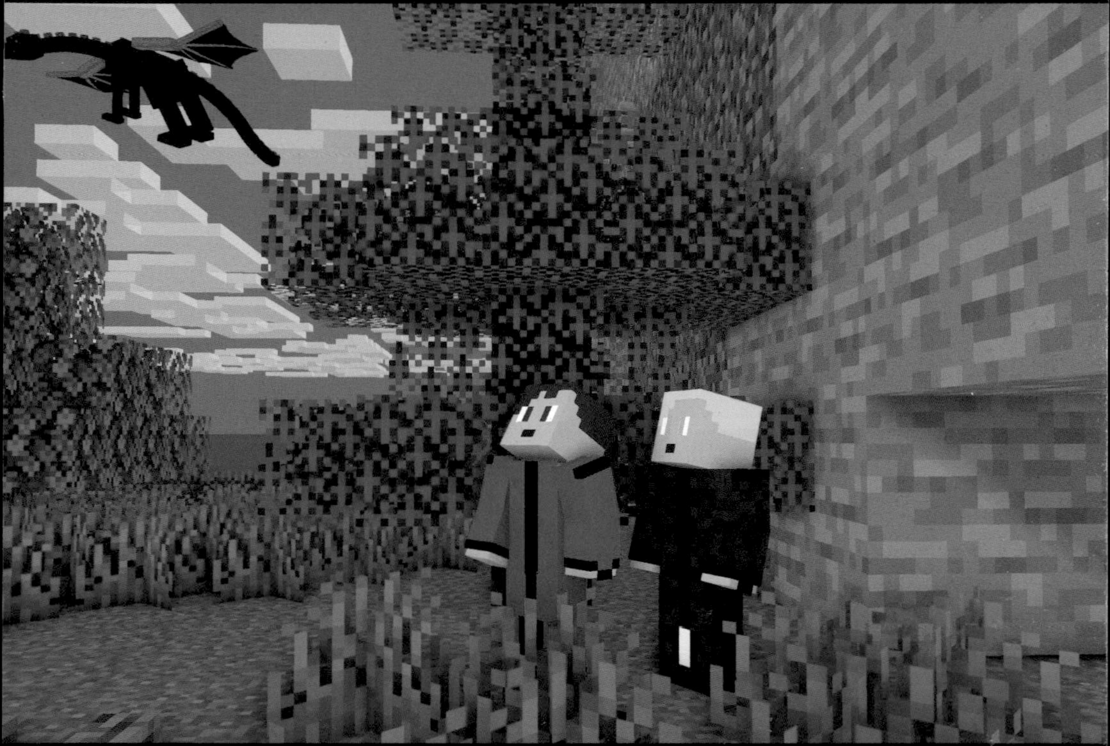

THE NEW MASTERS

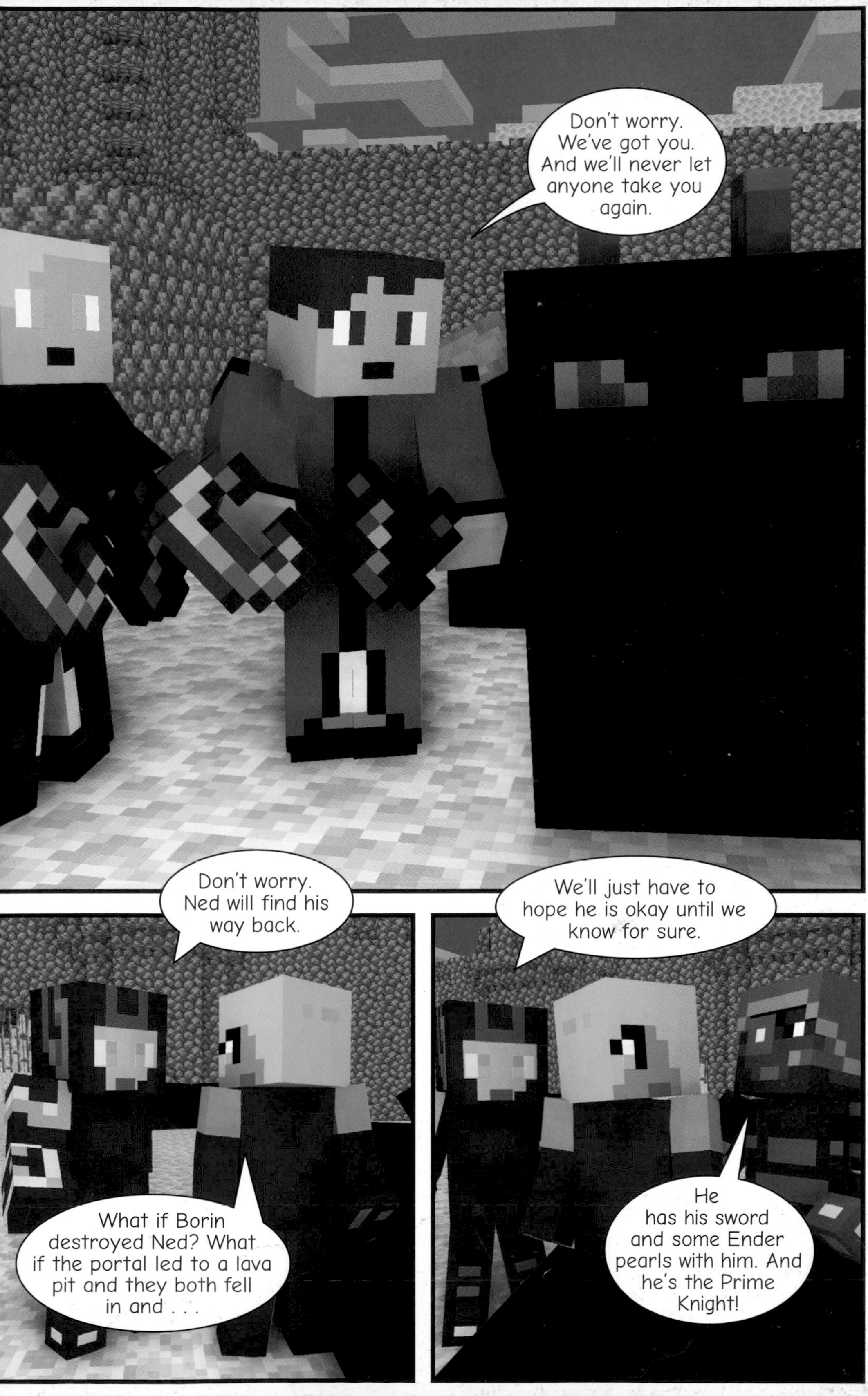
Don't worry. We've got you. And we'll never let anyone take you again.
Don't worry. Ned will find his way back.
What if Borin destroyed Ned? What if the portal led to a lava pit and they both fell in and . . .
We'll just have to hope he is okay until we know for sure.
He has his sword and some Ender pearls with him. And he's the Prime Knight!

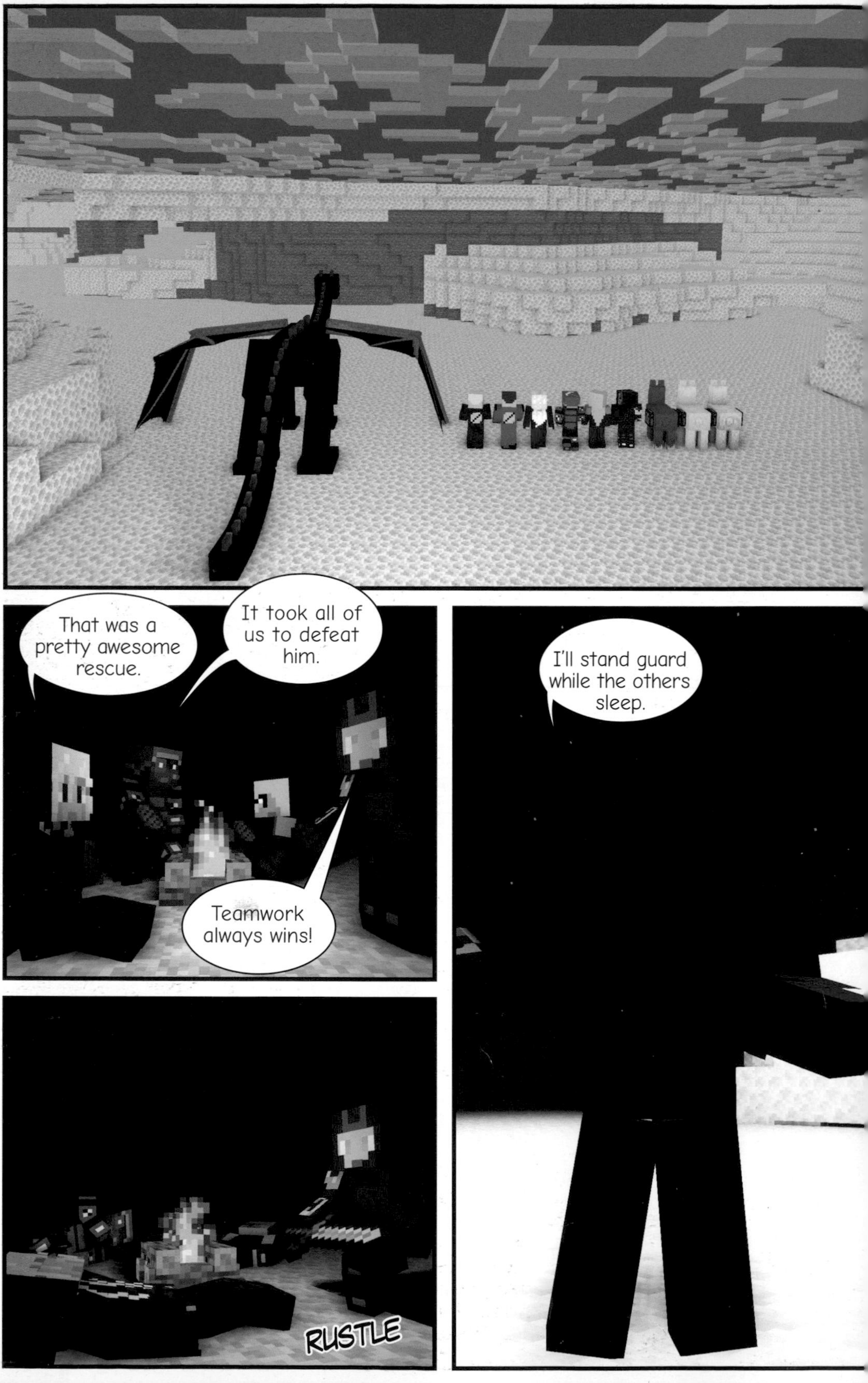

That was a pretty awesome rescue.
It took all of us to defeat him.
Teamwork always wins!
RUSTLE
I'll stand guard while the others sleep.

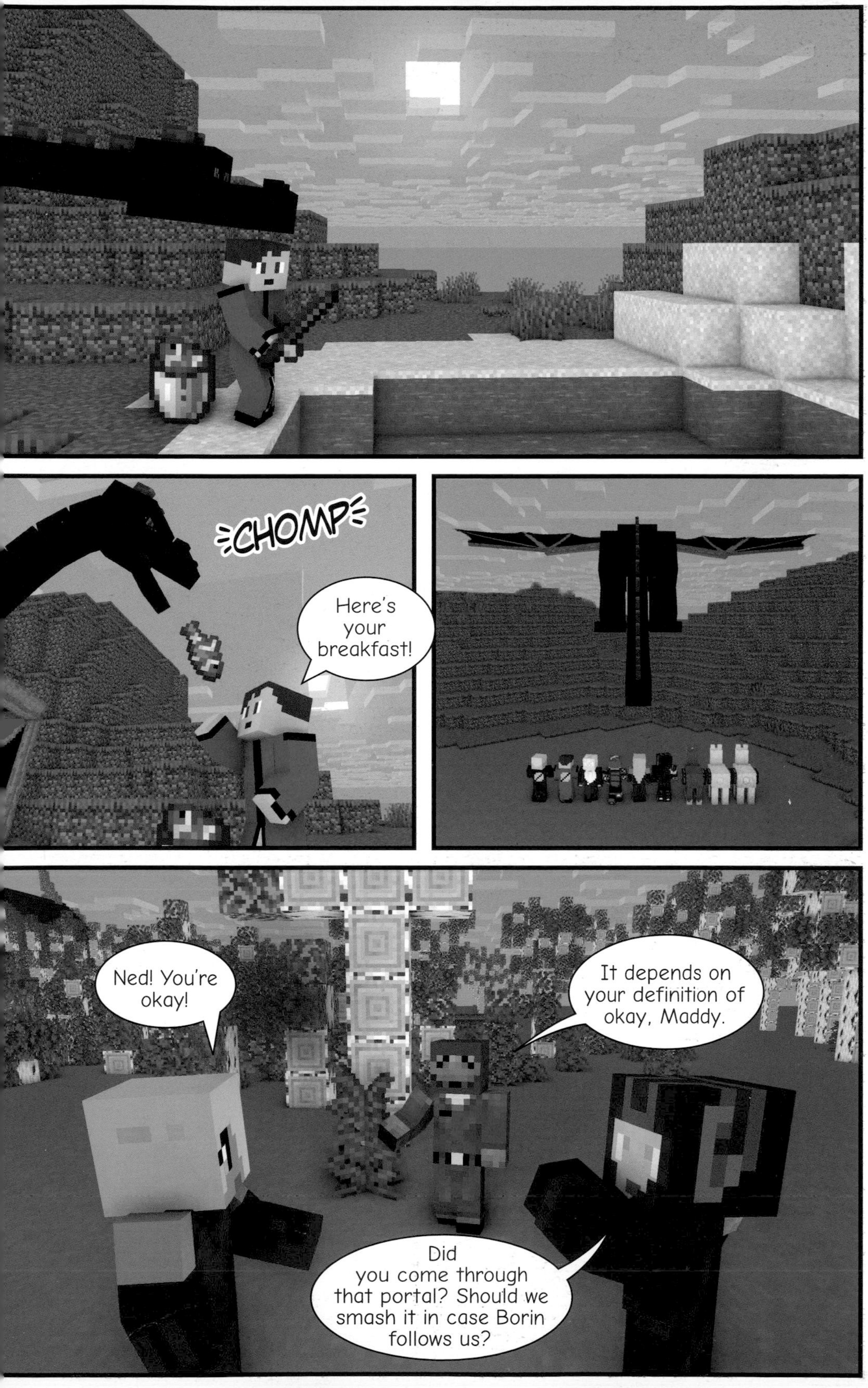
CHOMP
Here's your breakfast!
Ned! You're okay!
It depends on your definition of okay, Maddy.
Did you come through that portal? Should we smash it in case Borin follows us?

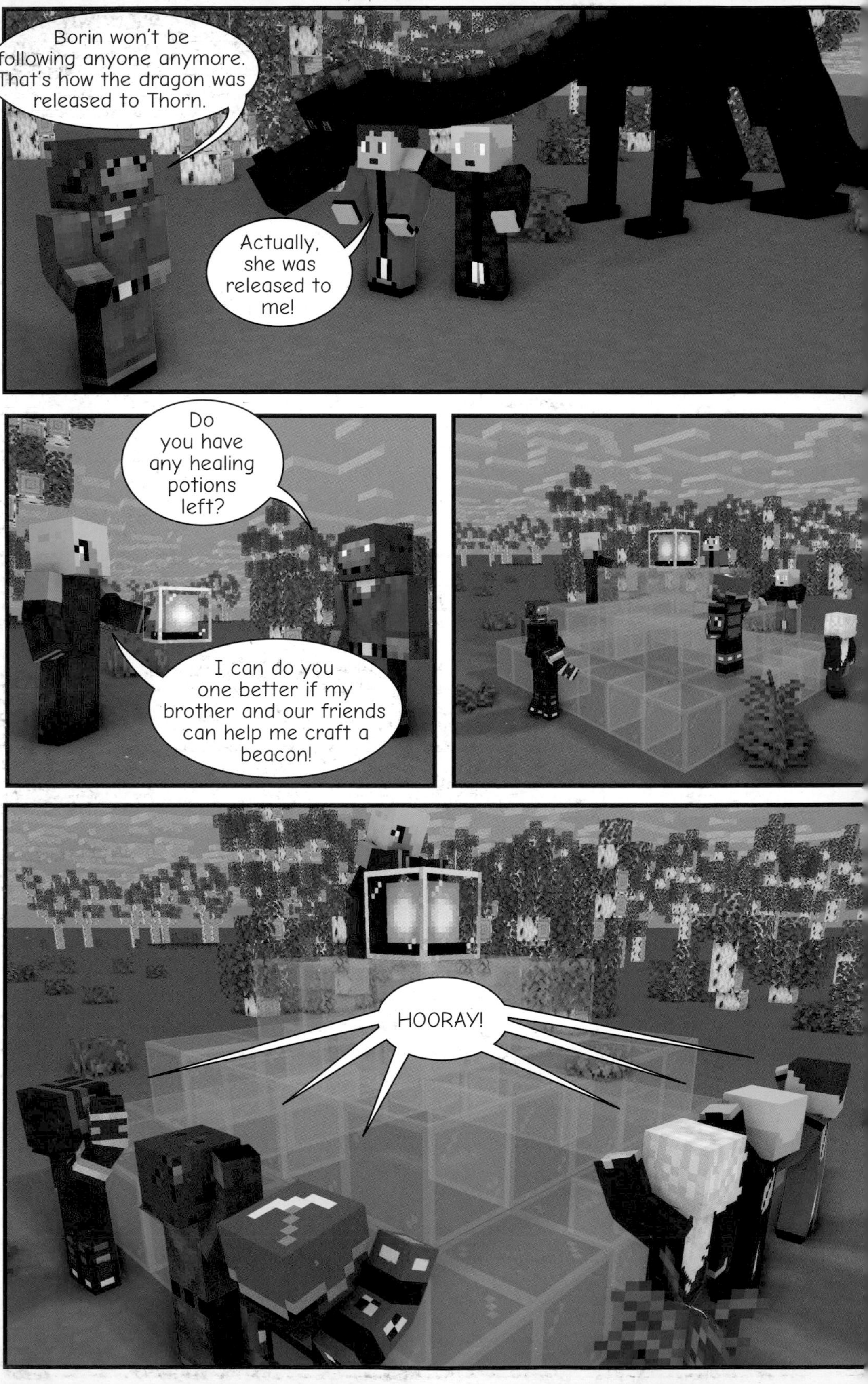
Borin won't be following anyone anymore. That's how the dragon was released to Thorn.
Actually, she was released to me!
Do you have any healing potions left?
I can do you one better if my brother and our friends can help me craft a beacon!
HOORAY!

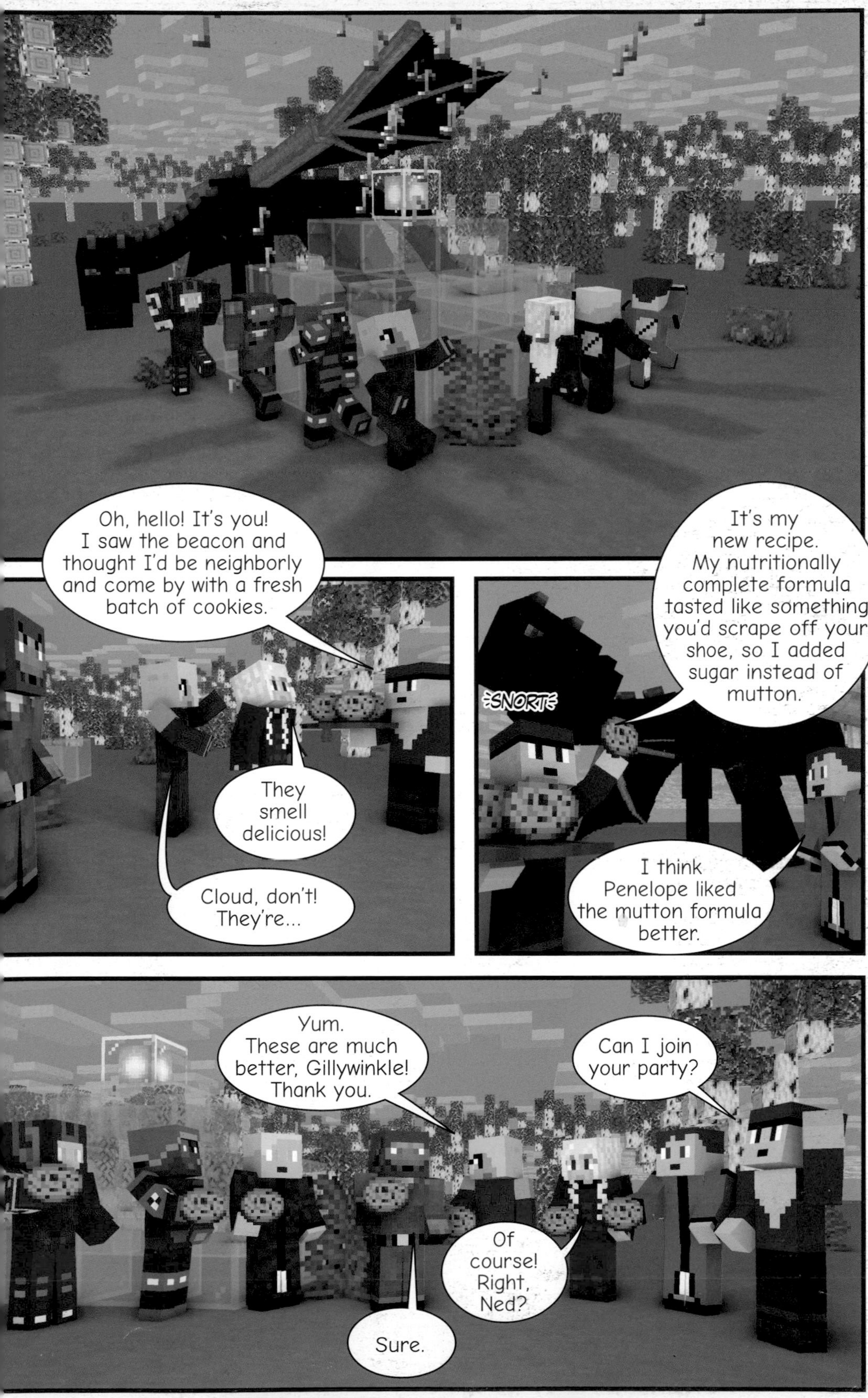
Oh, hello! It's you! I saw the beacon and thought I'd be neighborly and come by with a fresh batch of cookies.
They smell delicious!
Cloud, don't! They're...
SNORT
It's my new recipe. My nutritionally complete formula tasted like something you'd scrape off your shoe, so I added sugar instead of mutton.
I think Penelope liked the mutton formula better.
Yum. These are much better, Gillywinkle! Thank you.
Sure.
Of course! Right, Ned?
Can I join your party?

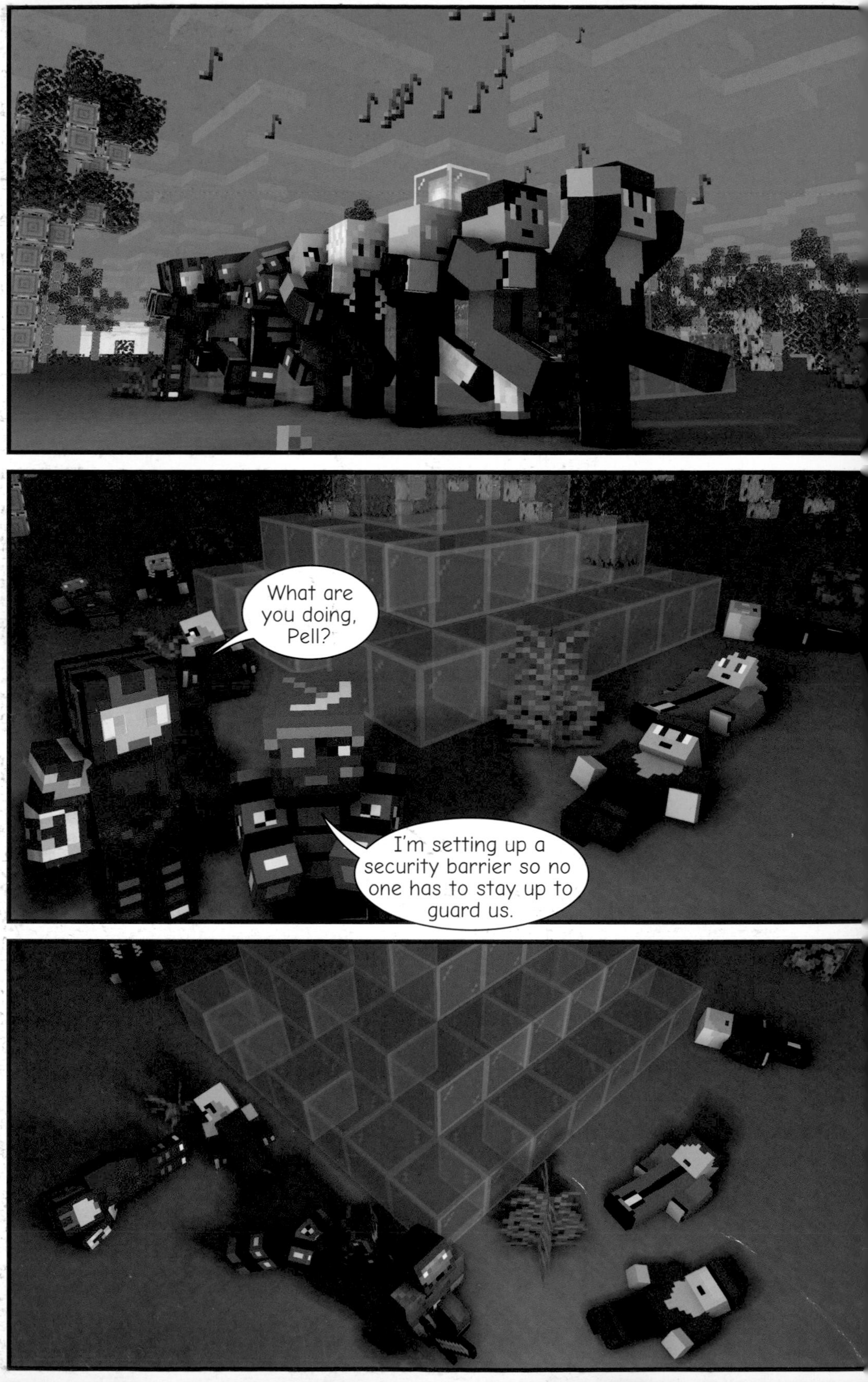
What are you doing, Pell?
I'm setting up a security barrier so no one has to stay up to guard us.

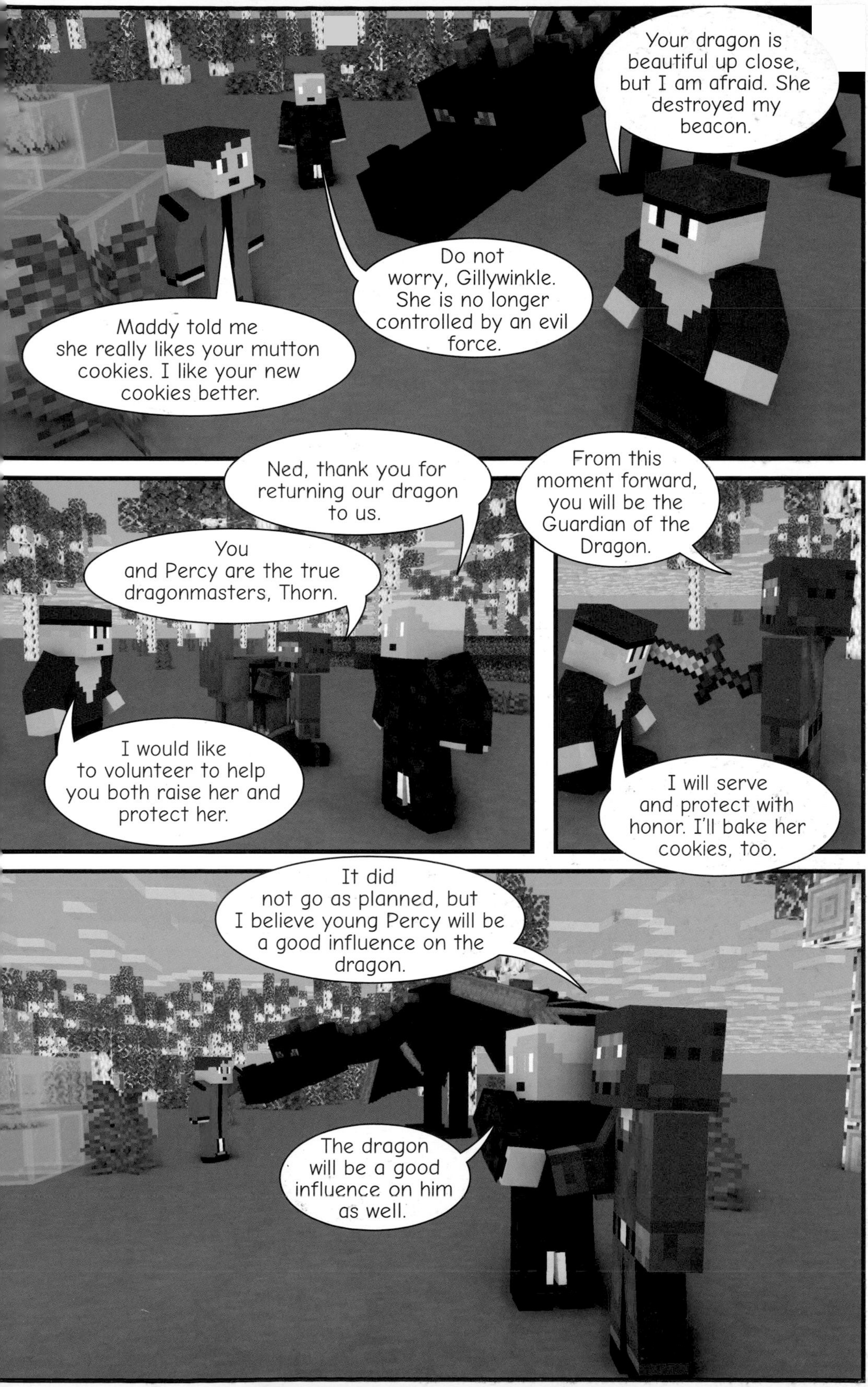
Your dragon is beautiful up close, but I am afraid. She destroyed my beacon.
Do not worry, Gillywinkle. She is no longer controlled by an evil force.
Maddy told me she really likes your mutton cookies. I like your new cookies better.
Ned, thank you for returning our dragon to us.
You and Percy are the true dragonmasters, Thorn.
I would like to volunteer to help you both raise her and protect her.
From this moment forward, you will be the Guardian of the Dragon.
I will serve and protect with honor. I'll bake her cookies, too.
It did not go as planned, but I believe young Percy will be a good influence on the dragon.
The dragon will be a good influence on him as well.

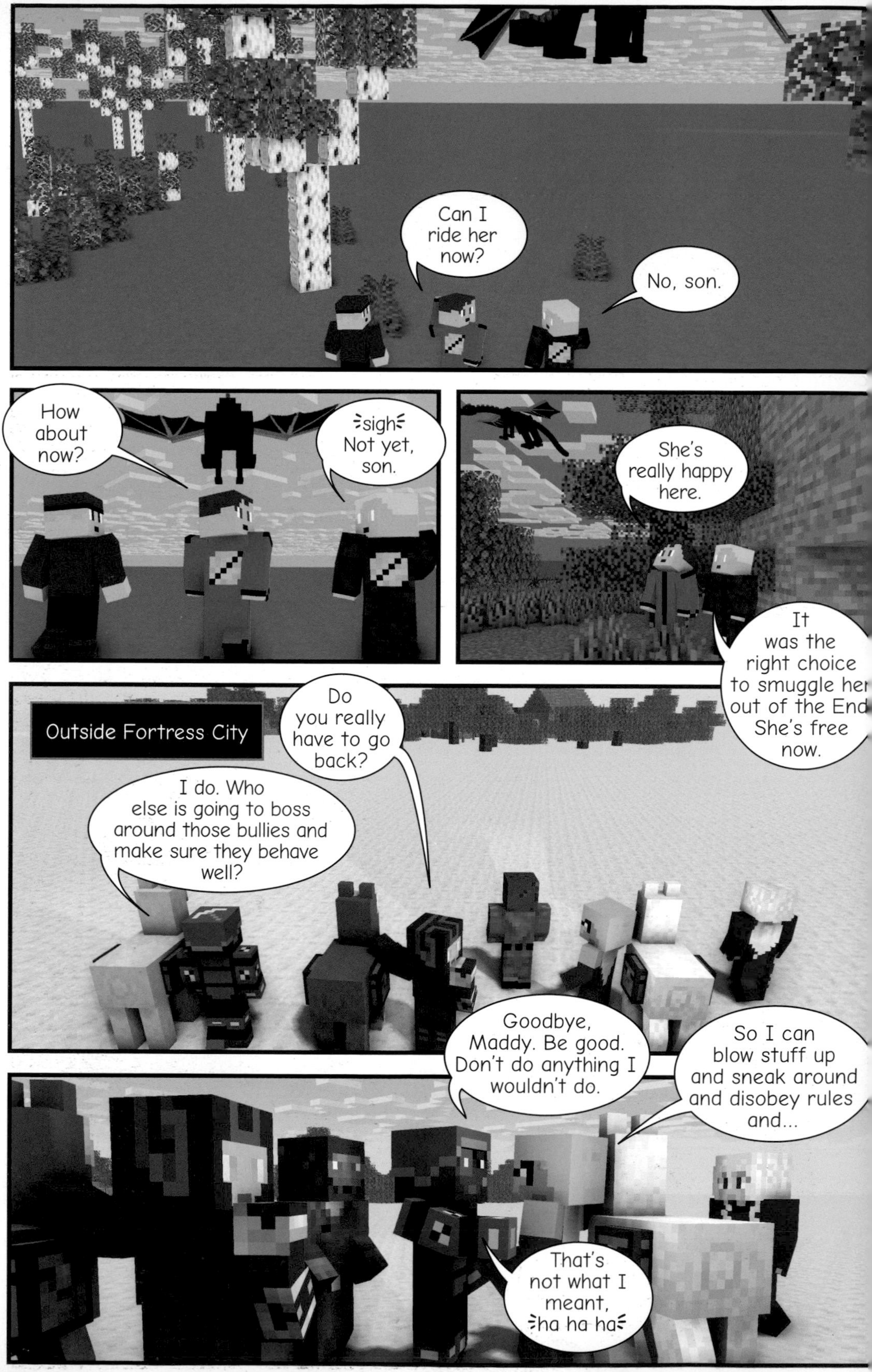
Can I ride her now?
No, son.
How about now?
≷sigh≶ Not yet, son.
She's really happy here.
It was the right choice to smuggle her out of the End. She's free now.
Outside Fortress City
Do you really have to go back?
I do. Who else is going to boss around those bullies and make sure they behave well?
Goodbye, Maddy. Be good. Don't do anything I wouldn't do.
So I can blow stuff up and sneak around and disobey rules and...
That's not what I meant, ≷ha ha ha≶

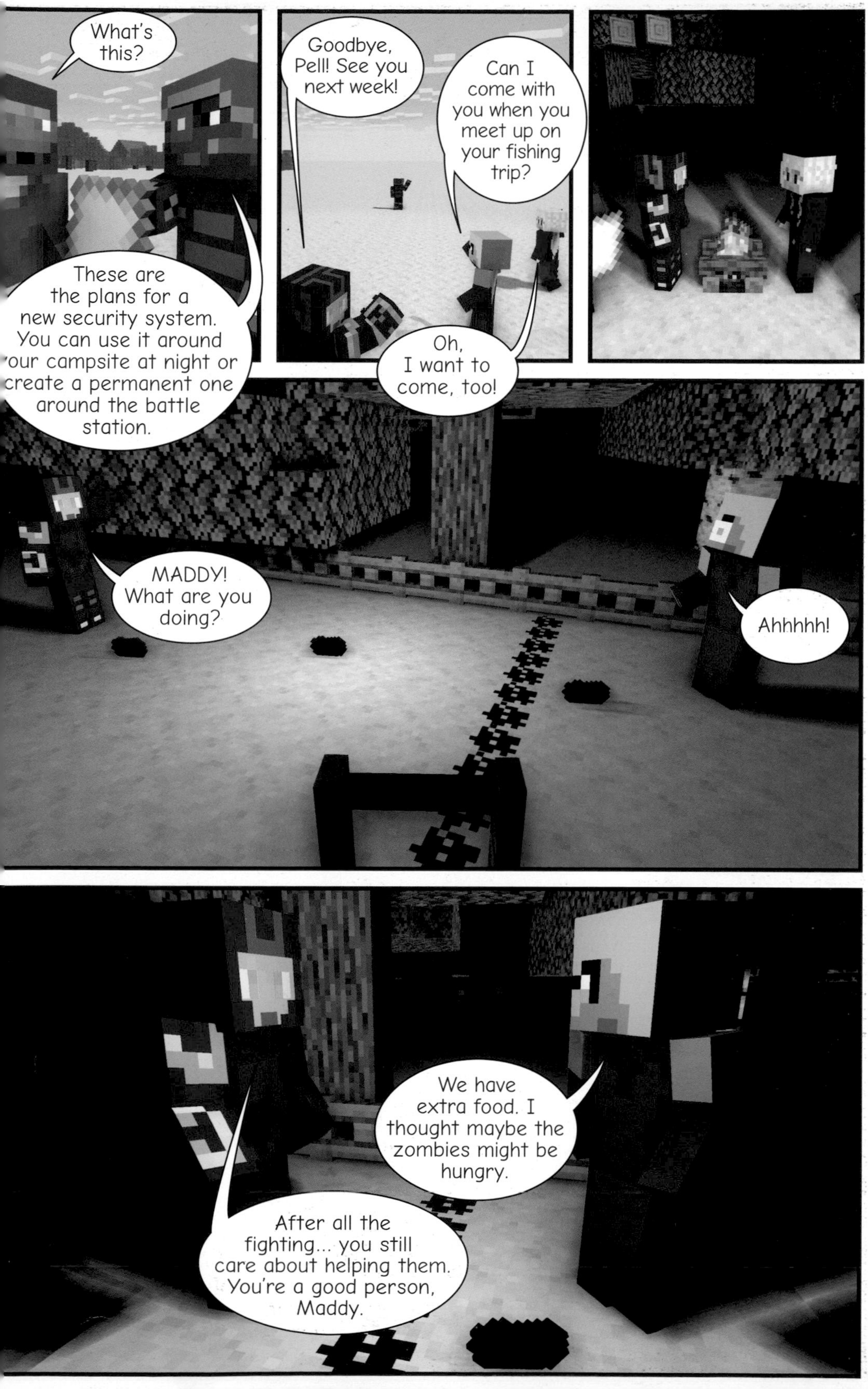
What's this?
These are the plans for a new security system. You can use it around your campsite at night or create a permanent one around the battle station.
Goodbye, Pell! See you next week!
Can I come with you when you meet up on your fishing trip?
Oh, I want to come, too!
MADDY! What are you doing?
Ahhhhh!
We have extra food. I thought maybe the zombies might be hungry.
After all the fighting... you still care about helping them. You're a good person, Maddy.

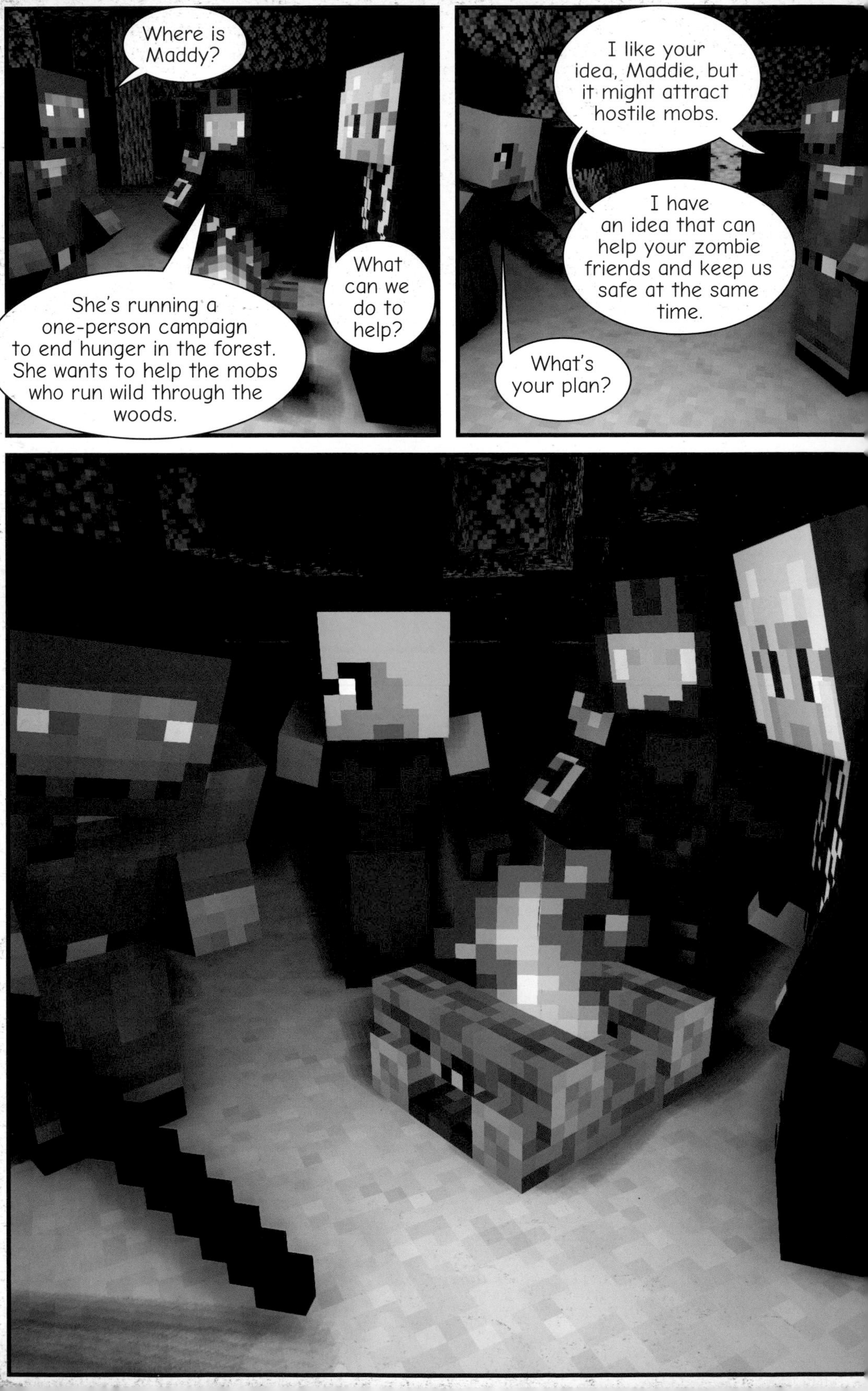
Where is Maddy?
She's running a one-person campaign to end hunger in the forest. She wants to help the mobs who run wild through the woods.
What can we do to help?
I like your idea, Maddie, but it might attract hostile mobs.
I have an idea that can help your zombie friends and keep us safe at the same time.
What's your plan?

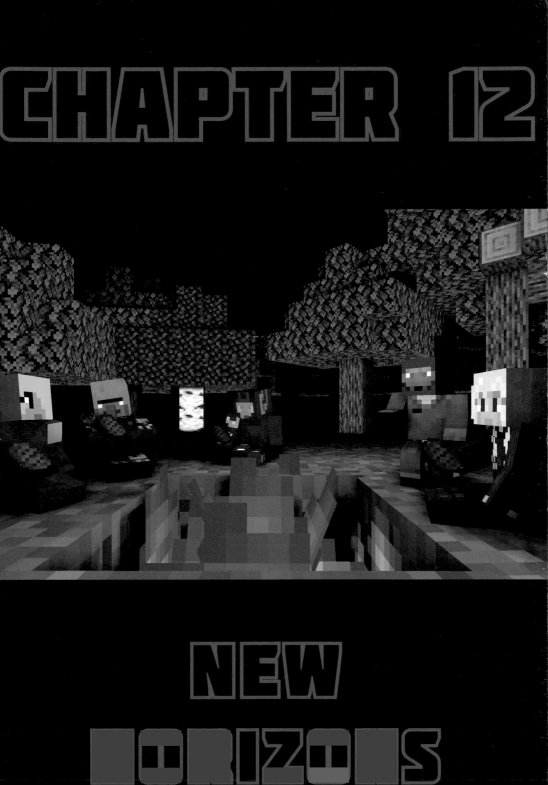

CHAPTER 12

NEW HORIZONS

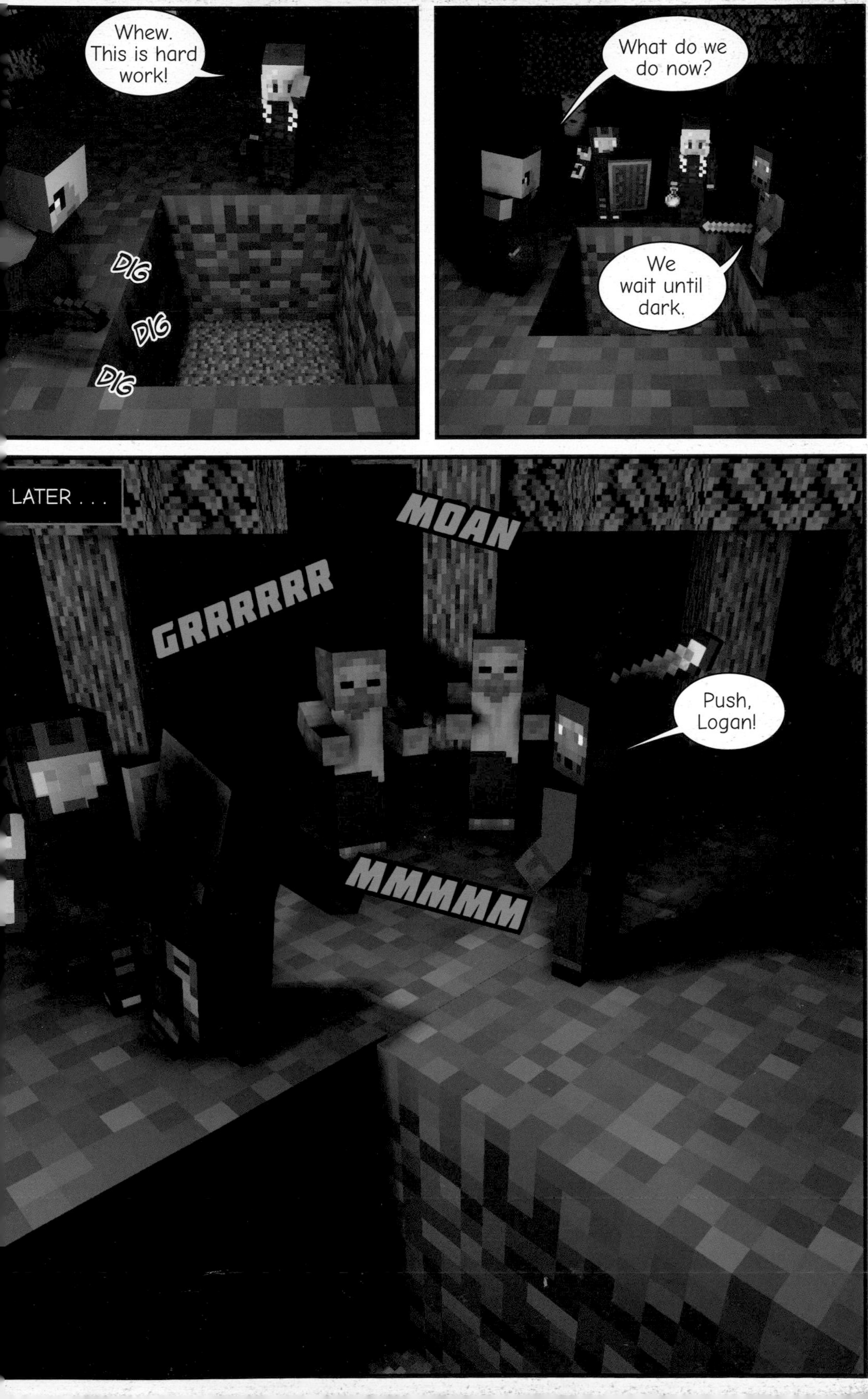

Whew. This is hard work!
DIG
DIG
DIG
What do we do now?
We wait until dark.
LATER . . .
MOAN
GRRRRRR
Push, Logan!
MMMMM

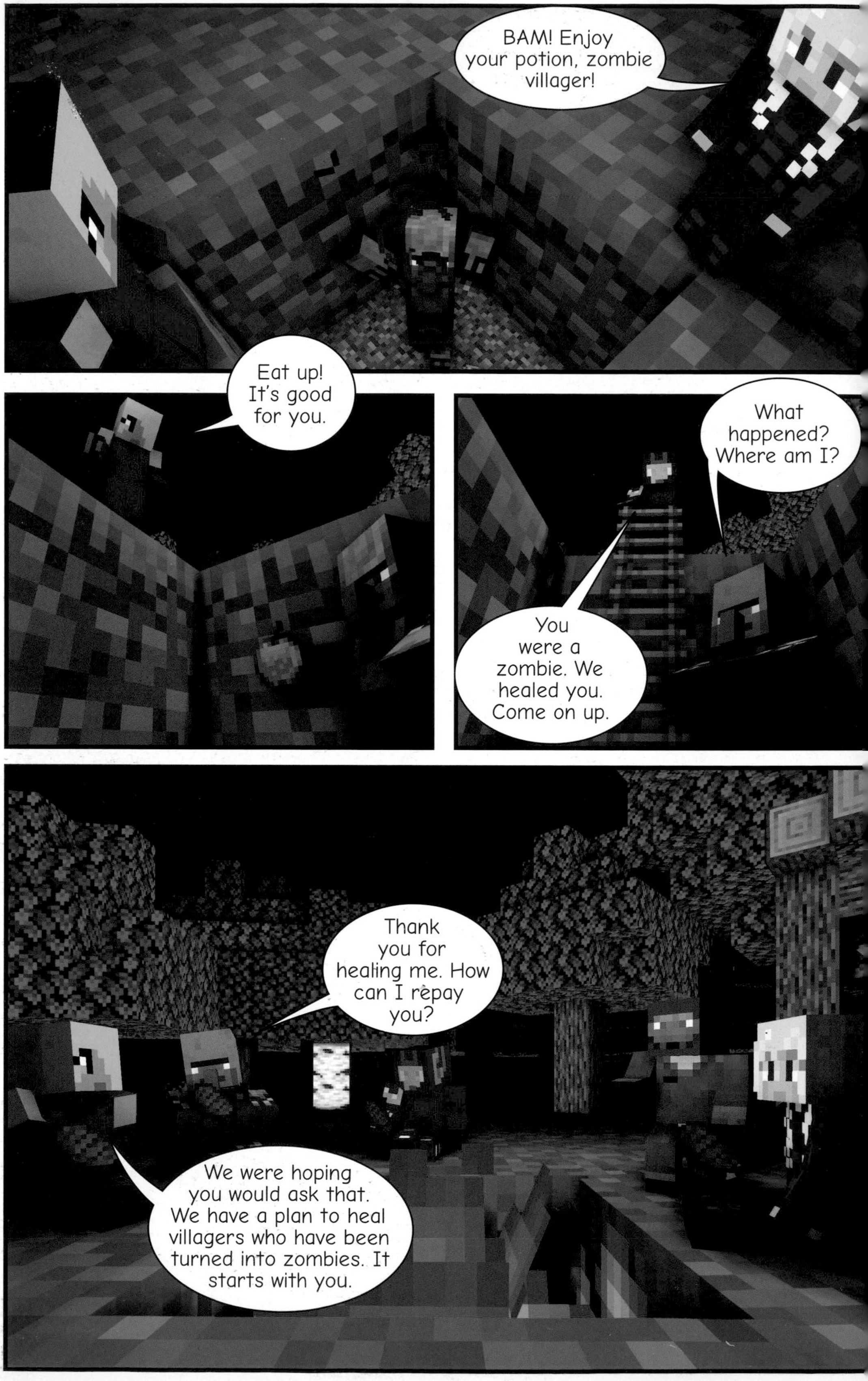
BAM! Enjoy your potion, zombie villager!
Eat up! It's good for you.
What happened? Where am I?
You were a zombie. We healed you. Come on up.
Thank you for healing me. How can I repay you?
We were hoping you would ask that. We have a plan to heal villagers who have been turned into zombies. It starts with you.

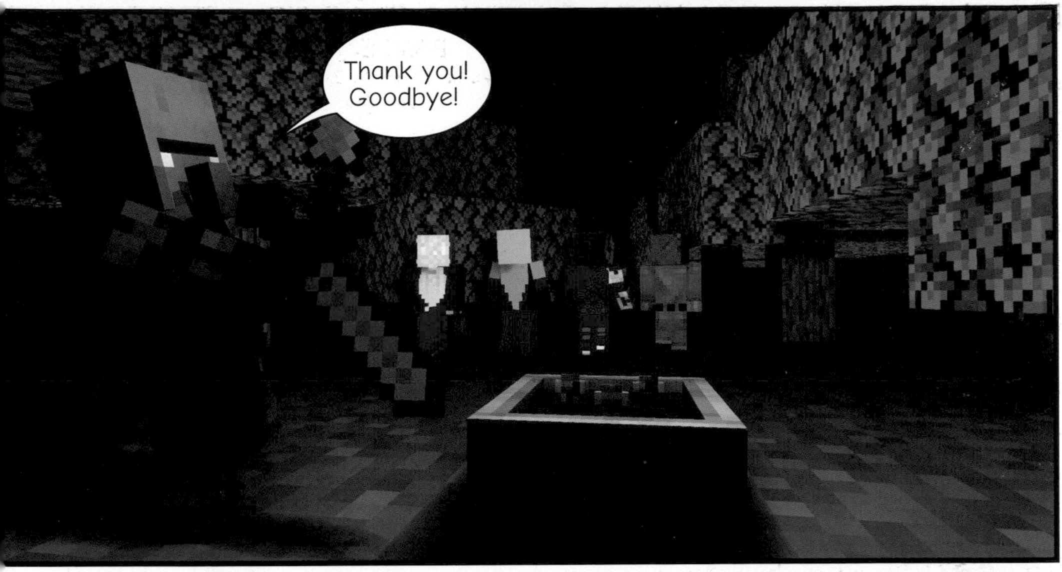
Thank you! Goodbye!

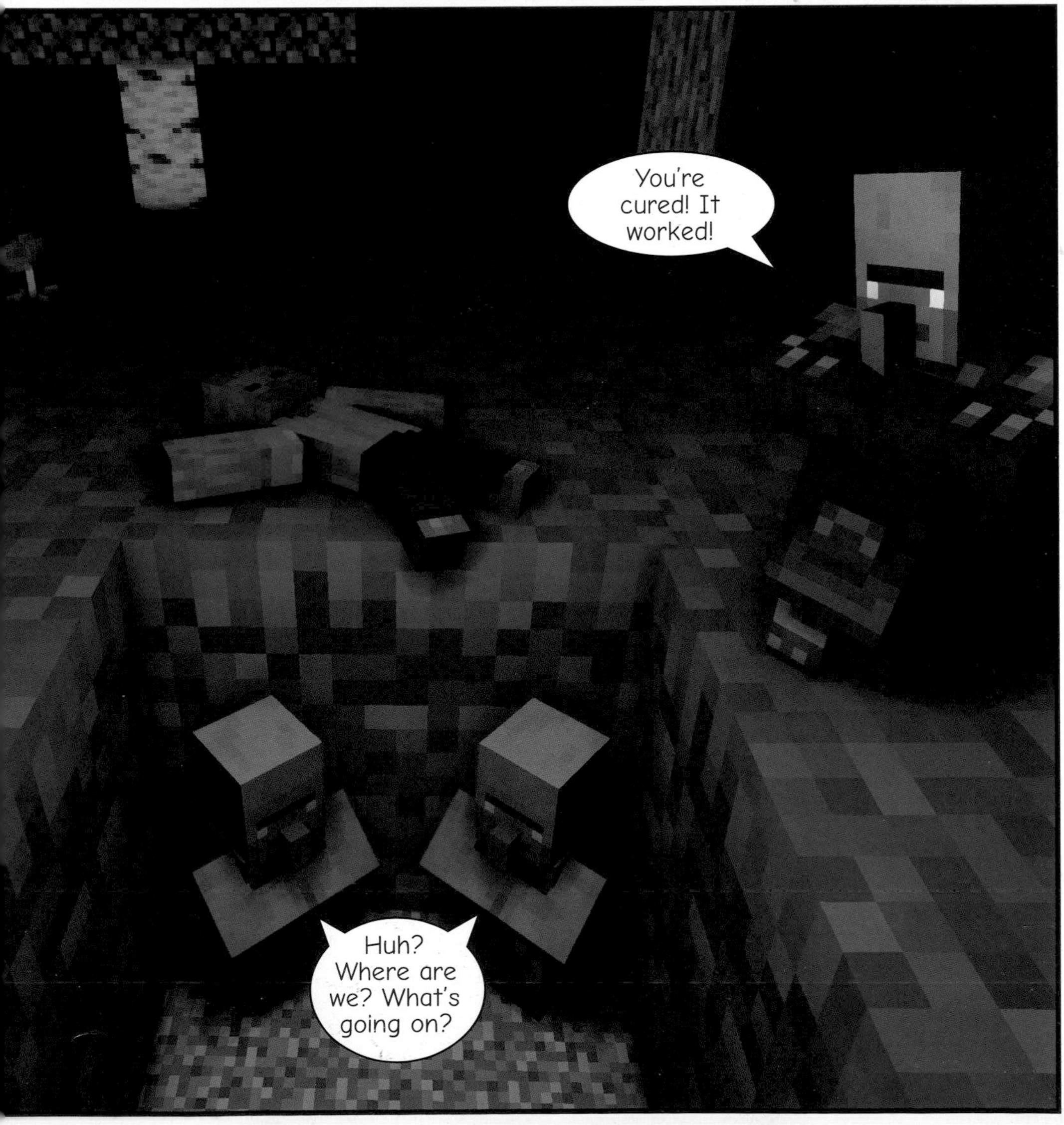
You're cured! It worked!
Huh? Where are we? What's going on?

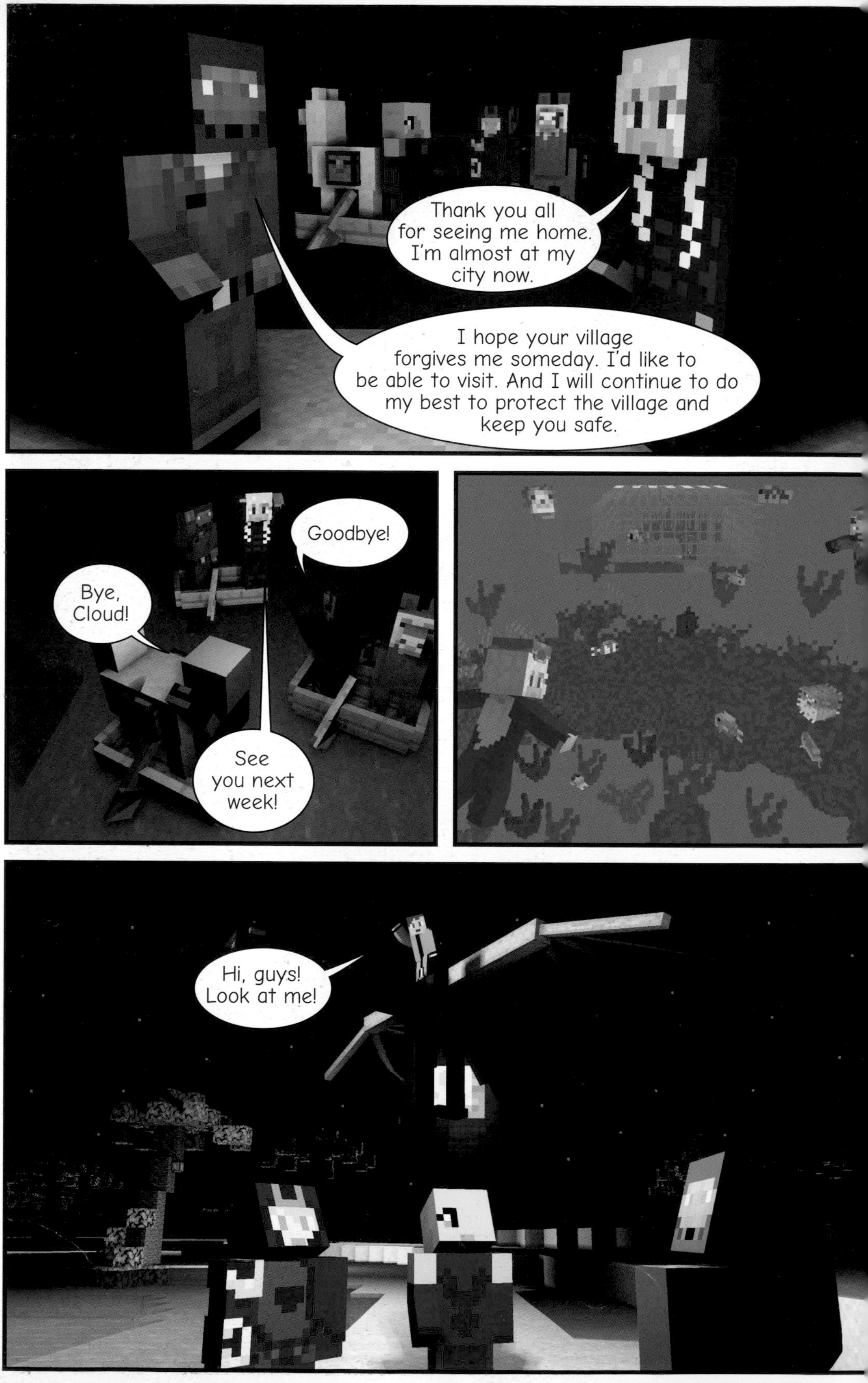
Thank you all for seeing me home. I'm almost at my city now.
I hope your village forgives me someday. I'd like to be able to visit. And I will continue to do my best to protect the village and keep you safe.
Goodbye!
Bye, Cloud!
See you next week!
Hi, guys! Look at me!

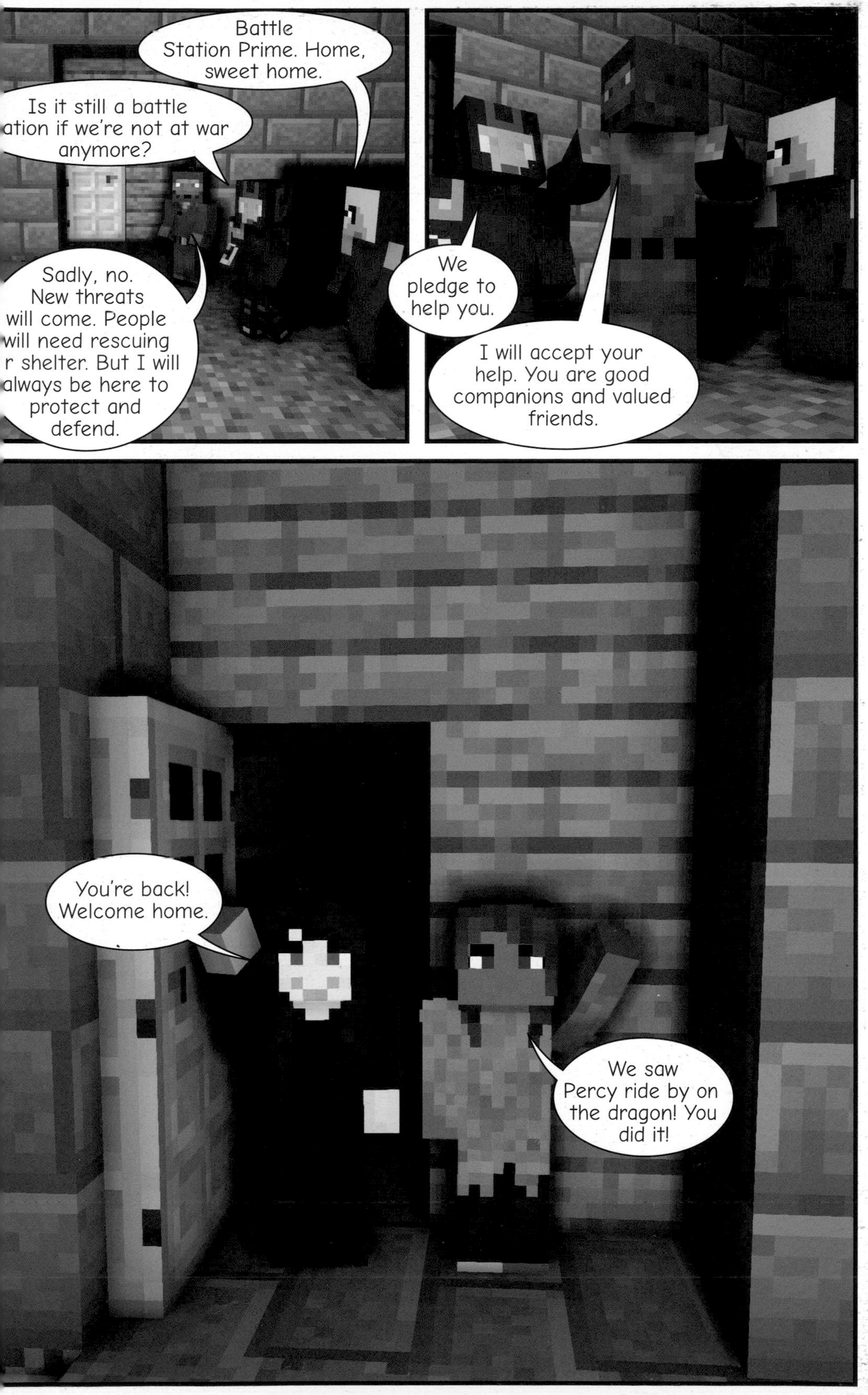
Battle Station Prime. Home, sweet home.
Is it still a battle ation if we're not at war anymore?
Sadly, no. New threats will come. People will need rescuing r shelter. But I will always be here to protect and defend.
We pledge to help you.
I will accept your help. You are good companions and valued friends.
You're back! Welcome home.
We saw Percy ride by on the dragon! You did it!

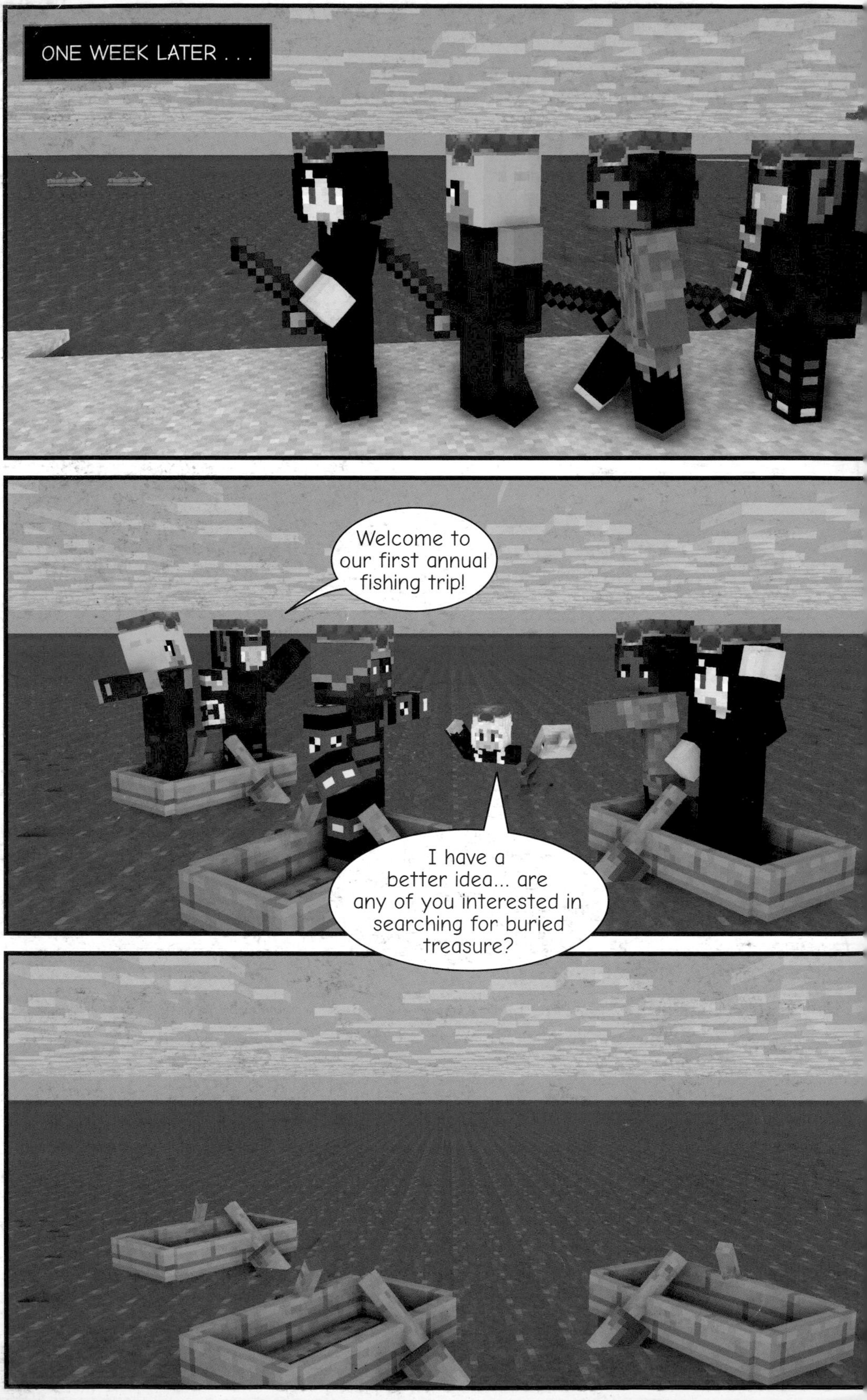
ONE WEEK LATER . . .
Welcome to our first annual fishing trip!
I have a better idea... are any of you interested in searching for buried treasure?

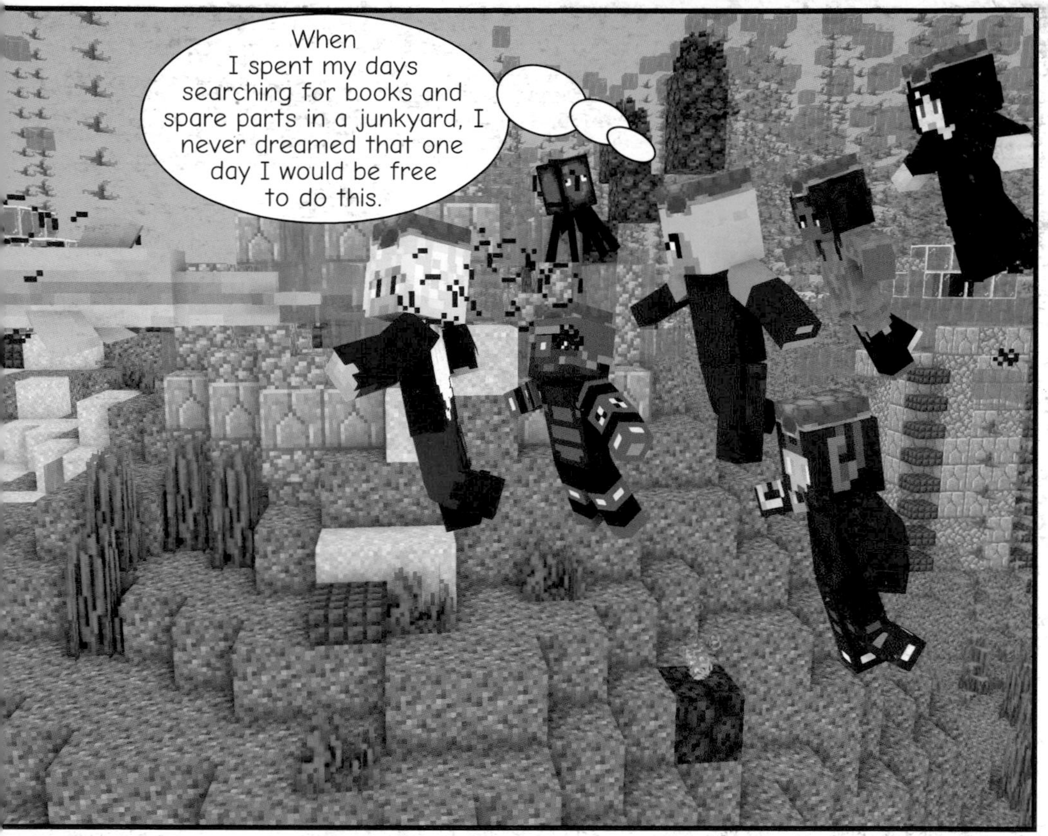
When I spent my days searching for books and spare parts in a junkyard, I never dreamed that one day I would be free to do this.

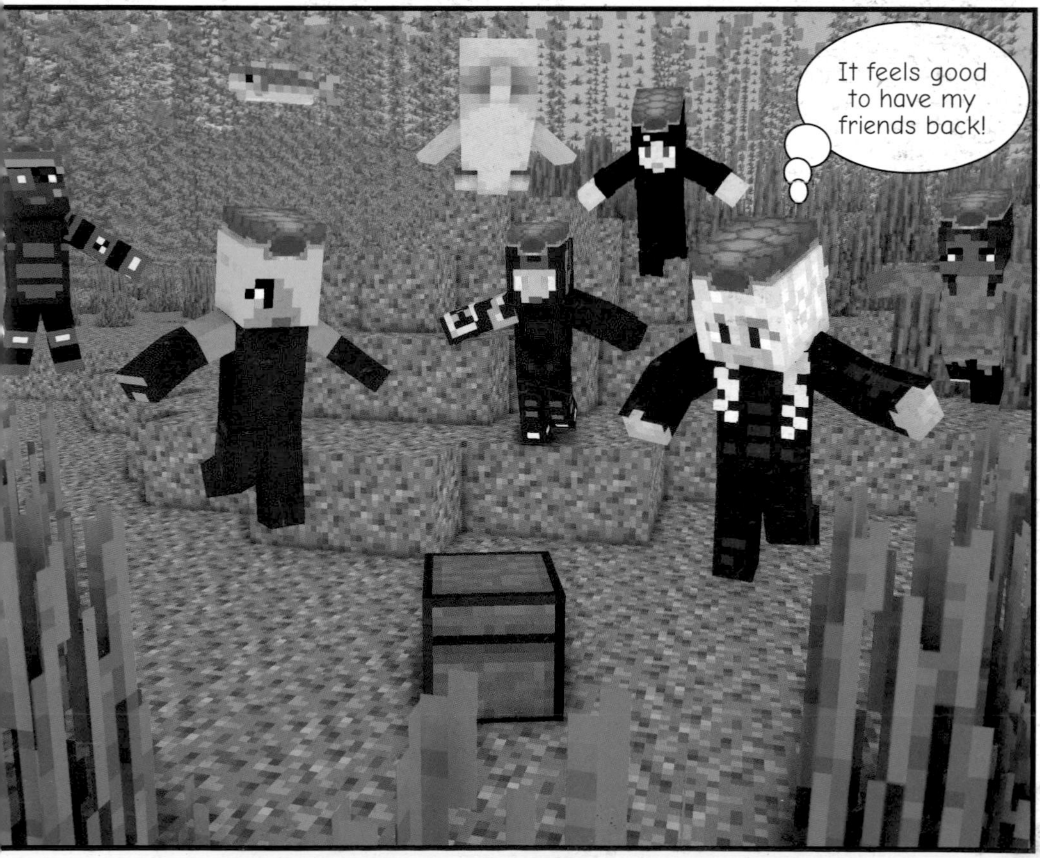
It feels good to have my friends back!

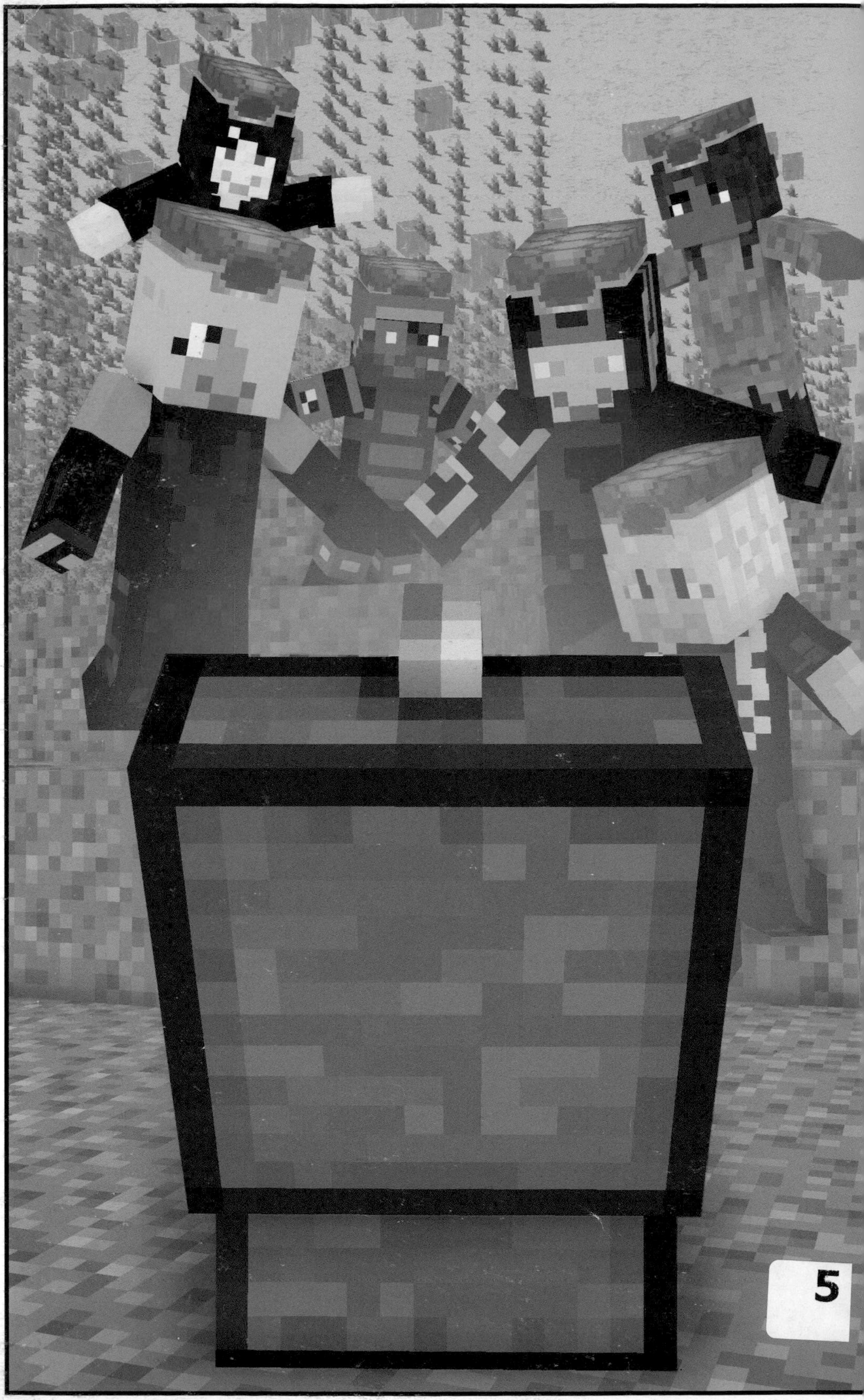
5